认知诗学

第九辑

熊沐清/主编

西南交通大学出版社
·成 都·

图书在版编目（CIP）数据

认知诗学. 第九辑 / 熊沐清主编. —成都：西南交通大学出版社，2021.12
ISBN 978-7-5643-8523-1

Ⅰ. ①认… Ⅱ. ①熊… Ⅲ. ①诗学－中国－文集
Ⅳ. ①I207.2-53

中国版本图书馆 CIP 数据核字（2021）第 275199 号

Renzhi Shixue (Di-jiu Ji)
认知诗学（第九辑）
熊沐清 主编

责任编辑	居碧娟
封面设计	曹天擎
出版发行	西南交通大学出版社 （四川省成都市金牛区二环路北一段 111 号 西南交通大学创新大厦 21 楼）
发行部电话	028-87600564 028-87600533
邮政编码	610031
网址	http://www.xnjdcbs.com
印刷	成都勤德印务有限公司
成品尺寸	170 mm × 230 mm
印张	15.25
字数	226 千
版次	2021 年 12 月第 1 版
印次	2021 年 12 月第 1 次
书号	ISBN 978-7-5643-8523-1
定价	68.00 元

编委会

目　录

儿童文学的认知研究

认知诗学"关键词"

前沿译介

名家特稿

Does Cognition Translate? Predictions, Plot, and World Literature①

Karin Kukkonen
(University of Oslo, Norway)

【Abstract】 Comparative literature and cognitive literary studies both consider literature as a worldwide phenomenon. The move toward world literature in comparative literature made salient the issue of reading some texts in translation, and world literature turned its attention to whether texts are entirely translatable and how center and periphery in the "world republic of literature" are organized around languages that are predominantly translated (or translated into). This article proposes that cognitive literary studies and comparative literature could enter into conversation around the topic of language differences and translation. For cognitive literary studies, the approaches of predictive processing and embodied cognition have in recent years developed the conceptual means to include these differences in our discussions without falling back on the Sapir-Whorf hypothesis. Language shapes thought, but it does so in a flexible exchange between verbal markers and language-created contexts. The author models this exchange for literary texts by means of salient verbal markers that indicate plot events and outlines

---

Author: Karin Kukkonen is professor in comparative literature at the University of Oslo.

① This article was written while I was a fellow at the Wissenschaftskolleg zu Berlin. I thank Merja Polvinen, Gisle Sapiro, Mads Rosendal Thomsen, and especially Lisa Zunshine for their generous and incisive comments on earlier versions of the manuscript. A first version of this article was presented at the Centres, Peripheries, and Zones of Contact workshop at the University of Oslo inJune 2019.

possible shared avenues of future research for cognitive literary studies and comparative literature along these lines. The examples discussed are the Finnish national epic *Kalevala*, its French and English translations, and the contemporary novel *Sankarit* by Johanna Sinisalo.
【Key word】 translation; cognitive literary studies; predictive processing; plot; *Kalevala*; Johanna Sinisalo

Comparative literature and cognitive literary studies share a global perspective on literature. In the last decades, comparative literature has ventured beyond the European canon and into the system of world literature, where transnational streams of literary texts are investigated. Cognitive literary studies sees in principle all of literature as its domain, since thoughts and emotions are features involved in texts from any language or country. While the global perspective of comparative literature has constantly grappled with whether and how texts can be translated, cognitive literary studies has stayed clear of the issue of language differences and drawn on a general, universal sense of "literature." In establishing a point of connection between cognitive literary studies and comparative literature, I revisit the issue of language differences and translation. My particular interest here lies in how language-specific aspects of literature contribute to the abstraction of plot and how they travel in translation. From my discussion of plot, I then develop a preliminary proposal for an approach to cognitive literary studies that is attentive to language differences and thus might enter into dialogue with comparative literature.

1 Universals, Translation, and World Literature

The Finnish epic *Kalevala*, collected by Elias Lönnrot in eastern Finland in the first half of the nineteenth century and published in 1835—1836 (*Old Kalevala*) and in a revised version in 1849 (*New Kalevala*), easily makes the cut for Finland's contribution to world literature. It is perhaps the Finnish literary text that most readers outside of Finland know, ahead of classics like Aleksis Kivi's *Seven Brothers* (*Seitsemän veljestä*, 1870) and Väinö Linna's *Unknown Soldier* (*Tuntematon sotilas*, 1954) and contemporary favorites like works by Sofi Oksanen and Arto Paasilinna.① The stories around the culture hero Väinämöinen, the hunt for the magic mill Sampo, and the tragic fates of Aino, Lemminkäinen, and Kullervo have shaped Finnish national identity and have been translated in many different languages.

To my knowledge, cognitive literary studies have not yet analyzed *Kalevala* to any significant extent. Such studies could easily be imagined, though. Embodied approaches could make much of the implied and actual movements when Väinämöinen sings his rival Joukahainen into the ground; social cognition and theory of mind could address the different competitions throughout the poem, and cognitive stylistics could shed light on the ways in which songs and direct speech intersect. Patrick Colm Hogan (2011: 212) briefly mentions the song of Kullervo as an example of the sexual plot, that is, physical love without attachment, and then as an example of the revenge plot (228), when he discusses"narrative universals" and how they appear to emerge from emotional patterns. ②

Both cognitive literary studies and comparative literature can make an argument about *Kalevala*, related to shared cognitive processes or the condition of having entered world literature. An interesting link

① I take a simple measure ofcanonicity here, as it is also deployed inJschke and Fischer 2016: the number of different language entries a given text has in Wikipedia. Kalevala has entries in sixty-six languages, Seitsemn veljest in twelve languages, and Tuntematon sotilas in ten languages. Sofi Oksanen's 2008 novel Puhdistus (Purge) also has ten languages, and Arto Paasilinna's most referenced novel isJniksen vuosi (The Year of the Hare), published in 1975, with eleven languages.

② See Hogan's article in this issue for his account of how such narrative universals shape emplotment.

between these two lines of argument arises, however, when we consider the issue of translation.

Before Kullervo can become an example in Hogan's *Affective Narratology* (2011), *Kalevala* needs to gain sufficient prominence in the international world of letters for a translator to undertake the massive work of turning it into English, German, French, and so forth, and for a publisher to print and promote it. Pascale Casanova (2004, 2015) and Gisèle Sapiro (2010), taking a sociological perspective on world literature, underline that the question of who gets translated and who does not depends on the power relationships among different languages in the "republic of world literature" (Casanova 2004). In the mid-nineteenth century the stock of texts that might contribute to the national identity of peoples that were hitherto dominated by a colonial language (such as Swedish in Finland) was riding high, and this arguably increased the probability that *Kalevala* would get translated into languages of the center, gaining what Casanova calls *authorization* from the capital. ①

Translators themselves also need to make a range of choices, for example, whether to keep the particular meter of *Kalevala* or to turn the entire oral poem into a prose narrative, and whether to translate particular Finnish terms or to let them stand in the Finnish. Consider the verses from Kullervo's death song, when the perspective shifts and the sword that Kullervo had been addressing suddenly responds:

---

① Casanova (2004) writes mainly about Paris as the capital of literary prestige and about how translation into French and acknowledgment in French literary circles gave authors "authorization" and "consecration" in the world republic of letters.The case of *Kalevala* is slightly different because it is not a text by an individual artist, cashing in on the artistic autonomy and literary prestige that comes with Parisian approval. However, the patterns appear to be similar. While *Kalevala* was not a success in Finland(the original print run offive hundred copies lasted for more than twelve years; see Karkama 2008: 145), it was relatively quickly translated into Swedish(1841/1864—1868), German (1845 in parts), and French (1845/1867) and saw much interest in the European centers.

Miekka mietti miehen mielen
Arvasi uron pakinan
Vastasi sanalla tuolla.

(*Kalevala*, 2015, runo 36: 327–29)

This is translated in the Oxford World Classics edition of Kalevala as

The sword followed the man's drift
It guessed the fellow's chatter
And answered with this word.

(Bosley, 1989: 495)

The translator, Keith Bosley, chose to stay close to the convention that content from the first line of a verse is repeated with different words in the second line. However, he did not attempt to reproduce the initial rhyme in the first line (*mie*kka, *mie*tti, *mie*hen, *mie*len), even though Old English epics, like *Beowulf*, share this feature with *Kalevala*.

The French translator L. Louzon Le Duc (1867: 367), on the other hand, chooses to present the passage in prose: "Le glaive pressentit le dessein de l'homme, il comprit la question du hros, et il lui rpondit." Even though the meter and rhyme are lost in the French, it is closer to the original in other respects. In the French, Kullervo is dubbed a *héros*, more like the Finnish *uros* (which refers to a rather manly and almost brutish protagonist), whereas the English *fellow* gets a lighter quality, especially when combined with *chatter*.

In comparative literature, a significant debate has arisen around languages and their importance as boundaries and conduits of literary text. David Damrosch (2009) argues that it is necessary to read in translation, since translations make a much greater variety of texts available to readers than such readers' language capacities could feasibly allow. Translation makes literature as world literature available: "Read intelligently, an excellent translation can be seen as an expansive transformation of the original, a concrete manifestation of cultural exchange, and a new stage in a work's life as it moves from its first home out into the world" (66). In particular, the French translation of *Kalevala* could be described along these lines.

There are, however, dissenting voices. In particular, Emily Apter (2013) stresses moments of untranslatability when concepts in one language apparently cannot be translated into another language without loss of accuracy, feel, and sharpness. We have already seen the slippery semantic ground around *uros, héros*, and *fellow* in the *Kalevala* translations. Kullervo's epithet *sinisukka* is perhaps an even better example. The term sinisukka literally translates to "bluestocking"but has no feminist meaning in the Finnish, where it refersvctova "fineboy."The term itself cannot be translated literally into English, but that does not necessarily mean that it is untranslatable. Lawrence Venuti (2016) criticizes Apter and argues that, in practice, translators have an entire range of well-established strategies to deal with such problems. Indeed, as Apter herself also acknowledges, texts that are difficult to translate provoke frequent translation attempts. Language itself comes to feature in discussions of world literature through their "knowledge repertoires" (Saussy, 2017) and through the recognition that some literary texts are already "born translated," either because authors translate their own writing or because they already write in order to be translated (Walkowitz, 2015).

The different *Kalevalas* might offer an intriguing case study for world literature and the ways in which cultural capital moves from an early French translation that attempts to make *Kalevala* accessible, to a much later English translation in the Oxford World Classics series that attempts to maintain some feeling of reading a "prehistoric epic" (as the blurb has it) while nevertheless working toward semantic ease. The French translator Le Duc also produced novelistic works such as *L'Odyssée galante d'une princesse russe* (1879), and therefore might have chosen to present his *Kalevala* in a mode more similar to the tradition of adventure literature. Depending on which translation you use, Kullervo is conceived in rather different tones as a chattering *fellow* or a gallant *héros*, and arguably, this inflects how you understand the plot of his tale. While it is easy to make a case for the differences in tone, and for the respective assimilation and differentiation strategies of these *Kalevala* translations, how can we make such an analysis relevant for the encounter between world literature and cognitive literary study?

2 Predictions, Language, and Cognitive Literary Study

Even though many areas of cognitive literary studies, such as cognitive poetics and cognitive stylistics (Semino and Culpeper 2002; Stockwell 2002; Brne and Vandaele 2009), build on linguistics, attention to language differences is rare in the field. The models of linguistics that cognitive poetics and cognitive stylistics draw on, however, are not the only possible way to discuss language from a cognitive perspective. Recent moves in psychology have come to think of cognition as a predictive phenomenon. The approach, named predictive processing, proposes that perception, emotion and thought unfold along a feedback loop between predictions and the ways in which we constantly revise them in our exchange with the environment. ①

Language is a much-discussed example for these predictive processes (see Dehaene 2012). As we learn a language, we learn

① For an introduction, see Wiese and Metzinger 2017; for comprehensive treatments from different positions in philosophy of mind, see Hohwy 2013 and Clark 2015.

regularities and patterns that inform the preconscious and unvoiced predictions underlying later language use. When you read a sentence like this, you can predict, within a reasonable margin of error, the next couple of words that are likely to follow on the basis of the semantic and syntactic principles of English. The words *margin of* already make you predict, on grounds of semantics, that the next word is going to be *error* and, on grounds of syntax, a noun or noun phrase. If I were to write *within a reasonable margarine of error*, presenting you with apredについては error, you would need to decide whether you have a case of malapropism, an autocorrection gone wrong, or a regrettable lack of spelling skill on my part. Fluency in English in the predictive processing account would mean that you get your predictions about this language right, and the better you get at a foreign language, the more easily and effortlessly you predict the words likely to follow. What I have described here are general principles of language according to predictive processing. However, it should be readily apparent that the predictive patterns for English do not transfer to Finnish; different languages require distinct knowledges of predictive patterns.

The predictive patterns related to different languages are not irrelevant variants, but as Gary Lupyan (2012a, 2012b) and Andy Clark (2008) argue, they also shape thought in different ways. The mind is understood to extend into the material, social, and linguistic environment. In the account of the extended mind, we think through the pen in our hand, with our partners in conversation, and, perhaps, through the very sentences we utter. Language is understood as a mode of scaffolding thought. Language points toward particular aspects of the world by giving words to objects, experiences, and concepts, and it thereby parses our perception of and communication about the world in particular ways. The traditional image is that language emerges from the rich soil of thought. The philosopher Clark (2008), however, suggests that it might be the case that language, like the floating roots of a mangrove tree, catches, shapes, and accumulates thought and thereby builds its own context. Thought and language become inextricably entwined. The linguist Lupyan (2012a, 2012b) argues for a theory of language-augmented thought. According to this model, words make real-world phenomena easier to perceive and to recall. It appears to be the case, for example, that verbal cues (such as the word *barking*) lead us to think of a concept faster than a nonverbal cue (such as the sound of a dog barking) (see Lupyan 2012b).

Lupyan and Clark then deploy predictive processing to further model thought augmentation through language. Words that we learn provide us, in the parlance of predictive processing, with top-down predictions regarding the things we perceive, experience, and think about. The verbal cue barking highlights a particular element, providing a verbal marker within the continuity of our auditory perception. Words thereby parse perception and lay fast tracks into our conceptual knowledge. These top-down predictions that come from words are specific to different languages, of course.

In classical cognitive linguistics, words do not affect the working of other cognitive systems, such as perception, memory, and attention (for a much-cited statement, see Pinker 1994), and cognitive literary studies therefore was justified to consider them independently from language. The predictive-processing perspective I have outlined above changes this, because it conceives of a feedback loop between a bottom-up perceptive stream and top-down predictions in verbal markers. When we speak, listen, or talk to ourselves, language creates an auditory environment. The perspective from predictive processing and the extended mind now proposes that language itself not only scaffolds thought but also creates an "artificial context" (Lupyan and Clark 2015: 282-283), a kind of conceptual environment to match the auditory. In this artificial context, words can direct our attention or affect our perception, and language can to some extent "program" the mind by manipulating sen-sory experience (Lupyan and Bergen 2016). Language, then, clearly intercon-nects with general and specific cognitive capacities.

Not only perception and attention but also emotion has been conceptually linked to language in this framework, and thereby another core point of interest for cognitive literary studies comes to be language connected and language specific. Lisa Feldman Barrett (2017) proposes that words invite the formation of emotion concepts and that these emotion concepts, by providing the kind of attention-guiding and perception-shaping predictions mentioned above, then enable us to understand inner bodily states in terms of meaningful emotions. [①] She discusses several examples of emotion words from different languages that lead the speakers of these languages to categorize their bodily experience differently:

Emotion words are not about emotional facts in the world that are stored like static files in your brain. They reflect the varied emotional meanings you construct from mere physical signals in the world using your emotion knowledge. You acquired that knowledge, in part, from the collective knowledge contained in the brains of those who cared for you, talked to you, and helped to create your social world.

Emotions are not reactions to the world; they are your constructions of the world. (104)

Anil Seth (2014: 567) argues, on the same grounds, that based on the regularities we develop from predictions about our bodily states, an "embodied self" emerges, namely, the kind of bodily state "most likely

---

① Casey Schoenberger's article in this issue highlights other aspects of Barrett's work, in particular her notion of the "body budget" as it applies to performance. For a discussion of the body budget in relation to the reading process, see Kukkonen 2020.

to be you."

Language-augmented thought stretches across the entire spectrum of cognitive and affective engagements. Let me illustrate with an example the relevance that this proposal from predictive processing has for matters of translation. Books about particular Nordic embodied selves are selling very well at the moment, in particular those on Danish *hygge* (cozyness). Finland has rather belatedly joined the publishing wave with books on *sisu (*a state of stubborn courage often hailed as a core Finnish personality trait) and *kalsariknni* (Rantanen 2018). *Kalsariknnit* is the ritual of getting drunk in your underwear as you unwind in the evenings. *Kalsarit* are the underwear, and *känni* is the state of intoxication. Miska Rantanen (2018) translates this term in the singular as "pantsdrunk," which works well enough for speakers of US English. However, when you put *kalsarikänni* in the plural, as is commonly the case, *kalsarikännit* evokes the fact that parties and occasions for going out are conventionally rendered in the plural in Finnish, as in *juhlat* (party, celebration). With *kalsarikännit* you ironically make it an occasion by yourself, a twist which would be hard to reproduce with the English translation. However, just through this explanation, your conceptual repertoire has already been extended. If you then read the book on *kalsarikännit* or create such an occasion for yourself in Finland, you will develop a thick set of top-down predictions that relate to the word. A translator might let the Finnish word stand or use the English neologism *pantsdrunk*, and rely on the *realia* of the literary narrative (Leppihalme 2011), the culture-bound elements in a text, to allow readers to glean the predictions necessary to embed the word.

Translation studies prompts us to take the next step in this argument. Venuti (2016) points out that the relevant unit of translation is often not the individual word, which usually appears to be untranslatable, but the sentence, the paragraph, and sometimes the text itself. The perspective from predictive processing works along exactly this kind of trade-off between the individual word and the linguistic context of sentences and *realia* in which it is embedded. The Finnish word *kalsarikännit*, taken by itself, works as a verbal marker that lays a conceptual shortcut once you know it. In a longer prose text, a "larger unit of translation" (Venuti 2016: 189), readers can glean the predictions that come with familiar words, or indeed, it might reconfigure these predictions.

The links between words and the predictions that they provide for our perception of and thinking about the world are not fixed. Indeed, throughout our lives we learn new words in our own languages and from other languages that expand and adjust our repertoires of concepts, even though our first languages themselves prefigure a certain range of predictions. The predictive processing perspective on language and thought therefore does not correspond to the Sapir-Whorf hypothesis (or, rather, its foreshortened interpretations). As Daniel Casasanto (2008) points out in "Who's Afraid of the Big Bad Whorf?", the claim that language shapes our thoughts (which is held in predictive processing) is not the same as the claim that we think in language (which is usually imputed to be Whorf's stance). It seems quite likely that thought does not coincide with language, but this does not mean that language would not have an effect on the ways in which we think. Through the processes of parsing, attending, and categorizing, language can still impact thought. There is controversy around the extent to which language shapes thought; however, it appears that different languages and their conceptual systems can prime our attention in different ways.

The perspective I have outlined here does not lock speakers of a language in their own conceptual world, as would a strict version of linguistic relativity (such as the Sapir-Whorf hypothesis). It rather shows how language enables usto pay attention to different aspects of our experience and to conceptualize it. Arguably, language in literature also works along these lines, even though its emphasis, specificity, and room for ambiguity will differ from everyday language use. Indeed, we might think of literary texts as a "designed sensory flow" that constantly challenges and adjusts the top-down predictions we carry through our linguistic, cultural, and literary knowledge (see Kukkonen 2020). What does such a perspective on language in cognitive approaches to literature mean for the issue of translation and world literature?

3 Kullervo's Knife and Kalevala's Rhyme: On the Translatability of Plot

The plot of a literary narrative might appear a long way from concerns of translation and language. But what if we were to consider the possibility that predictive processing might depend on probabilistic predictions that resemble the predictions we make in understanding plots? Readers' predictions, as they arise from the words and the sentences, contribute to the large predictive links we call *plot*, while in turn, the plot markers (i. e. , verbal cues indicating plot events) provide orientation for readers' inferences as the narrative progresses. The designed sensory flow of the text, in other words, teaches readers how it should be read, and the predictions involved here have a language-specific dimension. Recall that Hogan describes Kullervo's tale on the one hand as a sexual plot (referring to Kullervo's sexual relationship with a woman he meets in the woods and who turns out to be his sister) and on the other hand as a revenge plot (referring to Kullervo's revenge on his uncle Untamo for killing his family, even as it turns out that they are alive and well). There is another way for looking at the plot of Kullervo's story, though. We can think of plot events as prediction errors, that is, unexpected events that lead readers to reconfigure their predictions for how the story will continue. The major plot events yield a trajectory of reconfigured predictions, that is, moments at which readers' emotional investments also change. For example, while Kullervo discovering that his family is still alive is a prediction error that makes a happy outcome more likely, the following prediction error that the woman he just slept with is in fact his sister makes a tragic outcome more likely (and, in fact, sets Kullervo on the path to suicide). The configuration of a plot in the model of predictive processing is a complex constellation of these epistemic (what is likely to happen) and emotional (what we want to happen) probabilities (see Kukkonen 2014).

Plot events are moments that change the predictions and probabilities in a narrative. They are not only salient in this respect but also often marked in the language of the narrative. In modern novels this may happen through shifts in focalization (see Kukkonen 2020). In *Kalevala*, readers' attention is pointed toward plot events through particular verbal markers. For instance, it is striking how often blades are mentioned when major plot events occur. Kullervo decides to break his bondage to Ilmarinen when his father's knife breaks on the stone bread that Ilmarinen's wife had given him. When Kullervo finds out that the woman he just slept with is his sister, he cuts the links to his horses with a knife, and when he has killed his uncle Untamo, he decides to take his own life, talking to his sword (the passage discussed earlier). The blade is clearly the focal point of Kullervo's emotional engagements, and it arguably signals plot events to readers. These are the moments when Kullervo snaps.

The blades amount to more than a traditional motif, however. Throughout reading the Kullervo cycle, readers learn to assign a particular conceptual and emotional relevance and meaning to the blades[1]. It starts to prime readers' attention, prepares particular top-down predictions, and generally marks moments of highly emotional involvements. Just as I have introduced the word *kalsarikännit* to you earlier, so have you learned about the relevance of the blade in *Kalevala*, and so would you have learned about it easily and unobtrusively while reading the narrative itself. The blade plays a role in all three versions of *Kalevala* discussed. In Le Duc's (1867: 342) French prose version, Kullervo mentions the broken knife three times to Ilmarinen's wife: "Mon couteau s'est ébrèché contre la pierre, il s'est brisé contre le rocher, le couteau, seul héritage que j'ai reçu de mon père, le couteau qui appartenu à ma famille." In the Finnish, it is mentioned twice:

> Ve'in veitseni kivehen,
> Karahutin kalliohon
> ——Ainoan isoni veitsen,
> Sukukuntani kuraksen.
>
> (*Kalevala*, 2015, 33: 235-238)

In the English, we have again three mentions:

> I took my knife to the stone
> And upon the rock
> Scrunched my matchless father's knife
> My kinsfolk's dagger!
>
> (Bosley, 1989: 465)

It is at this moment that Kullervo's relationship to his family is

① As research in concepts shows, the learning of concepts is closely linked to emotions (see Ponari, Norbury, and Vigliocci 2017).

broken properly. The repetition ("father's knife" and "kinfolk's dagger") establishes the relevant parallelisms. The breaking of the family relationship happens to "Kullervo, son of Kalervo" because of a stone in his bread, but it is Kullervo himself who wields and breaks the knife. With the breaking of the knife, Kullervo thinks his family finally gone, even though he finds his father, Kalervo, and his mother and siblings alive in the next song of the poem.

The second appearance of the knife occurs at the moment when he realizes that he has ravished his sister and that a return to his family is impossible. The knife joins the first episode to the second, and arguably, it allows readers to make sense of the connection between the two events by linking their changing probabilities (even though they will probably not articulate this) and moving seamlessly through a narrative that stretches across two very different plot prototypes in Hogan's account. The blades in Kullervo's story refer back to earlier moments that similarly work as plot events, and they arguably draw readers' attention to the changing relevance of the blade as the plot develops.

The fact that whenever Kullervo snaps there are blades involved is striking, but it does not presuppose that such central plot concepts necessarily refer to sharp and dangerous objects. Johanna Sinisalo ([2003] 2015) introduces a very different plot marker in the novel *Sankarit*, her version of *Kalevala*. In *Sankarit* the mythical heroes of *Kaleval*a are reimagined in the present day through the personas of rock stars. Sinisalo assumes a basic familiarity of her readers with the characters and narrative of *Kalevala* (though, arguably, this does not exceed the familiarity of most Finns with *Kalevala*). The magic smith Seppo Ilmarinen is readily recognizable in the character Ile Aerosmith, Väinämöinen in Vesa Kuningas, and Joukahainen in his rival Joakim. *Sankarit*, like *Kalevala*, is patterned by the songs of the heroes. For the issue of plot, however, it is the rhyme of Kalevala itself that serves as a marker. When in Sinisalo's *Sankarit* Kullervo's uncle Untamo destroys the family (by building a skiing resort on their land), the paragraph begins: "Kaivinkone kirnuaa kuoppaa kiviseen maahan, se on kirkkaankeltainen kirppu Unnastunturin taivaaseen ulottuvan töyrään varjossa" (277; The digger churns holes into the stony ground, it is a bright yellow flea in the shadow of the banks of Unnastunturi hill that stretch into the sky).

In her prose narrative Sinisalo reproduces typical features of *Kalevala*, both the initial rhyme and the repetition of the first line in the second. The wife of Ilmarinen begins her contradictory relationship with Kullervo with the following line: "Tytti Pohjola-Ilmarinen katsoo Karelia [=Kullervo in *Sankarit*] ja hänen käsivarsiensa karvat pörhistyvät pystyyn, kurkuu kuivuu voimattomasta vihasta" (289; Ilmarinen's wife looks at Kullervo and the hairs on her arm stand on end, the throat dries from powerless rage). And when the passage begins where Kullervo realizes that he slept with his sister (and she commits suicide), Sinisalo writes: "[I]kkunalaudalla kasteessa näkyy paljaan jalan jättämä juova, ja jossakin yhdeksän kerrosta alempana, hämäryyden verhoamana, häämöttää harmaan ja valkoisen kirjavalla kivetyksellä epä määräisen muotoinen vääntynyt kuvio; se muistuttaa niitä outoja olentoja, joita Karel piirsi pienenä puotipaperit täyteen" (315-16; On the window sill in the dew the track of a naked foot could be seen, and there below, nine stories farther down and obscured by the gloom, an irregularly shaped and twisted figure is barely visible on the gray and white speckled pavement; it resembles the strange creatures that Kullervo drew all over the wrapping paper). Such instances of initial rhyme can be found elsewhere in Finnish prose, too, for example, in Aleksis Kivi's *Seven Brothers* (1870). But Sinisalo does not use it to create lyrical impressions. Throughout *Sankarit*, the narrator and the protagonists (we also find this in direct speech) themselves signal plot events when the narrative approaches the model of *Kalevala* by reproducing the particular initial rhyme in the prose. We have here a stylistic device different from Kullervo's blade, which nevertheless marks plot events, their emotional involvements, and conceptual relevance.

With Kullervo's knife and Sinisalo's rhymes, the narratives create their own artificial contexts, as Lupyan and Clark (2015) would have it. The word or the stylistic device serves as a marker; they scaffold readers' pursuit of the plot as they make their way through the linguistic environment of these texts. The probability design of the text develops readers' understanding progressively. When the knife appears for the second time or when Sinisalo launches into *Kalevala* verse, readers learn that these linguistic features relate to plot events. Just as you got to know *kalsarikännit* from my explanations, so do readers of *Kalevala* and *Sankarit* learn about the conceptual structure of the plot from the artificial context of language that these literary texts build. We have to place a question mark after the notion that plots are universal and not relevant for translation if we start considering these texts from the point of view of predictive processing. Words or stylistic devices in the text mark the points at which plot events occur; they guide attention and facilitate between the concrete flow of the text and the abstraction of the plot configuration. If we start paying attention to these points of transfer between text and plot, we might well find plot markers that make plot a matter of translation, too.

Indeed, words in a foreign language draw attention to and might highlight related plot events even more strongly. Readers do not necessarily have to understand the words for them to work as plot markers, but there tend to beknowledge. If Kullervo snaps when his knife comes into play or if *Sankarit*'s plot aligns with *Kalevala* when the verse appears, plot markers arguably work more effectively when readers know what they mean. Texts, however, do not leave readers alone with this task, and translators arguably can work with the artificial context of larger stretches of text when they need to translate plot. From this point of view, plots are not narrative universals but an important component of a cognitive approach that takes language differences into account.

4 A Cognitive Approach to World Literature through a Cognitive Approach to Translation

The way I seek to combine world literature and cognitive approaches goes through language difference and textual traditions rather than through narrative universals. The perspective from predictive processing will not lead to a certain number of plot prototypes that can be surveyed and compared; the number of potential markers of plot events (and the configurations that emerge from them) is as infinite as the number of potential narratives. What I propose is to draw attention to the moments when plots configure and when readers' emotional involvement is heightened to do particular conceptual work in translation (or not, depending on the decision of the translator). My own translations of Sinisalo's text elide the rhymes, but it is not inconceivable that a more gifted translator could retain them in the English.

The present article is only a preliminary proposal, for a number of reasons. First, a cognitive account of language differences has not yet been integrated in cognitive approaches to literature. Drawing on work in predictive processing, I have begun to sketch an alternative account where language differences really make a difference, but a lot of work remains to be done. Second, the relationship among predictions, prediction errors, and the plots of literary narratives needs to be developed in much more detail. Elsewhere I have worked toward a general account of such probability designs, the tensions between creating and breaking readers' expectations (Kukkonen 2020). In this article, I have merely highlighted how plots can relate to issues of translation. Third, cognitive translation studies has not been brought into contact with cognitive literary studies. It appears to me, though, that cognitive processes of translators, such as metacognition and uncertainty management, expert processes and bilingualism (which are a mainstay of discussion in cognitive translation studies; Shreve and Angelone 2010), could enter into an interesting dialogue with cognitive literary studies. Moreover, Sandra L. Halverson's (2003: 218) account of linguistic features that typically appear in translated texts and the "gravitational pull" of highly salient lexical and semantic structures in language could be discussed through predictive processing. In these final paragraphs, I attempt to outline what insights and impulses such a cognitive approach to literary translation could provide for world literature.

Literature, Rebecca Walkowitz (2015) argues, is "born translated" because some writers are polyglot (her examples are the usual suspects: Coetzee, Beckett, etc.). One might extend Walkowitz's argument to literary language itself as born translated in the sense that the markers of plot events can refer to salient concepts and stylistic devices from other authors and other languages. In the case of Sinisalo, this translation happens across the historically different uses of Finnish as a literary language from Lo¨nnrot's Kalevala in the nineteenth century to Sinisalo's novel in the twenty-first century. ① Plot markers could be a way to identify salient concepts imported by authors who themselves

① *Kalevala* was originally a set of oral epics collected by Lönnrot on his travels through eastern Finland, but Lönnrot transformed the the dialect-based oral poetry considerably, making it more "literary," when getting the text ready for publication.

might not be polyglot.

More generally relevant, a cognitive literary translation studies would need to account for (1)strategies of domestication and alienation (rendering foreign), (2)concepts and contexts, and (3)the relationship between textual strategies and the power dynamics of the world republic of letters. Lawrence Venuti (1995) distinguishes between translational strategies of domestication and foreignization. The *Kalevala* translation in French would be an example where the Finnish epic is familiarized for French readers in the second half of the nineteenth century. The *Kalevala* translation in English, in turn, would be an example where the text is made strange and its foreignness is foregrounded for the Oxford World Classics series. Such domestication and foreignization can unfold through all levels of the text. From the point of view of predictive processing, a cognitive translation studies could investigate whether the translation draws on familiar cultural patterns of prediction or introduces readers to new prediction patterns, and which expository modes are deployed. Are these new predictive patterns linked to particular concepts from other languages? Are they placed at prominent plot points, thus drawing the attention of readers to how they are ingrained in the shape of the narrative? Or are they tied to the idiosyncratic speech of a character? Through these distinctions, a cognitive translation studies could arrive at an account of familiarized/foregrounded foreignness in the conceptual shape of the narrative versus familiarized/foregrounded foreignness that pertains to particular characters, while the narrator maintains a different stance.

Translational norms, that is, the regularities that pattern regimes and practices of translation, have been a center of debate in translation studies between culturally oriented and linguistically oriented approaches (see Vandaele, forthcoming). The French and English translations of *Kalevala* already indicate a profound difference of translational norms. Gideon Toury (1995) and Itamar Even-Zohar (1990) have done important work on translational norms through discussions of diverse textual features, but they have not explored the relevance of plot. It appears to me, however, that plot, especially because of its importance for the narrative's conceptualization, could contribute to the understanding of how translations develop their own norms.

The discussions around translatability can also be developed through the particular attention to plot markers I propose. The conceptual salience is arguably heightened when untranslated terms serve as plot markers. The question arises whether or not the translator then chooses to create an artificial context in the rest of the text that will make readers understand the relevant predictions connected to the untranslated word. For such cases, one could distinguish between embedded and isolated untranslatables. With embedded untranslatables the rest of the narrative proves some kind of explanatory context for the untranslated word; for isolated untranslatables it does not. Then, following Apter (2013), one could investigate whether embedded untranslatables defuse the disruptiveness or continue to function as a checkpoint of translation. Predictive processing and the account of plot markers could further contextualize these effects. Since plot events are conceptualized as prediction errors that revise readers' expectations, their integration into the rest of the narrative and its artificial context could smooth over the surprise of the prediction error and make the oddness of the untranslated word disappear, or it could emphasize the oddness and underline its salience.

Plot markers and the ways in which they are translated might also provide a way to talk about larger power distributions in the world republic of letters in relation to the dynamics within the texts themselves. Casanova (2004) mainly discusses statements about literature (manifestos, reflections, etc.), but it appears to me that her observations could also be applied to the prestige economy between plot markers, prominent elements of the text, and other aspects of narrative discourse. Taking into account the role that writers and translators play in the articulated field of globalized literature (see Sapiro 2010), we could ask, Are writers from the periphery of the literary field more likely to introduce plot markers that are very culturally specific words? And do writers who write to be translated opt for conceptually more unobtrusive plot markers, while they might keep culturally specific modes of writing for the discourse of characters? Looking at the inverse direction of translation, will translators from central into peripheral languages keep culturally specific plot markers (given the prestige that might be linked to the source language)?

Do these choices reveal explicit strategies of resistance and assimilation, and how do these relate to authors' and translators' self-understanding? And, finally, it would be interesting to investigate how plot markers feature in what Casanova (2015) calls *minor literature*: literature written in a language of the center that nevertheless subverts the values of the center. Are plot markers perhaps the knives that these authors stick into the back of mainstream language, thereby developing their particular mode of literariness?

Does cognition translate? I have approached this question through the issue of how different languages might shape thought differently and how these differences become salient for the study of plot. As I hope I have shown, predictive processing is a cognitive model that is well suited for the purpose. It allows for language differences to make a difference and also accommodates the ways in which literary texts both create and disrupt our expectations and norms. Along the avenues I have outlined above, cognitive literary studies could expand its repertoire and relevance and enter into a new interdisciplinary exchange, this time with comparative literature and translation studies.

References

[1] APTER EMILY. Against World Literature: On the Politics of Untranslatability. London: Verso, 2013.

[2] BARRETT LISA FELDMAN. How Emotions Are Made: The Secret Life of the Brain. London: Macmillan, 2017.

[3] BOSLEY KEITH, trans. The Kalevala. Oxford: Oxford University Press, 1989.

[4] BRÔNE GEERT, JEROEN VANDAELE, eds. Cognitive Poetics: Goals, Gains, and Gaps. Berlin: Mouton de Gruyter, 2009.

[5] CASANOVA PASCALE. The World Republic of Letters. Cambridge, MA: Harvard University Press, 2004.

[6] CASANOVA PASCALE. La langue mondiale: Traduction et domination. Paris: Seuil, 2015.

[7] CASASANTO DANIEL. "Who's Afraid of the Big Bad Whorf ? Crosslinguistic Differences in Temporal Language and Thought." Language Learning, 2008, 58, suppl. 1: 63-79.

[8] CLARK ANDY. Supersizing the Mind: Embodiment, Action, and Cognitive Extension. Oxford: Oxford University Press, 2008.

[9] CLARK ANDY. Surfing Uncertainty: Prediction, Action, and the Embodied Mind. Oxford: Oxford University Press, 2015.

[10] DAMROSCH DAVID. How to Read World Literature. Malden, MA: Wiley-Blackwell, 2009.

[11] DEHAENE STANISLAS. "Le cerveau statisticien: La re´volution Baye´sienne en sciences cognitives." Lectures at Colle`ge de France, 2012, January 10-February 21. Http: //www. college-de-france. fr/site/stanislas-dehaene/course-2011-2012. htm.

[12] EVEN-ZOHAR ITAMAR. "Gnessin's Dialogue and Its Russian

Models." Poetics Today, 1990, 11 (1): 131 -152.
[13] HALVERSON SANDRA. "The Cognitive Basis of Translation Universals." Target, 2003, 15 (2): 197-241.
[14] HOGAN PATRICK COLM. Affective Narratology: The Emotional Structure of Stories. Lincoln: University of Nebraska Press, 2011.
[15] HOHWY JAKOB. The Predictive Mind. Oxford: University of Oxford Press, 2013.
[16] JÄSCHKE ROBERT, FRANK FISCHER. "Contributors to World Literature—Identifying Writers in Wikipedia, Part II." weltliteratur. net (blog), 2016, August 19. Http: //weltliteratur. net/Contri butors-to-World-Literature-Identifying-Writers-in-Wikipedia- Part-II.
[17] Kalevala ja opas sen lukemisen. Helsinki: Suomalaisen Kirjallisuuden Seura, 2015.
[18] KARKAMA PERTTI. "Kalevala ja kansallisuusaate." In Ulla Piela, edited by Seppo Knuuttila and Pekka Laaksonen, Helsinki: Suomalaisen Kirjallisuuden Seura, 2008: 124-169.
[19] KUKKONEN KARIN. "Bayesian Narrative: Probability, Plot, and the Shape of the Fictional World." Anglia, 2014, 123 (4): 720-739.
[20] KUKKONEN KARIN. Probability Designs: Literature and Predictive Processing. New York: Oxford University Press, 2020.
[21] LE DUC, L LÉOUZON, trans. Le Kalevala, épopée nationale de la Finlande et des peuples finnois. Paris: Librairie internationale, 1867. https: //gallica. bnf. fr/ark: /12148/bpt6k65356671. texteImage.
[22] LEPPIHALME RITVA. "Realia." In Handbook of Translation Studies, edited by Yves Gambier and Luc van Dorselaer. Amsterdam: Benjamins, 2011: 126-130.
[23] LUPYAN GARY. "Language-Augmented Prediction." Frontiers in Psychology, 2012a (3): 422.
[24] LUPYAN GARY. "What Do Words Do? Toward a Theory of

Language- Augmented Thought." Psychology of Learning and Motivation, 2012b, 57: 255-297.

[25] LUPYAN GARY, BENJAMIN BERGEN. "How Language Programs the Mind." Topics in Cognitive Science, 2016, 8 (2): 408-421.

[26] LUPYAN, GARY, ANDY CLARK. "Words and the World: Predictive Coding and the Language-Perception-Cognition Interface." Current Directions in Psychological Science, 2015, 24 (4): 287 -294.

[27] PINKER STEVEN. The Language Instinct: How the Mind Creates Language. Harmondsworth: Penguin, 1994.

[28] PONARI MARTA, Courtenay Frazier Norbury, Gabriella Vigliocci. "Acquisition of Abstract Concepts Is Influenced by Emotional Valence." Developmental Science, 2017, 21 (2): e12549.

[29] RANTANEN MISKA. Kalsarika: The Finnish Path to Relaxation. London: HarperCollins, 2018.

[30] SAPIRO GISÈLE. Globalisation and Cultural Diversity in the Book Market: The Case of Literary Translation in the US and France. Poetics, 2010(38), no. 4: 419-39.

[31] SAUSSY HAUN. "Language as Knowledge Reservoirs." Know, 2017, 1 (2): 259-272.

[32] SEMINO ELENA, JONATHAN CULPEPER, eds. Cognitive Stylistics: Language and Cognition in Text Analysis. Amsterdam: Benjamins, 2002.

[33] SETH ANIL. "Interoceptive Inference, Emotion, and the Embodied Self." Trends in Cognitive Science, 2014, 17 (11): 565-573.

[34] SHREVE GREGORY, ERIK ANGELONE. "Translation and Cognition: Recent Developments." In Translation and Cognition, edited by Gregory Shreve and Erik Angelone. Amsterdam: Benjamins, 2010: 1-16.

[35] SINISALO JOHANNA. Sankarit. Helsinki: Teos, 2003/2015

[36] STOCKWELL PETER. Cognitive Poetics: An Introduction. London: Routledge, 2002.

[37] TOURY GIDEON. "The Nature and Role of Norms in Translation." In Descriptive Translation Studies and Beyond. Amsterdam: Benjamins, 1995: 53-69.

[38] VANDAELE JEROEN. "A Science of the Times? Descriptive Translation Studies and History." In The Routledge Handbook of Translation History, edited by Christopher Rundle. London and New York: Routledge, forthcoming.

[39] VENUTI LAWRENCE. Translator's Invisibility: A History of Translation. London: Routledge, 1995.

[40] VENUTI LAWRENCE. "Hijacking Translation: How Comp Lit Continues to Suppress Translated Texts." Boundary 2, 2016, 43 (2): 179-204.

[41] WALKOWITZ REBECCA. Born Translated: The Contemporary Novel in the Age of World Literature. New York: Columbia University Press, 2015.

[42] WIESE WANJA, THOMAS METZINGER. "Vanilla PP for Philosophers: A Primer on Predictive Processing." In Philosophy and Predictive Processing, vol. 1, edited by Thomas Metzinger and Wanja Wiese. Frankfurt am Main: MIND Group, 2017.

认知是否可译？预测、情节与世界文学

卡琳·库克伦 著　李丹云 译

【摘要】比较文学研究和认知文学研究都将文学视作世界范围内的普遍现象。比较文学领域的“世界文学”转向使得阅读文学翻译文本的适切性问题更为突显，世界文学将注意力转向文本是否完全可译，关注“世界文学共和国”的版图是如何围绕源语和译语来构建分布。本文提出认知文学研究和比较文学研究可以围绕语言差异与翻译这一话题展开讨论。近年来，预测加工和具身认知的方法发展了认知语言学研究的概念手段，而让我们不必依赖于萨皮尔-沃尔夫（Sapir-Whorf）假说。语言塑造思维，但却是在语言标记和语言创造的语境间进行灵活交换的方式来进行的。本文通过能够突显情节事件的语言标记（verbal markers）来模拟文学文本的这种交换，并勾勒出未来认知文学研究和比较文学研究可能的共同途径。文中以芬兰民族史诗《英雄国》（*Kalevala*）的法文和英文译本，以及乔安娜·西尼萨洛（Johanna Sinisalo）的当代小说《英雄》（*Sankarit*）为例，进行相关探讨。

【关键词】翻译；认知文学研究；预测加工；情节；《英雄国》；乔安娜·西尼萨洛

比较文学与认知文学都着眼于全球文学研究。在过去的几十年里，比较文学已经走出了欧洲经典研究，进入跨国文学的世界文学

作者简介：卡琳·库克伦（Karin Kukkonen），女，挪威奥斯陆大学比较文学方向教授，主要从事比较文学和认知文学研究。

译者简介：李丹云，女，海南医学院外国语学院副教授，四川外国语大学英语学院博士研究生，主要从事认知诗学和文体话语分析研究。

体系研究，文学文本的翻译成为研究重点。因为任何语言和国度的文学都离不开其思维和情感这两个特点，因此，认知文学本质上将所有文学研究都视为其研究对象。当全球视角下的比较文学一直在争论文本是否可译以及如何翻译之时，认知文学研究一直在回避语言差异这个问题，而从更为广义的层面上去讨论“文学”这个话题。鉴于此，为了建立认知文学研究与比较文学之间的联系，我重新讨论了语言差异和翻译问题。令我特别感兴趣的是特定语言的文学如何促成情节的抽象化，以及它们如何在翻译中传播。在对情节的讨论中，我初步提出了关于语言差异的认知文学研究的方法，进而可能与比较文学展开对话。

1 普遍性、翻译与世界文学

芬兰史诗《英雄国》（*Kalevala*），又译作《卡勒瓦拉》，是由 19 世纪诗人伊莱亚斯·伦罗特（Elias Lönnrot）长期深入民间收集芬兰东部地区的民谣润色汇编而成，于 1835—1836 年出版，被称为《老英雄国》（*Old Kalevala*），1849 年修订版出版《新英雄国》（*New Kalevala*），是芬兰民族文学对世界文学的一大贡献。它或许是除芬兰民众以外最为世人所熟知的作品了，超越了后来的经典名著阿列克西斯·基围（Aleksis Kivi）的《七兄弟》（*Seitsemän veljestä*，1870）、维因内·林纳（Väinö Linna）的《无名战士》（*Tun-tematon sotilas*，1954）以及当代最受欢迎的索菲·奥克萨宁（Sofi Oksanen）和阿托·帕西林纳（Arto Paasilinna）的作品。史诗围绕芬兰文化英雄维纳莫宁（Väinämäinen）展开，寻找神磨桑波（Sampo），故事中阿伊诺（Aino）、莱明基宁（Lemminkäinen）和库勒沃（Kullervo）的悲惨命运已经成为芬兰的民族身份象征，并被翻译成多种语言。

据我所知，认知文学研究领域还没有对《英雄国》进行过重要分析。尽管这样的研究是很容易想象的。当维纳莫宁以歌唱的方式将他的竞争对手朱卡海因（Joukahainenen）引到地面时，通过具身方法有助于充分理解其中许多隐含的和实际的行动；社会认知和心智理论能够解读全诗中许多不同冲突，而认知文体学可以为我们理解诗中歌谣和直接引语是如何交叉贯穿提供线索。帕特里克·科尔姆·霍根（Patrick Colm Hogan，2011：212）在讨论“叙事共性”以及它们是如何从情感模式中显现出来时，简要提及将库勒沃的歌谣作为性爱情节以及复仇情节的例子，认为这是一种没有依恋关系的物欲之爱（Hogan，2011：228）。

认知文学研究和比较文学研究都涉及共同的认知过程或与进入世界文学的条件有关，因而都可以就《英雄国》进行讨论。然而，当我们在考虑翻译问题时，这两种观点之间出现了有趣的联系。

在霍根把库勒沃当作其《情感叙事学》（*Affective Narratology*，2011）中的一个例子之前，《英雄国》还并未引起国际文学界的关注。因此，若要将其译成英语、德语、法语等多种语言，并供出版商印刷制作，译者还需要做大量工作。帕斯卡莱·卡萨诺瓦（Pascale Casanova，2004，2015）和吉赛尔·萨皮罗（Gisèle Sapiro，2010）从社会学的角度看待世界文学，强调在“世界文学共和国”（Casanova，2001）中，译与被译取决于不同语言之间的权力关系。19世纪中期有关民族身份的文学创作风头正起，而这一时期的民族身份一直都受殖民语言（比如芬兰的瑞典语）支配，这就有可能增加了这部史诗被译为主导语言的可能性，即需要获得卡萨诺瓦所称的来自首都的所谓“授权”。

译者本人也需要做出一系列的选择，比如，是保留本诗特定的韵律还是把整首口语化的诗变成散文叙事诗，是翻译成某些特定的芬兰词汇还是不做翻译保持不变。例如库勒沃的死亡之歌这一节，当视角转变，库勒沃正在演讲时，那把剑突然回应道：

Miekka mietti miehen mielen
剑想知道男人的心灵
Arvasi uron pakinan
猜到了乌罗的包

Vastasi sanalla tuolla.
那边的字回答。

（*Kalevala*, 2015, runo 36: 327-29）

而在《牛津世界经典》版本中，*Kalevala* 被翻译为：

The sword followed the man's drift
那把剑跟着那人的动向
It guessed the fellow's chatter
它猜到了那家伙的喋喋不休
And answered with this word.
并以此答语。

（Bosley, 1989: 495）

译者基斯·博思利（Keith Bosley）选择了保持惯例，即从第一行开始，在第二行重复使用不同的单词。然而，他并没有试图重现第一行的首韵（miekka mietti miehen mielen），即使像《贝奥武夫》（*Beowulf*）这样的古英语史诗与《英雄国》也有同样的特征。

法国译者莱奥桑·勒杜克（L. Léouzon Le Duc）（1867：367）选择以散文形式呈现这一段。尽管法语中没有韵律和韵脚，但它在其他方面更接近原文。在法语中，库勒沃被称为“英雄”（héros），更像芬兰语的“男性”（uros）（指的是一个相当有男子气概、近乎野蛮的主人），而英语中的 fellow（男人）一词则显得比较轻松，尤其与 chatter（唠叨）一词搭配使用的时候。

在比较文学中，有关语言及其重要性是否应该作为文学语篇的界限和路径，成为研究者们争论的焦点之一。戴维·达姆罗施（David Damrosch，2009）认为有必要阅读翻译作品，因为翻译为读者提供了比读者自身语言能力所能达成的更丰富的文本。翻译使得文学走向世界成为可能：“（翻译）能使阅读明智，一部优秀的翻译作品可以被看作是原作品的延伸和拓展，是文化交流的具体表现，是作品从最初的归宿走向世界的一个新阶段。”（Damrosch，2009：66）特别是《英雄国》的法文译本堪称此类作品代表。

然而，其中也有反对的声音。艾米莉·阿普特（Emily Apter，2013）特别强调了某些情况下的不可译性，即在一种语言中出现的概念在另一种语言中没有可以对等的概念，这就未免会使其丧失准确性、感觉和清晰度。我们已经在《英雄国》的翻译中看到了 uros、héros 和 fellow 的模糊语义基础。库勒沃的绰号 sinisukka 或许是一个更好的例子。“sinisukka”一词的字面意思是“bluestocking”（女学者，装作有学问的女人），但在芬兰语中没有女权主义之意，指的是“好男孩”。然而，有学者认为虽然这个词不能按照字面意思翻译成英语，并不等于它不能被翻译。劳伦斯·韦努蒂（Lawrence Venuti，2016）批判了阿普特的观点，认为在实践中，译者有一整套行之有效的策略来处理这些问题。事实上，阿普特本人也承认，那些很难翻译的文本往往还会引发频繁的翻译尝试。语言本身是通过他们的“知识库”（knowledge repertoires）（Saussy，2017）来讨论世界文学的特色，我们得认识到某些文学文本本身已经“生来具有可译性”，一方面是因为作者自己翻译自己的作品，另一方面是因为他们为了翻译而写作（Walkowitz，2015）。

《英雄国》不同的翻译版本或许为世界文学提供了一个有趣的案例研究，它体现了文化的中心是如何转移的，早期的法文翻译还只是让《英雄国》浮出水面，为世人所见，而后来的《牛津世界经典文学》中的英文版本翻译则给人一种“史前史诗”的感觉（正如书的简介所宣扬的），然而实际上却是在朝着语义功能的方向前进。法国翻译家勒杜克自己也创作了小说作品，例如《奥德修斯的冒险》（1879），因此他本可以选择以一种更接近冒险文学的传统来翻译他的《英雄国》。根据译者使用的翻译方式，库勒沃可以被理解为一个健谈的小伙子，或者是一个勇敢的英雄，两种翻译的感情基调差异极大，且可以说，这种基调能反映出译者是如何理解故事的情节。要举出一个翻译的感情基调不同的例子很简单。但是，就《英雄国》这本民谣集采取同化或是异化翻译策略而言，我们如何从世界文学和认知文学研究角度做出相关的分析呢？

2 预测、语言与认知文学研究

尽管认知文学研究的许多领域，如认知诗学和认知文体学是建立在语言学基础之上（Semino & Culpeper 2002；Stockwell 2002；Brône & Vandaele，2009），但在此领域内鲜有关注语言差异的。然而，认知诗学和认知文体学所借鉴的现代语言学模式并不是从认知学角度讨论语言的唯一可能方法。最近心理学的研究发现，认知是一种预测性的现象，被称为“预测处理”，提出感知、情感和思维会沿着一条预测“反馈环”（feedback loop）逐渐展开，在我们与环境的交流中不断修正我们的预测。

语言则是这些预测过程中一个被广泛讨论的例子（Dehaene，2012）。当我们学习一种语言时，我们学习的是其常见规律和模式，这些规律和模式为我们的前意识和无声预测提供了信息，这些预测正是后期语言使用的基础。当你读这样的句子时，根据英语语法和句法规则，你可以在误差范围内预测接下来可能会出现的几个单词；根据语义学规则，“误差”这个词让你能够预测到接下来的单词将会是“错误”；而根据句法规则，它应该是一个名词或者名词短语。如果我为了向你展示一个预测错误的例子，误把 margin 写成了 margarine，那么你需要确定是你词语理解错误，还是文本自动纠错功能出了问题，抑或是作者拼写错误。在预测过程中，英语流利将意味着你用这门语言做出的预测是正确的，你越擅长一门外语，你就越容易预测接下来可能出现的单词。我在这里所描述的正是基于预测处理的一般语言原则。然而，很明显，英语的预测模式不会自然而然地转移到芬兰语中，不同的语言需要不同的预测模式知识。

与不同语言相关的预测模式与其变体有关，但正如盖里·卢普言（Gary Lupyan）（2012a，2012b）和安迪·克拉克（Andy Clark，2008）所说，预测模式也以不同方式在塑造着思维。众所周知，心智已经延伸到物质、社会和语言环境之中。在扩展的思维中，我们通过手中的笔与我们的伙伴交谈，也许还通过我们所说的每句话进行思考。语言被理解为支撑思维的一种模式。语言通过描述事物、经验和概念，来认识来世界的特定方面，从而以特定的方式解析我们对世界的感知和交流。传统观点认为，语言是从理性思维中产生的。然而，哲学家克拉克（2008）认为，语言可能像红树林漂浮的根一样，可以捕捉、塑造并积累思维，并由此构建语境，思想和语言变得密不可分。语言学家卢普言（Lupyan，2012a，2012b）提出了“语言增强思维理论”（theory of language-augmented thought）。该理论认为，词汇使得现实世界的现象更容易被感知和回忆。例如，言语符码（如“吠叫”这个单词）比起非言语信息（比如真正的狗叫声音），会让我们更快地想到什么是“犬吠”的概念（Lupyan，2012b）。

卢普言和克拉克接着运用预测处理过程，通过语言进一步发展了他们的思维增强理论。我们所学的词汇为我们所感知、体验和思考的事物提供了自上而下的预测。“吠声”这个词汇提示突出了一个特殊的元素，在我们听觉感知的范围内提供了一个言语标记。因此，词汇有助于理解感知，让我们能够快速进入概念知识体系。当然，这些来自词汇的自上而下的预测会因特定语言而有所差异。

在经典的认知语言学中，词汇并不影响其他认知系统的工作，比如感知、记忆和注意力（Pinker，1994）。因此，认知文学研究过去被称为是独立于语言的研究不无道理。而上述我的预测过程理论改变了这一观点，因为建立了基于一个自下而上的感知流和自上而下的以语言为标记的“预测反馈环”。当我们说话、听话或自言自语时，语言创造了一个听觉环境。从预测加工和扩展思维的角度来看，语言本身不仅为思维搭建脚手架，而且创造了一个“人工语境”（Lupyan & Clark，2015：282-83），这是一种能够匹配听觉的概念环境。在这种人为的语境中，词汇能够引导注意力或者影响我们的感知，并且语言可以通过操控我们的感官体验，在某种程度上“编程”我们的大脑（Lupyan & Bergen，2016）。因此，语言与一般的认知能力和特定的认知能力是相互关联的。

在这个框架下，不仅是感知和注意，连情感都与语言在概念上相互关联，因此，认知文学研究的另一个核心兴趣点是与语言相关，而且是与特定语言相关的。丽莎·费尔德曼·巴瑞特（Barrett, 2017）提出，语言可以引发情感概念的形成，而这些情感概念是通过上文所提及的注意力引导和感知塑造而形成的，从而使我们能够从有意义的情感角度去理解身体的内部状态。她讨论了不同语言中的情绪性词汇，这些词汇导致操这些语言的人对他们的身体体验进行了不同的分类：

情绪性词汇并非存储在我们头脑中静止不变的情感事实而已。它们反映了你用情感知识从世界上仅有的身体信号所构建的各种情感意义。在某种意义上，你是通过那些关心你、与你交谈并帮助你构建社交世界的人的大脑中的集体知识来获得你自己那些知识的。

情绪不是你对世界的被动反应，而是你对世界的主动构建。（104）

阿尼尔·赛斯认为，同样，我们基于规律对自己身体状态做出预测。因此，一个“具身自我”出现了，也就是说，这种身体状态“最有可能是你”（Anil Seth，2014：567）。

语言增强思维理论涉及认知和情感交往的整个范围。我再举个例子说明这一提议对于翻译的重要性。目前关于北欧人具身自我的书籍很畅销，尤其是关于丹麦人的 *hygge*（cozyness，舒适惬意）的书籍。芬兰其实较晚才加入有关“sisu”和“kalsarikänni”（Rantanen, 2018）的书籍出版大潮，“sisu”意指一种天生的勇气，常被誉为芬兰人的核心性格特征，而“kalsarikänni”则是指在晚上解开睡衣喝得酩酊大醉。“Kalsarit”是“内衣”的意思，“känni”是喝醉的状态。米斯卡·兰塔宁将其译为单数形式的“pantsdrunk”（Rantanen, 2018），这种翻译对于说美式英语的人来说已经足够好了。然而，当你把“kalsarikänni”用复数形式表达时，这个词则会让人想起这样一个事实：在芬兰语中，聚会和外出的场合通常是用复数形式表达的，如

“juhlat”（聚会，庆祝）。讽刺的是，这样你就面临一种困境，即很难找到对等的英语翻译。然而，通过这种解释，你的概念库（conceptual repertoire）已经得到了扩展。如果你读了有关“kalsarikänni”的书或者在芬兰有过此亲身经历，你就能产生很多从上到下与这个单词有关的预测。译者可能会直接使用这个芬兰语单词，或者使用英语新词“喝醉了”，然后依靠“文学叙事”的直观教具功能（Leppihalme，2011），即文本中的文化因素，让读者能够收集所必要的预测信息来嵌入“kalsarikänni”这个单词。

翻译研究促使我们对这一论点进行进一步的探讨。韦努蒂（2016）指出，相关的翻译单位往往不是单个单词，因为它通常看起来是不可译的，而是句子、段落，有时甚至是文本本身。预测处理的观点正是基于单个词汇和句子的语境之间的权衡而工作的。芬兰语“kalsarikänni”，就其本身而言，就像一个语言标记，一旦你知道了，它就会为你提供一个概念上的捷径。在一个更长的散文文本中，“更大的翻译单元”中（Venuti，2016：189），读者可以收集熟悉的词语带来的预测，或者可能会重新配置这些预测资源。

词语及其为我们的感知和思考提供的预测之间的联系并不是固定不变的。诚然，尽管我们的母语本身就会为我们预设一系列的预测知识，但是，我们的一生中会不断地从母语和新的语言中学习新的词汇，而这些词汇会不断扩展和调整我们所积累的概念。因此，对语言和思维的预测加工观点与萨丕尔-沃尔夫假设（或者更确切地说，对这个概念的缩略语的阐释）并不相关。正如丹尼尔·卡萨桑托（Daniel Casasanto）（2008）在《谁怕那只坏的大 Whorf》中指出的那样：“语言塑造我们的思维（预测加工理论也持有这种观点）和我们用语言来思考的观点是不一样的（这通常被认为是沃尔夫的立场）。也许思想很可能与语言不一致，但这并不意味着语言对我们的思维方式没有影响。通过解析、参与和分类的过程，语言仍然可以影响思维。语言在多大程度上塑造了思维，这一问题存在争议，然而可以确定的是，不同的语言及其概念系统似乎可以以不同的方式引导我们的注意力。

我在此所概述的观点，并不像严格意义上的语言相对论那样，把一门语言的使用者锁定在自己的概念世界里（比如萨丕尔-沃尔夫假说），而是说明语言是如何使我们的注意力集中在不同的方面，也就是集中注意我们所经历的，并使之概念化。可以说文学中的语言也遵循此法，尽管它的重点、特殊性和歧义空间不同于日常语言的使用。的确，我们可以把文学文本看作一种“设计好的感官流“，不断挑战和调整自上而下的、伴随语言、文化和文学知识的预测（Kukkonen，2020），那么，这种认知文学方法中的语言视角对于翻译和世界文学研究意味着什么呢？

3 库勒沃的刀与《英雄国》的韵律：论情节的可译性

文学叙事的情节可能看似与翻译和语言的关注点相去甚远。但是，我们是否可以考虑到这种可能性的存在呢？即我们在预测过程中所依赖的概率预测和我们理解情节时所需的预测相似。读者从单词和句子中获得预测对于理解情节有所帮助；反之，那些情节标记（比如一些暗示情节事件的言语提示）会随着叙述的进行而为读者提供推测的方向。换言之，作者设计好的文本感知流会告诉读者应该如何阅读，这里涉及的预测有一个特定的语言维度。回想一下，霍根一方面把库勒沃的故事描述为性情节（指的是库勒沃和他在树林里遇到的一个女人发生性关系，后来发现她是他的妹妹），另一方面又把它描述为一个复仇情节（指的是库勒沃对他叔叔昂塔莫 Untamo 的报复，因为库勒沃认为叔叔杀害了他的家人，尽管后来证实家人还健在）。不过，我们还有另一种方式来解读库勒沃的故事情节。我们可以把情节事件看作预测错误，也就是说，意料之外的事件会引导读者重新设定他们预测故事将如何继续。主要的情节事件产生了一个重新配置的预测轨迹，也就是读者的情绪投入也发生了变化。例如，库勒沃发现家人还活着是一个预测错误，从而有可能带来了一个令人高兴的结局，然而接下来的另一个预测，他刚刚发生关系的那个女人其实是他的妹妹则更可能是一个悲剧的结局（而且实际上，这个悲剧让库勒沃走向了自杀的道路）。预测处理模型中的情节构建是一个复杂的认知（可能发生的事情）和情感（我们希望发生的事情）概率的集合（Kukkonen，2014）。

情节事件是指在叙述中改变预测和可能性的时刻，情节事件不仅有这个特点，而且通常具有明显的语言标记。在现代小说中，这可能通过焦点的转变来实现（Kukkonen，2020）。在《英雄国》中，读者的注意力通过特定的语言标记指向事件的发生。例如，我们发现当主要情节事件发生时，“刀”被提及的频率非常显著。当库勒沃父亲的刀在伊尔马林（Ilmarinen）妻子给他的石头面包上打破时，库勒沃决定不再受伊尔马林的束缚；当库勒沃发现和他发生关系的那个女人是他的妹妹时，他用刀子切断了马的缰绳；当他杀死了他的叔叔昂塔莫时，他对着自己的刀自言自语，决定结束自己的生命（此前有所讨论）。显然，刀是库勒沃情感活动的焦点，而且可以说它们在向读者传达着情节事件，这些就是库勒沃内心预测的情节事件。

然而，刀在此处不仅仅是一个传统母题。通过阅读库勒沃的预测环，读者学会了为刀赋予概念上和情感上的关联及意义。刀开始占据阅读者的注意力，为读者提供从上到下的预测准备，并且通常标志着高度情绪化的时刻。正如我之前向你们介绍了“kalsarikännit”（晚上解开睡衣喝得酩酊大醉）这个词，你们也已经了解了《英雄国》中刀的关联意义。因此，你们在阅读故事时能够轻松而不费力地读懂它。刀在我们讨论的《英雄国》的所有三个版本中都扮演着重要角色。在勒杜克（1867：342）的法语散文版本中，库勒沃三次向伊尔马林的妻子提及那把破损的刀：“Mon ***couteau*** s’est ébrèché contre la pierre, il s’est brisé contre le rocher, le ***couteau***, seul héritage que j’ai reçu de mon père, le ***couteau*** qui appartenu àma famille.”（10）。在芬兰语的版本中被提及了两次：

Ve'in ***veitseni*** kivehen,
Karahutin kalliohon
——Ainoan isoni ***veitsen***,
Sukukuntani kuraksen.

（*Kalevala*, 2015, 33: 235–238）

在英语版本中也是被提及三次：

I took my ***knife*** to the stone
And upon the rock
Scrunched my matchless father's ***knife***
My kinsfolk's ***dagger***!

（Bosley, 1989: 465）

恰恰就在此时，库勒沃与家人的关系破裂。此处重复"父亲的刀"和"亲属的匕首"使用了排比的手法。家庭关系的破裂碰巧发生在"库勒沃——卡莱尔沃的儿子"身上，因为他的面包里有一块石头，但是库勒沃自己挥舞并折断了这把刀。随着刀的折断，库勒沃认为他的家人死了，尽管他在下一首诗歌中发现他父亲卡莱尔沃、母亲还有兄弟姐妹都还活着。

刀第二次出现正是库勒沃意识到自己迷奸了自己的妹妹的时候，并且就是在此刻，他明白自己是有家再也不能回了。刀在一、二节之间起到了承上启下的作用，可以说，这使得读者能够通过不断变化的可能性和霍根对两个不同的情节原型游刃有余的表述，来理解这两个事件之间的联系（尽管读者可能不会明说）。在库勒沃的故事中，刀既可以回指早前类似情节事件，且随着情节发展，读者的注意力也随着刀的关联程度而有所变化。

事实上，虽然库勒沃的故事经常提及刀，但它并没有假设这样的中心情节概念必然会涉及尖锐和危险的物体。约翰娜·西尼萨洛（Johanna Sinisalo）（2003，2015）在小说《英雄》（*Sankarit*）中引入了一个非同寻常的情节标记，其库勒沃的神话英雄被重新想象为现代摇滚明星。西尼萨洛假定读者对《英雄国》的人物和叙述基本熟悉（尽管可以说，这并不超过大多数芬兰人对该诗的熟悉）。神奇的塞波·伊尔马林（Seppo Ilmarinen）所扮演的多个角色辨识度很高，比如所扮演的空中铁匠伊莱（Ile Aerosmith）（Aerosmith 为美国一摇滚乐队），在维萨国王（Vesa Kuningas）中扮演维伊内梅宁（Väinämöinen），和约基姆（Joakim）演对手戏时扮演朱卡海宁（Joukahainen）。《英雄》如同《英雄国》一样，遵循英雄赞歌的模式。但是在情节方面，《英雄国》的韵律本身成为一个显著的标记。在西尼萨洛的版本中，库勒沃的叔叔昂塔莫在家族土地上建立了一座滑雪度假胜地，从而摧毁了整个家族的那一段是这样开始的："**K**aivinkone **k**irnuaa **k**uoppaa **k**iviseen maahan, se on **k**irkkaankeltainen **k**irppu Unnastunturin taivaaseen ulottuvan töyrään varjossa"（277）（挖掘者钻入了布满石头的地面，它是一个明亮的黄色的跳蚤在一直延伸到天际的乌纳斯坦图里山的河岸阴影下）。

在西尼萨洛的散文叙事诗中，她在头韵和第二行中重复第一行都重现了《英雄国》的典型特点。伊尔马林的妻子与库勒沃的矛盾关系是从诗的这一句开始的："Tytti Pohjola-Ilmarinen katsoo Karelia [=Kullervo in Sankarit] ja hänen käsivarsiensa karvat pörhistyvät pystyyn，kurkuu kuivuu voimattomasta vihasta"［289：泰蒂·波乔拉-伊尔马琳看着卡雷利亚（《英雄》中的库勒沃）和她的手臂的汗毛直立起来，喉咙因无力的愤怒而干燥］。当段落开始时，库勒沃意识到他和他的妹妹上了床（她自杀了），西尼萨洛写道："kkunalaudalla kasteessa näkyy paljaan jalan jättämä juova, ja jossakin yhdeksän kerrosta alempana, hämäryyden verhoamana, häämöttää harmaan ja valkoisen kirjavalla kivetyksellä epämääräisen muotoinen vääntynyt kuvio; se muistuttaa niitäoutoja olentoja, joita Karel piirsi pienenä puotipaperit täyteen"（315-16：在露珠下，窗台上可以看到一只光着脚的脚印；在那里，再往下九层楼，在昏暗中，一个形状不规则、

扭曲的人影几乎看不见，出现在斑驳的灰白色路面上；它就像库勒沃在包装纸上画的那些奇怪的生物）。这种首韵的例子在芬兰散文中也随处可见，例如，阿莱克西斯·基威（Aleksis Kivi）的《七兄弟》（1870）。但是西尼萨洛并没有用头韵来创造抒情的印象。在《英雄》中，当叙述通过在散文中重现特定的首韵来贴合原著《英雄国》的文体风格时，叙述者和原叙述者（我们在直接对话中也发现了这一点）本身就标志着情节事件。我们这里有一种不同于“库勒沃的刀”的文体表现手法，它标记了情节事件，体现了人物情感变化以及关联的概念。

随着库勒沃的刀和西尼萨洛的押韵，故事创造了他们自己的人工语境，正如卢普言和克拉克（2015）所做的那样。作者运用文字或文体手法作为显著标记，帮助读者通过文本中的语言环境来读懂情节。读者的理解是随着文本的可能性预测设计而循序渐进地发展的。当刀再次出现，或者当西尼萨洛进入与刀有关的诗句时，读者了解到这些语言特征与情节事件有关。正如你从我的解释中了解了kalsarikännit（晚上解开睡衣喝得酩酊大醉）一样，《英雄国》和《英雄》的读者也从这些文学文本所构建的人工语言语境中了解了情节的概念结构。如果我们开始从预测处理的角度来考虑这些文本，那么我们有必要质疑这些普遍存在的情节真的与翻译无关吗？文本中的词汇或文体手段标记了情节事件发生的时刻；它们在具体的行文和抽象的情节配置之间具有引导注意力和促进理解的作用。如果我们开始注意文本和情节之间的这些转移点，我们很可能会发现情节标记，这就使情节也值得翻译（言外之意，情节也是可译的）。

的确，外语词汇更能吸引人们的注意，并可能更强烈地突出相关情节事件。读者并不一定要理解这些文字才能作为情节标记，但是在情节标记和情节所需的知识之间往往会存在概念上的关联。如果库勒沃突然折断他的刀时，或者当有关刀的诗节出现时，《英雄国》和《英雄》的情节恰好能对应上，而读者也知道其意，那么情节标记的作用可能会更明显。然而，徒有文本并不能让读者独自完成这个任务，译者在需要翻译情节时，可以根据文本的具体内容和上下文来进行翻译。从这个角度来看，情节并非叙事的普遍性，而是需要考虑语言差异的认知方法的重要组成部分。

4 世界文学的认知研究方法：认知翻译方法

我是从语言差异和文本传统的角度，将世界文学和认知方法结合起来的，而并非从叙事共性角度展开。预测过程的视角并不会产生出可以调查和比较的某种数量的情节原型，情节事件的潜在标记（以及由此产生的结构）的数量与潜在叙事的数量是无限的。我只是提醒大家在翻译某些特定概念时，注意那些情节设置和读者情感参与被强化的地方，我自己翻译西尼萨洛的经典诗歌时，删去了那些押韵词，但一个更出色的译者也有可能在英文版本的翻译中将其保留，（是强化还是弱化，这取决于译者的决定）。

鉴于几方面原因，本文只是做了一个初步提议。第一，对语言差异的认知解释还没有被整合到认知文学研究当中来。参考可预测过程的相关文献，我开始考虑语言差异是否真的会产生影响，但还有很多工作要做。第二，预测、预测错误和文学叙事情节之间的关系需要更详细地进行论述。除此之外，我还就预测概率设计、建立和打破读者预期之间的紧张关系进行了整体描述（Kukkonen，2020）。在本文中，我仅强调了情节是如何与翻译相关的。第三，认知翻译研究尚未与认知文学研究联系起来。然而，在我看来译者的认知过程，比如元认知和不确定性管理、熟练过程和双语因素（这是认知翻译研究的主要论题论）（Shreve & Angelone，2010）可以成为认知文学研究非常有趣的话题。此外，我们还可以从预测过程的角度来讨论桑德拉·霍尔沃森（Sandra L. Halverson，2003：218）所说的翻译文本中出现的典型特征和高度突显的词汇语义“引力”。在最后几个段落，我试图概述文学作品的认知翻译方法给世界文学研究所能带来的启示和借鉴。

丽贝卡·沃尔科维茨（Rebecca Walkowitz）（2015）认为，文学“生而被译”（born translated），是因为一些作家会说多种语言（她引用的例子是常见的怀疑对象：Coetzee，Beckett 等）。有人可能会把沃尔科维茨的论点延伸到文学语言本身，把它理解为：对于其他作家和语言而言，情节事件标记能够指示某些突显的概念和文体表现手法。以西尼萨洛为例，从 19 世纪的伦罗特的《英雄国》到 21 世纪的西尼萨洛的小说《英雄》，芬兰语作为一种文学语言的用法在历史上存在着很大的差异，情节标记可以作为一种手段来识别非多语作家引入的某些突显的概念。

更普遍相关的问题是，认知文学翻译研究需要考虑以下几个方面：（1）归化和异化策略；（2）概念与语境；（3）语篇策略与世界文学界权力的动态关系。韦努蒂（1995）对归化和异化的翻译策略进行了区分。《英雄国》的法文译本就是一个正面例子，19 世纪下半叶芬兰史诗为法国读者所熟悉，而《英雄》的英文译本则是一个反面例子，它的译本语言奇怪，其异域性在牛津世界经典丛书中尤为明显，这种归化和异化在文本的各个层面都有所体现。从预测处理的角度来看，认知翻译研究可以研究翻译是否利用了熟悉的预测文化模式，还是向读者介绍了新的预测模式，以及采用了哪些解释性模式。这些新的预测模式是否与其他语言的某些特殊概念相关？它们是否被放置在突出的情节点上，从而吸引读者注意它们是如何为叙述铺垫的？或者他们是否与某个角色的特殊语言有关？通过这些区别，认知翻译研究可以得出两种不同的解释，一种是叙述概念形成中的熟悉的（familiarized）/前景化的（foregrounded）异化，另一种是与某些角色有关的熟悉的/优先的异化，即属于普通人物的熟悉的/优先的异化，而叙述者仍保持着不同的立场。

翻译规范，即翻译模式体系和翻译实践的规定，其争论的焦点一直是翻译到底该以文化为导向还是以语言导向（Vandaele，即将出版）。《英雄国》的法语和英语译本已经说明了翻译规范的巨大差异。吉迪恩·图尔利（Gideon Toury）（1995）和伊塔马尔·埃文·佐哈尔（Itamar Even-Zohar）（1990）通过讨论不同的语篇特征，在翻译规范方面做出了重要的贡献，但他们还未探究情节翻译的重要性。然而在我看来，情节，尤其因为它对叙事概念化的影响，能够有助于我们理解翻译如何发展自己的规范。

关于可译性的讨论也可以关注我所提出的情节标记。当某些无法翻译的表达作为情节标记发挥作用时，毫无疑问，其概念的突显也是被强化的。问题在于，译者是否选择在文本中创造一个人工语境，以使读者理解与未翻译词汇相关的推测。对于这种情况，我们可以区分嵌入的和孤立的不可译部分。由于嵌入了不可译的词汇或表达，其余的叙述为未译词提供了某种解释性的上下文；对于孤立的不可翻译部分，则没有这种上下文的解释。然后，根据阿普特（2013）的观点，人们可以考虑嵌入的不可译部分是否会有助消除干扰，还是继续成为翻译难点，预测处理和情节标记的说明可以进一步使得这些效果情境化。由于情节事件可以作为预测错误来修正读者预期，因此，将预测错误融入其他叙事部分和人为增加的上下文中，反而可以缓和预测误差带来的惊诧度，让那些不可译词汇不会显得那么突兀。

情节标记及其翻译方法也为我们从更广层面上来探讨与作品本身地位相关的、世界文学领域的权力分布问题。卡萨诺瓦（2004）主要讨论了关于文学的命题（宣言、反思等），但在我看来，她的观察也可以应用于情节标记、文本突出元素和叙事话语其他方面之间的“威望经济”（prestige economy）。考虑到作家和译者在全球化文学中所扮演的角色（Sapiro，2010），我们可能会问，处于文学领域边缘的作家是否更倾向于引入具有文化特异性的词汇作为情节标记？而那些为翻译而写作的作家，是否会选择在概念上并不引人注目的情节标记，却保留文化特定的写作模式来表达角色的话语？反之，将主流语言的原著翻译为外围语言的译者是否会保留文化上特定的情节标记（考虑到可能与本土语言相关的声望）？这些选择是否揭示了抵制和同化的显性策略？而这又与著者和译者的自我理解是如何相关的？最后，情节标记在卡萨诺瓦（2015）的“非主流文学”（minor literature）中具有什么特点，这类研究也将会很有意思。所谓“非主流文学”，就是用主流语言写作，却颠覆了主流文化的价值观。情节标记或许是这些作家用主流语言写作时使用的妙招，从而形成他们独特的文学风格呢?

关于认知到底是否可译，我试图通过探讨不同的语言如何形成不同的思维，以及这些差异在研究情节时如何突显来回答这个问题。综上所述，预测过程是能够很好地服务于这个研究目的的认识模型理论，因为预测过程模型允许语言差异产生影响，也包容文学文本创造和打破我们的期望和规范的方式。通过上述途径，认知文学研究还可以扩展其研究范围，进入新的跨学科研究，与比较文学和翻译研究展开学科交流。

多模态认知诗学

《你好，灯塔》的多模态互文性研究
——认知文体学视角

雷　茜　周玉艳

【摘要】绘本是一类独特的文学语篇，它不仅是文字、图像、字体、布局和色彩等多种模态共同建构意义的结果，也是互文的产物。因此，绘本的产生和理解既离不开其多模态文体特征的建构，也离不开对其他文本的借鉴和改造。本文将《你好，灯塔》的多模态文体特征分析与互文性分析相结合，基于心理空间理论和概念整合理论，探讨绘本主题意义的解读过程。

【关键词】《你好，灯塔》；多模态文体特征；互文性；认知文体学

0 引　言

《你好，灯塔》是美国绘本作家索菲·布莱克尔（Sophie Blackall）2019 年凯迪莱克金奖作品。绘本选题巧妙、形式多样、内容丰富，吸引了包括儿童和成人在内的大量读者。目前，对这部绘本的研究主要从主题意义解读（蔡朝阳，2019；陈园，2019）和多模态文体特征（史琪，2020；孙梦晨，2021）两个角度展开，还没有互文性角度对绘本意义的生成和解读的研究，更没有从多模态特征与互文

基金项目：国家社会科学基金项目“多模态语篇文体分析综合理论模型的建构及其应用研究”（2019K0198）的阶段性研究成果。

作者简介：雷茜，女，西安外国语大学英文学院教授，博士，博士生导师，主要从事系统功能语言学、文体学和多模态话语分析研究；
周玉艳，女，西安外国语大学英文学院硕士研究生，主要从事多模态文体学研究。

结合视角的研究。众所周知，文学作品的意义生成和理解都离不开与其他文本之间的多重关联。作为图像、文字、字体、布局和色彩等形式共同参与意义建构的一种文学体裁（Gibbons，2012：1），绘本意义的产生也离不开多模态互文。本文以多模态文体特征和互文性为切入点，借用概念整合理论探索绘本意义解读的认知机制，为绘本的认知研究提供新视角。

1 多模态文体研究

南丹麦大学的诺加德（N. Norgaard）教授是首个对文学作品多模态文体特征展开研究的学者。她认为多模态文体学是文体学理论和符号学理论的联姻（Norgaard，2011）。多模态文体学主要研究文学语篇和非文学语篇意义建构过程中语言模态和非语言模态前景化特征（雷茜，2018：36）。目前的多模态文体学有功能和认知两大研究方向，其中多模态功能文体学主要探讨多模态文体分析的理论建构（张德禄、穆志刚，2012）和不同模态在实现语篇三大功能中的作用（王红阳，2007；雷茜，2015）。张德禄、穆志刚（2012）以功能文体学理论为基础，建了一个功能、语境、模态间关系、前景化特征和意义整合为核心、以突出特征和前景化特征分析为路径的多模态功能文体分析框架，并在一则漫画的多模态文体分析中检验了框架指导文体分析的有效性。基于这一理论框架，学者们以现有的模态语法（Haliday，1995；Kress & van Leeuwen，1996，2006；van Leeuwen，2002）和模态间表现关系理论（张德禄，2009）为工具，研究小说和绘本的多模态文体特征（雷茜，2015；史琪，2020）。多模态认知文体学以概念隐喻理论、概念整合理论、文本世界理论等为基础，研究广告和电影语篇的认知（Forceville，1996，2002，2006）和多模态文体学作品的主题解读（Gibbons，2012）。雷茜（2017）以图式理论和概念隐喻理论为出发点，解读了多模态小说《女性世界》中复杂人物的认知过程。但是，以上研究并不涉及绘本多模态文体特征的认知研究。

2 互文性研究

互文性（intertextuality）概念是法国符号学家克里斯蒂娃（Kristeva）在20世纪60年代提出的。受巴赫金（Bakhtin）对话理论的启发，克里斯蒂娃认为“所有文本都是由无数引语拼凑而成的，任何文本都是在前语篇吸收和改造”（Kristeva，1986：37）。费尔克拉夫（Fairclough，1992）将互文性分为显著互文性（manifest intertextuality）和构成互文性（constitutive intertextuality）。前者指语篇中标明的与其他语篇的互文关系，后者指语篇中不同体裁、话语和风格之间的互文关系。辛斌（2000）把互文性分为具体互文性（specific intertextuality）和体裁互文性（generic intertextuality）。具体互文性不仅囊括了 Fairclough 的显著互文性，而且包括不加标明而引用他人话语产生的互文性；体裁互文性指一个语篇中不同风格（style）、语域（register）或体裁（genre）的混合交融，也可以看作来自不同群体的声音之间的相互作用（同上：15）。何伟、郭笑甜（2020：42）把互文性分为指涉文化语境的篇际互文和指涉情景语境的语篇内互文。在多模态语篇的互文性研究中，侯建波（2016：175）提出冲突型互文、概括型互文、互构型互文和延伸型互文四个类型。在以上的互文性类型区分中，体裁互文更多地关注不同体裁、话语和风格之间互文的语言表征而忽视了文本间的语境因素；多模态语篇互文主要研究语篇内模态间的互文，缺乏对语篇外的模态互文的研究。对语境依赖性强的多模态语篇意义建构需要不同模态协同参与，需要重视语境的互文意义，因此，冲突型、概括型、互构型和延伸型互文是本文进行多模态互文分析的理论框架，语篇内互文和篇际互文在考虑语境时也是本文分析的重要工具。

互文性的应用研究主要有三类路径：一是系统功能语言学的语境、语域理论和互文性结合（张春燕，2015；侯建波，2019）；二是利用认知隐喻理论和概念整合理论阐释互文根源（黄婉冬，2012；高原，2010；张立新，2017）；三是互文性在具体语篇解读中的研究（王莹、辛斌，2016；陈贵才、原一川，2019）。此外，互文性的研究对象包括诗词、广告、新闻漫画、网络视频、杂志封面、汽车标语（李勇忠、陈慧珍，2014）和企业微博（徐燕、冯德正，2020）等。尽管，以上研究对象涵盖面很广，但是还没有对绘本互文性的研究。Van Heerden（2009）认为互文意义的建构依赖百科知识和对前文本的体验经验（转引自 Stella Bullo 2017：3-4）。互文性参与文本的意义建构，并且需要读者的文化背景知识为理解现文本作桥梁，由此读者解构文本意图过程中介入的互文性本质上是认知思维的过程。绘本是儿童喜闻乐见的读物，因此研究绘本的认知机制对培育儿童感知世界具有重要的启发意义。然而，现有的绘本文体研究主要是基于功能文体学理论的多模态特征分析（史琪，2020；孙梦晨，2021），少有研究关注绘本文体特征与互文性的关系及其认知。本研究将从多模态文体特征和互文性入手，考察绘本意义建构和解读中的多模态互文机制。

3 《你好，灯塔》的多模态文体特征

《你好，灯塔》讲述了守塔人一家在灯塔中的平凡生活，包括刚到灯塔每日料理灯塔内事务、接来新婚妻子一同登塔、援救三位遇难水手并迎接新生命、被告知自动化装置将取代人力和守塔人一家搬离灯塔等情节。

基于系统功能语法（Halliday，2004）、视觉语法（Kress & Van Leeuwen，1996，2006）、字体语法（Van Leeuwen，2005b/2006）、颜色语法（Kress & Van Leeuwen，2002）和模态间关系理论（张德禄，2009），笔者首先分析了与绘本概念意义建构相关的前景化文体特征。

3.1 《你好，灯塔》的语言模态文体特征

对绘本语言模态及物性过程的统计显示，全书有 93 个物质过程、32 个言语过程，7 个行为过程、4 个关系过程、2 个心理过程和 1 个存在过程。书中大量的物质过程和灯塔需要人日夜不停地守护形成语境照应，前景化动词“tend”“polish”“trim”“refill”“give”“write” “pull”“help”等表现了守塔人繁忙的工作、守塔人夫妇救助三位遇难水手的过程、妻子替换丈夫日夜操劳（不仅照顾丈夫还要料理灯塔）的过程，动词“run”“tend”“walk”“write”的使用表明了守塔人妻子为丈夫的事业所做的牺牲；守塔人一家被告知自动化灯塔将要代替人力灯塔时，重复出现的动词“polish”“tend”“write”表明守塔人默默坚守，站好最后一班岗的精神风貌。绘本封面的标题“Hello，Lighthouse”和文中反复出现的问候“...Hello，Lighthouse”首尾呼应，频繁出现，构成失衡突出，使得灯塔被前景化。32个言语过程都是反复出现的“...Hello，Lighthouse!”。言语动词“Hello”并无具体的动作发出者，“Lighthouse”是言语目标，这和茫茫大海、人来人往的语境一致，表明经过灯塔的航海人员和船只是不计其数的，找不到具体的动作发出者，灯塔为无数人指明方向，更加衬托了灯塔的前景化。反应过程中的“look”“sneeze”“sit”是守塔人视察灯塔、守塔人生病和妻子照顾生病的守塔人时的行为，与海上恶劣的天气和环境照应，突出守塔人夫妇为守护灯塔的奉献精神。

3.2 《你好，灯塔》的非语言模态文体特征

绘本中的非语言模态包括图像、字体、布局和色彩。通过人工标注发现绘本图像有61个行动过程、14个反应过程、3个象征过程和1个分析过程。其中，行动过程和反应过程是突出过程，结合守塔人的工作环境，构成前景化叙事过程，表明图像中守塔人依旧处于忙碌的工作中，救助水手时大量的动作过程还表明守塔人的勇敢和无私。这和故事语境契合，动作过程使得守塔人前景化，为读者呈现出繁忙的奉献者形象。反应过程主要出现在守塔人视察灯塔、妻子坐在生病的丈夫旁、妻子凝视丈夫、丈夫看着新生儿、守塔人一家注视灯塔、守塔人注视孩子等语境中，表明守塔人一家在灯塔中的点滴琐碎生活细节，联系情景语境守塔人夫妇的现实生活在灯塔中被前景化。少量的概念表征都用来凸显灯塔的核心地位，封面的灯塔是对灯塔象征性的第一次表现，故事开头和结尾分别是同样的图像，灯塔孤零零地屹立在海面上，强调了灯塔的孤独，封面首

尾 3 次强化灯塔的重要地位。就字体模态而言，斜体的“*Lighthouse*”在绘本中出现了 2 次，构成失衡突出的字体特征。其中，“Hello, *Lighthouse!*”和“Good-bye, *Lighthouse!*”分别表现了守塔人初次登塔的愉悦欢快和守塔人一家同灯塔告别时的留恋，其轻盈的斜体外形，强化字体的前景化特征，给人愉悦的阅读感受。绘本结尾的“*Hello?*”斜体加问号暗含了灯塔对守塔人一家搬离灯塔后的问候和怀念。此外，“HELLO!”一词有 3 次大写，它们并没有与“Lighthouse”一同出现，而是单独使用，也构成主图字体特征，大写的“HELLO!”成为前景化字体特征，凸显了灯塔对海上航行人员的指引作用。就布局模态而言，首先，“Hello，Lighthouse”在狂风吹拂时字体随风飘扬和守塔人妻子照顾生病的丈夫时，“everywhere”字母分离、“up”“down”一上一下的排版都是突出的布局特征。将字母排列成物体的形状，产生与语言模态所指吻合的效果。由此，两个前景化布局特征能渲染环境、增强妻子忙碌的动态感和即时感。此外，绘本 10 次使用圆形图像定框，构成另一个重要的布局突出特征。它们分别出现在守塔人登塔、夫妻团聚、迎来新生儿等重要语境中，表明守塔人一家在灯塔内的幸福圆满生活，表明了灯塔的包容性，构成绘本前景化布局特征，凸显绘本追求圆满幸福的美好生活的主题。色彩模态中红色、黄色和绿色频繁使用，构成失衡突出，表征灯塔塔顶和塔门、灯塔的光芒和小孩的衣服以及孩子出生时的祥瑞征兆与语境联系密切，构成色彩的前景化特征，表明了灯塔指引方向、美好希望、传承精神和生命活力等主题意义。

3.3 《你好，灯塔》的模态间关系文体特征

Bateman 认为图文关系的确立与话语类别相关，语类是决定图文关系的关键因素（转引自汪燕华，2010：74）。图像是先于语言出现的最直接、最简单的人类感知方式（同上），也是更容易吸引儿童注意力的模态。绘本《你好，灯塔》的图像主体是灯塔，守塔人是灯塔活动的参与者，环境成分仍以灯塔为主，分析图文模态发现，绘本中有 6 次图文互补强化关系、3 次图文互补扩充，10 次非互补

交叠和 2 次非互补语境交互。在以上图文互补强化关系中，图像模态是主模态，语言模态为图像模态服务，强化守塔人工作的繁重机械，补充了守塔人被告知离开灯塔的信息。红色的灯塔门、黄色的光线、小孩手中的黄色马灯和挂着的黄色衣服都与文字模态形成互补扩充关系，不仅表达了温暖和友爱的字面意义，还将灯塔给航行船只的帮助、带给航海人的希望以及守护精神的传承等主题蕴含在这些色彩背后。灯塔发出的光芒、冰雪覆盖的海面、游走的鲸鱼、妻子繁忙的场景、守塔人怀抱新生儿与文字模态形成非互补交叠关系，一方面表现了海上四季的变换，另一方面还反衬出守塔人夫妇的坚守。最后，迷雾中灯塔不停地发出的“Clang”声响、字体模态的圆形布局都与字体模态形成语境交互，共同表达灯塔在暴风雨中的坚守和守塔人三口之家的喜悦和圆满。

4 《你好，灯塔》的互文性分析

尽管《你好，灯塔》是绘本，但它与文学文本的互文关系和其他文学体裁一样丰富。下面是对这部绘本和三部与灯塔有关文学作品的内容互文分析。

4.1 与绘本《灯塔守护人》的冲突互文

绘本《灯塔守护人》（*The Lighthouse Keeper*，2019）是新西兰著名儿童文学家朗达·阿米塔奇（Ronda Armitage）创作、大卫·阿米塔奇（David Armitage）作插画的系列儿童绘本，讲述了故事主人公格瑞林夫妇守护灯塔的场景。格瑞林先生非常热爱自己的灯塔守护工作，他对生活的热爱和乐观态度让灯塔上平淡乏味的日子丰富精彩，夫妇两人同贪吃的海鸥、搁浅的鲸鱼等斗智斗勇，生活幸福而有趣。同样，绘本《你好，灯塔》同样讲述了灯塔守护人和妻子平淡充实的灯塔守护生活。在故事的内容上，《你好，灯塔》与《灯塔守护人》是完全同质的，两者坚守本职工作的守正精神如出一辙，然而前者欢快愉悦，后者单调乏味，两者在内容上形成冲突型互文。

这种内容基调的不同形成一种反衬，能引发读者对灯塔守护人生活的阅读兴趣。因此，对《灯塔守护人》故事情节的知识积累能够为《你好，灯塔》的理解做出铺垫和回应。

4.2 与小说《到灯塔去》的互构

英国作家弗吉尼亚·伍尔夫（Virginia Woolf）的《到灯塔去》（*To the Lighthouse*，2011）讲述了拉姆齐先生一家在海边度假的故事。小说由“窗”“岁月流逝”和“灯塔”三部分构成，在第一部分“窗”中，拉姆齐太太和儿子詹姆士在窗口眺望着远处的灯塔，并承诺儿子如果明天天气好的话，带着他去灯塔。然而，事与愿违，第二天天气骤变，他们一家并未成行。小说第三部分“灯塔”讲述了男主人公齐拉姆先生在数年后和一双儿女到灯塔去的过程。虽然，小说大量篇幅围绕灯塔展开，但是读者并没有真正登上灯塔，也不知道灯塔里面是何光景。主人公因去灯塔去的心愿未了而对灯塔念念不忘，小说的描写最终还是没有涉及灯塔内部的生活。相比之下，绘本《你好，灯塔》中的故事情节完全围绕守塔人实际的生活事实，守塔人独自一人登上灯塔，感受到料理灯塔内事务的无聊和情感上的孤独，随后接来陆地上的妻子，与之团聚。因此，绘本《你好，灯塔》完成了小说《到灯塔去》的心理意象填补，放大镜式的绘本图像跨越体裁帮助齐拉姆一家实现了到灯塔去的愿望，因此，两者在内容上是互构的。

4.3 和电影《海王》的延伸互文

电影《海王》（*Aquaman*）是美国华纳兄弟影片公司 2018 年出品的动作奇幻片，故事从海底世界亚特兰蒂斯王国的女王亚特兰娜和大陆世界海岸某处一个灯塔守人的爱情故事开始，讲述了这对恋人所生儿子亚瑟的故事。亚瑟具有海陆两栖属性，面对海陆的存亡时刻，他勇敢担负起保护陆地的使命，与同母异父的弟弟相抗争，在海陆大战时夺回统治海洋的武器三叉戟，成为海王，保卫海陆平衡（丁卫真，2020）。尽管，电影《海王》的情节围绕亚瑟展开，对发生在灯塔上的爱情故事轻描淡写，读者依然对主人公亚瑟父母在灯塔的相遇和相爱充满了好奇和想象。因此，电影中的神奇爱情满足了读者对远方灯塔的诗意想象。然而，绘本《你好，灯塔》讲述的是发生在灯塔中的平淡现实生活，是守塔人和妻子相濡以沫的真实生活。因此，电影《海王》是有关《你好，灯塔》现实描写在想象领域的补充，二者构成延伸型互文。

5 《你好，灯塔》的多模态互文性分析

当单一文字模态不能很好地实现其语用交际功能时，就需要整合其他模态，丰富信息传递渠道，则形成了多模态互文（武建国、刘艾静，2020）。绘本不仅是多种模态共同建构意义的语篇，也含有丰富的互文信息。下面从标题、语言和图像等方面探讨绘本《你好，灯塔》的多模态互文特征。

5.1 标题的多模态互文

标题素有“题眼”之称，能向读者传达故事的主旨。《你好，灯塔》的标题互文包括语篇内互文和篇际互文。语篇内互文首先表现为标题文字与封面非语言模态间的互文。封面标题“HELLO，LIGHTHOUSE”与同属封面的图像灯塔照应互文，达到强化故事主旨的目的。同时，标题“HELLO，LIGHTHOUSE”与正文反复出现的“Hello, Lighthouse”形成概括型互文。在文中“Hello, Lighthouse”是语言过程。尽管没有固定的发话人，但是言语内容是向灯塔表达问候和致以敬意。因此，标题的问候和文中的问候能通过复现达到唤起敬意和深化主题的目的。与此同时，围绕灯塔的环形布局和亮黄色灯光，与绘本故事的圆满主题和希望寓意形成隐性篇内互文，很好地透露了故事的主要参与对象和主题。除了语篇内部的多模态互文外，《你好，灯塔》的篇际多模态互文性也很明显。篇际互文性容纳了超越文本的体裁、风格和语域等特征。首先，标题“Hello，Lighthouse”与小说《到灯塔去》的标题“To the Lighthouse”形成

了互构型互文。两者不仅采用同样的意象——灯塔，而且在意义上还有补充关系，从而实现了绘本与小说间的体裁互文。其次，索菲绘本《你好，灯塔》和绘本朗达·阿米塔奇《灯塔守护人》构成同一体裁不同故事情节的冲突互文。如果《灯塔守护人》聚焦守护灯塔的夫妇勇敢和有趣的守塔生活，那么绘本《你好，灯塔》则重新演绎了守塔人的故事，突显守塔人生活的平淡和他对本职工作的热爱。因此，尽管两者都使用了多模态表达主旨，但是在语场和语旨上都有明显不同，属于不同语篇之间的多模态互文。

5.2 图像互文

图像在绘本中占据重要篇幅，对图像互文的分析也可以更好地帮助读者建立知识联系，了解绘本的交际意图。绘本《你好，灯塔》的图像互文包括文外图像互文和文内图像互文。

文外图像互文指绘本中的图像与读者知识积累中相关图像的互文。据索菲本人陈述，为了完成绘本中灯塔（图 1）的创作，她查阅了大量海洋生活和海上灯塔的绘画，包括有关灯塔的版画（图 2），观察了灯塔在不同时间下展现出来的浪漫，并亲自前往 Quirpon 岛观察那里的灯塔（图 3）。因此，从创作的角度看，绘本中灯塔的图像是在作者观察到各种灯塔形象的基础上生成的。构成语篇外图像互文关系，为语篇的解读就提供了思路。此外，《你好，灯塔》中守塔人对小孩殷切的目光和电影《海王》中灯塔守护人和亚特兰娜之子亚瑟的故事构成语境延伸型互文，表达了对未来的无限期望。

图 1

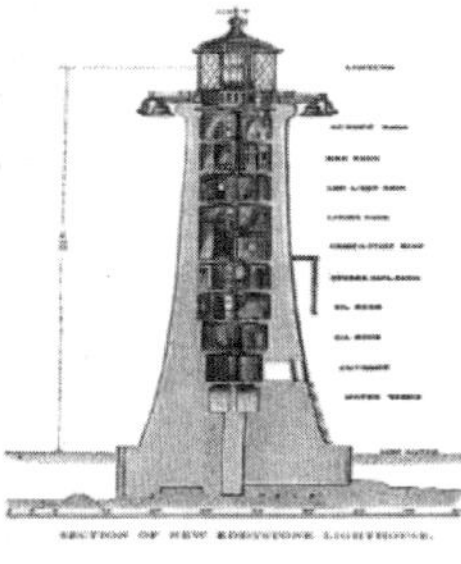

图 2

图 3

文内图像互文性主要体现在文内图像模态之间，图像与文字、字体和布局之间的相互关联。从图像模态的角度出发，封面的灯塔、海浪与灯光同文中的灯塔、海浪和灯光呼应，直观展示了守塔人料理灯塔内事务，如擦拭望远镜（He polishes the lens）、记录灯塔日志（He writes in the logbook）等的生活细节，与文字对故事的讲述呼应，共同帮助读者理解绘本的主旨。当守塔人一家在临行前同灯塔告别时，“*Hello*?”一反常态使用斜体，与后面的问号表达了守塔人一家对守塔时光的怀念和不舍。最后，绘本的图像与布局模态的互文尤其明显。在绘本中，当海面乌云漫卷、海浪拍岸时，文字模态呈现随风飘散的无序状态，活灵活现地呈现了海上的景象，是图像和文字的照应互文。图像中共出现了 10 次原形排版和 3 次半圆形排版。刚到灯塔上，守塔人每日机械的工作让守塔人只能对着妻子的相片睹物思人，靠着信件和妻子交流，这时半圆形的定框和守塔人孤身一人的状态形成语境互文。而当守塔人与妻子汇合后，出现在不同情景中的圆形排版定框和图像，表明守塔人一家在灯塔内的圆满生活，灯塔为守塔人一家提供了生活空间，灯塔反哺守塔人的辛苦付出，同样体现了语境互文。

5.3 色彩互文

绘本中的色彩互文主要表现在红色、黄色和绿色与图像的情景语境互文。色彩模态文体特征分析显示，红色、黄色和绿色是绘本的前景化特征。首先，灯塔的塔顶和灯塔门都是醒目的红色，其功能是便于来往船只辨识灯塔位置，为海上航行者指引方向。当守塔人一家告别灯塔、搬入新家后，图像中守塔人新家的门也是红色，位于图像的右边且尺寸较大，守塔人家门的红色和灯塔的红色构成语境互文，表达怀念和守候的概念意义。此外，守塔人小孩手中提的马灯和墙上的小外套都是黄色，与灯塔发出的黄色光线形成色彩互文，表达传递希望和责任的主题意义。最后，守塔人妻子分娩时天空出现形似祥云的绿色彩带，同灯塔内绿色墙纸、极光互文，新生命通过极光颜色表征，共同表达生命的活力与希望。

6 多模态互文与《你好，灯塔》概念意义的多元整合

心理空间理论和整合理论为语篇意义的理解提供了模型，下面从《你好，灯塔》的多模态文体特征和互文性相结合，讨论绘本意义的多元整合。

6.1 心理空间理论和概念整合理论

心理空间（1994：13）指人们在交谈和思考时为了达到局部理解和行动目的临时储存于工作记忆的概念集合（conceptual packet）。基于心理空间建构过程需要空间内各个要素之间互动关联这一理论基础，Fauconnier（1997）提出概念整合理论，该理论旨在揭示自然语言中的意义实时（on-line）建构及连接各个心理空间的映射过程（王文斌、毛智慧，2011：Ⅳ）。概念整合理论是一个“四空间”交互的认知模型，包括两个输入空间（input space），由两个输入空间映射而成的类属空间（generic space），最后形成的整合空间（blending space），该理论一方面揭示了跨空间的语义映射，另一方面呈现语义生成的动态机制，对来自不同空间的语境语义特征的整合，尤其是多模态意义建构的认知过程有着天然的优势。

6.2 《你好，灯塔》的多模态意义

《你好，灯塔》是一部由图像、文字、字体、布局和色彩共同建构意义的语篇。文字模态描述了守塔人在灯塔内繁忙地工作、对海上同胞的热心帮助，强化了夫妻二人的履职敬业。图像模态贯穿始终，封面的灯塔与正文反复出现的灯塔图像，表征灯塔的核心地位；故事中人力灯塔被自动灯塔取代，灯塔守护人离开岗位，预示着社会发展带给人类的创新。图像中手提马灯的小孩和温暖的黄色相照应，喻指守塔人默默奉献精神的延续；灯塔黄色灯光直射远方，暗含对未来的无限希望。到最后，绘本中美丽丰富的图像、变换的字体、圆形和随风飘动的文字布局、蓝色海水和黄色灯光，与文字模态相互强化和相互补充，在向读者传达深刻故事内涵的同时，也给读者带来了美好的视觉享受。

6.3 《你好，灯塔》的互文意义

在图文并置的话语中，图像和文字并非各自独立，而是在争执、对话、延异的过程中产生的（汪燕华，2010：74）。《你好，灯塔》与多重文本在内容上互文和不同模态在语篇内外的互文丰富了绘本的内涵。首先，在内容上，《你好，灯塔》中守塔人和妻子的琐碎生活细节与小说绘本《灯塔守护人》的守塔生活在内容上的冲突互文，成功向读者展现守塔人兢兢业业的守正精神；《你好，灯塔》与小说《到灯塔去》和电影《海王》在内容上的互构型互文和延伸型互文，预设出人们对灯塔的期待向往。其次，在多模态互文方面，封面标题、封面图像和正文文字的失衡突出构成的概括型互文，凸显了灯塔的坚固永恒；守塔人新家红色的大门与灯塔的红色，守塔人小孩手中提的黄色马灯和墙上的小外套与灯塔发出的黄色光线都是图像与色彩的互构，共同表达了传递责任的主题意义；绘本中文字随风飘散的无序状态、守塔人与妻子汇合时文字和图像的圆形布局都是图像和布局的互构，描绘了美丽的环境和温馨的场面，也凸显了绘本的审美效果。

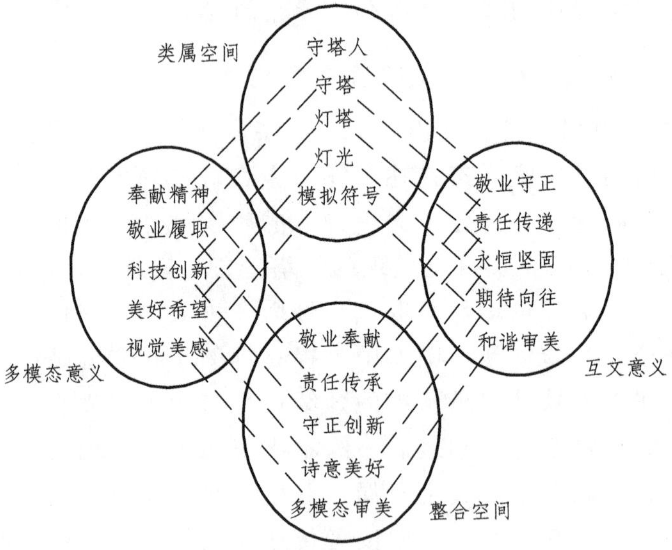

图 4

6.4 基于心理空间理论的概念整合

根据概念整合理论，类属空间中的概念向两个输入空间映射，来自不同输入空间的概念在类属空间映射下整合成新的空间，产生新义。从以上的分析可以看出，绘本的多模态意义和互文意义是两个不同输入空间，类属空间中的守塔人、守塔、灯塔、灯光、模态符号等元素分别映射到多模态意义空间和互文意义空间，使绘本的多层主题意义得以实现。首先，多模态意义表达了的守塔人奉献精神，与互文意义表达的是守塔人的敬业精神在整合空间形成了守塔人敬业奉献的精神风貌，这是绘本传达的第一层意义。此外，守塔在多模态意义空间展现出的敬业履职与在互文空间表达的责任传承在新的整合空间表达了责任传承的绘本主题。昔日要人工看守的灯塔被自动灯塔取代，灯塔在多模态意义空间是科技创新的对象，而互文分析显示灯塔是坚固永恒的代表，二者在新的整合空间表达了守正创新的绘本主题。同时，灯光在多模态空间表达的意义是对美好未来希望，互文表达的意义是期待和向往，二者在整合空间中得到的意义是灯光代表诗意美好。最后，多模态符号在多模态空间的意义是视觉美，在互文意义空间的意义是趣味性与和谐性，二者在新的整合空间指向绘本带来的视觉享受，很好地阐释了绘本文学的多模态审美主题。综上所述，绘本《你好，灯塔》的多模态意义和互文意义在心理空间的多元整合成功建构了敬业奉献、责任传承、守正创新、美好希望、视觉享受的多层主题，为绘本理解提供了新的视角和深度。

7 结 语

多模态文体特征是绘本的自然属性，语言和非语言模态的协同作用能够借助多种感官辅助意义建构和理解，而互文性也是绘本作为文学作品的重要特征，能更好地阐释绘本的生成过程。本文对这部优秀绘本的多模态互文性的认知研究不仅加深了读者对绘本的多模态文体特征和互文性质的认识，揭示了绘本的多重主题，而且为绘本认知研究提供了新的视角。但是，本研究仅是多模态互文性认知机制的个案探索，建立绘本语料库和研究不同体裁语篇的互文认知机制可以加强互文性在多模态语篇中认知解读的说服力。

参考文献

[1] S BLACKALL. Hello, Lighthouse. Orchard Books, 2019.

[2] S BULLO. Investigating Intertextuality and Interdiscursivity in Evaluation: The Case of Conceptual Blending. Language and Cognition, 2017, 1-19.

[3] N FAIRCLOUGH. Discourse and Social Change. Cambridge: polity press, 1992.

[4] G FAUCCONNIER. Mappings in Thought and Language. Cambridge: Cambridge University Press, 1997.

[5] G FAUCCONNIER. Mental Spaces: Aspects of Meaning Construction in Natural Language. Cambridge: Cambridge University Press, 1985/1994.

[6] C FORCEVILLE. Non-verbal and Multimodal Metaphor in a Cognitive Framework: Agendas for Research //G. Kristiansen, M. Achard, R. Driven, & I. de Mendoza. (Eds.), Cognitive Linguistics: Current Application and Future Perspectives. Berlin/New York: Mouton de Gruyter, 2006: 379-402.

[7] C FORCEVILLE. Pictorial Metaphor in Advertising. London/New York: Routledge, 1996.

[8] C FORCEVILLE. The Conspiracy in the Comfort of Strangers: Narration in The Novel and the Film. Language and Literature, 2002, 11 (2): 119-135.

[9] A GIBBONS. Multimodality, Cognition and Experimental Literature. London/New York: Routledge, 2012.

[10] M A K HALLIDAY. An Introduction to Functional Grammar

(2nd). London: Edward Arnold, 1994.

[11] G KRESS, T VAN LEEUWEN. Colour as a Semiotic Mode: Notes for a Grammar of Color. Visual Communication, 2002, 1 (3): 343-368.

[12] G KRESS, T VAN LEEUWEN. Reading Images: The Grammar of Visual Design. London: Routledge, 1996/2006.

[13] J KRISTEVA. Word, Dialogue and Novel, The Kristeva Reader. Oxford: Blackwell Publishers, 1986: 36-37.

[14] N NORGAARD. Multimodal Stylistics: The Happy Marriage of Stylistics and Semiotics //S. C. Hamel (ed.). Semiotics: Theory and Applications. New York: Nova Science, 2011: 255-260.

[15] T VAN LEEUWEN. Towards a Semiotics of Typography. Design Journal & Document Design, 2006, 14 (2): 139-155.

[16] T VAN LEEUWEN. Typographic Meaning. Visual Communication, 2005b, 4 (2): 137-143.

[17] 蔡朝阳.《你好，灯塔》：一本孤独、守望与勇气之书 [EB/OL]. [2019-06-14]. [2021-04-06]. https：//mp.weixin.qq.com/s/Wk9pn-Q_s_baaBrF34APwQ.

[18] 陈贵才，原一川. 劳伦斯诗歌中的再生隐喻与英国诗歌死亡叙事传统的互文性. 重庆交通大学学报，2019（3）：102-107.

[19] 陈园. 一座灯塔，一个守护人——评《你好，灯塔》[EB/OL]. [2019-09-19]. [2021-04-06]. https：//mp.weixin.qq.com/s/Bh__qA0uYty2l61oSGLigg.

[20] 丁卫真.《海王》景观电影的新神话建构. 电影文学，2020（5）：149-151.

[21] 弗吉尼亚·伍尔夫.《到灯塔去》. 瞿世镜，译. 上海：上海译文出版社，2011.

[22] 高原. 用概念整合理论分析诗歌的互文性——以李清照词《临江仙》为例. 广东外语外贸大学学报，2010（1）：72-74+87.

[23] 何伟、郭笑甜. 语言系统的复杂性和语篇功能的体现方式. 当

代修辞学，2020（1）：39-47.
[24] 侯建波. 电视公益广告的多模态互文研究. 广西民族大学学报（哲学社会科学版），2016（4）：175-178.
[25] 侯建波. 网页新闻漫画的多模态互文功能研究——以凤凰网“大鱼漫画”为例. 外语教学，2019（4）：39-43.
[26] 黄婉冬. 从概念整合角度看诗歌的互文性——以李白的两首送别诗为例. 苏州教育学院学报，2012（1）：61-63.
[27] 朗达·阿米尔奇（文），大卫·阿米塔奇文（图）.《灯塔守护人》. 孙淇，译. 贵阳：贵州人民出版社，2019.
[28] 雷茜，张德禄. 格林海姆·洛雷拼贴小说《女性世界》两版封面的多模态文体对比研究. 当代外语研究，2015（9）：20-25.
[29] 雷茜. 多模态功能文体学理论建构中的几个重要问题探讨. 外语教学，2018（2）：36-41.
[30] 雷茜. 格林海姆·洛雷拼贴小说《女性世界》人物认知研究——多模态认知文体学视角. 北京第二外国语学院学报，2017（6）：57-68.
[31] 李勇忠、陈慧珍. 多模态视下视阈下互话性“越界”——以汽车尾部标语为例. 江西理工大学学报，2014（6）：76-80.
[32] 史琪. 儿童绘本《你好，灯塔》的多模态功能文体特征研究[D]. 西安：西安外国语大学，2020.
[33] 孙梦晨. 索菲·布莱科尔绘本多模态文体特征研究[D]. 西安：西安外国语大学，2021.
[34] 汪燕华. 多模态话语中的图文关系. 外国语文，2010（5）：73-75+121.
[35] 王红阳. 卡明斯诗歌“1（a”的多模态功能解读. 外语教学，2007（5）：22-26.
[36] 王文斌、毛智慧. 心理空间理论和概念合成理论研究. 上海；上海外语教育出版社，2011.
[37] 王莹，辛斌. 多模态图文语篇的互文性分析——以德国《明镜》周刊的封面语篇为例. 外语教学，2016（6）：7-11.

[38] 武建国、刘艾静．国家形象宣传片《角度篇》解说词翻译中的互文性策略研究．西安外国语学院学报，2020（2）：22-25.
[39] 辛斌．语篇互文性的语用分析．外语研究，2000（3）：14-16.
[40] 徐燕，冯德正．新媒体商务话语中的多模态体裁互文：语域类型学视角．外语教学，2020（3）：23-28.
[41] 张春燕．新媒体语篇的多模态互文性分析——以一则网络配音视频为例．外国语文研究，2015（4）：23-30.
[42] 张德禄，穆志刚．多模态功能文体学理论框架探索．外语教学，2012（3）：1-6.
[43] 张德禄．多模态话语分析综合理论框架．中国外语，2009（1）：24-30.
[44] 张立新．互文性与隐喻——中美外交话语隐喻互文性比较研究．语文学刊，2017（2）：34-38.

后现代绘本对经典童话的颠覆性解构与重构：认知叙事学视角

赵秀凤

【摘要】后现代绘本是后现代主义儿童文学的重要组成部分。后现代绘本充分利用多模态符号资源，全方位颠覆经典童话叙事图式——故事图式、体裁图式和表征图式，形成了其独特的语类特征和核心认知建构策略。该类绘本在解构传统儿童文学交流范式和意义的僵化感知的同时，淋漓尽致地模拟展演文学创作的虚构性本质和元认知过程，以此重构和培育儿童在文学叙事、心理及情感感知和空间认知等方面的创新性元认知能力，引领儿童读者切身感知和体验到对僵化图式进行反思和颠覆带来的快乐和成就，培养自由、开放和创新的生活态度和艺术鉴赏习惯。

【关键词】绘本；后现代；儿童文学；认知叙事；多模态

1 引 言

兴起于20世纪中后期的后现代哲学思潮，高举解构文本、反传统、去中心的大旗，以消解现代社会中的话语霸权为宗旨，掀起了声势浩大的后现代文化运动，撼动了后现代社会的文化根基（王治河，2006；王寅，2012；赵秀凤、黄洁，2013）。风靡社会各领域的

基金项目：教育部人文社会科学规划基金项目“多模态能源舆情话语的认识批评研究”（21YJA740055）和北京市社会科学基金规划项目“多模态视域下中西能源话语比较研究”（21YYB006）的阶段性成果。

作者简介：赵秀凤，女，中国石油大学（北京）外国语学院教授，博士，博士生导师，主要从事认知诗学多模态认知研究和认知分析研究。

后现代主义思潮也侵入了儿童文学的领地，尤其是曾经长期由经典童话独霸天下的绘本王国。

绘本，又称图画书，是图像、文字、物质载体、构型设计等多模态资源协同创造的有机艺术整体。凭借其多模态符号资源优势，绘本得以实现叙事能指化和感官刺激，在后现代主义思潮的影响下，被视为消解文字霸权、解构传统、对抗确定性的强有力武器（赵秀凤，2020）。著名的绘本叙事学家诺德曼（Nodelman，2000）曾一针见血地指出，儿童图画书早已和后现代主义建立了特殊的关系。在“去经典”“不确定”“碎片”“多元”“无序”等后现代精神感召下，一批绘本如《三只小猪的真实故事》《青蛙王子变形记》《三只小狼和大坏猪》等运用“戏仿”“自我指涉”“拼贴”等后现代文学手法，以颠覆经典童话、打破常规叙事的后现代姿态，登入了儿童文学的殿堂，打破了长期被浪漫主义主宰的童话世界。

这种后现代儿童绘本是对经典童话的颠覆性解构，也是解放性重构，是“理解后现代颠覆权力结构的一把钥匙”（Chambers，1985：38），自然也引起了学者的广泛关注。从研究广度和深度来看，最有影响力的后现代绘本研究主要集中于文学批评领域，代表性成果包括刘易斯（Lewis，1990，2001）、格里夫（Grieve，1993）、德雷桑（Dresang，1999）、西普和潘塔莱奥（Sipe & Pantaleo，2010）、潘塔莱奥和西普（Pantaleo & Sipe，2008）、潘塔莱奥（Pantaleo，2014）等，它们重点探讨后现代绘本在叙事方式、表现形式、后现代主题等方面的鲜明特征。“相对后现代主义成人文学批评，后现代绘本研究更关注成人作者和儿童读者的不平等权力关系、对传统童话式绘本常规的颠覆性及其多模态实现过程”（赵秀凤，2020：15）。除文学批评外，儿童教育领域聚焦后现代绘本的教育意义和价值，展开了广泛讨论，如崔蒂斯（Trites，1994）、陶恕和周（Tozer & Chou，1997：822-828）、戈德斯通（Goldstone，1998，2001/2002）、麦吉尔（McGillis，1999：111-126）、安斯蒂（Anstey，2002a，b）、沃森（Watson，2004）、潘塔莱奥（Pantaleo，2007）等（赵秀凤，2020：15）。

现有研究加深了我们对后现代绘本鲜明特征和教育意义的认

识，但是，传统文学批评范式下的特征描写和意义阐释，无论有多充分，都没有触及因而无法解答后现代绘本“何以能够”通达读者心理，形塑价值，即其生成机制和文学交流过程中的心理表征问题。就这一问题，赵秀凤（2020）以《臭起司小子爆笑故事大集合》（以下简称《臭》）（1992）为例，采用多模态认知诗学研究路径，做了初步探讨，但是，该文所分析的认知机制类型仅局限于或基于《臭》这部绘本本身，没有把后现代绘本作为一种独特的文学体裁（或类型）进行整体性考察，对认知生成机制的探讨也仅局限于认知图式。

本文拟在赵秀凤（2020）基础上，采取认知叙事学视角，把后现代绘本视为一个文学样类范畴，将绘本视为读者感知和体验的符号媒介，“关注叙事被感知和被识别时读者的心理过程”（Fludernik & Olson，2011：3）。我们把后现代绘本的叙事交流置于语境（包括文化语境、情景语境、认知语境等）作用下的作者与读者的认知协商和互动，审视其颠覆性过程，揭示其背后的元认知操作。“从读者认知加工的角度，揭开该类绘本后现代性的产生机制，有助于从根本上理解其文学和文化价值”（赵秀凤，2020：15）。

2 认知叙事学与认知图式

作为认知科学和叙事学交叉融合形成的新兴研究领域，认知叙事学经过几十年的发展，已经成为“当代西方叙事学前沿发展领域中的重要分支，是后经典叙事学发展历史过程中极具生命力的一大理论思潮”（陈礼珍，2020：51）。认知叙事学领域内部尽管研究角度和侧重点不尽相同，但都一致“关注叙事被感知和被识别时读者的心理过程，而不是语言叙事，尤其是散文叙事的功能分类”（Fludernik & Olson，2011：3），即认知叙事学把文学的认知交流过程确立为焦点研究对象，力图利用认知心理学、神经认知科学、认知语言学等领域的研究成果丰富和充实对文学交流活动及其效果的阐释。

从广义的角度来说，认知叙事学也是认知诗学的重要组成部分，其核心思想的典型代表是戴卫·赫尔曼（David Herman），他认为叙事是“一种认知风格”，“叙事理解就是建构和更新人脑中的认知模式的过程，文中微观和宏观的叙事设计均构成认知策略”（转引自申丹，2004：4）。赫尔曼（赫尔曼、尚必武，2009：100）指出，研究者可以聚焦话语模型提示的认知过程或判断，如绘本叙事中图像和语言激发的认知过程、故事世界的本体地位、存在物及时空等要素，考察叙事建构世界的方式。换句话说，叙事文本是激活读者心理体验的媒介和符号，特定的符号形式（包括图像、文字、声音、动作等多模态符号）和叙事结构会诱发读者启用或更新使用特定的认知模式，启用特定的认知策略。

在文学交流过程中，文学常规，包括文学的体裁、主题、人物、结构、语言风格等文学要素在内的已有习惯性组合模型，会像那些基础性概念结构的基本组成单元一样，在读者心里形成特定的心智模型，用莱考夫（Lakoff，1987）提出的认知语言学术语来说，形成文学交流的“理想认知模型”，成为读者文学记忆的重要组成部分，组织和控制着读者的文学阅读和理解。当然，该类认知模型不是一成不变的，事实上，正如库克（Cook，1994）所言，阅读文学的过程就是不断刷新图式（schema-refreshing）的过程；在文学阅读过程中，基于现实世界或已有文学知识所形成的已有认知图式，往往被不断更新，从而影响文本的体验、接受与评价。但是，就文学体裁特征而言，某类特定文学经典，从叙事形式到故事内容、人物塑造、语言风格等往往会形成特定的模式化图式，即相对稳定的结构和特征，也会激活读者相对稳定的阅读期待。从某种意义上来说，特定文学样类的特征组构成某种相对稳定的原型（Prototype），依照认知经济原则和被感知的世界结构原则指引着读者对该类文学的理解和体验。某一具体的文学作品是否具有原型效应，也潜在于读者的阅读期待视域，担当可供随时比对的预制心理模型。

从这一角度来说，图式是文学交流过程中最为重要的认知模型，图式理论是研究文学语篇理解的重要方法（Emmott，1997；Culpeper，2001）。作为概念知识的框架组织，图式可以解释文本信息如何在读者的思维记忆里形成连贯的有意义的整体，因而，我们可以从图式入手，关注文学文本如何调用和刷新读者的认知心理模型，创造特定的文学认知体验。从认知图式角度考察后现代绘本对传统经典童话叙事的创新或突破，有助于从根本上揭示后现代性绘本阅读效果的生成机制，是解答后现代体验何以能够的密钥。

3 后现代绘本的认知叙事分析

文学文本世界往往通过偏离性语言、结构或内容，挑战或颠覆既定图式，改变既定认知图式，激活新的感知体验。整体而言，后现代绘本正是通过“颠覆性”更新常规认知图式这一基本认知策略，实现对经典童话的颠覆性解构，打造其“后现代性”身份的。从绘本阅读和接受来说，读者也正是通过对常规图式偏离所引发的“陌生化”认知体验，刷新对原有童话故事世界的认知，创造性建构新的故事世界，获得新奇的“后现代”文学体验。参照封宗信（2014），以下分析分为三类图式：故事图式、体裁图式和多模态表征图式。

3.1 颠覆故事图式

后现代绘本最突出的特征就是打破原童话故事内容，把耳熟能详的经典童话彻底改写，冲击读者所熟悉的认知模型。故事内容图式上的解构或再语境化（recontextualization）包括背景场景错位或挪用、人物角色翻转、情节重置、结尾颠覆和开放多元。

改变原童话的背景图式，使读者对故事世界在时间、空间和人物角色关系的感知产生错位性穿越，穿越时间和空间的既定边界，不得不启用新的认知模型，重新建构和体验故事世界。如在著名的后现代绘本小说《三只小狼和大坏猪》中，故事发生的背景元素全部“与时俱进”，组合构建出一幅现代生活场景，小猪盖房子用的材料不再是原童话中的结草，而是水泥、沙子、钢板、铁栅栏、铁锁，甚至还有防弹玻璃；小狼房间里的家具设备还有电器如冰箱；小猪的户外活动也完全是现代的典型活动场景，如打网球，玩槌球。这种故事场景的故意移位，一方面模拟现代生活现实，拉近与读者的距离，增强对故事世界可信度的感知体验，同时也诱使读者按照当下的现实生活逻辑，对绘本故事世界进行推理和评判，“将故事的意旨转向现实的道德判断，挑战和质疑童话历史所建立的传统认知范畴”（钱淑英，2006：55）。

与故事背景错位设置密切关联，后现代绘本还经常颠覆经典童话中的“人物原型”，冲击刻板印象图式结构，诱使重新思考和评价。如在经典童话中，狼凶残狡猾、威猛高大，而小猪则憨厚可爱、矮小柔弱。在《三只小狼和大坏猪》中，两者的身份完全逆转，狼被表征得憨厚可爱，被不断建房子的“大坏猪”打扰，深受其苦，不得不默默忍受躲避。《臭》中“青蛙王子”中的青蛙，伸着吞噬各类小昆虫的硕大无比的长舌头，贪婪狡猾，骗到了公主的吻，没有变成王子，跳到池塘里游走了。同样，《臭》中的丑小鸭没有变成白天鹅，长大后依然还是地地道道的丑小鸭。颠覆人物原型图式是最为普遍的后现代手段，也是后现代绘本最常用的颠覆性标志特征，重新设定不同于经典童话故事里的人物，是解构和颠覆传统认知、消解僵化价值判断模式的强有力手段，也是后现代向确定性、常规性现代思维开炮的最佳爆破口。

人物角色设定的逆转颠覆势必直接影响故事情节发展脉络和故事结局。如大卫·威斯纳的《三只小猪》，以经典童话故事为起点，但又偏离其原有既定故事情节脉络：大灰狼也是想把小猪的房子吹倒，但居然把小猪吹到故事外面去了，由此，创造性虚构出第一层故事边界裂痕。继而，三只小猪还把《三只小猪》这本物理意义上的童话故事书给拆解了，做成了玩具，纸飞机。这个飞机居然还飞到了另外两个童话故事里——《鹅妈妈童谣》和《武士屠龙》，由此创造出连环跨界，把物理空间、虚构故事空间进行了层级套嵌。但这些空间之间原有的具有阻隔性的边界，在读者的心理表征空间彻底销毁，故事情节得以在其中畅通无阻穿行，于是，三只小猪逃脱了老被狼吃掉的命运，来到了故事之外的故事里，读者得以在图文符号的协同作用下，重新组织叙事进程，重构出全新的故事世界。

后现代绘本不但对经典童话故事情节延展脉络进行了大胆的再情景化重置，颠覆性刷新读者熟知的故事图式，而且对故事结尾进行了颠覆性解构。如《臭》中“青蛙王子”和“丑小鸭”的故事结尾“大跌眼镜”，青蛙还是那只青蛙，丑小鸭长大后依然很丑，这样的故事结局消解了定势思维图式中“脱胎换骨”式的身份转换，漂白了经典童话的浪漫主义色彩，诱使读者重新审视和质疑经典童话的僵化思维本质。再如，在大卫·威斯纳《疯狂星期二》的结尾，小猪居然打破了枷锁，摆脱了引力束缚，飞上了天空，留给读者无限的想象空间。更奇特的是，在贾尼·罗大里的《童话故事游戏》里，作者居然列出了三个结局，读者可以根据自己的喜好，自行选择或干脆直接重写。由此可见，后现代绘本也擅长对经典故事结尾大做文章，打破固定范式结局，消解“圆满”型定势心理期待，为读者提供崭新的、开放的、多元的情节可能，诱发读者充分调用个人经验感知，重构故事情节。该类对经典故事情节的解构与重构是提升读者审美感知体验的最直接通道，读者的个体体验和意识活动获得了一种前所未有的尊重。

以上是在故事内容维度上的创新和颠覆，是最具冲击力的图式颠覆手段，对习惯执着于故事情节的小读者来说，也是最易引发新鲜感和警觉意识、刷新图式、放慢阅读进程的有力操控器。

3.2 颠覆体裁图式

“体裁图式”指经典童话惯用的相对定型的交流模式和语类结构。在交流模式方面，经典童话绘本把儿童读者定位为受教育或被教化的对象（赵秀凤，2020：15），作者及陪伴儿童阅读的成人读者是合谋关系，绘本只是对儿童开展道德教化的媒介或手段，所以，经典童话故事也往往具有固定的图式，从起点、矛盾冲突、变化到完美结局，这一经典童话故事脉络执念于浪漫主义或超现实主义价值追求，以近似机械的方式强行浇筑一种简单而统一的理想主义情愫。从某种意义上来说，经典童话的成人作者与儿童读者之间是一种不平等权力关系，儿童绘本只是道德教化工具。

在该类传统定位作用下，绘本作为一种独特的儿童文学样类，其突出特征就是故事情节的线性、结构的简单性和意义的给定性，这些都构成了绘本这一文学体裁的常规，即原型性图式。然而，后现代文化思潮影响下的后现代绘本对这一原型体裁图式进行了颠覆性解构。

首先，后现代绘本颠覆常规文学交流模式。绘本不再被定位为道德教化的工具，读者不再只是被动的接受者，而应邀参与文学交流的全过程，参与意义创造。定位不同，导致了交流模式的重构：读者、作者之间变成了一种合作和协同共谋关系，从情节设置、人物认知到意义提取都不是给定的或一成不变的；道德教化不再是儿童绘本的唯一旨趣，传统上被极端边缘化的"审美性"和"体验性"提升为核心要素，儿童读者成为具有独特体验和审美能力的平等个体。就文学交流的认知过程而言，后现代绘本所激活的认知图式更倾向于调用主体间性（intersubjectivity），作者与读者处于平等地位，对故事意义乃至叙事行为或图书编辑制作行为本身进行协商（赵秀凤，2020）。关于后现代绘本对经典童话叙事体裁图式的颠覆，潘达莱奥和西普（Pantaleo & Sipe，2008：3）指出，后现代绘本颠覆了文学传统和常规，削弱了故事与外面的真实世界之间的隔断。"后现代绘本具有强烈的自我指涉性，不再诱发读者的间接体验，相反，是摆出一副元虚构的姿态，引导读者去关注文本本身的符号性、虚构性"（赵秀凤，2020：15）。

其次，后现代绘本"反客为主"，彰显元小说叙事或元虚构本身。元小说叙事是"一种创作手法，它自觉而系统地彰显文本作为人工产品的本质，以质疑小说与现实之间的关系"（Patricia，1984：2）。元小说是后现代小说"后现代性"的重要标志，通过"自我指涉"，"使读者产生虚实难辨的错觉，并获得阅读中的互动体验感"（梁斌，2020：76）。就其认知本质而言，元小说叙事是一种典型的元认知活动，是对小说创作或叙事过程本身认知活动的自涉；就其体现形式而言，往往表现为故事讲述本身的主题化，如何讲、什么时间讲、由谁讲本身构成了小说故事世界内容的一部分，如在《臭》中，讲述行为或过程本身甚至成为不同叙事人物争夺或争论的焦点，甚至成为重要的规训手段，如以下文字所示：

（1）Why don't you disappear for a few pages? 你为什么不消失几页呢？（还没轮到你讲）

（2）Hey，you are not in this story. 嗨，你不在这个故事里。（还没讲到你呢，你先不要出场）

（3）You have to start with "once upon a time". 你必须先说"很久很久以前"。（你的故事开头不对）

（4）You just told the whole story. 你都已经讲完了整个故事。（还让我们讲什么？）

从某种意义上来说，元叙事其实是对固化体裁图式的一种颠覆性力量，如《臭》中的"巨人讲述的故事"对经典童话结构顺序进行了彻头彻尾地颠覆：以"THE END"开始，以"Once upon a time"结束，这是后现代绘本对固有结构性秩序的反叛（赵秀凤，2020：25），也是作者元认知能力自身的概念化呈现。

最后，后现代绘本消解常规边界，刻意打破常规叙事技巧。如前文所述，《三只小猪》与《鹅妈妈童谣》和《武士屠龙》之间居然可以穿行无阻，叙事世界与故事世界之间也再无阻隔：三只小猪居然游荡在故事之外，竟然把书拆了，把有故事的纸折成了纸飞机，坐上纸飞机，在故事框之外飞翔。这种常规边界的消解，也是一种元叙事手段，意在打破读者对故事模式的僵化认知，在彰显故事虚构性本质的同时，提升读者对故事背后常规隐性存在的叙事者身份的认识。如按照常规体裁图式，故事集内的不同故事应各自独立，各自形成封闭的故事内环。但是，在《臭》中，在小红鸡的故事结尾处，小红鸡问道："Who thinks they're going to help me EAT the BREAD?"（谁能帮我吃新做的面包？）本来不在这个故事世界的巨人（the Giant）突然应答道："BREAD?""EAT?"画面上呈现出张着大嘴的巨人正在吞下左侧页上呈现的小红鸡手举的那盘面包。次页画面上刻画的是剩下的半块面包，巨人正在剔牙，嘴角处飘落着小红鸡蓝色的帽子，而且剩下的那块面包变成了三明治。图像表征以转喻的形式表达了巨人对小红鸡及其面包的吞并行为。这样的安排，使得在不同故事之间原应有的界限和隔离被彻底打破，人物可以穿越到其他故事世界内，参与故事情节，改变故事发展脉络，创造结局。这样的叙事确实是对常规叙事图式的彻底解构（赵秀凤，2020：25）。该类便于穿越的边界的消解，也非常符合儿童的思维模式与心理机制，"对他们来说，真实与虚幻之间并不一定存在着清晰的界限，他可以从这个世界跳到那个世界，好像从一个窗户前跑到另一个窗户前一样"（史密斯，2014：218）。

如同其他类型的后现代主义文学，以非线性、跨界性、互文性等特征大大颠覆了现代主义文本的叙事方式（Lewis，2001：94），后现代绘本对经典绘本叙事模式的颠覆性创造给儿童文学和儿童绘本带了巨大的冲击和洗礼。谢瑞·阿兰（Cherie Allan）在专著《与绘本游戏：后现代主义与后现代性》（2012）的结论中写道："后现代主义对绘本的影响就如后现代现象本身：是含混的、片段式的、去中心化的，拒绝固定的界限、同质化的阐释和既定的归类理论。"按照罗兰·巴特尔（Roland Barthes，1974）在《S/Z》中的分类，后现代绘本是典型的"可写性文本"（scriptable，writerly），打破了传统的"可读性文本"（lisible，readerly）的常规模式，能指与所指之间的关系不再一目了然，文本的意义变得游离，排斥卒读下的简单赋值，也相应为儿童读者创造了想象或自由发挥的空间。在参与后现代绘本文学交流的过程中，读者的主体性得到最大程度的释放，颠覆经典图式带来的新奇感、游戏感，与故事图式颠覆所带来的延迟的张力与未完成的期待一起，构成了一种后现代绘本阅读独有的情感狂欢，令儿童读者体会到摆脱约束后的开放与自由，从而可以实现激发创造力，提升审美体验，刷新认知图式的艺术价值。

3.3 颠覆表征图式

从表征角度来说，绘本是图画和文字协同叙述的完整故事，是图文合奏的艺术作品，对此，松居直（2009：122）用以下公式对插图读物和绘本（图画书）形象地进行了区别性概括：图+文=插图读物、图×文=图画书。正是基于这一区别性认识，英语学术界往往用“Picturebook”这一合二为一且大写首字母P的英文术语强调其独立性。关于图画和文字的协同作用，两次获得过凯迪克金奖的美国画家芭芭拉·库尼也用了一个非常形象的比喻：绘本是一串珍珠项链，其中，图画是珍珠，文字是穿起珍珠的线。项链的艺术性存在源自两者的完美结合。与插图读物、识字图画书等不同，作为一种单独的叙事文学样类，“绘本”的独特之处就在于图画本身不再处于附属地位，服务于解释文字内容，相反，对于绘本整体而言，图画本身具有极其重要的、不可或缺的叙事功能，否则就不能称其为“绘本（小说）”。

关于绘本中的图文关系，苏瓦兹（Schwarcz，1982）概括为两种：“叠合式”和“背离式”。“叠合式”就是图画和文字之间和谐一致，相互补充或衬托，合作完成故事叙事；而“背离式”就是图画和文字之间存在语义冲突或张力，比如文字和图画分别讲述相冲突的事件（潘多灵、夏成，2019：49）。当然，也有学者反对这种划分，如诺德曼（2000）则认为，绘本中的图画和文字是相互制约的关系，使意义延迟，生成任何一方单独所不能传达的意义。这里诺德曼只是强调了图画和文字的不可分割性，苏瓦兹提出的上述分类是在承认图画和文字协同作用前提下所做的细分，具有一定的合理性。

整体而言，传统经典绘本多沿用“叠合式”，页面设计以图像为主，文字相对较少，字体排版统一规整，多位于页面边缘位置，有时候也位于页面图画中间。在图-文表征及其相互关系上，后现代绘本也在很大程度上打破或颠覆传统表征图式，呈现出更多组合样态，突出表现为以下几种情况。

第一，文字的物理符号属性得到最大程度的突显，包括字体、颜色、大小、排版等在内的多模态符号成为具有本体价值的表意或叙事资源，服务于绘本整体叙事。

如在《臭》中（见图 1），分别用不同颜色和字体表征“小红鸡”与 Jack 的对话：小红鸡的言语与她身体的颜色相同，均为亮眼的红色，而 Jack 的回话用黑色和小号字体呈现，与图像上小红鸡与 Jack 的形体和姿态对比相呼应，彰显小红鸡作为第一个故事讲述者的霸气（赵秀凤，2020：18）。再如，在《臭》的致献页中（见图 2），致献文字采用黑色加粗大字体，但方向上却违反读者的阅读常规图式，采用倒置方式，诱使读者手动，在物理空间意义上颠倒图书方向，从而实现读者的合作性涉身叙事；此外，该致献词被置于一块白板上，是故事讲述者 Jack 所在的故事世界内的一个物理实体，是故事内容的一部分，也可以解读为聚光灯下的一块宣传板，“其亮度与右侧和底部标示故事世界的暗色形成鲜明对比，这一白板不但在物理属性上彰显了其人工加工特质，凸显其物质性，而且，该白板上的文字同图像中 Jack 的表情姿态——与故事外的读者有视线接触，共同创建了一种直接对话情景”（赵秀凤，2020：19）。再如图 3 所示，《臭》中论文集题目文字居然设计成为独立的物理实体，在力量作用下，纷纷跌落。

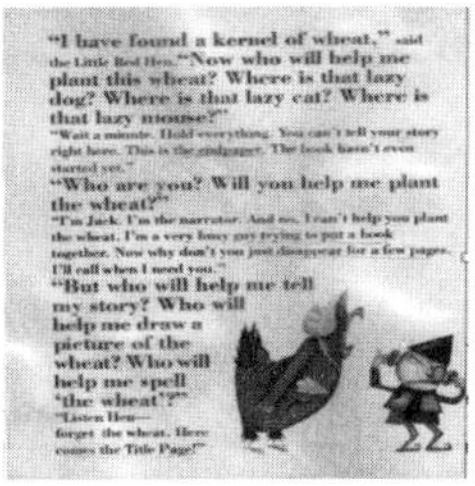

图 1

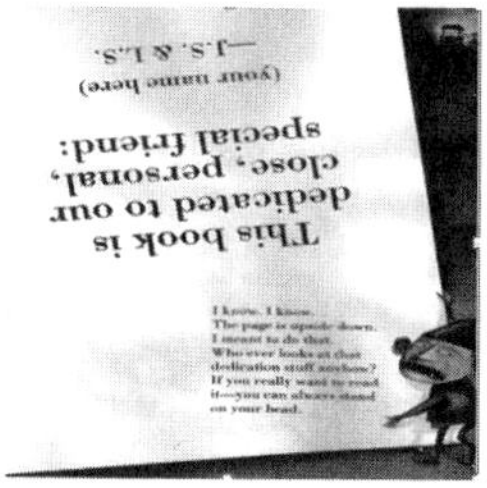

图 2

图 3

除了打破文字本身的印刷常规图式外，后现代绘本还混合图画与文字的边界，故意模糊两者之间的常规范畴，如图 4《三只小猪的真实故事》中，用“砖、树枝、稻草”组合成大写字母“E”，与文字“verybody”一起代替常规单词“everybody”，图 5 中，图画与文字的边界消解得更彻底，文字“This is the real story”中的每一个字母都是由故事内与小猪相关的各类物质表征的，包括小猪的鼻子、尾巴等。

图 4

图 5

第二，图画本身的表征方式也往往打破规整常规，如图画框本身成为故事世界边界消解的表征手段。如图 6 选自《谁害怕那本大坏书？》（*Who's Afraid of the Big Bad Book?*），充分利用文字形体、标点符号、颜色、图形形状，组合成符号层级叠加和套嵌的立体复杂网络，故事讲述者的世界、不同叙事者所讲述的不同的故事世界之间可以随意穿越。通过对符号主体性表征地位的核准确认，构建边界消失的多维世界，象似性表征后现代思想中的去中心和反霸权思想。

第三，图书的材质物理属性也成为叙事符号，而不只是绘本故事交流的载体。例如纸张的形状、颜色、材质类型、图书的装订、设计版式等，都从幕后搬到台前，进入绘本叙事的内容。如图 7 选自《令人难以置信的吃书男孩》（*The Incredible Book Eating Boy*），该绘本充分利用各类图书的材质颜色和形状，表征绘本故事内所讲述的被男孩囫囵吞枣吃掉的各类图书。

图 6

图 7

图 8

第四，图文视角不一，建构后现代性断裂与游移。如《母鸡萝丝去散步》中，文字和图像是沿用不同的视角定位建构表征的：文字部分用一连串第三人称简单叙事小句——“母鸡萝丝出门去散步，她走过院子，绕过池塘，越过干草堆，经过磨坊，穿过篱笆，钻过蜜蜂坊，按时回到家吃晚饭”表征故事主角之一母鸡完整的散步事件，如果仅看文字，读者只能在心理构建出一幅母鸡萝丝平凡无奇的故事地图，只有仔细看图画（如图 8），才能感知到故事世界内部母鸡和狐狸之间的张力，因为图画部分采用了另外一种远远大于母鸡有限眼光的表征视角，突显对立角色狐狸的眼光及叙事者的全知眼光。正是图画与文字在叙事视角上的割裂，创造出后现代绘本的去中心性和不确定性，也在一定程度上揭示出语言的困境或语言再现的局限性。

4 后现代绘本解构与重构的元认知价值

关于后现代绘本解构经典，运用多模态展开后现代重构的教育意义和价值，已有不少学者从文学批评的角度进行了阐述，其教育功用概括起来包括：为儿童提供更多想象空间、激发儿童的创造力、调动儿童的主体性、培育批判思维，重塑价值，拒绝霸权控制等（Brooker，1992；史菊鸿，2009）。这些功能是成人研究者以专家身份对该类绘本文学价值的理论分析和探讨，虽然很有道理，但是，我们认为，这些教育功能的概说本身并没有直抵本质，因为其功能的通达和实现归根结底需要儿童读者自身的心理感受或体验。从这一角度来说，我们以上的认知叙事分析是对后现代绘本多模态符号在儿童心理激活的心理感知过程的模拟性重构，有助于从根本上揭示后现代绘本的认知功用。

基于以上的认知叙事分析，我们可以说，后现代绘本解构和重构经典童话的最根本的价值是培养儿童的“元认知能力”。借用布劳（Blau）的定义，元认知（metacognition）是“关于思维的思维”（2014：46），也就是关于认知本身的认知或反思性认识。文学阅读有助于培养学生的元认知能力，这被视为文学作品的普遍功能，布劳发现学生在阅读文学过程中有获得元认知能力的习惯（转引自肖谊、谢梦昕，2021：123；Blau，2014：46）。我们赞同肖谊和谢梦昕把元认知能力从学习者的学习能力扩展到小说创作中的叙事机制。可以说，正是由于作者在小说创作过程中，启用元认知能力，创造出颠覆经典认知图式的艺术作品，才能极大推动读者元认知能力的提升。从这一角度来看，后现代绘本叙事的上述全方位的图式颠覆正是充分发挥元认知能力，开展元认知叙事行为的结果，反过来也是对儿童读者进行元认知能力培养和训练的最佳舞台。

作为一种隐性的认知策略，包括认知过程、认知方式与认知活动在内的元认知关涉知识接受与认识的机制与规律。按照元认知的这一属性——“将其作为对象或调节任何认知活动的知识或认知活动”（转引自肖谊、谢梦昕，2021：124；Flavell，2004：275），后现代绘本创作者把经典童话故事图式、体裁图式和表征图式进行了大胆地颠覆性再情景化挪用，把传统经典童话置于一个全方位立体环绕审视批判的境地，不但颠覆其故事内容，更主要的是颠覆其虚构性这一根本属性，使虚构之虚构、讲述之讲述成为再创造的焦点，通过连环颠覆和套嵌，最大限度地彰显文学艺术创造的元认知活动或过程本身。正是由于创作者元认知能力的最大彰显，使元认知行为本身也成为后现代绘本的主题内容，因而成为读者感知和体验的重要组成部分。元认知创作过程的彰显，清楚地向儿童读者展示了反思性认知和元认知推理的形态和价值，从而使后现代主义的核心思想——“反思和批判”超脱了空洞抽象的宣扬，而是以元认知的形态展演给儿童读者，让他们感知到该类绘本对僵化图式的反思性和批判性，潜移默化地引导和培养儿童自由创造，质疑权威，拒绝有限性和确定性，充分发挥个体的主体性，创造意义和价值。

5 结　语

本文立足认知叙事学立场，从认知图式角度，结合实例，考察分析了后现代绘本颠覆经典童话叙事的三个方面——颠覆故事图式、颠覆体裁图式、颠覆表征图式。这些构成了后现代绘本独特的语类特征和核心认知建构策略。后现代绘本通过颠覆作为读者概念组织结构的常规图式，解构传统文学交流范式和意义的僵化感知。

这类绘本通过全方位的立体化、系统化打破和颠覆传统绘本童话，试图对儿童及伴读成人进行感知、思维和价值重构，敦促读者运用后现代思维重新审视世界和人生，重点重构和培育儿童在文学叙事、心理和情感感知和空间认知等方面的创新能力。后现代绘本对经典童话解构和重构的重要价值是培养儿童的“元认知能力”，引领儿童读者切身感知和体验到对僵化图式反思和颠覆带来的快乐和成就，鼓励和培养自由、开放和创新的生活态度和艺术鉴赏习惯。

参考文献

[1] C ALLAN. Playing with Picturebooks: Postmodernism and the Postmodernesque. Houndmills, Basingstoke, Hampshire: Palgrave Macmillan, 2012.

[2] M ANSTEY. “It’s not All Black and White”: Postmodern Picture Books and New Literacies. Journal of Adolescent and Adult Literacy, 2002a, 45 (6): 362-271.

[3] R BARTHES. S/Z: An Essay. Translated by Richard Miller. New York: Hill and Wang, 1975.

[4] S BLAU. Literary competence and the experience of literature. Style, 2014 (1): 42-46.

[5] P BROOKER. Modernism/Postmodernism. London: Longman, 1992.

[6] A CHAMBERS. Booktalk: Occasional Writing on Literature and Children. London: The Bodley Head, 1985.

[7] G COOK. Discourse and Literature. Oxford: Oxford University Press, 1994.

[8] J CULPEPER. Language and Characterisation. London: Longman, 2001.

[9] E DRESANG. Radical Change: Books for Youth in a Digital Age.

New York, NY: The H. W. Wilson Company, 1999.

[10] C EMMOTT. Narrative Comprehension: A Discourse Perspective. Oxford: Oxford University Press, 1997.

[11] J FLAVELL. Theory-of-Mind Development: Retrospect and Prospect. Merrill-Palmer Quarterly, 2004 (3): 274-290.

[12] M FLUDERNIK, G OLSON. Introduction // G. Olson. Current Trends in Narratology. Berlin and New York: De Gruyter, 2011: 3.

[13] B GOLDSTONE. Ordering the Chaos: Teaching Metafictive Characteristics of Children's Books. Journal of Children's Literature, 1998, 24 (2): 48-55.

[14] B GOLDSTONE. Whaz up with Our Books? Changing Picture Book Codes and Teaching Implications. The Reading Teacher, 2001 / 2002, 55 (4): 362-370.

[15] A GRIEVE. Postmodernism in Picture Books. Papers: Explorations into children's literature, 1993, 4 (3): 15-25.

[16] G LAKOFF. Women, Fire and Dangerous Things: What Categories Reveal about the Mind. Chicago: Chicago University Press, 1987.

[17] D LEWIS. Reading Contemporary Picture Books: Picturing Text. New York, NY: Routledge Falmer, 2001.

[18] D LEWIS. The Constructedness of Texts: Picture Books and The Metafictive. Signal, 1990, 62: 131.

[19] R MCGILLIS. "Ages": All Readers, Texts, and Intertexts in The Stinky Cheese Man and Other Fairly Stupid Tales // S. Beckett. Transcending Boundaries: Writing for a Dual Audience of Children and Adults. New York: Garland Publishing, 1999: 111-126.

[20] P NODELMAN. Words about Pictures: The Narrative Art of Children's Picturebooks. London: The University of Georgia Press, 2000.

[21] S PANTALEO, L SIPE. Postmodernism and Picturebooks //L. Sipe et al. (eds.) Postmodern Picturebooks: Play, Parody, and Self-referentiality. New York, NY: Routledge, 2008: 3.

[22] S PANTALEO. Scieszka's the Stinky Cheese Man: A Tossed Salad of Parodic Re-versions. Children's Literature in Education, 2007, 38: 277-295.

[23] S PANTALEO. The Metafictive Nature of Postmodern Picturebooks. The Reading Teacher, 2014, 67 (5): 324-332.

[24] W PATRICIA. Metafiction: The Theory and Practice of Self-Conscious fiction. New York: Methuen & Co. Ltd, 1984.

[25] J SCHWARCZ. Ways of Illustrator: Visual Communication in Children's literature. Chicago: American Library Association, 1982.

[26] J SCIESZKA, L SMITH. The Stinky Cheese Man and Other Fairly Stupid Tales. New York: Scholastic Inc., 1992.

[27] L R SIPE, S PANTALEO. Postmodern Picturebooks: Play, Parody, and Self-Referentiality. Routledge, 2010.

[28] S TOZER, V CHOU. Playing against Conventions: The True Story of the Stinky Cheese Man //J. Flood, S. Heath, & D. Lapp. Handbook of Research on Teaching Literacy Through the Communicative and Visual Arts. Mahwah, NJ: Lawrence Erlbaum Associates Publishers, 1997: 822-828.

[29] R S TRITES. Manifold Narratives: Metafiction and Ideology in Picture Books. Children's Literature in Education, 1994, 25 (4): 225-242.

[30] K WATSON. The Postmodern Picture Book in the Secondary Classroom. English in Australia, 2004, 140: 55-57.

[31] 陈礼珍. 当代西方认知叙事学研究的最新走向与远景展望. 解放军外国语学院学报，2020（1）：51-58.

[32] 戴维·赫尔曼，尚必武. 叙事学研究的新发展：戴维·赫尔曼访谈录. 外国文学，2009（5）：97-105.

[33] 封宗信. 日常语篇的文学性与片段随意拼接中的叙事性. 认知诗学，2014（1）：46-55.

[34] 梁斌. 后现代主义视角下的儿童绘本创作及其教育价值. 学前教育研究，2020（11）：75-80.

[35] 钱淑英. 互文性透视下的儿童文学后现代景观——以改编自《三只小猪》的图画书为考察对象[J]. 浙江师范大学学报，2006（4）：54-58.

[36] 申丹. 叙事结构与认知过程：认知叙事学评析. 外语教学，2004（9）：1-8.

[37] 史菊鸿. 从乔恩·钱斯卡的两本图画书看美国儿童文学的后现代性. 宁夏大学学报（人文社会科学版）2009（1）：103-108.

[38] 史密斯·李利安. 欢欣岁月，梅思繁，译. 长沙：湖南少年儿童出版社，2014.

[39] 松居直. 我的图画书论. 上海：人民美术出版社，2009.

[40] 王寅. 哲学的第四转向：后现代主义. 外国语文（四川外国语学院学报），2012（2）：9-15.

[41] 王治河. 后现代哲学思潮研究（增补本）[M]. 北京：北京大学出版社，2006.

[42] 肖谊，谢梦昕. 元认知与英美小说对莎士比亚的挪用. 外语与外语教学，2021（2）：123-129.

[43] 赵秀凤，黄洁. 后现代语境中的认知诗学学科定位和发展前景. 外语学刊，2013（5）：26-30.

[44] 赵秀凤. 多模态认知诗学视域下的后现代绘本叙事——以《臭起司小子爆笑故事大集合》为例. 英语研究，2020（2）：13-27.

儿童绘本图文信息耦合与读者心理表征

任 政

【摘要】本文运用图式、原型和心理模型理论分析美国漫画艺术家慕斯的绘本《禅故事》(2005)里图文信息耦合及其激发的读者心理表征。虽然图文相互补充构成独特的信息耦合，并同步推进主线与内嵌故事的进程，但文字信息激发的理想心理模型或原型图式与图画呈现的形象有明显冲突，给读者造成认知加工困难和心理表征困惑。本文认为，这些冲突代表着禅的一系列矛盾统一，恰恰是慕斯要达到的艺术效果。整个绘本建构了一个图文信息交替、主线故事与嵌套故事穿插、副文本与正文相配、作者与读者互动的系统网络，旨在刷新读者的语言图式、故事图式和真实世界知识图式，寓教于乐。
【关键词】绘本；图文信息；图式；心理表征；禅

0 引 言

绘本是结合象形（iconic）符号和规约（conventional）符号进行两个层面交流的艺术形式（Nikolajeva & Scott，2001：1）。绘本通常指儿童绘本。与文中插图的成年人读物不同，儿童绘本是图中插文，通过大量连续图画配以少量文字（甚至没有文字）为儿童传播信息或讲故事（Nodelman，1988：vii）。绘本与其他视觉艺术不同，其中的图画不仅具有美学价值，而且能够帮助文字共同讲述故事。象形符号的能指直接表征所指，规约符号的能指依靠约定俗成的规则表征所指。图以空间为轴，具有瞬时的静态特征；文以时间

作者简介：任政，女，清华大学外文系博士研究生，主要从事多模态文体学研究。

为轴，具有连续的动态特征。图善于展现整体，文善于描写细节并表现其间关系。图文有着各自的特点，在呈现信息时交替发挥作用，因为从读者角度，读文和赏图不能同时进行。两种符号或模态有机配合，展示了绘本独特的节奏、形状和结构规约（Nodelman，1988：Ⅷ）。

Painter 等人（2012）指出，绘本有教育价值，对儿童的文字识读、文学素养和价值观的形成有重要影响，不但为儿童学前教育做必要准备，而且引导儿童接触文学、认识社会。Stephens（1992）指出，绘本还是儿童形成世界观的重要信息来源。近些年来，越来越多的绘本涉及较为深奥和严肃的话题，如《战争爆发的那天》（Davies & Cobb，2018）、《我们是水的保护者》（Lindstrom & Goade，2020）、《黑是一种彩虹色》（Joy & Holmes，2020）、《与爸爸一起回家》（Lyons & Minter，2019）等。著名美国漫画艺术家琼·穆斯（Jon J. Muth）创作的绘本《禅故事》（*Zen Shorts*）讲述了一个关于东方“禅”的故事，该绘本荣获 2006 年凯迪克绘本银奖并连续 41 周上榜《纽约时报》畅销书单。它集绘画与叙事于一身，创造了一个个与现实若即若离的虚构人物形象，在人物交流主线中，内嵌了三个植根于东方文化、改编给西方读者的小故事，在娱乐中启发读者思考取与舍、得与失、拿起与放下等深刻关系，领略“福兮祸兮”“静思”等精神内涵。本文拟在认知诗学视角下，运用图式、原型和心理模型理论分析图文信息耦合及其激发的读者心理表征。

1 图式、原型与心理模型

图式是概念结构的基本组成单元。例如，人对“空间”的经验和概念大致通过“容器”“来源—路径—目标”“部分—整体”“上—下”“前—后”等图式来组织，或者说，这些结构组织着我们的理想认知模型或心智模型（Lakoff，1987）。图式理论已发展为认知语言学研究语篇（包括文学语篇）理解的重要研究方法（见 Emmott 1997；Culpeper 2001）。作为概念知识的框架组织，图式可以解释文本信息如何在读者的记忆里重新组合。来自不同文化的读者有不同的期待和概念知识或心理图形，读者把文本信息与记忆里的心理图形进行对比并重新组合，构成新的图式。在这一过程中，读者推断文本中的情节或填补其逻辑空白才能达到顺畅阅读，但这些环节都要依靠已有知识图式。Cook（1994）指出，文学是最显著的具有图式刷新（schema-refreshing）功能的文本，即人们感知世界的常规方法经常被文学文本里的偏离性语言、结构和内容挑战或颠覆。换句话说，文学作品表征的虚构世界与我们对现实世界的感知不完全相同，阅读文学就是更新我们的图式，改变我们对世界的感知。封宗信（2014）分析了文学作品刷新读者语言图式、故事图式和体裁图式的效果，并指出文学阅读还可以让我们进一步思考“文学”和“叙事小说”等概念。

原型理论来自 Eleanor Rosch 等学者在 20 世纪 70 年代认知心理学实验中的发现，即人类最善于罗列出一个范畴的共同特征。范畴理论的核心是范畴化的两个基本原则：认知经济原则和被感知世界结构原则。前者指人类以最省力的方式获得尽可能多的信息，换句话说，人类能够将所经历过的相似刺激划归为同一范畴，而非单独存储每个刺激信息，以达到认知表征中的经济性。后者指世界具有相关关系结构（如鸟类的翅膀经常与羽毛和飞行能力相关，而非与皮毛或水下呼吸能力共现），人类依赖这种相关关系结构才能形成并组织范畴。这两个原则构成了人类的范畴化系统。Lakoff（1973）在模糊论的框架下讨论了范畴的原型概念和边缘概念，如知更鸟、鸡、企鹅在“鸟”范畴里的典型性程度不同，知更鸟最典型，企鹅最靠边缘。所以“企鹅是鸟”的命题不完全正确，但“企鹅算鸟”（A penguin is sort of a bird）的命题接近正确。Rosch & Mervis（1975：575）认为，原型是概念的抽象表征，是被试判断某些事物与其相关“图像”匹配程度时产生的范畴或心理结构。但 Rosch（1978：261）后来认为，原型效应不能解释特定的加工模型，也无法提出一套范畴认知表征的理论。Gibbs（2003）认为原型不是抽象、预先存在的概念结构，而仅是意义识解的结果。

Lakoff（1987）提出了心理模型（mental models）理论，认为原型或典型效应是表面现象，不同于认知表征，而是一系列复杂的心理模型结合后的结果。Lakoff（1987：68-75）从认知层面构建了范畴结构并提出“理想化认知模型”理论，即所有范畴都与理想化认知模型有联系，也是世界理论的相对稳定的心理表征。他同时还提出了另一种认知模型——群集模型（cluster models），并以“母亲”概念为例解释了群集模型包含的一系列次范畴模型：生育模型、遗传模型、养育模型、婚姻模型、宗谱模型。他指出，在同一概念的众多群集模型中，总有一个理想认知模型凸显，因此就产生了典型性效果，从而暗淡了其他次范畴。尽管很多词典把“生育模型”看作“母亲”概念的主要特征，但Lakoff发现，有的词典突出其养育模型，有的词典突出这一概念的宗谱模型。这就意味着，读者看到一个特定词项，对其所指的特征进行概念化的侧重点也不一样。因此，原型理论强调的典型与非典型关系对解释词汇概念具有重要意义。Geeraerts（1989：591）指出，原型理论是产出型理论，对词汇范畴结构的精辟分析不仅能运用于词汇研究的各个领域，而且能运用于语言学的其他领域。已经有研究证明，该理论作为认知语言学的重要基石，能够解释所有语言结构层面的语言与认知互动。

2 绘本及其图文信息

绘本《禅故事》按画册装帧设计，没有普通图书常用的目录和页码。绘本封面和封底为满页全彩色，内有33个页面，其中主线故事占23页面，内嵌故事占10页面。除正文外，绘本还包括扉页、版权页、致献页、跋页等页面。主线故事和内嵌故事在色彩和画风等方面有着明显不同。主线故事页面以白边为画框，色彩丰富，人、物、景逼真，绘画风格为水彩画；内嵌故事满页无框，分别以蓝灰、淡绿和淡黄为底色，人、物、景形象简单，以水墨勾勒，主要人物形象无色彩填充。扉页、版权页、致献页、跋页采用内嵌故事页面的底色，扉页与跋页插图均为水墨黑白色。

绘本讲述的是一家三个孩子安迪（Addy）、迈克尔（Michael）、卡尔（Karl）与一只名叫“静水”（Stillwater）的大熊猫如何成为朋友的故事。三个小朋友每次去拜访大熊猫，大熊猫都会给小朋友分享一个简单而又充满哲理的小故事:《良叔叔与月亮》(“Uncle Ry and the Moon”)《农夫的运气》(“The Farmer’s Luck”)《重负》(“A Heavy Load”)。《良叔叔与月亮》讲的是独居山顶的良叔叔家徒四壁，却偏遇盗贼。良叔叔没有赶走盗贼或与之搏斗，而是把仅有的一件破袍送给了他，并哀叹没能把一轮皓月给他。《农夫的运气》是传统故事《塞翁失马焉知非福》的改编版。农夫失马，因祸得福，第二天失马归来，带回两匹马。接着因福得祸，农夫的儿子骑马跌下摔断腿。后来因祸得福，躲过了应征上前线的厄运。《重负》讲两个和尚赶路，遇见一位少妇因一深水坑阻碍了去路，老和尚背起少妇蹚水而过，少妇未说一个谢字。两个和尚继续赶路，小和尚百思不得其解，问老和尚为什么要背少妇过河。老和尚答，他早已把她放下，反而责问小和尚为什么还没“放下”。这三个短故事均未明确指出其中的寓意，这正反映了禅的最基本特点“不依赖言辞”（Abe，1985：23）。“思悟”、心与心之间的交流是禅内涵传播的途径（Suzuki，1973）。在绘本最后的跋页上，“作者注”（Author’s Note）提供了很多信息，回答了“何为禅？”之问。作者依次介绍了“禅”（Zen）的来源及含义、大熊猫名字“静水”(“心静如水”“心若止水”)、良叔叔形象（源自日本著名诗人良宽）和本书标题“禅故事”的来龙去脉，以及三个故事源远流长的出处（第一、三个取自有数百年历史的禅宗文学，第二个植根于已有数千年历史的道家文化）。最后指出，这些故事有很多版本，作者选择了最易于儿童理解的版本。

3 图文信息互补与冲突

《禅故事》中的文字与图像信息互补是主流，但图文分别提供的信息在许多结构分析层面发生冲突，文字激活的典型概念与图画呈现的形象有明显差别，不符合读者已有的典型认知图式。标题里的 shorts 是“短小精悍”（的故事），与“短裤”的语义双关，而图画提供的信息是一只穿着大短裤的熊猫。图文合作既点名了绘本的主要内容，又描绘了故事中重要人物角色。作者在致献页中写道：此绘本是献给曾在家里门廊上跳过舞的一只大熊猫。绘本开头讲道：小朋友卡尔意外地发现窗外有一只熊（bear），但图画是一只打着红色雨伞的熊猫（panda）。这说明小朋友们也许不认识熊猫。熊带着一丝熊猫的口音解释说他来取被风刮过来的雨伞。三位小朋友向熊猫做了自我介绍。叙述者说这是三位小朋友与“静水”相遇的过程。读者通过图文信息知道，图中熊猫的名字就是“静水”，但故事里的三位小朋友不知道，他们与熊猫互动中没用过称呼语或直呼过其姓名。

第二天，安迪去跟静水用茶。她被静水先“请进”后“请出”屋子，原来他在后院一顶帐篷里。屋内陈设和墙上的两幅水墨竹画，文字对此并没有描述。静水告诉安迪帐篷是良叔叔送的生日礼物。静水看到安迪带来了蛋糕，一问一答才发现两人都没在过生日。静水要给安迪讲个故事，作为送给他叔叔的生日礼物。接下来，文字告诉读者在“讲”故事，而图画显示在“画”故事。随着绘本页面由彩色变为黑白，文字信息量也加大。良叔叔有一天晚上发现住处有一位“访客”（visitor），原来是个入室盗贼在搜寻财物。与之匹配的图片展示的是一只狐狸正悄悄从窗户中钻进房间里。这显然是“入室盗贼”（burglar）形象，与文字所描述的“访客”或“强盗”（robber）不符。此外，文字提供的故事人物是良叔叔和盗贼，而图画显示的是两只动物。主人（熊）高大魁梧，强盗（狐狸）渺小单薄。主人以礼相待，盗贼反而不知所措。整个互动过程都由文字完成。图画信息仅是两人握手言和，穿着破袍的狐狸在夜幕下落荒而逃。月光下的良叔叔坐在山顶沉思，所有内心活动也都由文字完成：良叔叔感到非常不安，哀叹没有更好的东西施舍给那个“可怜的人”。随后，画面回到了主线故事的色彩页面，图画显示熊猫和安迪都画了不少画，其中有一幅与《良叔叔与月亮》的配图相似。

次日，迈克尔去见静水。迈克尔看到熊猫坐在一棵高大的树上，也爬到树上。接下来的两个画面采用平视和仰视两个不同视角，展示了他们既可以飞向天空也有可能摔落地面的可能性。迈克尔认为如果他们摔到地上，那就太糟糕了。静水只回复了他一个词“可能”。紧接着的内嵌故事《农夫的运气》里，文字信息呈现的人物有农夫、他儿子、邻居、征兵的军官等，但图画描绘的却是一只只身着人衣、直立行走的动物。在田间劳作的是兔子形象，从马上一跃而下的也是兔子形象。农夫家厄运好运相互转换，邻居们或来安慰或来庆贺。图画对邻居只描绘了一次，在养伤的小兔子和若有所思的老兔子不远处，有一群隔栏相望毫无面部表情的动物：猪、鸡、狼、鹿、山羊、羚羊、青蛙、松鼠、猫头鹰等。这些具有明显特征的动物是农夫的“邻居”，但跟农夫不是同类。图文唯一保持一致的动物形象就是马。第一个内嵌故事占四个黑白页面，而第二个内嵌故事只有两个黑白页面，文字和插图都很集中，凸显了福与祸之间的快速转化效果。接着又回到主线故事，彩图占满整个内跨页，恰如特写，文字仅仅起点缀作用。

接下来的一天，卡尔去见静水。文字中，卡尔因对迈克尔有怨言，带来很多玩具。但是静水家的泳池放不下，清空后他们玩得很开心。随后他们一起用了茶，图画中熊猫和卡尔用茶壶茶碗喝茶，与安迪的茶点不同。在静水送卡尔回家的路上讲了《重负》的故事。图中，熊猫骑着小车、背着卡尔，卡尔背着玩具，“背负”（carry）的信息明确，为嵌套故事埋下了伏笔。两个和尚遇见一位少妇和两个抬轿的仆人被一深水坑拦住去路。仆人抬着轿，拿着行李，无力让少妇安全过去。少妇“等着迈出轿椅”，怒气冲冲地责骂仆人。而图画信息是，水坑对面有两只拟人化的老鼠，一边拿着重物一边抬轿，轿椅上稳稳地站着一位“女性”老鼠，衣着打扮入时，面带怒色。深水坑这边两只老鼠的态度截然不同，一个直面对岸，一个背对他们，读者难以判断哪个是文中的老和尚哪个是小和尚。第二页的文字信息是，小和尚看了看少妇，从她身边走过，而老和尚一言未发，不假思索背起少妇蹚水而过，放在对岸，但少妇未说一个谢字。文字信息有过程细节，而图画信息仅呈现了一瞬间："女性"老鼠悠然地坐在一只老鼠的背上，老鼠正踩水而过，另一只老鼠满脸的疑惑。第三页的文字信息是，两个和尚继续赶路，小和尚心事重重，几个小时后才忍不住开口问老和尚：那妇女自私无礼，你背她过河，可她连声谢都没说。图画信息只有两只动物一前一后在赶路，看不出有任何互动。接下来的一页文字信息是，老和尚回答：我几个小时前就放下了，你为什么还背着她？而图画信息是在草丛中，两只老鼠相向而立，没有任何对话的动作和神情。嵌套故事结束后，再次回到主线故事。全书最后一页彩图上的文字信息告诉读者，三个小朋友与静水成了朋友，图画信息同步渲染，故事结束。

4 图文信息与心理表征

原型理论认为，概念是范畴的复杂心理表征，是与该集（set）或类（class）里典型成员所具有特征足够相似的成员身份（Adajian，2005：231）。心理模型由外部信息和内在知识两种来源支撑。外部信息是通过感知、理解得到的数据，内在知识是已有的图式或脚本。心理模型涉及人的具身体验方式，如视、听、感知等，因此具有多模态性，而且能提供一个认知框架，把文字和视觉理解结合起来进行解释。文本加工过程需要读者语篇结构知识，不仅是事件模型、语境模型、文类模型等知识，还需要读者运用认知策略进行选择和推理。语篇描写细节信息充分程度、物体的外貌、人的类型、事件和行为动作的特征等都对语篇理解有很大作用。认知诗学研究发现，所有神话故事情节的颠倒都可以从认知视角来解释：读者在阅读过程中一直在建构、监控并维持着语境图式，因此会对所读故事进行预测（Emmott，2003）；读者需要经过一些认知加工过程才能对一个故事建立心理表征（Semino，2003；Gavins，2003）。

《禅故事》里文字提供的一些概念与其激活范畴里的代表性概念不符，或与图画提供的形象有冲突，直接与读者已有的原型概念和图式发生矛盾，给读者造成认知困惑。安迪找静水用茶时，图画中，带去的蛋糕上插着的竹子，其形象与生日蛋糕相似，激活了读者“生日蛋糕”图式，同时，安迪与静水同食蛋糕，但人兽各取其所需，合二为一又刷新了该图式。熊猫屋内墙上挂着的两幅水墨竹画可以激活两种图式：人的精神食粮和熊猫的物质食粮，雅俗合一生成了新的“画”图式。故事中，静水告诉安迪帐篷是良叔叔过生日时送给他的；静水给安迪讲故事当作送给良叔叔的礼物。绘本中的生日礼物是自己过生日送给他人的礼物，所送生日礼物为精神礼物，并且庆祝生日的人不在场。这些都与读者已有的“生日礼物”图式相冲突，构成复杂的心理表征，刷新了人们的认知，突出了“给”的内涵，暗含着“禅”的精神，加强了与后面内嵌故事的联系。

内嵌故事《良叔叔与月亮》中的不速之“客”激活的是包括来访的客人、亲戚、朋友、商友、生意伙伴、顾客等的范畴概念。强盗虽属“来客”的语义范畴，但不具有“访客”范畴成员的原型或典型特征。访客的典型特征是“来访”“看望”“探访”，而强盗的典型特征是“以暴力或恐吓为手段偷窃或抢劫”。读者认知经验中的典型图式是强盗蒙面劫财，并手持利器以威胁他人，而图画呈现的“入室盗贼”与这一原型概念或典型图式不符。强盗重点在将物品占为己有，入室盗贼强调非法入侵的过程。图画中盗贼狐狸矮小猥琐，胆战心惊，与高大威猛的主人熊形成鲜明对比。在读者的认知中，抢劫歹徒是强势一方，受害者是弱势一方，而图画信息是主强客弱，颠覆了两者之间的身份和权力不对等关系。故事中，盗贼好逸恶劳，不顾主人家徒四壁，依然拿走主人唯一一件破袍；主人失去最后一件物品，并不感到难过，反而希望能给盗贼更美好的东西——月亮。这与常规丢失物品人的心态有强烈的反差，使得故事所要传达的“给予”概念凸显。“给”的语义是“交付，送与”，其典型搭配对象是当事人有处置权的物品。良叔叔希望送给盗贼的月亮，既不是可以交付的物品，也不是他可以处置的财产。良叔叔与盗贼从受害与施害关系反转为施惠与受惠关系，瓦解了入室盗贼的原型概念，提供了新的“给予”心理模型，刷新了读者的故事和知识图式。

故事《农夫的运气》中，农夫对于丢失马儿、失马归来、儿子受伤、险避征兵等一系列的事情，邻居们或来安慰或来祝贺，但他的回应总是“可能”。这与人们的常规态度不同，面对如此跌宕起伏、具有戏剧性的生活，正常情况下很难保持一颗平常心。但农夫处事不惊的态度刷新了读者的认知图式，引发读者思考。“农夫”的原型范畴化概念和理想认知模型包括在田间劳作，拥有农舍畜圈，屋内有陈设、家具及生活用品；“邻居”包括外貌与农夫同质同形；“马”包括拉车、驮运、农用、军用、体育运动等；“军官”包括佩枪、制服、军马等。图中的马、枪械、军旗、沙发、电视、绷带等形象可以唤起读者的现实世界知识图式，但这些信息是文字部分未提及且在有限空间无法表达的细节。文字读者会运用已有图式进行推理：骑马—跌下—骨折—卧床……有因果关系；房间—沙发—电视—家具……以及征兵—军官—队伍—操练—枪械—军旗……有联想关系，都可以通过读者的逻辑推理得出，图画信息使这些细节更为明确和具体。

内嵌故事《重负》里有三个“重负”的概念，一是仆人不仅手拿行李而且抬轿，二是老和尚背负少妇，三是小和尚心里的重负，与主线故事里，图画描绘的熊猫背负卡尔、卡尔背负玩具的形象和文字中展现的卡尔的烦心事形成多模态语义连贯。嵌套故事中，不仅文字而且图画向读者讲述的主要内容都是背少妇蹚过一深水坑，激活了读者“物理负重”的图式。然而，在故事的结尾颠覆了读者的认知，老和尚的一句话“几个小时前我已经把她放下了，为什么你还放不下呢？”激活了“精神负重”图式，与原激活的原型概念图式不同，构建了不同的心理表征。对比“物理负重”和“精神负重”两个图式，能够启发读者思考禅的精神内涵。对于这个故事，东方读者的已有故事知识是：老和尚携小和尚游方，途遇一女子不敢过河，老和尚便背她而过，放下后继续赶路。小和尚心事重重，走了几十里地才问是不是犯戒。独行少妇有难，老和尚相助，发生男女授受不亲的价值冲突才是关键。慕斯的改编虽有大致相似的地方，但在细节上弱化了老和尚背少妇的必要，而且丑化了少妇的相貌和人品，把故事焦点带到另一个走向，启示变成了以德报怨、与人为善，小和尚对佛戒的肤浅理解也变成了对禅宗的不解。

三个小故事都有一个共同点：文字中人物指称词所激发的图式是人，而图画呈现的是动物，仅借用了现实世界里人的典型特征和行为举止。例如，在《农夫的运气》中，文字中的人物包括农夫、他儿子、邻居、军官等，而图画所描绘的农夫父子、部队官兵的形象都是身着人衣、可以直立行走的兔子，农夫的邻居们是羊、猪、鸡、狼、鹿、青蛙、松鼠、猫头鹰等动物。图画中人物形象打破了文字信息所激活的概念图式，导致读者认知加工困惑。作者将文字中的人物角色描绘为动物，调用人外貌动作特征，激活了读者的理想心理模型。减弱了人类的社会属性，规避了人类的年龄、性别与社会地位等方面的问题（Nikolajeva，2002），使被叙述对象简单化，增强符合儿童天性的成分。相比于成年人，儿童的行为和心智更接近动物（Zipes，2006），因此对儿童读者来说从动物形象里更易理解人的世界。文字保留了禅故事原汁原味的色彩，图画用寓言和童话手段创造偏离正常的人物形象，降低了原故事的难度，增强了赏图的乐趣，传达了深奥的寓意。从多模态视角来看，两种符号各司其职，互为补充，文字信息激发的原型概念和图式与图画信息展示的直观图像冲突，挑战读者的已有图式，激发读者对比不同图式，推理内在逻辑，构建出新的图式，从而理解作者意图，领略绘本的艺术魅力。

Beaugrande（1980）将信息度分为三个等级，第一等级信息是普通的、平常的信息，没有特别之处；第二等级信息是不寻常、不太可能发生的事情但依然可以想象，通过对原有图式稍稍调整仍可以解释；第三种信息是不可能发生的事情，打破原有图式，在这种情况下，读者期待一种合理的解释，或者认为他们阅读的是完全虚拟的世界。图文表征信息不一致促使读者思考，寻求合理的解释。绘本故事里没有一处提到禅，似乎与标题没有关联。但绘本最后所附的“作者注”用另一种声音为读者点明了主题。整个绘本故事以拉波夫等（Labov & Waletzky，1972）定义的“结局”（resolution）结束，缺少“结束语”（coda），即使得读者回到现实世界的话语。但是“作者注”发挥了“结束语”的作用，帮助读者将虚拟故事与现实世界相联系，用现实世界信息补充了绘本正文留下的语义和认知空白。叙事学家 Genette（1997：1-2）写道，副文本（paratext）是使文本成书并呈现给读者及大众的材料，是作者表达评论性话语的载体，是文本与文本外文字（off-text）之间的一个地带。它不仅具有过渡（transition）功能，而且还有交易（transaction）功能，直接影响文本的理解和接受。“作者注”在虚构世界与现实世界之间架起了一座桥梁，把讲故事与解释故事和说明故事主题结合起来，点出了禅和道的悠久历史及关键词“思”。如果说绘本正文页是通过虚构故事传达禅的精神，那么致献页和跋页是通过现实世界的真实信息为正文服务，同时也为读者提供知识。作者话语与叙述者话语的紧密配合，绘本主题既明确又含蓄，将禅的思想内涵表现得淋漓尽致。

5 结 语

语篇加工不仅需要词汇语法和语篇知识，而且需要有关世界知识。这些知识来自我们与世界的互动和具身体验。理解日常语言原理适用于理解文学语言，已经是认知诗学的共识和基本原则（Turner，1991：20）。我们需要调用已有对现实世界的体验和认知模型理解虚构世界，一旦虚构世界的表征与我们对现实世界的感知有差异，那么这些差异会促使读者调取更多的相关知识进行判断，结合人的文学心智和文学能力，更新知识，刷新图式，产生新的心理模型，改变对现实世界的感知或升华对现实世界的认识。McEwan（1997）指出，教育类话语里有两个常见的功能：强制性（coercive）叙事与解放性（emancipatory）叙事。前者具有劝说性，意在束缚人的信念；后者具有表达性，意在提供创造新意义的过程。《禅故事》图文并茂，双模态表征既矛盾又统一，主线故事与嵌套故事、文本与副文本、虚构世界话语与真实世界话语配合形成了一个既对立又互补的立体网络，实现了作者与读者、叙述者与受述者、意向读者与真实读者之间的多层次交流，把图文符号各自的表面意义与象征意义结合在一起，充分发挥了绘本叙事艺术的寓教于乐功能，巧妙地阐释了东方哲学中禅的概念和内涵。慕斯的绘本用虚构表征现实，用日常表征禅道，用动物世界表征人类世界，用可言说表征不可言说，用看似浅显的故事把禅的真谛——静思、沉思、反思——润物细无声地传递给了读者，既对西方儿童有教育意义，也对东方儿童乃至全世界成人读者有教育意义。

参考文献

[1] M ABE. Zen and Western Thought. London: Macmillan, 1985.

[2] T ADAJIAN. On the Prototype Theory of Concepts and the Definition of Art. The Journal of Aesthetics and Art Criticism, 2005, 63 (3): 231-236.

[3] G COOK. Discourse and Literature. Oxford: Oxford University Press, 1994.

[4] J CULPEPER. Language and Characterisation. London: Longman, 2001.

[5] N DAVIES, R COBB. (illus.). The Day War Came. London: Walker Books, 2018.

[6] R DE BEAUGRANDE. Text, Discourse and Process: Toward a Multi- Disciplinary Science of Texts. Norwood, NJ: Ablex, 1980.

[7] C EMMOTT. Narrative Comprehension: A Discourse Perspective. Oxford: Oxford University Press, 1997.

[8] C EMMOTT. Reading for Pleasure: A Cognitive Poetic Analysis of “Twists in the Tale” and Other Plot Reversals in Narrative Texts//

Gavins, J & G. Steen (eds.). Cognitive Poetics in Practice. New York: Routledge, 2003: 145-160.

[9] J GAVINS. Too Much Blague? An Exploration of the Text Worlds of Donald Barthelme's Snow White// Gavins, J & G. Steen (eds.). Cognitive Poetics in Practice. New York: Routledge, 2003: 129-144.

[10] D GEERAERTS. Introduction: Prospects and Problems of Prototype Theory. Linguistics, 1989, 27 (4): 587-612.

[11] G GENETTE. Paratexts: Thresholds of Interpretation. trans. by J. E. Lewin. Cambridge: Cambridge University Press, 1997.

[12] R W GIBBS. Prototypes in Dynamic Meaning Construal // Gavins, J & G. Steen (eds.). Cognitive Poetics in Practice. New York: Routledge, 2003: 27-40.

[13] A JOY, E HOLMES. (illus.). Black Is a Rainbow Color. New York: Roaring Brook Press, 2020.

[14] W LABOV, J WALETZKY. Narrative analysis: Oral Versions of Personal Experience // Helm, J (ed.). Essays on the Verbal and Visual Arts. Seattle: University of Washington Press, 1967: 12-44.

[15] W LABOV. Language in the Inner City. Philadelphia: University of Pennsylvania Press, 1972.

[16] G LAKOFF. Hedges: A Study in Meaning Criteria and the Logic of Fuzzy Concepts. Journal of Philosophical Logic, 1973, 2 (4): 458-508.

[17] G LAKOFF. Women, Fire and Dangerous Things: What Categories Reveal about the Mind. Chicago: Chicago University Press, 1987.

[18] C LINDSTROM, M Goade. (illus.). We Are Water Protectors. New York: Roaring Brook Press, 2020.

[19] K S LYONS, D Minter. (illus.). Going down Home with Daddy.

Atlanta: Peachtree Publishers, 2019.

[20] H MCEWAN. The Functions of Narrative and Research on Teaching. Teaching and Teacher Education, 1997, 13 (1): 85-92.

[21] J J MUTH. Zen Shorts. New York: Scholastic Press, 2005.

[22] M NIKOLAJEVA. The Rhetoric of Character in Children's Literature. Oxford: Scarecrow Press, 2002.

[23] M NIKOLAJEVA, C Scott. How Picturebooks Work. New York: Garland Publishing, 2001.

[24] P NODELMAN. Words about Pictures: The Narrative Art of Children's Picture Books. Athens, GA: University of Georgia Press, 1988.

[25] C PAINTER, J R MARTIN, L Unsworth. Reading Visual Narratives: Image Analysis in Children's Picture Books. London: Equinox, 2012.

[26] E ROSCH, C MERVIS. Family Resemblances: Studies in the Internal Structure of Categories. Cognitive Psychology, 1975 (7): 573-605.

[27] E ROSCH. Principles of Categorization // E. Rosch & B. Lloyd (eds.). Cognition and Categorization. Hillsdale, NJ: Erlbaum, 1978: 27-48.

[28] E SEMINO. Possible Worlds and Mental Spaces in Hemingway's "A Very Short Story"// J. Gavins & G. Steen (eds.). Cognitive Poetics in Practice. New York: Routledge, 2003: 83-98.

[29] J STEPHENS. Language and Ideology in Children's Fiction. London and New York: Longman, 1992.

[30] D T SUZUKI. Zen and Japanese Culture. Princeton: Princeton University Press, 1973.

[31] M TURNER. Reading Minds: The Study of English in the Age of Cognitive Science. Princeton, NJ: Princeton University Press,

1991.

[32] J ZIPES. (ed.). The Oxford Encyclopedia of Children's Literature: Vol. 1. Oxford: Oxford University Press, 2006.

[33] 封宗信. 日常语篇的文学性与片段随意拼接中的叙事性. 认知诗学，2014（1）：46-55.

认知女性主义批评

《他们眼望上苍》：女性主义的解构与重构

刘玉红　王　珊

【摘要】赫斯顿的长篇小说《他们眼望上苍》是美国 20 世纪文学经典之作。传统女性主义观点和 Shawn E. Miller 的解构都有不足之处，本文以认知女性主义为视角，运用可能世界、具身性和隐喻这三个认知诗学工具重读该作品，认为文本的女性意识主要表现为珍妮的可能世界与三任丈夫的可能世界的冲突或融合。贯穿于这一两性关系的是两个隐喻："人生是走向地平线的旅程（Life is a journey to the horizon）"和"珍妮是一棵树（Janie is a tree）"。它们承载了文本的具身性，即珍妮以身体去体验生活的风风雨雨，去理解人生的内涵，最终获得内心的成长。

【关键词】《他们眼望上苍》；认知女性主义；可能世界；具身性；隐喻

0　引　言

长篇小说《他们眼望上苍》（*Their Eyes Were Watching God*, 1937，下文简称《他们》）是佐拉·尼尔·赫斯顿（Zora Neale Hurston，1891—1960）最著名的作品，它被誉为黑人文学经典、女性文学经典和 20 世纪美国文学经典（程锡麟，2005：110），当然也是美国南方文学的经典。故事脉络清晰：混血儿珍妮先后嫁给三个黑人男性洛根、

基金项目：本文系国家社科基金项目"认知女性主义视域下美国南方女作家的焦虑书写"（19BWW074）的阶段性成果。

作者简介：刘玉红，女，广西师范大学外国语学院教授，博导，主要从事认知诗学和英语教学研究；
王珊，女，北部湾大学国际教育与外国语学院讲师，硕士，主要从事英语教学和认知诗学研究。

乔和甜点心。二段婚姻烙刻了打动人心的爱恨情仇。故事最后以甜点心意外死亡、珍妮返回黑人城结束。小说对话活泼，笔调幽默，不乏诗情画意，处处渗透对生命、责任、自由、黑人文化、种族关系的感知和思索。美国黑人著名作家艾丽丝·沃克说，“对我来说，再也没有比这本书(《他们》)更重为重要的书了”(王家湘，译后记，229)。

大量的评论多集中于女主人公珍妮这一形象，肖恩·E. 米勒(Shawn E. Miller，2008)总结传统的女性主义观点为“珍妮·克劳福德是一个思想稳定的女性主义英雄，她努力摆脱男性压迫，视之为自我实现的必要前提。她和洛根·基利克斯、乔·斯塔克斯的两次婚姻都失败了，因为他们过于强求珍妮顺从他们，强势坚持传统的性别角色和阶级角色。珍妮勇敢反抗强加于她的被动角色，终于，她当初在梨树下憧憬的爱情在甜点心身上找到了。他们的婚姻与之前的不同，夫妻平等，自由自在，于是，她完成了从物体到主体的生命升华之旅”(Miller，2008：186)。国内评论多与之类似。肖恩认为这一观点难以解释一些文本细节，值得商榷。

1 解构：另一种女性主义

肖恩的文章《“试走另一条路”:〈他们眼望上苍〉之从抗争到创造性顺从》(“‘Some Other Way to Try’：From Defiance to Creative Submission in Their Eyes Were Watching God”，2008，以下简称肖文)旨在从女性主义框架内解构传统的女性主义观点，另寻出路。肖文认为，虽然传统的女性主义观点在赫斯顿评论中仍占正统地位，但它不得不至少面对两个令人困扰的问题，其一，作品的全知视角导致对女性遭受的暴力不加批评，其二，甜点心这一形象存在含混之处(Miller，2008：186)。该文反对把这些问题视为作品的缺陷，提出如果另辟蹊径，问题便可迎刃而解。她提出两条路子，一是否定甜点心是珍妮的解放者，他和珍妮的前两任丈夫一样都是大男子主义者，二是珍妮依靠顺从的策略而非战斗的精神最终得偿所愿。

首先，珍妮的三桩婚姻并不是从完全失败到失败再到成功。在前两次婚姻中，珍妮受到的压迫是具体的，如洛根要求她赶骡犁地，压制珍妮，甚至威胁使用暴力。乔也一样，他把珍妮摁进他设计的模子里，还家暴了珍妮不止一次（同上：188）。甜点心也差不多，他“表现出基利克斯和斯塔克斯受到批评的缺点，如果我们不看珍妮对三个男人不同的反应，那么甜点心对待珍妮和其他两个对待她非常相似”（同上：189）。这个相似就是丈夫要求妻子遵循传统的性别角色：妻子由丈夫养活（哪怕珍妮在银行里有不少钱），要她下地干活，因为“其他女人都这么做”（155）[①]。像乔一样，甜点心也打了珍妮，为的是“再度证明她属于他”（171）。

肖文指出，甜点心虽然比珍妮的前两任丈夫更像她理想的丈夫，但他并非她的解放者，那两位丈夫也并非史诗或罗曼司中的恶棍（Miller，2008：191）。故事的核心部分采用第三人称的全知视角，这样读者可看清珍妮是如何理解洛根和乔行为的动机，换言之，全知视角让我们把他们当人而不是当魔鬼看（同上：191-192）。他们伤害珍妮，她也伤害他们。珍妮威胁洛根要跟人跑走，洛根忌妒害怕，便口出恶言，气得他“半抽泣半喊叫”（38）。乔压制珍妮，多半因为她攻击他。他不许珍妮去参加骡子的葬礼，他回来后她脸色难看，两人为货单争吵，也是珍妮引起的。珍妮对他们有攻击性，因为她怀疑他们要控制自己，对甜点心则完全不同，她对他言听计从，鲜有逆言，因为此时她已四十，明白了婚姻不可能像她不成熟时所想象的一模一样，婚姻要顺心，她得先控制自己的好斗（fighting spirit），但这并不能抹掉甜点心的大男子形象（Miller，2008：193）。

其次，珍妮不是传统观点认为的强势的女权主义英雄。故事结尾时，她的确成了女性主义者声称的一个有尊严有力量的女性，但这不是甜点心的功劳，而是珍妮自己一人所为（同上：194）。她在前两次婚姻中遭到强力压迫，意识到直接抵抗难以成功，“为了获得理想的婚姻，她必须抛弃自己的‘战斗精神’”（同上），于是转而采

① 本文中只标注页码的引文均来自佐拉·尼尔·赫斯顿的《他们眼望上苍》，王家湘译，浙江文艺出版社 2017 年版。

用服从（submission）战术。她对甜点心有求必应，处处服从，“她对他如此服从，真是一个好妻子，他不得不开始思考自己是否对得起这样的妻子，于是他必须在言行上展示自己是一个好丈夫”（同上：195），由此，珍妮反而由被动变主动。在那场飓风灾难中，赫斯顿再次用了全知视角，展示珍妮如何继续以服从策略来降服甜点心。在逃难中，她总是听他的，让他直到被狂犬病吞噬时还深感羞愧（200）。直到甜点心病情再发，在狂乱中朝她举枪开火，珍妮的顺从才告终，她不得不打死了甜点心。不过在陪审团面前，她的“忠实的妻子”这一形象仍助她达到免于判刑的目的。

2 女性主义之再解构

肖文对传统女性主义观点的解构有合理之处，如甜点心也有大男子主义的表现，珍妮不是强势的女权主义者，不过，肖文也要面对一些不符合其观点的文本细节。

其一，洛根和乔伤害珍妮，不是肖文所说的因为珍妮伤害他，而是因为他们坚持自己的价值观，并强迫珍妮认同，伤害她在前。肖文认为，洛根害怕珍妮跑走，便出言恶毒。他没有考虑珍妮为什么想跑走。其实肖文指出了原因：洛根要珍妮干男人干的活。这不符合珍妮“你干的是你的活，我干的是我的活”（37）的夫妻分工原则。洛根嘴仗打不过珍妮，便以暴力相威胁，珍妮坚决离家而去。市长乔比富农洛根更甚，一开始就不许珍妮和城里人交往，不许她说话，“她（珍妮）可真不怎么说话，她出了点错，他那个大喊大叫劲儿真有点让人无法容忍”（59）。这话来自熟人琼斯的评论，更显客观。乔不让珍妮去参加骡子的葬礼，是极度限制她的自由，珍妮脸色难看，这很自然，不是对乔的伤害。

其二，珍妮的顺从不是传统意义上无主见的顺从。珍妮一开始就有自己的主见，有自己的声音，她敢于向外婆说不想嫁人，说出对新婚丈夫洛根的不满。她和洛根的对话不卑不亢，有理有据，丝毫不落下风。当时她不过十七岁左右，便有如此口才，把洛根逼得泼妇似的破口大骂，还差点哭出来，可见珍妮本质上并不顺从，只不过在善于经商、强于弄权的乔面前，她的声音一时被压住了。在乔的高压下，她心态分裂，“……她坐在那里，看着自己的影子料理着店务，拜倒在乔面前，而真正的她一直坐在阴凉的树下，风吹拂着她的头发和衣服”（90）。这种分裂说明她内心并不顺从，如果是真顺从，她就不会对病床上的乔绝地反击，把他活活气死。她对甜点心言听计从，原因有二：她没有他见世面多；她真心爱他，愿意和他一起干活。她嫉妒时照样敢打甜点心，这样的行动就是一种强力发声。可见，珍妮既不像传统女性主义观点所说的“珍妮经历了一次从沉默到发声的自我实现过程”（King，2008：114），也不是肖文所说的以顺从获得生存和权力，她一开始就有自己的声音，这声音渗透在众多的自由间接话语中，这表明她没有真正顺从过哪一个丈夫，而是通过争论、吵架、沉默、打架等多种形式发出强声。

必须指出的是，在洛根压迫珍妮这个问题上，其他学者同样忽视文本细节，如 Sharon L. Jones 认为，“洛根一跟珍妮结婚，就很想叫她去干活，甚至叫她去干其他人认为是男人干的活，比如劈柴或赶骡犁地。她干活的时候，想起外婆说过的话，黑女人给人当骡子使唤”（2009：198）。我们如细读文本，就知道洛根是叫珍妮劈柴，但她不干，还回嘴，“……你要是坚持不劈、不把柴抱进来，我猜你没饭吃也挺得住。你请原谅我这样说，基利克斯先生，不过我一根柴都不打算去劈。”他也没办法，只能嘴硬，“哪，你知道我会给你劈柴的，即使你对我要多刻薄有多刻薄。你姥姥和我已经把你惯坏了，看来我不得不继续惯下去了”（31）。洛根是打算买头骡子让珍妮犁地，可接下来既没看到他把骡子买回来，也没看到珍妮去犁地，倒是当天珍妮遇到乔斯塔克斯后，“此后他们每天都设法在大路对面栎木丛中相会，谈论着当他成为大人物时她坐享其成的日子”（35）。正因为洛根在珍妮身上找不到发挥大男子主义的空间，才失控地大吼起来，因此，“黑女人给人当骡子使唤”这句话是不符合文本原意的。

其三，甜点心虽有一些大男子主义表现，但与洛根、乔有本质的不同，他是真爱珍妮，不像洛根只在意妻子干不干活，也不像乔只在意妻子听不听话。如不是这样，珍妮也不会对甜点心有“撕心裂肺的爱”（150），不会万般不舍他，不会在故事结尾回到乔留给她的屋子，呼唤的却是甜点心。他们的爱主要表现为一起做事：钓鱼、打猎、摘豆子、玩乐。两人关系平等。甜点心叫珍妮一起去摘豆子，“下工后甜点心帮着她准备晚饭”（156）。他们晚上跳舞跳得晚，“……他就不让珍妮和他一起下地干活了。他要她休息好”（179）。飓风来时，他因不愿离开大沼泽，害得珍妮不得不跟他一起逃难，他很自责，担心珍妮怪他，“他低声下气地说，‘你嫁给我的时候绝对没有指望会落到这一步吧’”（195）。他从疯狗嘴里救下珍妮，并不居功，而是“因为我（甜点心）在这儿，而且我还要你知道这儿有个男子汉”（195）。

笔者认为，对《他们》的读解，既要修正传统女性主义一元论的不足，不能只强调珍妮受到压迫，而没有看到她一直在发出自己的声音，又要弥补肖文和其他学者对文本细节的疏忽，为此，认知女性主义文学批评可提供一条有效的途径。

3 重构：认知女性主义

认知女性主义（feminist cognitivism）是约翰·帕特里克·林斯特罗斯（John Patrick Linstroth）提出的，他说，“我把对女性主义与认知的关系理解称为‘认知女性主义’或‘女性认知主义’”。虽然他并未对认知女性主义做系统性阐述，但从认知人类学视角论述了性别身份，探讨“性别实践如何创造一个心智、认知和记忆的本体论和认识论框架以及结构化的实践模型”（xxvii）。目前与认知女性主义最为相关的是神经女性主义。《神经女性主义：女性主义理论与认知科学的交叉问题》（*Neurofeminism: Issues at the Intersection of Feminist Theory and Cognitive Science*，2012）是第一个将脑科学视角引入女性主义研究的成果，明确提出将女性主义研究与认知科学结合，主要讨论四大问题：性与性别的差异、伦理道德、科学哲学和具身体验。必须说明的是，认知女性主义是一种元批评，它的分析方法是一个开放的体系，可取百家之长，但需遵循两个基本原则：一是认知科学原则。认知女性主义可以借用认知文体学、认知叙事学、认知修辞学的文本分析方法研究文本的形式，也可以借用认知科学的理论方法，如心智阅读、社会认知、认知心理学、文学达尔文主义等，对文本和文学活动提出某种意义阐释；二是女性主义原则。认知女性主义的研究方法和内容都应服务于女性主义研究的基本目的和任务，如探讨情感、伦理道德在女性主义知识生产中的地位和作用，考察具身性文本以及图像的力量以何种强度的身体方式感动读者，并可结合个体特点、性别差异、社会语境来阐释作品中性别歧视话语、女性体验、父权文化等问题。据此，本文尝试以认知女性主义为视角，运用可能世界、具身性和隐喻这三个认知工具来分析《他们》中的女性意识。

可能世界是“模态逻辑的基本概念，指一种可以想象的事物状态的总和，它既可以指我们生活在其中的现实世界，也可以指与现实世界不同但可以思议的其他世界”（熊沐清，2011：12）。因为“每一个世界在其自身当中都是现实的，从而所有的世界都具有同等的地位”（陈波、韩林，2005：666），可能世界当然也“具有逻辑的一致性，具有完整的空间内容和完整的时间历史”（熊沐清，2020：35），可与真实世界并行不悖。在小说文本中，人物的可能世界主要有五类：知识世界（epistemic worlds 或 knowledge worlds，指虚构世界里人物相信他们的世界是真实的）、意图世界（intention worlds，指人物有意识地计划改变他们的世界）、欲望世界（desire worlds 或 wish worlds，指人物希望或想象他们的世界有改变）、责任世界（obligation worlds，指经过人物的道德观过滤出来的种种观念）和幻想世界（fantasy worlds，指人物的梦想、幻觉、想象或自我虚构）（Stockwell，2002：95）。可能世界这一研究方法“特别适用于描述文本宇宙的内在结构和解释情节的发展”（盖文思，2020：79）。故事中的可能世界如同真实世界一样时时存在冲突，既有人物之间个人世界的冲突，也有某一人物的不同世界的冲突，如欲望世界和责任世界的冲突（Ryan，2013），这些冲突推进情节发展，进而形成文本宇宙的内在结构。

从可能世界观照小说人物，可看出文本与读者的独特关系。马戈林（1989）认为，我们可以从四个方面来理解虚构文本中的人物：① 语言表述对象（姓名、指称、具体描写等）；②“义子”即文本具体化的各种特性的集合体；③ 思想的载体，如寓言中的人物；④ 在情节中承担行动功能的个体，如施动者、欲望的对象、帮助者和对立者；⑤ 非真实个体，由指称来确定，属于某一非真实的事态。第5种源于可能世界，这样的人物是作者想象出来的仿真人物，他或她“拥有内心世界、知识、信仰、记忆、态度和意图，换言之，拥有意识、内心世界和人格”（转自 Ryan，2013：22）。可见，只有第 5 种人物形象才能解释为什么虚构文本可以激起读者的情感共鸣（同上）。这样的情感共鸣与读者的脚本知识密切相关，读者需要依据自己对真实世界的了解（脚本知识）来理解和认同虚构文本中的可能世界。因此，“可能世界理论”（possible worlds theory）是关注文学阅读的认知诗学一个非常重要的理论领域（熊沐清，2011：12）。

具身性是人认知世界一个重要的工具。Karin Kukkonen 指出，我们的认知是具身的，“因为思维植根于我们的身体及其活动”（2019：1）。身体不再是一副“臭皮囊”，而是一切知识的基础。不仅思考，而且情感都深深地具体化为我们身体的物理状态、活动、态势等（1）。具身是女性主义理论的核心问题，因为身体是性别差异的象征性建构的一个场所（Threadcraft，2016：207）。在达尔文进化论、神经生物学或量子物理学理论指导下的物质女性主义（material feminism）的目标只是解决身体的生物学方面问题（Grosz，2004），因此它不可避免地将女性主义对身体的研究进行“二分”：在探索文化、社会或语言如何塑造身体时只依赖于社会建构理论，无视生物学模型，反之亦然。当然，物质女性主义观点不可能失去其影响力，因为它涉及女性主义思想的根本问题——身体的重要性。现在，越来越多的女性主义者从现象学视角思考具身性，以对生命体的关注为基础，探究女性怀孕、分娩和育儿的生活体验，也重新关注我们作为有血有肉的人的体验（Schott，2010）。这种体验指出了认知女性主义未来研究的一个主要方向：将女性主义的身体认识与生理学、药理学、进化理论、神经科学、认知科学等对生物性身体描述相结合，为探索“进入身体”提供新途径，对身体进行更有活力、更符合生物性和社会文化性的描述。在文学研究中，“小说的情节和事件，只有作用于人物，成为人物的体验，才有意义”(Palmer, 2010：203)。

20世纪下半叶兴起的“认知转向”是隐喻获得极大关注的原因之一，因为它使我们意识到“有必要重新思考心智研究的一些最为基本的观念：意义、真理、思维的本质，以及身体在塑造心智中的作用”(Lakoff，2003：243)。方向隐喻可能是具身与修辞结合最为紧密的一个例子，例如，“高兴是向上的（happy is up)”和“悲伤是向下的（sad is down)”(Lakoff，2003：15) 就是以人的身体状态为基点：人高兴时精神抖擞，昂首挺胸，悲伤时垂头丧气，低首下心。

基于以上理论认识，本文提出，《他们》的女性意识主要表现为人物的可能世界发生多种关系：珍妮的幻想世界和洛根的责任世界、乔的意图世界有冲突，和甜点心的知识世界走向融合。贯穿于这一两性关系的是两个相辅相成的隐喻，一是“人生是走向地平线的旅程(Life is a journey to the horizon)”，二是“珍妮是一棵树(Janie is a tree)”。这两个隐喻承载文本的具身性，即珍妮以身体去体验生活的风风雨雨，去理解人生的内涵，最终获得内心的成长。

《他们》由四个文本真实亚世界构成：洛根的六十英亩农庄、乔的伊顿维尔、甜点心的杰克逊维尔和大沼泽。这些可能世界体现出三个男性不同的价值观、不同的生存逻辑。洛根的可能世界是责任世界，他一心勤劳致富，相信为妻之责是屋里屋外的活儿都要干，不仅要做饭持家，还要劈柴犁地。乔的可能世界是意图世界。他一开始就有目的地设计自己未来的生活，“他一直想成为一个能说了算的人”(33)。这个“说了算”涵盖家里家外。家外，建起黑人城，开商店，发财致富，当上市长，操弄权力；家里，他很早就宣称，“她（珍妮）是个女人，她的位置在家庭里”(51)，她要做的是少说话，顺从他，看好商店。甜点心的可能世界是欲望世界。他的生活观很明确："干活—挣钱—玩乐—干活"，这一循环模式的本质即"生活就是自由"。他唯一想改变的是与心爱之人分享这样的生活，他要珍妮随他到大沼泽去，因为"那儿的人什么也不干，就是挣钱和玩乐。咱们一定得上那儿去"（150）。珍妮是故事的中心人物，她的可能世界有幻想世界，也有欲望世界。她的幻想世界始于她 16 岁时躺在梨花树下，从蜜蜂进入花朵这一动态意象感悟到婚姻的喜悦和痛苦（14），由此铺垫出婚姻携带的矛盾情感。她的欲望世界是前两任丈夫促成的，他们对她的要求和压制促使她产生改变生活的渴望，欲望世界由此形成。

按照可能世界理论，"人物的各种可能世界构成了一个个私人的嵌入叙事（private embedded narrative），而这些叙事相互又构成了复杂的关系……作为一部小说，这些可能世界之间必须有某种关联。换言之，人物、事件、题材、主题等方面均应具有内在统一性或关联性，否则整部小说就会显得散漫"（熊沐清，2011：20-21）。在《他们》中，串起多重可能世界的"通达策略"（熊沐清，2011：20）是围绕珍妮的两个隐喻："人生是走向地平线的旅程"（Life is a journey to the horizon）和"珍妮是一棵树"（Janie is a tree）。旅行隐喻以时空交错和套嵌叙事勾勒出珍妮的人生旅程和心理变化，主要集中于她 16 岁到 40 岁出头即青春期到中年，以及她生活过的四个地方，最后又回到她在黑人城的家。她的可能世界通过婚姻这一媒介和三个男性的可能世界发生接触、碰撞或融合。她追求浪漫婚姻的幻想世界被洛根的责任世界打破，她追求夫妻平等的幻想世界被乔的意图世界击碎，直到甜点心出现，两人追求自由生活的可能世界才融合在一起，珍妮才成了"开心骡子"，她做饭持家，下地干活，不累也不烦，她对甜点心说"我的生活有了意义"（195）。甜点心死后，她埋葬他，这意味着她的半生旅程结束，她总结道，"现在我又回到家里来，待在这里我也就满足了。我已经到过地平线，又回到这里"（224）。对女性而言，婚姻是最直接的具身体验，死亡是最直观的具身感受，珍妮的故事就是女性体验生活的一个过程。

在四个人物的可能世界互动的过程中，珍妮不断成长，这可用树隐喻来表达。其一，树的成长总要经历风风雨雨，珍妮承受了洛根和乔的风吹雨打，也沐浴了甜点心的阳光雨露。其二，树在成长中不仅外形发生变化，其内在结构也会发生变化。珍妮每一次情感的生发和转折都与树有关。16 岁的她在开花的梨树下憧憬婚姻生活，产生了树的幻想："能做一棵开花的梨树——或随便什么开花的树多好啊！有亲吻它的蜜蜂歌唱着世界的开始"（15）。她邂逅乔也是在春天的大栎树下，两人偷偷在大路对面的栎木丛中相会时，她把自己当成了树，"从现在起直到死去，她的一切将洒满花粉与春花。她的花上会有一只蜜蜂"（39）。被乔打后，她意识到自己这棵树不再美丽，"她不再有怒放的花朵把花粉撒满自己的男人，在花瓣掉落之处也没有晶莹的嫩果"（84）。甜点心的到来让珍妮一下回到当年对梨树的感觉，"他会是花儿的蜜蜂——是春天梨花的蜜蜂"（124），这暗示她就是狂喜地迎接蜜蜂到来的梨树。实际上，杂草丛生、林木茂盛的大沼泽野性十足，与黑人城的等级和秩序截然不同，象征珍妮（和甜点心）的个性本质和生活追求。结婚后，她曾以为甜点心和南基相好，焦虑不已，"一粒恐惧的种子正在长成一株树"（159）。最后，珍妮自己揭示出树隐喻的内涵，她"感到自己的生命像一棵枝叶繁茂的大树，有痛苦的事、欢乐的事，做了的事、未做的事。黎明与末日都在枝叶之中"（10）。可以说，珍妮的爱恨情仇都与树相融相交，她这棵树饱经风霜，生命力依然旺盛，她眼里的生活依然是丰富的、多彩的（226）。可见了，她的内心获得了生长，对生活有了成熟的认识，这是珍妮体验人生后结出的硕果。

旅行隐喻是一种普适性认识，树隐喻是一种个性化体验。珍妮独特的具身体验和情感波折与美国南方的历史变迁相伴相随的。美国内战结束后，黑人的生活环境有了很大改善，但"就种族问题而言，历史仍以种种形式挥之不去"（Jones，2009：189）：外婆痛苦的回忆、特纳太太内化的本族歧视、乔模仿白人做生意和弄权、甜点心被白人用枪逼着收尸。然而，对生活在既自由又受到很大压制的环境中的珍妮，历史的阴影没有笼罩住她，反而催生了她追求独立和平等的意识，这是一棵树不惧风雨而勇于成长的信念，故事结尾，这样的意识传达给了她的好友费奥比，费奥比回以誓言“他们最好别在我面前批评你”（225）。读者可以猜到，费奥比将在街坊邻居的闲谈中将珍妮的观念辐射出去，由此，珍妮的人生之旅由个体的感性认识上升人性的普遍意义，这为赫斯顿在自传《路上的尘迹》（*Dust Tracks on a Road*，1942）中所坦言的“我没有种族偏见”（232）提供了一个引人注目的脚注，这是小说女性意识的深度，也是它超越族裔文学的表现。

4 结　语

《他们》的情节设计有一不寻常之处：珍妮年届四十还没有孩子。相关评论对此几乎置之不理。本文认为，这暗示美国南方进入新时代后，珍妮摆脱了母亲这一传统身份的沉重负担，同时作品可以专注于她的心路历程，这是情感认知的焦点所在，即珍妮首先是活生生的人，然后才可能是文化符号和思想载体。当然，本文只是众多解读中的一种。雷恩·西蒙斯（Ryan Simmons）警告说，“我不是说《他们眼望上苍》不可读解，而是说任何读解都不能视为定论”（2008：180）。经典之作着墨微妙，意蕴丰富，主题多元，留白若隐若现，《他们》就有这样的特点，看似不经意的比喻、随手拈来的插科打诨，越琢磨越有味道，研究空间仍然很大。肖文的题目说得好，“试走另一条路”，笔者相信，如果运用图形/背景、范畴化、脚本等其他认知诗学工具，这部作品还会呈现出新的内涵和意蕴。

参考文献

[1] DAMASIO ANTONIO. The Feeling of What Happens: Body, Emotion and the Making of Consciousness. London: Heinemann, 2000.

[2] GROSZ ELIZABETH. The Nick of Time: Politics, Evolution and

the Untimely. Durham: Duke University Press, 2004.

[3] HURSTON ZORA NEALE. Dust Tracks on a Road. New York: Harper Perennial, 2005.

[4] JONES L SHARON. Critical Companion to Zora Neale Hurston: A Literary Reference to Her Life and Work. New York: Facts On File, Inc., 2009.

[5] KING LOVALERIE. The Cambridge Introduction to Zola Neale Hurston. Cambridge: Cambridge University Press, 2008.

[6] KUKKONEN KARIN. 4R Cognition and Eighteenth-Century Fiction: How the Novel Found its Feet. Oxford: Oxford University Press, 2019.

[7] LAKOFF GEORGE AND Mark JOHNSEN. Metaphors we live by. London: The University of Chicago Press, 2003.

[8] LINSTROTH JOHN PATRICK. Marching against Gender Practice: Political Imaginings in the Basqueland. Lexington: Lexington Books, 2015.

[9] MILLER E SHAWN. "Some Other Way to Try": From Defiance to Creative Submission in Their Eyes Were Watching God. Harold Bloom ed. Zora Neale Hurston's Their Eyes Were Watching God, New Edition. New York: Infobase Publishing, 2008.

[10] PALMER ALAN. Social Minds in the Novel. Columbus: The Ohio State University Press.

[11] RYAN MARIE-LAURE. Possible Worlds. the living handbook of narratology, http: //www. lhn. uni-hamburg. de/node/54. html, 27. September 2013.

[12] SCHOTT ROBIN MAY. Birth, Death and Femininity: Philosophies of Embodiment. Bloomington: Indiana University Press. 2010.

[13] SIMMONS RYAN. "The Hierarchy Itself": Hurston's Their Eyes Were Watching God and the Sacrifice of Narrative Authority. Harold Bloom ed. Zora Neale Hurston's Their Eyes Were Watching

God, New Edition. New York: Infobase Publishing, 2008.

[14] STOCKWELL PETER. Introduction to Cognitive Poetics. London: Routledge, 2002.

[15] THREADCRAFT SHATEMA. Embodiment. Lisa Disch and Mary Hawkesworth (eds.) The Oxford Handbook of Feminist Theory. New York: Oxford University Press, 2016: 207-226.

[16] 陈波，韩林. 逻辑与语言——分析哲学经典文选. 北京：东方出版社，2005.

[17] 程锡麟. 赫斯顿研究. 上海：上海外语教育出版社，2005.

[18] 赫斯顿，佐拉·尼尔. 他们眼望上苍. 王家湘，译，杭州：浙江文艺出版社，2017.

[19] 盖文思，乔安娜，杰拉尔德·斯蒂恩. 认知诗学实践. 刘玉红，译，北京：教学与研究出版社，2020.

[20] 熊沐清. 认知诗学的可能世界理论与《慈悲》的多重主题. 当代外国文学，2011（4）：11-23.

[21] 熊沐清. 爱米丽的心理障碍与福克纳的人格冲突. 黔南民族师范学院学报，2020（5）：34-44.

图形-背景理论下《呼吸课》的焦虑解读

陈湘柳

【摘要】美国当代著名作家，安·泰勒在她的长篇小说《呼吸课》中打破单一线性的时间顺序，以玛吉和艾勒的双性视角和跳跃的故事情节来突显婚姻生活中的不满与焦虑，这种复杂的结构给读者带来一定的认知困难。认知诗学中的图形-背景理论认为图形具有前景化文体特征，图形与背景具有动态的转换关系。图形-背景理论能够帮助读者厘清本小说中图形人物与背景人物发生转换的主题意义，理解贯穿故事的玛吉这一焦虑的女性形象，以及她是如何走出焦虑的。

【关键词】图形-背景；焦虑；《呼吸课》；女性形象

0 引 言

安·泰勒（Anne Tyler，1941—）被认为是新一代美国南方女作家的代表人物（李美华，2003：147），她很多小说的背景都是美国南方城市巴尔的摩，一个她自1967年起就生活在其中的地方，因此她的作品有强烈的南方女作家的特点，例如以女性为中心，以家庭关系为主题。泰勒的小说总会让人想到“寻常家庭有着非同寻常的烦恼，这是她伟大的主题”（Salwak，1994：Ⅸ）。目前泰勒已出版21部小说，其中1989年出版的第11部小说《呼吸课》（*Breathing Lessons*）获普利策奖。小说主人公玛吉是一名中年妇女，她与丈夫

基金项目：本文系国家社科基金项目“认知女性主义视域下美国南方女作家的社会焦虑研究”（19BWW074）的阶段性成果。

作者简介：陈湘柳，女，桂林电子科技大学外国语学院教授，硕士，主要从事认知诗学、英美文学研究。

艾勒已有 28 年的婚姻，小说主要讲述了玛吉和艾勒去参加朋友葬礼的一天的行程。虽然故事发生在短短的一天，但作者细致地描述了玛吉和艾勒的婚姻生活，从他们最初相恋的激情到漫长婚姻中的疲惫与焦虑。泰勒的作品关注现代社会中个体的迷惘和对自我认同的追寻，能够引起读者的共鸣与反思。《呼吸课》被《时代》杂志评为年度好书，被《洛杉矶时报》认为是泰勒作品中最有力也最令人感动的一部。

国内外对泰勒作品的研究主要集中于婚姻、家庭、亲子等主题，不少学者对泰勒的作品进行文本比较研究，认为泰勒在创作主题和表现手法上继承了美国南方文学的传统（Bond，1986；Eckard，1985；Elkin，1985）。也有学者将泰勒与其他女性作家相比较，阐述其在现代女性作家中的重要地位（Wolpert，1988；Quiello，1991）。此外，学者们还热衷于从女性主义视角分析泰勒的作品（Lovenheim，1991）。事实上，泰勒有很多作品都试图通过男性视角或者双性视角进行创作（赵岚，2015：8）。《呼吸课》也采用了双性——玛吉和艾勒——的叙述视角，它打破单一的线性因果顺序，更为有效地推动情节发展，体现出泰勒卓越的叙事能力。Peter Prescott 评价泰勒有惊人的能力，能将结构复杂的小说表现得不费吹灰之力，甚至随意（Salwak，1994：173）。由于小说结构复杂，图形-背景理论能够帮助读者更好地解读作品，更深入地理解生活中的焦虑问题。

1 图形与背景的转换

图形-背景理论最初源于格式塔心理学，认为人在观景辨物时之所以能够形成三维立体图像，是因为他具有辨别图形和背景的能力（刘玉红，2014：137）。认知诗学借用了这一概念，认为图形和背景是文学文本分析时应关注的基本特征（熊沐清，2008：303）。图形具有如下一个或多个特点：图形自成一体，边界清晰；相对于静止的背景，图形是移动的；图形在时间和空间上先于背景；图形原为背景的一部分，后脱离出来，成为图形；图形细节更清楚、焦点更清晰、更明亮或更具吸引力；图形在背景顶上或前面或高处，或大于背景。在文学文本阅读过程中，图形-背景之间的关系不是静止不变的，而是处于动态变化中（Stockwell，2002：18）。在某些章节处于图形位置的人物或事件在另一些章节有可能变成背景，反之亦然。图形与背景的这种动态变化，不但是刻画人物、突显主题的需要，同时还能避免情节推进的呆板，吸引读者的注意，引发阅读兴趣。

图形和背景在文学研究中的运用主要表现为前景化（foregrounding）。读者在阅读进程中，随着情节的推进而关注某一人物、某一事件、某一景观等，每个被关注的对象都是暂时的图形，其他部分则是背景。（Stockwell：15）。《呼吸课》中图形人物是玛吉和艾勒，在小说的构架中，这两个人物与其他人物构成图形与背景的关系，他们作为图形，获得读者的特别关注，其他人物作为背景隐藏在图形后面。在情节推进过程中，他们二人的叙事位置会互换，有时玛吉为图形，艾勒为背景；有时艾勒为图形，玛吉为背景。

图形人物是占据最多文本空间的人物，某个人物的持续在场或频繁登场将时时提醒读者该人物的存在，唤起读者对这一人物的关注。《呼吸课》由三个部分组成，第一部和第三部从玛吉的视角展开故事，第二部从艾勒的视角叙述，因此玛吉和艾勒符合图形人物的前景化文体特征。小说中还出现了玛吉的丈夫艾勒、儿子杰西、儿媳菲奥娜、女儿戴茜、孙女勒罗伊、朋友赛琳娜、丈夫的父亲和姐姐，以及玛吉自己的家人、同学等人物，这些人物与玛吉和艾勒夫妇相比都是背景人物。但是，当小说要突出玛吉或者艾勒的不同身份时，有些背景人物就会与他们同时成为图形人物，例如，要强调玛吉或者艾勒的父母身份时，他们与儿子和儿媳都成了图形人物。玛吉和艾勒之间也有图形与背景的互换，因为处于静止状态的客体很难让认知主体持续保持注意力，这样的动态转换，能够更新读者的阅读注意，随时跟随图形人物的动态发展向前迈进。在某些章节，次要人物成为图形，使得小说中人物关系趋向复杂，人物形象更显完满。

《呼吸课》的结构貌似简单，仅由三个部分构成，但是这三个部分由许多时间跳跃的情节组成，而这些情节则以玛吉和艾勒的视角串联起来，他们的视角所观照出来的生活时时有焦虑。小说叙述了玛吉和艾勒去参加赛琳娜丈夫的葬礼，整个故事结构就是他们一天的行程，但是泰勒没有按照物理时间和空间来安排情节发展，而是交错展开，玛吉和艾勒 28 年的婚姻生活通过图形与背景的对比呈现出来。在故事中，玛吉具有妻子、母亲、祖母三重身份，但是她的情感付出没有得到想要的回报，她对婚姻的认知与艾勒有很大的反差，因此她的生活充满焦虑。

认知诗学的根本任务或存在根据是从解释到发现（熊沐清，2012：448）。本文将根据图形-背景理论分析文本，探究图形人物之间、图形人物与背景人物之间的关系，解读女主人公玛吉的情感焦虑和认知焦虑，探讨缓解焦虑的方法。通过图形与背景的对比，读者能够充分感受到婚姻生活中夫妻之间细微的情感变化和绵延的情绪起伏，理解婚姻中的焦虑现象。

2　焦虑解读

焦虑是人对现实或未来事物的价值特性出现严重恶化趋势所产生的情感反映（仇德辉，2018：19）。在心理上，焦虑会使人陷于紧张、不安、忧虑、烦恼等不愉快的复杂情绪状态。艺术上的焦虑指由某种内在冲突引发不安忧虑的内心状态。在文学中，布鲁姆著名的“影响的焦虑”揭示了经典、焦虑、误读和文学创新之间的辩证关系。在《呼吸课》中，玛吉的焦虑主要源于情感和认知两个方面：她对家人付出的感情没有回报，她对婚姻的认知与艾勒有极大的反差。

2.1　情感焦虑

阿兰·德波顿（Alain de Botton）指出，焦虑的第一个起因就是对爱的渴求，爱的缺乏会强烈影响我们，被人漠视会让我们愤怒、绝望，对自己产生怀疑，觉得自己一无是处（2004：8）。玛吉的焦虑来自她想对亲人付出所有的爱，但是她付出的爱都得不到回应，她想象出来的肥皂泡总是被无情地戳破。作为妻子，玛吉希望与艾勒能够思想和行为达成一致，但是艾勒总是在指责她；作为母亲，玛吉想要安排儿子的一切，结果儿子的生活和工作都与她的期望背道而驰；作为祖母，玛吉连见到孙女的机会都几乎没有。

在《呼吸课》中，当玛吉和艾勒同为图形时，泰勒主要强调玛吉被艾勒忽视。在去参加葬礼的路上，玛吉一直想与艾勒谈论前儿媳准备再婚的问题，而艾勒只顾着抱怨玛吉撞了汽车。玛吉哭泣的时候，艾勒一直走在前面，她能感觉到他的不耐烦。“那就好像有一片东西，玻璃一样平而硬的东西，把她挡在外面”（泰勒，2017：35）。为了发泄她的愤懑，她冲着他嚷道，“你必须一再强调我多么没逻辑，我多么没脑子，而你又是多么聪明，多么有先见之明（36）”。艾勒的自尊心和冷漠一直对她是一种威慑。有时候，她忍受着艾勒因为对她不满而流露的冷漠，进而变得麻木、疲倦。玛吉在婚姻中不时涌起暗淡、无望、愤怒、走投无路的感觉。

当玛吉需要支持时，艾勒经常选择视而不见。在葬礼上赛琳娜安排玛吉和艾勒唱歌，艾勒却拒绝了，玛吉只好自己站起来唱，结结巴巴，洋相百出，而艾勒无动于衷地看着她，好像他们没有任何关系似的。两人发生争执时，艾勒总是有理，总会逼玛吉认输。一旦他认为是玛吉的错，他总是以阴沉严厉、带着批评意味的目光审视她，所以玛吉总是对艾勒不抱希望，她甚至想着要是她临终前待在医院里，他大概不会来送她。如果她先死，他大概就装聋作哑，当什么都没发生，生意照做，口哨照吹，一如既往。在女性眼里，她们不明白为什么男性总是不能接收到她们发出的信号，或者总是理解错误她们的信息，还固执地不听她们的解释，以至于当女性跟男性同时出现时，总是会担心自己出什么差错。

玛吉的生活逻辑是：“爱”带来婚礼，婚礼带来孩子，孩子重复同样的生活：婚礼，然后孩子（Salwak，1994：169）。当玛吉的视角是母亲时，她的儿子与儿媳也成为图形人物，玛吉呈现出一个焦虑的母亲形象。在整部小说中，让玛吉无法抑制、非常冲动的是一种最普通的母亲幻想：她希望自己的孩子留在家中（Salwak：103）。但是，她的女儿高中毕业后选择离家去外地上大学，儿子租房自己住，儿媳离婚后带着孩子离开了巴尔的摩。玛吉编造了一堆理由想撮合离异的儿子和儿媳，希望他们能带着孩子一起回家，却无法成功。她不想放手，她觉得是别人硬把这些从她手里抢走。她不再是孩子依赖的母亲，这引起玛吉的焦虑，并且这种失落感充满她的整个生活。

小说的开头是玛吉误以为电台广播中想要再婚的女子是儿媳菲奥娜，这时玛吉和艾勒是图形，菲奥娜是背景，这个部分突出的是玛吉和艾勒的矛盾。当小说叙述到杰西和菲奥娜的故事时，他们和玛吉共同成为图形，强调玛吉作为母亲的焦虑，艾勒变成了背景。图形背景的转换使读者能够感受到故事重点的变化，符合阅读审美规律。杰西和菲奥娜是高中生，却未婚先孕。菲奥娜坚持要堕胎，杰西想要留下孩子，于是杰西请求玛吉去劝说菲奥娜。玛吉到诊所找到菲奥娜，夸张地说杰西如何爱她，如何为迎接孩子做好了准备。两个十七八岁的小年轻，自己还是孩子，却在玛吉的劝说下稀里糊涂地结婚生子了。

在儿子结婚前，玛吉不断地在两个年轻人面前说对方的好话，不惜夸大其词。杰西什么都没做，玛吉却拿了一个木销来欺骗菲奥娜，说他已经着手做婴儿床。儿子离婚后，玛吉完全不顾儿子与儿媳的意愿，一门心思撮合他们复婚。她在儿子面前说菲奥娜思念他，见不到他非常伤心；在儿媳面前说杰西舍不得她，时常会打开她的香皂盒闻一闻。玛吉想要用这些言语来打动他们，却不知这些只是她自己编造的谎言。他们见面后，谎言被揭穿，一家人又一次闹翻。从葬礼上出来，玛吉要求艾勒专门改道去菲奥娜家，劝说她带着女儿一起去巴尔的摩。她对菲奥娜说杰西仍然爱着她，一直想着她，终于说动了菲奥娜答应去一天。玛吉立刻偷偷打电话给杰西，说菲奥娜非常想见他。一个操碎心的老母亲，不停地在两边劝慰、说和，努力粘合一个支离破碎的家庭。

焦虑的特点是难以控制的担忧（Stein，2003：29）。玛吉是一个典型的美国南方母亲形象，她总是在担忧孩子们的生活，在她的心里，她的儿女一直是小孩子，不谙世事，弱小无力，她从没接受孩子们已经长大这一事实，对她来说，不能成为儿女依赖的母亲让她深感沮丧。

玛吉不仅是母亲，还是祖母。当她以祖母身份出现时，她与菲奥娜成为这个视角的图形人物。因为儿子与儿媳离婚，玛吉身为祖母却很难见到孙女勒罗伊，为此她想了很多办法去探望孙女。刚开始她一个人偷偷去，觉得自己鬼鬼祟祟，躲躲闪闪，可是那些探望一次比一次令人失望，直到最糟糕的那一次，勒罗伊只寻找外祖母而不要她。玛吉终于死了心，从此只和艾勒一起去正式探访，可没多久，正式探访也停止了，因为她在孙女三岁时送的小猫引起孩子过敏，于是菲奥娜不愿意让她再接近孩子。偶然听到一段广播，玛吉就认定儿媳菲奥娜要再婚，于是她不顾艾勒劝阻，自作主张要把孙女接到身边。

玛吉是一个充满爱心但心怀焦虑的祖母，她希望能时时刻刻守在孙女身边。勒罗伊刚出生时，她痛恨每天早晨不得不放开小娃娃去上班，她对艾勒抱怨菲奥娜根本不懂怎么照管孩子。她一天要往家里打好几回电话，看看家中情况如何。为了获得孙女的欢心，玛吉使劲问勒罗伊想吃什么，而她心里明白自己听上去多么聒噪，多么虚伪，多么刻意，但是她希望勒罗伊能够透过她年老的面孔看见她的内心依然年轻（泰勒：303）。

整部小说的高潮出现在玛吉一家和艾勒的父亲、姐姐一起去匹姆里科赛马场，给艾勒的父亲过生日。在这一部分中，作者画了一个突出的图形，把玛吉作为妻子、母亲、祖母这个综合身份的焦虑情绪完整地体现出来。作为妻子，玛吉必须照顾艾勒两个不健康的姐姐，而艾勒自顾和他的父亲去给赛马下注。两个姐姐一个把棉花糖摆满整排座位，把场地弄得乱七八糟；另一个姐姐晕倒在座位上。作为母亲，她需要安排全家八个人的午餐，可是没有一个人帮她，每个人都忙着干自己的事。作为祖母，她还要帮助菲奥娜照顾孩子，因为杰西跑去跟朋友聊天喝酒，菲奥娜抱着大哭的孩子朝着远处的杰西尖叫。玛吉不得不负责所有的事情，但是所有人都来责备她，戴西向哥哥告状说妈妈和菲奥娜吵架，艾勒批评她没有管好自己的事，菲奥娜觉得她只会多管闲事。这时玛吉只想扔下这群人一走了之，就当她和这群人没关系。最后大家不欢而散，菲奥娜带着孩子离家出走，杰西也很少回家，戴西经常在别人家里待着，家里只剩下玛吉和艾勒。

生活就是用一种焦虑代替另一种焦虑，用一种欲望代替另一种欲望的过程（德波顿：221）。玛吉试图用祖母的焦虑代替母亲的焦虑，却不知这种祖母的焦虑就是母亲身份的延伸。这种分离的焦虑促使她希望通过孙女能将儿子一家重新拉回家中，以此缓解作为母亲的焦虑，却以失败告终。

2.2 认知焦虑

身份的焦虑是一种担忧，担忧我们处在无法与社会设定的成功典范保持一致的危险中，从而被夺去尊严和尊重（德波顿：6）。正如玛吉向来暗地里觉得外人是羡慕她的婚姻，却被菲奥娜无情戳穿，“我烦透了你们俩，总是为同样无聊的事唠叨、计较，吵个不停。艾勒永远有理，而玛吉永远犯错（泰勒：329）。”身为妻子的玛吉和身为丈夫的艾勒对婚姻有不同的认知。当她嫁给艾勒时，她以为他会“用新婚之夜望着她的那种眼神看她一辈子。她以为他会永远那样看下去呢”（泰勒：39），然而，经过多年的婚姻，艾勒已经不再这样看她了，他觉得玛吉总是不认真对待自己的人生，经常胡来，“总是一拍脑袋就毫无目的地莽撞地冲出去——走走岔路，随便逛逛”（泰勒：133）。所以，艾勒总是和玛吉唱反调，他不配合葬礼上的合唱，不愿意顺路去探望前儿媳和小孙女，不想在路上帮助车子坏掉的老人。玛吉在出发前撞坏汽车，上路后忘记带上地图，与艾勒争吵时跳下车就走。她想要找回早期的艾勒，那个还没让她失望的他。但是，现在她不得不忍受着艾勒的自尊心和冷漠，进而自己变得麻木、疲倦。她羡慕朋友塞琳娜的婚姻生活，就像一出最赏心悦目的家庭喜剧，哪怕在为人父母之后，他们对彼此仍旧那么专注，那么一往情深。当我们的朋友比我们更加优越，更有成就时，我们的焦虑甚至愤恨会接踵而来。

在婚姻中，玛吉和艾勒都是图形人物，泰勒把他们结婚初期和结婚 28 年后进行了对比。根据审美对照原理，在量或质方面可以比较的两件事往往能够给予审美主体（即读者）以深刻、强烈的印象，引起主体的审美注意（aesthetic attention）（熊沐清，2012：453）。在塞琳娜的婚礼上，艾勒配合玛吉一起合唱，环抱玛吉给她支持；28 年后，在塞琳娜丈夫的葬礼上，塞琳娜再一次安排玛吉和艾勒合唱，当玛吉站起身时，艾勒坐着不动，他就像一个根本不认识的人——完全陌生的人，只不过凑巧和她坐在同一排长椅上。她不明白他怎么能坐在那里一动不动，让她一个人难堪地应付整首歌。这两个相隔 28 年的图形放在一起对比，更衬托出玛吉婚后的焦虑。

在对待孩子方面，玛吉和艾勒也有很大的差异。在玛吉心里，儿子杰西一直是一个漂亮的、惹人怜爱的小男孩，他身上的问题不过是小孩子的通病而已，哪怕他已经结婚生子。艾勒关注的是儿子高中退学，五音不全，却想去当摇滚歌星。玛吉记得的是他总是哈哈大笑，而艾勒记得的却是他发脾气。玛吉觉得艾勒总是贬低杰西。杰西还是小孩的时候，艾勒总是说："别一哭就抱他，别一饿就喂他，你会宠坏他的。"（泰勒：233）玛吉却希望自己能有更多的东西给儿子，能一直陪伴他。

杰西高中辍学后，艾勒要求他独立生活，去找工作，自己找房子搬出去住。可是儿子离开后，玛吉觉得家里显得多么无趣，多么肤浅，毫无生气，无精打采。玛吉和艾勒一个在客厅这头，一个在那头，阴郁地大眼瞪小眼。他们互相责怪，玛吉怪艾勒，怪他太严厉；艾勒怪玛吉，怪她太心软。从杰西出生以来，他们就不断为他争吵，态度和立场从未改变。艾勒总是批评，玛吉不断辩解。艾勒说杰西讲话没大没小、不懂礼貌、犟头倔脑、笨手笨脚。玛吉说，他等长大就好了，有些孩子成熟得快，有些孩子成熟得慢。到了十几岁时，杰西与艾勒的距离越来越远，偶尔说几句话，也只对玛吉讲。连玛吉自己都觉得跟艾勒隔着很远的距离，他们之间已有太多的争斗与不和，关于杰西的吵闹重复了千万遍。

在小说中，杰西是背景，总是被动地出现，很少直接发声，与他有关的情节主要由玛吉或者艾勒的视角展现出来，从而形成了三种图形-背景的关系：玛吉-杰西（图形-背景）、艾勒-杰西（图形-背景）、玛吉-艾勒（图形-图形），这样的关系比照凸显出玛吉和艾勒对亲子关系的认知差异，玛吉想要亲密的母子关系，艾勒却是冷漠的父子关系。

3 缓解焦虑

我们对爱的需求保持稳定不变，因而在我们的需求和世界的不确定条件之间产生了一种不平衡，而这种不确定性构成了我们身份焦虑的关键原因之一（德波顿：114）。如果我们所期待的远超出我们所获得的，那么我们付出的代价就是永远都挥之不去的焦虑，我们永远都不能安于现状，永远都有无法完成的梦想。阿兰·德波顿说，治疗身份的焦虑没有灵丹妙药，但我们可以尽量去了解它、讨论它（4）。就像玛吉和艾勒，尽管他们的婚姻有冲突、有争执，但是他们也在努力互相理解、互相支持，共同经营着婚姻。

泰勒以性格迥异的夫妻之间的矛盾来表现婚姻中的冲突，从而凸显忍耐和妥协在人生中的重要作用。尽管艾勒在婚后喜欢对玛吉有各种指责，但是他知道妻子爱他，他也时时宽慰妻子。在去往葬礼的路上，玛吉与艾勒发生争吵，她自顾自地从车上跳下来，一个人在便利店里闲逛，这时艾勒来到她的身后说："嘿，小妞，想不想陪我一起去参加葬礼。"（泰勒：50）黑夜里，玛吉去寻找离开家的菲奥娜和勒罗伊，艾勒一直跟在她的身后。回到家，玛吉翻着她们留下的东西，艾勒闷声不响地站在她背后。当玛吉认为所有的人都离开了他们（儿子搬出去与新女友同居，儿媳带着孙女到另一个城市很难见面，女儿去上大学很少回家）时，她问艾勒："我们俩以后为什么活着啊，我们还剩下那么多日子？"艾勒回答她："为今天，亲爱的。"（泰勒：345）所以，即使他们互相有各种不满、愤懑，但他们的婚姻能够持续下去，因为他们知道对方会是自己身后的依靠。

经过 20 多年的婚姻，玛吉和艾勒的性格都有了互换，玛吉原来是急性子，艾勒原来更有耐心。可是有了孩子后，玛吉会对艾勒说："耐心点儿，艾勒（泰勒：250）。"玛吉有一支爱唱的歌，每回他俩出门，她就喜欢和艾勒一起唱。她哼着调子，艾勒打着节拍。哪怕再尖锐的痛苦，迟早都会被磨平，也许是因为艾勒在身边，有个同盟。

泰勒通过玛吉和艾勒去参加赛琳娜丈夫的葬礼一天的行程，向读者展现了她们28年的婚姻。28年里，玛吉和艾勒重复着同样的争吵、同样的指责、同样的怨恨，但是他们也重复着同样的玩笑、同样的情话。婚姻就像菲奥娜怀孕时参加的呼吸课，她以为呼吸是天生的、不用学习、人人都会的，实际上需要通过学习，才能在生产时顺畅地呼吸，舒缓疼痛。婚姻需要相互配合、共同经营，才能减轻焦虑，维持下去。

4 结 语

本文运用图形-背景理论对泰勒的小说《呼吸课》中焦虑的女性形象进行解读，通过探讨图形人物来深入理解焦虑的产生和表现。这样的文学作品可以帮助我们解决生活中隐藏在心灵深处的紧张和焦虑，有助于引导我们更正确、更审慎、更理智地理解世界。首先，我们要认识到，生活中焦虑无处不在。当今社会，身份的焦虑比以往任何时候都强烈，因为每个人获取成功的可能性比以往任何时候都大，我们都不想成为"失败者"，我们时时刻刻都被成功人士的故事所包围。其次，我们要理解，一个人怀有身份焦虑，意味着他抱有一定的追求，期待取得某些成果。如果我们对焦虑有所了解，那么当我们面对别人的漠视或者成功，我们的反应就不会仅仅是痛苦和内疚，并且知道世界上不是只有一种证明生活成功的方式。

参考文献

[1] BOND ADRIENNE. From Addie Bundren to Pearl Tull: The Secularization of the South. Southern Quarterly, 1986 (24): 64-73.

[2] ECKARD G PAULA. Family and Community in Anne Tyler's Dinner at the Homesick Restaurant. Southern Literary Journal, 1985 (22): 33-44.

[3] ELKINS J MARY. Dinner at the Homesick Restaurant: The Faulkner Connection. Atlantis: A Women's Studies Journal, 1985 (10): 93-105.

[4] LOVENHEIM M PATRICIA. Dialogues with American: Androgyny, Ethnicity, and Family in the Novels of Anne Tyler, Joanne Greenberg and Toni Morrison. Rochester: University of Rochester, 1990.

[5] QUIELLO M ROSE. Breakdowns and Breakthroughs: The Figures of the Hysteric in Contemporary Novels by Women. Storrs: University of Connecticut, 1991.

[6] SALWAK DALE, ed.. Anne Tyler as Novelist. Iowa: University of Iowa Press, 1994.

[7] STEIN J DAN. Cognitive-Affective Neuroscience of Depression and Anxiety Disorders. London: Martin Dunitz, 2003.

[8] STOCKWELL PETER. Cognitive Poetics: An introduction. London and New York: Routledge, 2002.

[9] WOLPERT P ILANA. Crossing the Gender Line: Female Novelists and Their Male Voice. Columbus: Ohio State University, 1988.

[10] 阿兰·德波顿. 身份的焦虑. 陈广兴，南治国，译. 上海：上海译文出版社，2018

[11] 安·泰勒. 呼吸课. 卢肖慧，译. 天津：百花文艺出版社，2017.

[12] 李美华. 安妮·泰勒在美国当代女性文学中的地位. 当代外国文学，2003（3）：145-149.

[13] 刘玉红. 文学中图形/背景的动态关系与偏离. 社会科学家，2014（1）：137-140.

[14] 仇德辉. 数理情感学. 北京：中共中央党校出版社，2018.

[15] 熊沐清."从解释到发现"的认知诗学分析方法——以 The Eagle

为例. 外语教学与研究，2012（3）：448-459+481.
[16] 熊沐清. 语言学与文学研究的新接面——两本认知诗学著作述评. 外语教学与研究，2008（4）：299-305+321.
[17] 赵岚. 诗性想象的共同体：安·泰勒小说研究. 南京：南京师范大学，2015.

“图形-背景”理论下《最初的爱情，最后的仪式》之女性悲剧命运研究

张媛飞

【摘要】短篇小说集《最初的爱情，最后的仪式》是英国当代著名作家伊恩·麦克尤恩的处女作与成名作，本文运用认知诗学中的图形-背景理论，通过对小说叙事手法、叙事视角、舞台模型偏离等的分析，阐释了小说女性人物的悲剧性命运及其根源：男权意识主导下女性的弱势地位、女性话语权的缺失和女性在小说焦点中的隐退，揭示了隐藏在作品里面的深刻意义。

【关键词】图形-背景理论；《最初的爱情，最后的仪式》；女性悲剧命运

0 引 言

伊恩·麦克尤恩（Ian Mc Ewan，1948— ）是当代英国文坛最优秀、最具影响力的作家之一。短篇小说集《最初的爱情，最后的仪式》（*First Love, Last Rites*，1975），以下简称《最初》）是其处女作与成名作，荣获毛姆文学奖。该书由八个短篇小说构成，讲述了八段情节各异却又情感共通的故事。

国内外学者已从多个角度对麦克尤恩的作品进行研究。国外研究如罗纳德·海曼（Hayman，1978）、贝特霍尔德·舍尼（Schoene，

基金项目：本文系国家社会科学基金项目“认知女性主义视域下美国南方女作家的社会焦虑研究”（19BWW074）的阶段性成果。

作者简介：张媛飞，女，北部湾大学国际教育与外国语学院副教授，硕士。主要从事认知诗学、认知语言学、叙事学等研究。

2009）从伦理价值切入，探讨麦克尤恩作品中的道德混乱、家庭与世界对抗等主题。安哥拉·罗格（Roger，1996）从女性主义角度指出：麦克尤恩塑造的女性是神秘、自然、敏感的，与暴力、残酷和剥削性的男性形成直观的对照，男性和女性之间的冲突展示广阔的社会范围内两极分化的状况。布鲁诺·赛维柯（Zerweck，2001）从叙事学角度梳理了他的小说中“不可靠叙事”在历史文化中的演变。伯恩斯（Byrnes，2004）分析了《最初》中的性变态及情感发展。生态批评家雷格·杰拉德（Garrard，2009）指出麦克尤恩的小说蕴含了深刻的生态思想，麦克尤恩认为“父亲制”和“消费主义”是当代生态危机产生的思想根源。国内，朱秋玲（2012）从伦理学角度探讨麦克尤恩小说中的人类生存困境和伦理道德问题。刘思畅（2015）从叙事学角度研究他的作品中第一人称叙事和成长叙事。谢一榕和刘一静（2018）从生态女性主义角度揭示他的作品如何展示扭曲的人性、人与自然割裂的荒凉感。虽然国内外学者从不同角度对麦克尤恩作品进行了研究，但主要集中在他的中后期作品，对《最初》的关注主要体现在伦理价值、女性主义、性变态等，国内对《最初》进行了一些初步探索，主要是主题研究、表层文本分析及单一叙事方面。《最初》作为一部获奖短篇小说集，仍有不小的研究空间。

本文在国内外研究的基础上，选取《最初》中最有代表性的四篇小说为研究对象，分别为：《立体几何》（“Solid Geometry”）、《家庭制造》（“Homemade”）、《蝴蝶》（“Butterflies”）和《舞台上的柯克尔》（“Cocker at the Theatre”）。这四段共情共通的故事几乎涵盖了本集子中所有重要的人物关系：夫妻关系、兄妹关系、邻居关系、陌生人关系等，且小说中的女性人物都以悲剧结尾，或被丈夫杀害，或被哥哥诱奸，或被猥亵后溺水而死，或遭性侵后失去工作。她们的身体成为男性的附庸物而饱受摧残，内心痛苦无法言说。女性人物的这种境遇深刻地反映了社会现实，带给读者无尽的思考。本文运用图形-背景理论，对小说的叙事手法、叙事视角、舞台模型偏离进行分析，力图阐释作品中女性形象的悲剧命运及其原因，对作品的内涵进行延伸和拓展，揭示隐藏在作品里面的深刻意义。

1　图形-背景理论与文学研究

图形-背景理论（Figure-Ground Theory）是认知诗学中一个重要而影响广泛的理论，源于心理学领域，1915年由丹麦心理学家爱德加·鲁宾（Edgar Rubin）提出，后被完形心理学家用于研究知觉和描写空间组织方式。鲁宾通过设计“人面-花瓶图（Face-vase Illusion）”说明图形比背景更具凸显性，且不同的人会注意情景中不同的部分，就会产生不同的范畴化方法，获得不同的视觉效果（王寅，2006：217-218）。

美国认知语言学家伦纳德·泰尔米（Leonard Talmy）把图形-背景理论用于认知语义研究，指出“图形是一个移动的或概念中可移动的物体，其路径、位置或方向被视为一个可变量，其特殊值是相对值。背景是一个相对于参照框架静止的参照物，图形的路径、位置、方向是相对于背景而言的”（Talmy，2000：315-316）。

认知诗学代表人物彼特·斯托克韦尔（Peter Stockwell）突破传统语言学理论的局限性，将图形——背景理论拓展到文学研究中。他认为一个视觉场或文本场中最有可能被认为是图形的有以下特点：① 它自成一体，与背景界限分明；② 和静止的背景相比，它可以运动；③ 它在时间和空间上可以先于背景；④ 它成为已经脱离主体的背景的一部分；⑤ 它可以更详细、更好地被强调，更明亮，或比范围中其他部分更具吸引力；⑥ 它可以在背景的顶部、前面、上面或者比其他剩余部分更大些。（Stockwell，2002：15）

总之，图形-背景理论体现出一种认知观，即相同的认知对象，会因为注意焦点的差异而获得不同的知觉效果。因此，一个语篇在认知上可能包含了由于图形和背景变换而组成的多种不同层次的时空关系（Reuven，1983：1）。例如，小说的主人公因为其鲜明的性格特征、复杂的语言行为及心理发展变化等成为叙事的焦点，成为文本中的图形人物，而其他人物则成为背景人物。随着情节发展和叙事节奏的变化，某些次要人物也可能从背景中脱离出来成为图形，而主要人物暂时成为背景。因此在文本阅读过程中，读者因为注意焦点的不同，图形和背景会发生动态变化，研究这种动态变化有助于我们了解和理解作者的写作意图和文本特色。

2 图形-背景理论下女性悲剧命运的认知分析

在《最初》中，作者巧妙地运用多种叙事手法和叙事视角，深度刻画女性人物的行为和心理，揭示两性关系中女性的悲剧命运。

2.1 叙事技巧的认知分析

在大多数叙事小说中，人物是图形，是叙述的焦点，行走在不同的场景中，人物所处的场景是背景。绝大多数时候主要人物是图形，次要人物是背景；故事的主线是图形，辅线是背景等。图形-背景关系在四个短篇的叙事手法中主要体现在以下三个方面：

第一，利用图形巧设悬念并解开悬念。《蝴蝶》一开始就以“尸体”为引子探秘小女孩悲剧性死亡的原因。小说从邻居与“我”聊死者、“我”被叫去警察局辨认尸体和死者父母见面到警察告诉“我”：“你是女孩死前最后一个见到她的人……”等一系列事件，说明“我”是小说关注的焦点，即图形，同时也是悬念所在，读者要更多地了解“我”，才能解开悬念。从以上关于“我”的一系列事件可知：“我”与死者之间有一定关联，“我”是尸体的见证者，强推测就是“我”是杀人凶手。但“我”到底是不是杀人凶手，没有马上给出答案，这就引发读者强烈的好奇感，想追随“我”进一步剥开悬念，这时“我”是小说唯一的“图形”。随着情节发展，就在“我”签完笔录离开警局时，“我”后悔这么精心打扮来到这里，后悔洗了澡还留着香皂的气味，于是开始回忆当天和小女孩之间的交往过程，这为读者关注的另一焦点——小女孩——的出场做好了铺垫，小女孩自然成为另一“图形”。

小女孩的出场帮助读者最终揭开悬念，清楚小女孩是如何被“我”一步步杀害的：小女孩跟“我”搭讪、叫“我”跟她买东西—恋上小女孩、用“蝴蝶”的谎言诱骗她到运河边—强迫小女孩摸下体、她仓皇逃跑、摔晕—“我”把昏迷的小女孩丢入运河，清晰展现了诱骗、猥亵、杀害未成年少女的全过程。“我”和小女孩是小说的主要图形（primary figure），和我聊“小女孩死亡事件”的邻居修车工“查理”是推动情节发展的“次要图形”（secondary figure），小说的背景就是那条具有象征意义的肮脏运河，它是小女孩悲剧命运的终结点。

第二，倒叙区分第一图形和第二图形。《家庭制造》讲述了兄妹乱伦的故事，小说通过倒叙手法展现女性人物“康妮”的悲剧性。作为哥哥的“我”和妹妹“康妮”同为小说的焦点和图形，但是倒叙手法的使用，使妹妹康妮迟迟不能进入读者关注的视线，因此“我”长时间地占据了小说中心人物的地位，是乱伦关系的主要施动者，成为小说的主要焦点和第一图形（first figure），而康妮是被施动对象，成为第二图形（secondary figure），这预设了她的悲剧性结局。

小说一开始就描绘了康妮在浴缸边抽泣，“我”坐在水池边放热水的情景。接着用倒叙手法回忆了“我”和比“我”大一岁的玩伴雷蒙德之间的故事：“我”跟雷蒙德的交往，让“我”体验了青少年抽大麻、酗酒、偷东西、看黄片等的快感，加上“我”受到性学启蒙，渴望冲破成人世界的最后一道防线。受此不良思想的影响，加上缺乏成人世界的正确引导，最后酿成兄妹乱伦悲剧。“我”的活动贯穿在整个小说的情节安排中，占据了“第一图形”的主要位置，而妹妹康妮虽然在小说的开始就提到，但是由于倒叙的使用，她迟迟没有出场，直到有一次“父母外出、不在家”需要“我照看”的情况下，康妮才作为一个鲜活的人物形象真正进入小说故事中，处于“第二图形”的地位，在“我”一步步诱导下，和哥哥发生了性关系。康妮作为最后出场的人物，成为小说悲剧性的结尾。

第三，明线和暗线结合促使图形与背景发生转换。在小说《立体几何》中，故事的明线和暗线相互交织出现，使故事的层次更加清晰，信息更加完整。明线是“我”和妻子之间发生的日常琐事，作为故事的图形被聚焦；暗线是曾祖父日记里的事件以及和名叫 M 的人之间的故事，这看似故事的背景，却控制着图形。明线和暗线相结合，将曾祖父日记里的故事贯穿在文中“我”和妻子的一切日常生活中，图形与背景相互转化、交融交织，无时无刻不影响着享有男权思想的“我”，最终导致女性悲剧的发生。

文中在描写丈夫和妻子最后一次做爱时，丈夫把妻子的腿放到位，然后把妻子的头、腿放进臂环、相互对穿，直至妻子的身体像袜子一样翻转回来结束生命，丈夫欣赏着受尽折磨的妻子展现出的惊人美丽和人体结构的高贵，这是故事的明线，作为图形被凸显。暗线是夫妻做爱的过程受到他的曾祖父日记《立体几何原理》的启发，且超越了曾祖父的理论证明——性交姿势不可能超过素数 17，文中说到：“这是第十八种姿势”（麦克尤恩，2019：27）。从表面看作为丈夫的“我”是杀害妻子的凶手，事实上真凶却是曾祖父留下的“杀人手册”——日记。日记里记录着一些所谓的性交方式、立体几何原理等，作为丈夫的“我”深受这些“奥秘”影响并执迷于研究它们。明暗交织，明线受控于暗线，这时暗线从背景脱离、凸显为图形，而明线却退为背景，日记因而成了关注的焦点——丈夫——借刀杀人的工具，而妻子则成了这个工具的牺牲品。

2.2 叙述视角的认知分析

叙述视角是指叙述时观察故事的角度。视角是传递主题意义的重要工具。无论是在文字叙事还是电影叙事或者其他媒介的叙事中，同一个故事，若叙事时观察角度不同，会产生大相径庭的效果（申丹等，2010：88）。任何叙事都有一定的视角，小说也不例外。

第一，第一人称叙事强势控制图形话语权。申丹（1994）指出，第一人称主人公叙述，一般来说都是回顾性的叙述。这一类型中潜存两种不同的叙事眼光：第一种为叙述者现在的“我”追忆往事的眼光，第二种为被追忆的“我”的不同观察位置所看到的景象。具体来说，第一种为“外视角”或“外聚焦”（因为现在的“我”处于被追忆的往事之外），第二种为“内视角”或“内聚焦”（因为被追忆的“我”处于往事之中）。

小说《立体几何》第一人称主人公叙事控制了小说篇幅和情节

发展，故事叙事都建立在“我”（丈夫）的认知范围内，一切以“我”为中心，“我”拥有绝对的权威，讲“我之所讲”，看“我之所看”，因此，“我”的口吻下的“丈夫”成为小说的中心人物，成为焦点，即文本中的图形，因为丈夫控制着话语权，妻子梅西逐渐成为“一切听从丈夫的安排、服从丈夫的命令”的背景人物。夫妻做爱有如下描写：“我倚着身亲吻她的后颈，把她的两条手臂带到背后。她乐于顺服我如此摆布”（麦克尤恩，2019：27）。妻子想和丈夫分享她当天河边散步的景象，丈夫毫不理会，在男权中心意识支配下毫无顾忌地操纵和摆布妻子的身体：把妻子的头、腿放进臂环，相互对穿，直至她的身体再像袜子一样翻转回来，最终死去。妻子的挣扎、喊叫、悲号直至沉默换来的是丈夫的内心麻木。以妻子的生命为代价实践曾祖父日记里的“性交姿势”，说明丈夫从骨子里继承了男权思想，女性身体对他而言就是一几何物体，冷酷而残忍的“杀人犯”形象得以最大化凸显，妻子随着生命消失成为故事的背景，同时也成为一个社会悲剧。

第二，第三人称叙事内外巩固图形地位。在传统的第三人称小说中，处于故事外的叙述者通常采用第一人称视角，20 世纪初以来，第三人称小说的叙述者常常转而使用主要人物的视角，这样叙述声音与叙事视角不再统一于叙述者，而是分别存在于故事外的叙述者与故事内的视角人物这两个不同实体之中（申丹，1996）。换言之，虽然故事的主人公以第三人称出现，实际上他在叙述自己的故事。

小说《舞台上的柯克尔》的主人公“男导演贾斯敏”以第三人称出现在文本中，小说中既有故事外的叙事者讲述贾斯敏的故事，也有贾斯敏从自己的视角讲述他的所见所闻，因此，叙述者兼人物“男导演贾斯敏”是小说的焦点，是第一个出场的人物，是最主要的人物，是主要图形，其余人物的出场都在“他”的安排下，为配合“他”拍摄“舞台交媾戏”而出现。这些人物如女编舞师黛儿、舞台配乐杰克、舞台助理哈里以及舞台上的五对男女是“参与者（participants）”，是小说中的次焦点或次要图形。这是一场男性主导的舞台戏，更是被导演用金钱控制的一台戏。在舞台上，男角和女角在导演的安排下“假戏真做”，发生了性关系，结局是他们被驱逐下舞台，结束自己的表演生涯。在这对受“惩罚”的男女中，只有男演员被提到名字，导演与他有一次简单的对话，而女演员作为受害者，从头到尾没有展示任何语言和行为，在被忽视和遗弃中默默退场，她没有机会叙说委屈与伤痛，只能独自承受悲剧性后果。

2.3 舞台模型偏离与图形和背景的错位

根据兰盖克关于“舞台模型（Stage Model）”的描述，观察者如同在台下观看演员表演的观众，目光前视时形成了一个视觉注意区，也叫“舞台表演区（Onstage Region）”，舞台道具和背景都在这一区域之中，舞台的表演者是观众注意力的焦点（Langacker, 1991: 285）。因此，舞台上的表演者应是图形，而舞台、地板、布景、灯光以及台下的导演、工作人员、观众应为背景，这是从台下观察者的视角审视观察者与表演者的关系。然而小说《舞台上的柯克尔》却偏离了这一舞台认知模型。

小说以编排男女舞台交媾戏拉开序幕，舞台上的男女看似是注意力的焦点，在舞台的聚光灯下作为图形出现，然而情况并非如此，整个舞台交媾戏的语言交流发生在导演与编舞师、导演与舞台配乐及助理之间，舞台上的男女受到导演“我”的支配。导演穿越和行走在舞台及舞台背景中，成了真正的图形。如“拍摄交媾戏的准备工作”时，“我要‘交媾好时光’，杰克（舞台配乐师）”“这就是你们的性交音乐，姑娘小伙子们”“黛儿（编舞师）在哪里？我要黛儿”“我要那些假发，哈里亲爱的（舞台发型师）”（麦克尤恩，2019: 88-89）。从这些语言可以看出：导演拥有绝对的控制权，他的命令性语言得到执行，无不体现了导演在整场舞台剧中的重要地位，成为叙事的焦点和图形，而舞台上的姑娘小伙子们，却没有更多的语言及动作描写，只是机械地执行命令，成为舞台剧的背景。

随着故事的发展，一对男女在性交音乐和导演、编排的指导下真正发生了性行为，导演才把目光集中到他身上，问：“你叫什么名字？”男角回答：“柯克尔。”（麦克尤恩，2019：94）这是导演和演员之间的唯一一次对话，这对男女暂时成为图形出现，而和这名男角发生性行为的女角，从头到尾没有说过一句话，连姓甚名谁都不知道，就和男角一起被驱赶出了舞台，唯一的提及成了永久的退却和消失。舞台模型的偏离说明：在以金钱交易的经济社会下，社会各阶层分层明显，拥有权势者能打破规约成为图形，如拥有话语权和指挥权的导演贾斯敏；而劳动者，如舞台上辛勤的表演者，尤其是女性劳动者，人格丧失，命比纸薄，隐退为社会生活的背景。

3　女性人物悲剧的原因分析

第二次世界大战后，英国经济经历了短暂的繁荣，陷入了水深火热的境地，如美、法等经济实力增强，削弱了英国在世界工业的地位，英帝国逐步瓦解。短篇小说集《最初》创作于 20 世纪 70 年代初，呈现了一个混沌、破败、肮脏而污秽的世界，折射出第二次世界大战后工业化发展对英国社会的影响：人与人的关系已经物化为支配与被支配、征服与被征服的关系，人作为有血有肉的个体毫无情感可言。这种扭曲的关系就像毒瘤一样，侵蚀着西方社会的家庭生活。生态女性主义从自然环境的破坏入手寻找原因，但从社会认知角度看，其深层原因主要体现在以下三个方面：

第一，男权意识主导下女性的弱势地位。小说中男性在欲望的支配下，通过欺骗、谎言、力量占有女性，有的女性遭受身体、心灵的扭曲和折磨，有的甚至被杀害，她们处于绝对弱势地位，女性无论在思想上、力量上、行动上都无法与男性抗衡，结局大多悲惨，因此，“主体性缺失的女性，使女性成为取悦男人、依附男人的他者”（熊天玉，2018：32）。这是造成女性悲剧的根本原因。

第二，男性在小说中处于焦点地位。小说中男性人物占据较长的篇幅，他们的语言和行动强劲有力，从头到尾几乎全程在场，而女性人物占据的篇幅较短，出场时间不多。男性能充分表达思想感情，控制叙事，成为绝对焦点，而女性人物一般处于被支配、被控制的地位，在男性压迫下成为次要图形，甚至成为背景，这是女性悲剧形成的一个重要原因。

第三，女性话语权缺失。小说无论是第一人称还是第三人称叙事，几乎都是从男性视角出发，男性视角控制了话语权，因此，女性人物难有机会表达自己的思想和情感，更无法捍卫自己的权益，她们的思想感情备受压迫。话语是权力和地位的象征，是构成社会力量的重要组成部分，话语权的丧失，意味着一切权力的丧失，这是女性悲剧形成的另一主要原因。

4 结 语

短篇小说集《最初》以工业化背景下英国自然环境恶化、社会伦理价值体系坍塌、人性扭曲为创作背景，刻画了女性在男权意识主导下身心遭受压迫和侵害，以及男性践踏女性生命的种种可怕场景。图形-背景理论通过对小说叙事手法、叙事视角、舞台模型偏离等的认知分析，反映了资本主义社会残酷的社会现实，阐释了女性人物命中注定的悲剧性结果，揭示了作品的隐藏深刻内涵意义，展现了作品独特的魅力。

参考文献

[1] G GARRARD. Ian McEwan’s Next Novel and the Future of Ecocriticism. Contemporary Literature, 2009 (4): 695-720.

[2] BYRNES, C BERNIE. “McEwan’s Early Works: A Study in Sexual Deviance and Emotional Development.” Short Story Criticis, Vol. 106, edited by Jelena Krstovic. London: Paupers' Press, 2004: 6-19.

[3] R HAYMAN. Ian McEwan’s Moral Anarchy. Books and Bookmen, 1978: 15-16.

[4] R W LANGACKER. Foundations of Cognitive Grammar vol. Ⅱ:

Descriptive Application. Stanford, California: Stanford University Press, 1991: 285.

[5] I MCEWAN, R ROBERTS. Conversations with Ian McEwan. Jackson: University Press of Mississippi, 2010: 56.

[6] A ROGER. Ian McEwan's Portrayal of Women. Forum for Modern Language Studies, 1996 (1): 11-26.

[7] B SCHOENE. Families against the World: Ian McEwan. //Schoene B. The cosmolitan Novel. Edinburgh: Edinburgh University Press. 2009: 37-65

[8] P STOCKWELL. Cognitive Poetics: An Introduction. London: Routledge, 2002: 15.

[9] L TALMY. Toward a Cognitive Semantics: Concept Structuring Systems. Cambridge, Mass. MIT Press. 2000: 315-316.

[10] R TSUR. What is Cognitive Poetics?. Tel Aviv: Katz Research Institute for Hebrew Literature, 1983: 1

[11] B ZERWECK. Historicizing Unreliable Narration: Unreliability and Cultural Discourse in Narrative. Style, 2001 (1): 151-178.

[12] 刘思畅.《最初的爱情，最后的仪式》中的第一人称叙事与成长叙事. 北方文学，2015（7）：36-38.

[13] 申丹. 对叙事视角分类的再认识. 国外文学，1994（2）：65-74.

[14] 申丹. 论第一人称叙述与第三人称有限视角叙述在视角上的差异. 外国文学评论，1996（2）：14-23.

[15] 申丹，王丽亚. 西方叙事学：经典与后经典. 北京：北京大学出版社，2010.

[16] 王寅. 认知语言学. 上海：上海外语教育出版社，2006.

[17] 谢一榕，刘一静. 从“生态女性主义”视角看麦克尤恩小说集《最初的爱情，最后的仪式》. 新丝路，2018（8）：151-152.

[18] 熊天玉. 严歌苓《芳华》中女性的主体性建构. 文学教育（上），2018（8）：32-34.

[19] 伊恩·麦克尤恩. 最初的爱情，最后的仪式. 潘帕，译. 上海：

上海译文出版社，2019.
[20] 朱秋玲. 从伦理学角度分析伊恩·麦克尤恩的《最初的爱情，最后的仪式》. 南昌：南昌大学，2012.

儿童文学的认知研究

多维双域型故事：绘本的认知研究进路

石晓菲

【摘要】本文着重考察两个问题：一是绘本的样式是否与特定的认知方式有关；二是绘本如何通过成年共读者引导儿童读者形成认识与感受。这两个问题能够通过吉尔斯·福康涅和马克·特纳提出的概念整合理论以及基于此的双域型故事模型得到解释。本文认为，绘本在多个维度上具备双域型故事的特征，从绘本的双重叙事媒介中获取意义依赖于读者的概念整合能力，成年人和儿童都具备该项能力。概念整合无处不在，从日常行为到想象性创造，但具体如何实现整合却受到认知发展和人生经历等诸多因素的影响，这也引起了儿童与成人在阅读上的差异，从而造成他们之间互动的可能性与必要性。本文从双域型故事模式入手，勾勒绘本的认知研究进路，并且尝试通过纳入绘本该研究对象推动理论工具的创新。

【关键词】绘本；概念整合；双域型故事；文学的认知研究

0 引 言

儿童文学研究在近二十年里呈现出认知转向的趋势，开始借助认知诗学、认知叙事学和认知科学等分析文本，考察儿童文学的文类特征，研究儿童如何阅读文本（例如：Nikolajeva，2014；Seelinger Trites，2014；Moruzi et al.，2018）。认知研究的理论视角不仅能够

基金项目：本文是江苏省哲学社会科学基金青年项目“当代西方绘本理论批评研究”（18WWC005）的阶段性成果。

作者简介：石晓菲，女，博士研究生，副教授，主要从事英国儿童文学、绘本理论研究。

为阅读文学对儿童有益的信念提供科学证明，而且可以观照儿童文学的核心特征，即儿童文学作者和读者在认知和情感发展上的差异远大于一般文学作品的作者和读者（Nikolajeva，2014）。而对于绘本来说，这种差异更为复杂，因为在多数绘本阅读情境中，儿童和成人是共读者，绘本采取哪些策略和技巧、如何通过成年共读者引导儿童读者获得知识、形成认识和发展情感，是既具有理论价值又极富实践意义的研究话题。此外，绘本的基本特征为通过图文互动产生意义。通常认为，尚未识字的儿童读者可以借助图像理解文字，从而实现从读图到识字的过渡。除这个原因之外，绘本图文互动的叙事模式是否与特定的认知方式有关，是另一个值得思考的话题。因此，本文试图透过认知研究的理论视角探讨上述两个问题。

1　绘本的认知研究

劳特里奇出版社于 2018 年推出的《绘本研究指南》（*The Routledge Companion to Picturebooks*）专辟一章介绍绘本的认知研究。在该书中，贝蒂娜·库马林·梅堡和约格·梅堡（Kümmerling-Meibauer & Meibauer，2018：393）认为，绘本的认知研究致力于解决一个核心问题，即儿童阅读绘本能够学到什么。国内外相关研究通常聚焦于以下四个方面：① 描述性绘本（没有情节，只绘有日常物品的绘本）如何帮助儿童认识和掌握概念域（Kümmerling-Meibauer & Meibauer，2005，2011，2015）；② 绘本尤其是叙事性绘本如何描摹情感、促进儿童的情感发展（Nikolajeva，2012，2014；赵秀凤和李晓巍，2016）；③ 阅读涉及撒谎情节的绘本要求儿童具备至少是最初级的心理理论，心理理论指人们根据他人的外部表情、言语和行为推测、理解和应对他人意图的能力，这类绘本也促使儿童产生道德意识（Kümmerling-Meibauer & Meibauer，2013；Silva-Díaz，2015）；④ 绘本中的地图可以帮助儿童认识空间，形成认知地图（Kümmerling-Meibauer & Meibauer，2013，2017）。上述研究的关注点都在于文本某方面如何促进儿童读者某项能力的发展，但从更为宏观的角度考察绘本基本叙事模式与儿童认知之间的关联或许能够为发展绘本的认知研究进路提供新思考。

若要在宏观的层面考察绘本与儿童认知，需要关注三个问题：一是图像之间的关系；二是每页文字叙述之间的关系；三是图像与文字之间的关系（Kümmerling-Meibauer & Meibauer，2018：393）。然而，早在绘本的认知研究出现之前，这三个方面就已经构成了考察绘本的基本路径。例如，佩里·诺德曼（Nodelman，1988：184）指出，绘本的图像组合顺序可以传达时间上的因果关系，把图像和文字综合起来会改变其中任一叙事媒介讲述的故事。玛利亚·尼古拉耶娃和卡洛·斯科特（Nikolajeva & Scott，2006：12）总结提炼出多种图文关系，探讨绘本如何通过不同种类的图文互动塑造场景和人物、呈现叙事视角、表达时间概念、构建空间关系。彭懿（2011）关于世界经典绘本的介绍与研究也基本遵循读图与读文相结合的路径。如果库马林·梅堡和梅堡提出的构建绘本认知研究进路的基本方式早已存在，那么认知的视角到底能够给绘本研究带来什么？这是本文将着重回答的问题。

2　绘本的多维双域型故事模式

认知研究有助于思考关于绘本的两个基本问题：一是绘本的样式是否与特定的认知方式有关；二是绘本如何通过成年共读者引导儿童读者形成认识与感受。这两个问题能够通过吉尔斯·福康涅和马克·特纳提出的概念整合理论得到解释。福康涅和特纳（Fauconnier & Turner，2002：40-44）提出，人类在思考、交谈和行为的同时构建心理空间（mental space），心理空间是存储在思维中的人、事物和事件的集合，包括整体性的知识框架和特定的具体知识，两个心理空间可以被选择性地、有条件地融合为一个新的心理空间，这个过程被称为概念整合（conceptual blending），整合产生的新的心理空间能够催生创造性的结构和意义。因此，概念整合的过程包括三个步骤：① 在两个心理空间中寻找对应关系；② 把两个心理空间中的元素有选择性地投射到整合产生的心理空间中；③ 新的结构和意义在整合空间中产生。无论是成年人还是儿童都具备概念整合的能力，概念整合无处不在，从日常行为到想象性创造，人们运用这项能力通常在电光石火之间，甚至意识不到它的存在。

特纳（Turner，2003：128）基于概念整合理论，进一步提出了“双域型故事”（double-scope story），即建立在不同框架上的两个输入故事融合形成的第三个故事，整合形成的新故事综合吸收了两个输入故事框架里的部分元素，进而产生创造性的结构和意义，而这些结构和意义是单看任何一个输入故事都无法获得的，整合故事反过来也影响和改变输入故事的内涵。有意思的是，特纳（Turner，2003：133-140）接着以备受欢迎的儿童绘本《逃家小兔》（*The Runaway Bunny*）（1942）和《阿罗有支彩色笔》（*Harold and the Purple Crayon*）（1981）为例，说明即便是 2 至 3 岁的幼龄儿童也可以理解双域型故事，双域型故事代表了儿童文学的主流叙事模式。

相较于儿童文学的其他样式，绘本在多个维度上具备双域型故事的特征。一是人格化的动物与事物是绘本中图像的常见构成元素，例如会说话的兔子、有眼睛的小火车，人格化的形象本身就是概念整合的结果，即把具备思考、行为和语言能力的人和不具备这些能力的动物或者事物整合在一起。二是虽然不能绝对化地认为文字以时间为轴而图像则以空间为轴，但文字确实更适合表达时间，图像更利于建构空间，而且这确实是绘本创作的常见做法。因此，多数绘本是把时间维度的文字与空间维度的图像整合起来形成的双域型故事。三是从图文关系的角度来看，某些绘本在图像和文字中分别讲述了不同的甚至是互相矛盾的故事，因此整部作品综合吸收了图文两个输入故事里的对应关系，调和了它们框架里的对立之处，从而形成整合故事。四是考虑到儿童与成人共读的情境，双重读者最终形成的对一部作品的认识往往整合了他们各自的理解，而作品解读又会和读者们的现实整合起来，影响他们对世界、对彼此的看法。

特纳以两部儿童绘本为例阐释双域型故事主要是为了说明概念整合能力为人类所特有，无论他们处于哪个年龄阶段，这或许也可以解释为什么绘本经常被用于幼龄儿童的启蒙。然而，读者如何进行概念整合、从整合中获得了什么确实受到认知发展和人生经历等诸多因素的影响，这也引起了儿童与成人在阅读上的差异，从而造成他们之间互动的可能性与必要性。笔者接下来以绘本《格林爷爷的花园》（*Grandpa Green*，2011）为例，意在阐释绘本的双域型故事模式，并试图勾勒儿童与成人阅读绘本可能会出现的相似与差异及其之间的互动。

3 案例分析：细读《格林爷爷的花园》

《格林爷爷的花园》是美国著名绘本大师莱恩·史密斯的作品，于 2012 年获得美国图书馆协会颁发的凯迪克银奖（The Caldecott Honor Book）。这部绘本讲述了一位年迈的曾祖父在一生中拥有各种各样的经历，比如在农场上玩耍、上学的时候得了水痘、爱读关于秘密花园和巫师的故事、中学时偷偷亲吻了喜欢的女孩子、参加战争、结婚和生子等，并且把这些经历以园艺的形式呈现和保留在了自己的花园中。

整部作品里，图像直观呈现了概念域的整合。比如，在第一个跨页上，巨大的灌木丛被修剪成了婴儿的模样，灌木丛顶端伸出一小撮树叶，像新生儿的头发，灌木婴儿仰脸大哭，翻到下一个跨页，读者会发现婴儿的眼泪其实是灌木丛背后的水管里喷出的水花。第五个跨页描绘了老人还是孩子时喜爱的书中的人物，但这些人物都是用灌木塑造的。第七个跨页通过整合战争意象与灌木削弱了战争的残酷性，从大炮里射出的弹药变成了从树干里伸出的一团树叶，满地战火是散落的鲜红的花。因此，贯穿整本书的众多园艺形象自始至终融合了两个概念域，即植物与人、植物与小说人物、植物与战争。概念整合打破了读者习以为常的认知模式，即树是树、人是人、战争是战争，能够有效抓住读者眼球，引导读者以新的眼光看待原本熟悉的事物，产生去熟悉化的效果。此外，这些基于概念整合的园艺形象是一个小男孩玩耍的大背景，《格林爷爷的花园》在图像层面讲述了一个建立在空间和玩耍框架上的输入故事，在这个输入故事里，小男孩和老人一起在花园中游戏。

这部绘本的文字层面则建构了另一个以时间线索和人际互动为轴的输入故事。第一个跨页上写着，他“出生在很早很早以前”，这句话延续到了第二个跨页上，“比电脑、手机和电视还要早”。对于熟悉这三类电子产品历史的读者而言，绘本里的文字从一开始把故事的起始时间框定在19世纪末20世纪初，对于生活在当下背景、被电子产品包围的儿童读者来说，想象一个没有电子产品的世界需要额外的努力。文字继续按照时间顺序讲述发生在“他”身上的故事——上学、初恋、参加战争、结婚。到此为止，文字部分的叙述似乎采用了第三人称全知视角。然而，在第九个跨页上，第三人称全知视角变为了旁观者视角：“至少他是这样讲的”（原文中的强调），这句话表明文字部分的故事其实是某位人物的转述，直到第十个跨页，这位人物的身份才被揭示出来：“后来他们有了孩子，又有了好多孙子孙女。还有了一个曾孙，那就是我。”因此，这部作品中的文字叙述了一个小男孩转述其曾祖父的人生经历。

读者通过在两个输入故事之间寻找对应关系可以发现，图像中的小男孩就是文字里提到的曾孙，图像里的老人对应文字故事里的曾祖父，园艺形象则对应曾祖父人生经历中最重要的片段。这些对应元素和关系投射到整合故事中会产生新的意义：曾祖父与他的曾孙通过园艺的形式分享人生经历，曾孙是他人生故事的转述者，通过共同参与园艺创作，也延续了他的生命与记忆。透过整合故事的视角，输入故事也引发了全新的解读，花园空间被赋予了时间上的意义，即曾祖父无法重返的过去，花园空间也获得了人际和情感上的重要性，这是曾祖父与曾孙共享的内心世界的外部投射。此外，文字部分平铺直叙，以波澜不惊的语调讲述曾祖父的人生，但图像则以丰富多彩的园艺形象呈现他一生中的重要片段，考虑到文字里的故事是小男孩对曾祖父人生经历的转述，文字与图像截然相反的风格似乎是在暗示曾祖父讲述自己经历时刻意的自我压抑，或者小男孩无法完全理解曾祖父自述背后的浓烈情感。无论是哪种情况，这种处理手法直接影响现实情境中儿童读者与成年共读者的角色与定位，换言之，绘本作品又与双重读者的现实形成了另一重整合。

文本里老人与小男孩的互动构成了对现实中代际关系的摹仿。例如，在上面所举的第七个跨页的例子里，图像通过整合战争意象与植物隐晦地表达了战争的残酷性，这样做可能有以下几个原因：一是当代记忆研究显示，人们的记忆往往并非完全如实再现当时发生的情景，而是根据回忆者的需要建构甚至歪曲出来的产物（例如McGilchrist，2012：81；Panksepp & Biven，2012：217）。在老人创造的园艺形象中，战争的残酷性被隐藏起来，或许是因为老人自己无法应对这段创伤性的回忆，他的逃避在园艺作品中得到了体现。二是老人故意削弱了战争的残酷性，以避免给小男孩造成负面的影响，从而保护小男孩内心的稳定和安全感。不管是哪种解读，都涉及猜测人物的内心世界。在第一种情况里，读者推测老人害怕回忆战争。如果是第二种情况，读者推测老人不愿意小男孩知道战争的残酷。第二种情况涉及代际关系里的一个常见现象，即成年人出于他们眼里的保护儿童的目的隐藏了部分真相，也就是常说的善意的谎言。

《格林爷爷的花园》还有一处涉及善意的谎言。第九个跨页上的文字写道："他们在一起幸福地生活了很多年，从没吵过架。至少他是这样讲的"（原文中的强调）。成年读者或者见证过父母争执的儿童读者在看到这里时，通常会意识到几乎没有一对夫妇在共度一生的过程里从未吵过架，而且，文本在陈述"从没吵过架"的事实后，补充了一句"至少他是这样讲的"，给原本看似事实的话语贴上了来源的标签，似乎也是在鼓励读者质疑老人呈现在曾孙面前的没有争执的婚姻生活。

在真实的绘本阅读情境中，理解这两处善意的谎言可能会给儿童读者带来较大的挑战。库马林·梅堡和梅堡梳理众多相关研究后总结得出，理解谎言和撒谎与心理理论的发展紧密联系在一起，如前所述，心理埋论指人们根据他人的外部表情、言语和行为推测、理解和应对他人意图的能力，而善意的谎言更为复杂，因为它要求人们掌握至少两层嵌套的心理状态（Kümmerling-Meibauer & Meibauer，2013：152-153）。例如，在《格林爷爷的花园》这本书中，读者推测（第一层）老人不愿意（第二层）小男孩明白（第三层）战争的残酷，同理，读者推测（第一层）老人不愿意（第二层）小男孩知道（第三层）他婚姻生活里的争执，甚至更为复杂，读者推测（第一层）小男孩知道（第二层）他的曾祖父想让（第三层）他相信（第四层）婚姻中没有争吵。正常情况下，儿童在 3 岁半开始理解一层嵌套的心理状态,但处理两层嵌套心理状态的能力发展于 6 岁左右，直到 12 岁至 17 岁之间，青少年才逐渐懂得对于一个人的意图和信念等内心状态，存在多种不同的理解（Kümmerling- Meibauer & Meibauer，2013：152-153）。因此，儿童，尤其是幼龄读者，可能无法辨识老人善意的谎言。

尽管《格林爷爷的花园》在此处对儿童读者提出了挑战，但成年人眼里的善意的谎言充斥着儿童的生活，所以这部作品刻画了代际关系的复杂性，如果儿童读者无法识别蕴含在文字叙述中的善意的谎言，图像也提供了值得深挖的线索，供成年读者引导儿童透过善意的谎言，瞥见隐藏的真相。例如，在第九个跨页上，小男孩转述了曾祖父声称他的婚姻生活中没有争执，但在同一页上的图像里，修剪成爱心形状的树木被灌木迷宫包围，似乎是在暗示毫无争吵的幸福婚姻疑云重重。整部绘本里，曾祖父拥有直接经历，而小男孩则是曾祖父人生经历的聆听者和转述者，也是读者感知曾祖父人生的媒介，因此，整本书自始至终鼓励读者透过小男孩的视角看待他曾祖父言语行为背后的情感和想法。无论儿童读者是否完全相信曾祖父的人生故事，他们的认知和感受对象都是曾祖父，一个与自己不同代的人，认知与感受是共情的基础，而对代际关系而言，因为两代人在经历上的鸿沟，共情尤为重要。此外，成年共读者可以选择鼓励儿童读者质疑曾祖父的故事，也可以选择引导他们相信善意的谎言，在这里，成年读者的选择实质上复刻了书中曾祖父呈现人生经历时的犹豫，即究竟是诚实地再现真相，还是出于善意的目的掩盖部分真相。因此，绘本对代际沟通的刻画与真实共读情境中的互动形成了另一重整合，儿童与成人能够通过阅读绘本重新思考自己在代际关系中的定位与选择。

绘本这一形式的双重叙事媒介与双重读者属性决定了其在多个维度上具备双域型故事的特征，把《格林爷爷的花园》作为典型案例进行分析也涉及心理理论，这充分说明认知叙事学中的诸多理论视角与工具对绘本研究有助力作用，绘本的认知研究亟待拓展和深入。

4 结 语

国际叙事学发展的前沿流派包括认知叙事学、女性主义叙事学和修辞性叙事学等（尚必武，2012b；申丹和王丽亚，2010；熊沐清，2014）。惠海峰（2021）指出，国内的儿童文学叙事研究近些年蓬勃发展，但多采用经典叙事学，而结合后经典叙事学的研究成果，积极推动研究方法论的创新，能够将我国的儿童文学研究推向纵深发展。惠海峰（2021）也认为，融合了图像与文字双重叙事媒介的儿童作品往往具有丰富的文本层次，不同层次之间相互竞争，产生多重阅读方式与顺序，叙事理论在面对此类现象时具有独到的阐释优势。再加上融合认知科学和脑科学等领域新成果的跨学科优势，认知叙事学能够极大地丰富与拓展现有的绘本研究。

此外，尚必武（2012a）认为，图文互构故事世界的文本形式不仅给读者带来了全新的阅读体验，而且给批评家提供了诸多新颖的研究课题。将绘本这一研究对象纳入考察范围，也可推动认知叙事学理论工具的发展和完善。以双域型故事的理论为例，特纳在阐释该理论时恰恰借用了两部儿童绘本来说明幼龄儿童也能够进行概念整合，概念整合是人类共有的认知能力。本文的绘本案例分析也发现，双域型故事可以在多个维度上存在，而且，读者如何整合两个输入故事，从整合故事中获得了什么受到多重因素的影响，包括认知能力的发展（例如心理理论）、文学经验的积累（例如推测谁是叙述者、理解如何讲述故事)、人生阅历的沉淀和具体阅读语境里的选择等。总而言之，认知叙事学与绘本研究或者更大范围里的儿童文学研究的关系不应只是单向助益，理想关系是双向互补，若能做到双向互补，才可更好地推动儿童文学研究成为学术焦点。

参考文献

[1] M W BROWN. The Runaway Bunny. New York: Harper and Row, 1942.

[2] G FAUCONNIER, M TURNER. The Way We Think: Conceptual Blending and the Mind's Hidden Complexities. New York: Basic Books, 2002.

[3] C JOHNSON. Harold and the Purple Crayon. New York: Harpercollins, 1981.

[4] B KÜMMERLING-MEIBAUER, J MEIBAUER. First Pictures, Early Concepts: Early Concepts Books. The Lion and the Unicorn, 2005, 29 (3): 324-347.

[5] B KÜMMERLING-MEIBAUER, J MEIBAUER. Early-Concept Books: Acquiring Nominal and Verbal Concepts// Kümmerling-Meibauer, B. (ed.). Emergent Literacy: Children's Books from 0 to 3. Amsterdam: John Benjamins, 2011: 91-114.

[6] B KÜMMERLING-MEIBAUER, J MEIBAUER. Towards a Cognitive Theory of Picturebooks. International Research in Children's Literature, 2013, 6 (2): 143-160.

[7] B KÜMMERLING-MEIBAUER, J MEIBAUER. Picturebooks and Early Literacy. How Do Picturebooks Support Early Conceptual and Narrative Development?// Kümmerling-Meibauer, B., Meibauer, J., Nachtigaller, K. & K. Rohlfing (eds.). Learning from Picturebooks: Perspectives from Child Development and Literacy Studies. New York: Routledge, 2015: 13-32.

[8] B KÜMMERLING-MEIBAUER, J MEIBAUER. Mctaphorical Maps in Picturebooks// Goga, N. & B. Kümmerling-Meibauer (eds.). Maps and Mapping in Children's Literature: Landscapes, Seascapes, and Cityscapes. Amsterdam: John Benjamins, 2017: 75-91.

[9] B KÜMMERLING-MEIBAUER, J MEIBAUER. Picturebooks and Cognitive Studies// Kümmerling-Meibauer, B. (ed.). The Routledge Companion to Picturebooks. Abingdon: Routledge, 2018: 391-400.

[10] I MCGILCHRIST. The Master and His Emissary: The Divided Brain and the Making of the Western World. New Haven: Yale University Press, 2012.

[11] K MOZURI, M SMITH, E BULLEN. (eds.). Affect, Emotion, and Children's Literature: Representation and Socialisation in Texts for Children and Young Adults. New York: Routledge, 2018.

[12] M NIKOLAJEVA. Reading Other People's Minds through Words and Images. Children's Literature in Education, 2012, 43 (3): 273–291.

[13] M NIKOLAJEVA. Reading for Learning: Cognitive Approaches to Children's Literature. Amsterdam: John Benjamins, 2014.

[14] M NIKOLAJEVA, C SCOTT. How Picturebooks Work. London: Routledge, 2006.

[15] P NODELMAN. Words about Pictures. The Narrative Art of Children's Picture Books. Athens: The University of Georgia Press, 1988.

[16] J PANKSEPP, L BIVEN. The Archaeology of Mind: Neuroevolutionary Origins of Human Emotions. New York: Norton, 2012.

[17] R SEELINGER TRITES. Literary Conceptualizations of Growth: Metaphors and Cognition in Adolescent Literature. Philadelphia: John Benjamins, 2014.

[18] M C SILVA-DÍAZ. Picturebooks, Lies and Mindreading. BLFT:

Nordic Journal of ChildLit Aesthetics, 2015 (6).
[19] M TURNER. Double-scope Stories// Herman, D. (ed.). Narrative Theory and the Cognitive Sciences. Stanford: Center for the Study of Language and Information, 2003: 117-142.
[20] 惠海峰．儿童文学的叙事研究应大有可为．文艺报，2021-01-15：5.
[21] 莱恩·史密斯．格林爷爷的花园．南昌：二十一世纪出版社，2012.
[22] 彭懿．世界图画书：阅读与经典．南宁：接力出版社，2011.
[23] 尚必武．图像与文本互构故事世界：绘本小说潮．中国社会科学报，2012a-03-30：A05.
[24] 尚必武．后经典叙事学的第二阶段：命题与动向．当代外国文学，2012b，33（3）：33-42.
[25] 申丹，王丽亚．西方叙事学：经典与后经典．北京：北京大学出版社，2010.
[26] 熊沐清．论认知诗学分析方法的多维性——以《威尼斯商人》中夏洛克一段台词为例．认知诗学，2014，1（1）：3-22.
[27] 赵秀凤，李晓巍．叙事绘本中“愤怒”情绪的多模态转-隐喻表征——认知诗学视角．外语教学，2016，37（1）：10-14.

图画书虚构性叙事脚本的认知启蒙研究

赵一凡　徐德荣

【摘要】图画书作为低年龄儿童的文学读物，其虚构性叙事脚本对于儿童认知发展具有重要的启蒙作用。图画书中的虚构性叙事脚本对于儿童的认知启蒙是如何实现的，又体现在哪里？本文在尼古拉耶娃针对儿童文学展开的认知诗学研究基础上，提出图画书这一特殊门类中的虚构性叙事脚本作为知识载体能够通过为儿童提供常识知识、伦理知识、审美知识，使其更新并提升对于现实物理世界、伦理世界、美学世界的认知，具体表现为更熟悉日常物理世界中的基本生存生活常识与规则，深化伦理道德观念与责任意识，发展美学欣赏能力，从而实现其认知启蒙价值。同时，论文也探讨了图画书虚构性叙事脚本可能带来的认知壁垒及出路。

【关键词】儿童文学；图画书；认知诗学；脚本；认知教育

0　引　言

为何儿童应该读文学？这个问题就如同“为何文学是不可或缺的”一样，涉及人类认知深处的发展需要。兴起于 20 世纪 70 年代的认知诗学试图借用最前沿的认知科学研究成果对读者与文本、认

基金项目：本文系教育部重大课题攻关项目“中国儿童文学跨学科拓展研究”（19JZD036）、国家社科项目“百年中国儿童文学外译研究”（XXX）和中央高校基本科研业务费项目“儿童文学翻译的跨学科研究”（202042006）的阶段性成果。

作者简介：赵一凡，女，中国海洋大学外国语学院博士研究生，主要研究方向为儿童文学及其翻译；
徐德荣，男，中国海洋大学外国语学院教授，博士生导师，主要研究方向为儿童文学及其翻译。

知与文学的互动关系给出新的解答。“文学之用”这一老生常谈的话题也就再次成为讨论焦点。现有的脑科学研究证明，文学阅读特别是虚构文学阅读对于个人的认知、社交、情感发展至关重要（Nikolajeva，2014：226）。认知诗学对于读者认知的关注更多地侧重于成年人，对于儿童读者的特殊性涉及较少。玛利亚·尼古拉耶娃（Maria Nikolajeva）是较早将认知诗学应用到儿童文学领域内的学者，正如其著作《为学而读：儿童文学的认知进路》（*Reading for Learning：Cognitive Approaches to Children's Literature*，2014）的标题所显示，她明确主张文学对于儿童的功能性，强调了阅读对于儿童认知发展之大用，虚构文学作品为儿童提供了认识世界的知识，也提升了他们适应世界的认知能力。本文进一步认为，图画书作为低年龄儿童的文学启蒙读物，更是在其认知发展上发挥了重要的启蒙作用。那么，图画书中的虚构叙事对于儿童的认知启蒙是如何实现的，又体现在哪里？本文试图论证，图画书中的虚构性叙事脚本（scripts）为儿童认知加工过程提供了充分的知识资源，儿童通过阅读形成认知模式，获得认知更新与迭代，从而使认知能力得以启蒙与提升。在尼古拉耶娃针对儿童文学展开的认知诗学研究基础上，本文提出图画书这一特殊门类中的虚构性叙事脚本能够通过为儿童提供三类知识资源：常识知识、伦理知识、审美知识，使儿童更新并提升对于现实物理世界、伦理世界、美学世界的认知，具体表现为更熟悉日常物理世界中的基本生存生活常识与规则，深化伦理道德观念与责任意识，发展美学欣赏能力，成为真正认知成熟的个体——图画书虚构性叙事脚本的认知启蒙价值就此体现。最后，本文也将就此过程可能带来的认知壁垒及出路加以阐述。

1 脚本何以启蒙儿童读者？

图画书虚构性叙事脚本何以实现认知启蒙？正如前文所概括，图画书中的虚构性叙事脚本为儿童认知加工过程提供了充分的知识资源，儿童在知识积累中，初步获得认知判断的基础和动力，形成认知启蒙。虚构叙事的知识资源得以传递的基本路径便是脚本。在认知诗学研究中，脚本与图式（schemas）这两个概念往往成对出现。彼得·斯托克维尔（Peter Stockwell，2005：77）在《认知诗学导论》（*Cognitive Poetics：An Introduction*）中也明确说明，“图式作为帮助理解话语而从记忆中抽取出的概念性结构，最初被称为脚本”。可见，脚本与图式在定义上密不可分，而在实际的认知启蒙过程中，二者发挥的作用也相辅相成。二者的关系可以理解为，脚本是内心为某情景预设好的一整套规则，有其社会文化性；而图式则是这一整套规则组合成型的认知模式。就脚本而言，包括辅助日常生活的情景脚本（situational scripts）、辅助情景交流的人际脚本（personal scripts）、辅助技术操作的工具脚本（instrumental scripts）等（Stockwell，2005：77），其为我们的日常生活提供了高效、通约的前提预设。脚本并不是先在、先验的，而是通过经验积累的。图画书的虚构性叙事脚本同理，儿童通过阅读不同的叙事脚本，自觉不自觉地将现有叙事脚本与以往的生活经验、阅读经验加以联系，从而在不同的虚构叙事中获得认知练习，逐步迭代知识、扩充认知知识库，渐渐熟练分辨虚构与现实的差别，最终更好地认识、应对现实世界。同时，经过吸收的叙事脚本内化形成满足现实需要的认知模式，帮助儿童构建认知世界的框架性系统。在认知发展成熟阶段，图式为认知主体提供了高效快捷的认知通道，脚本与图式往往互为增知益智的前提；而在儿童认知发展初期，组织较为灵活的脚本，作为其理解世界、理解他人的认知性铺垫，发挥了不可替代的奠基作用。

图画书的目标读者通常为 8 岁以下儿童，处于认知发展初期阶段，承担其认知启蒙职责的便是虚构性叙事脚本。本文认为图画书能够向儿童读者传递三种知识资源，分别为常识知识、伦理知识、审美知识，其均透过作为知识载体的脚本运行得以开采。典型脚本所蕴含的认知模式，将会通过不断的重复阅读得到学习、内化、巩固。有效的认知模式能够在底层逻辑层面发挥普遍性的认知提升功能，兼具趣味性与教育性的圆形虚构性叙事脚本便是一例。

圆形虚构性叙事脚本，顾名思义，体现为首尾相接的圆形虚构性叙事，多见于电影叙事艺术中，典型代表如昆汀·塔伦蒂诺（Quentin Tarantino）执导的犯罪电影《低俗小说》（*Pulp Fiction*，1994）。在圆形叙事中，需要特定的标记物出现才能引发读者的认知连贯（coherence）。这类标记物在认知诗学中称为 slots。slots 在叙事脚本中体现为具体化的事物，如标志性的特定场景、特定物品、特定行动者等。劳拉·努梅罗夫（Laura Numeroff）的"要是你给老鼠吃饼干系列"图画书便是圆形虚构性叙事脚本的典型体现。在《要是你给老鼠吃饼干》（*If You Give a Mouse a Cookie*，1985，以下简称《吃饼干》）中，故事的开头为"要是你给老鼠吃饼干，他就会跟你要一杯牛奶。"（努梅罗夫，2017：5-6）在美国的日常饮食习惯中，"饼干"这一 slots 的出现，便意味着要"喝牛奶"加以搭配。而"喝牛奶"则进一步引发下文"要吸管"的认知连贯。顺着"要是你……他就……"的叙事链条，故事环环相扣抵达结尾："……他就会跟你要一杯牛奶。很可能，要是你给了他牛奶，他就会要一块饼干配着吃"（努梅罗夫，2017：30-32）。此设计完美咬合开头处的"要是你给老鼠吃饼干……"于是，一个一个单线的子脚本基于被普遍确认的社会规约，共同串联成一个大的圆形脚本。正是由于子脚本的社会规约性，叙事逻辑符合默认的认知语境，因此可以自然衔接，引发读者对后续情节的循环想象。这一过程便自然实现首尾相接，叙事模型勾勒出一个流畅的圆环。就儿童而言，便也是在阅读过程中，学习这种经成人苦心设计的圆形叙事，从而逐渐将此类叙事脚本内化于心，形成认知模式，以备使用。

实际上，这种认知模式的确大有用处，其反映出人类深层认知模式，体现人类认识世界的底层逻辑之一，具有文化通约性，在不同地域的文化中都可见此类圆形叙事脚本，如希腊神话中对西西弗斯、普罗米修斯惩罚的循环，佛教中的六道轮回，道家哲学中首尾相接的阴阳鱼，甚至黑格尔的"正反合"辩证法、马克思哲学中的辩证认识论也都带有圆形叙事脚本的痕迹。因此，圆形虚构性叙事脚本作为图画书知识传递的重要方式，能够极大地促进儿童认知启蒙与认知能力提升。《吃饼干》中呈现的圆形虚构性叙事脚本，一方面趣味性十足，另一方面也兼具教育性，成功向儿童传递了这一有效的认知模式。下文将以此系列图画书为例，阐述虚构性叙事脚本传递的常识知识、伦理知识、审美知识及其对于儿童适应物理世界、伦理世界、美学世界所发挥的作用。

2　脚本认知启蒙的具体体现

不谙世事的儿童从图画书中获取关于世界、关于他人、关于自我的基本知识并加以运用，从而更加适应现实世界，此为图画书虚构性叙事脚本认知启蒙价值的重要体现。

就知识资源价值而言，图画书虚构性叙事脚本所引发的知识积累为儿童提升认知提供了必要的基础与原动力。斯托克维尔（Stockwell，2005：31-34）认为，学习的过程包括收集新事实、吸收新事实，判断事实的真假性，将其分类整理并与已有的认知模式加以比较。在文学阅读中，儿童密集地接触新事实、新情况，其有限的生活空间被无限地扩大，儿童获得充足的机会来扩充自己的知识资源库，从而进一步迭代自己的认知判断能力。尼古拉耶娃（Nikolajeva，2014：22）在已有的研究基础上进一步论证：儿童虚构类文学作品比一般虚构类文学作品能更大程度上提供知识性价值。在她看来，儿童虚构文学能够为儿童提供的知识资源主要有两类，一类是事实性知识（factual knowledge 或 encyclopaedic knowledge），一类是虚构性知识（fictional knowledge 或 aesthetic knowledge）。事实性知识是指（被认为）真实反映现实世界（actual world）的知识，尼古拉耶娃认为这类知识多从非虚构类文学作品中获取；虚构性知识是指通过文学阅读活动获取的文学阅读愉悦（Nikolajeva，2014：22）。本文认为，就虚构类图画书而言，因虚构性图画书目标读者的特殊性，其仍可为儿童提供相当程度的事实性知识，非虚构类文学并非儿童获取事实性知识的唯一渠道。此外，由虚构类文学提供的虚构性知识也并非仅包括"文学阅读愉悦"，此"愉悦"仅指向了审美知识的一部分。而在审美知识之外，虚构叙事还可以传递指向以伦理关系、道德观念为代表的伦理知识。因此，本文认为，图画书中虚构叙事的知识资源有三类，分别是常识知识、伦理知识、审美知识，同时，通过虚构性叙事脚本的运行，此三类知识得以开采、积累、内化，帮助儿童认识、适应与其相对应的三个世界，即物理世界、伦理世界、美学世界。

现有的认知诗学研究已在神经科学特别是镜像神经元研究的支持下，证明阅读虚构文学作品的确能够影响读者大脑与现实生活的互动关系（Kidd & Emanuele，2013），读者对虚构情节做出的认知、情感反应与对现实世界做出的反应无甚差异（Zunshine，2006）；虚构作品对大脑认知、情感反应的刺激，可以加深读者对于现实世界的理解（Kidd & Emanuele，2013）。图画书的阅读群体大多为 8 岁以下的儿童，其认知能力的发展正处于关键阶段，图画书虚构性叙事脚本对于儿童的适应世界的认知启蒙价值作用尤为突出。通过为儿童提供常识知识、伦理知识、审美知识，图画书虚构性叙事脚本帮助其提升对于物理世界、伦理世界、美学世界认知的具体指向为：物理世界指向现实生存的物质世界，着重于对现实物理世界基本常识的介绍，使儿童更为适应日常现实生活，而适应伦理知识所对应的伦理世界，使其逐渐形成对于人际伦理关系的认识，明晰个人的伦理责任与义务，并养成是非分明的伦理道德观；虚构性叙事脚本所带来的美学世界，将一个超越现实世界的诗意空间呈现在儿童面前，通过使其获得更多的美学体验，从而拓展其生命体验，获得更广阔的人生。

下文将逐一对图画书虚构性叙事脚本所承载的常识知识、伦理知识、审美知识及其如何帮助儿童提升对于物理世界、伦理世界、美学世界的认知展开具体论述。

2.1 常识知识：认知物理世界

首先，何为常识知识？由于图画书的主要阅读主体为幼儿（朱自强，2008：336），这一阶段的儿童初步具备了表达及读写能力，正处于对于世界知识的狂热吸收阶段，同时对在成人世界里习以为常的规则、习惯仍在适应中，尚未内化成固有认知。因此，即便是最“不言而喻”“不证自明”的原理，对于儿童来说，仍必须经过一定程度的质询、验证才能得以确认，这也是为什么儿童在这一阶段常常提出对“既定事实”构成挑战的“不同寻常”的问题。因此，在我们看来不是“知识”的内容，对儿童而言却是难能可贵的认识世界导论。图画书中许多在成人看来“非知识性”的设定，从儿童的角度来判断，实属必要的生存生活知识，因此我们将这类知识归为“常识知识”，即与现实物理世界相关的基本生存、生活知识。不过，与真正科普类书籍不同的是，在图画书虚构叙事中出现的常识知识往往与日常生活的具体情景紧密相关，着重呈现现实生活中的基本生活规则，但不讨论这些规则本身的对错正误，亦不关注事物自身的科学属性或技术生产属性。因此，这一层面的常识知识含义覆盖范围较广，区别于尼古拉耶娃针对非虚构文学作品中“科普性”事实类知识所做的狭义定义。

在“要是你给老鼠吃饼干系列”图画书中，虚构性叙事脚本运载的物理世界生存生活知识便可得到体现。书中，各类食物（饼干、牛奶、蛋糕、冰激凌、甜甜圈、煎饼等）、日常用品（剪刀、扫帚、蜡笔、午餐盒、手套等）悉数登场，食物的搭配习惯、物品的使用规则一一通过紧密咬合的圆形叙事脚本得以介绍。系列图画书向儿童传递常识知识的认知启蒙价值并非体现为介绍某种事物的营养成分、科学搭配或制作流程等，而是西方社会中为大多数人所遵循的饮食传统，如饼干搭配牛奶、布朗尼蛋糕搭配冰激凌球、纸杯蛋糕搭配彩色糖粉等，这些惯例与中国不同地域所习惯的豆浆配油条、饺子配醋或蒜泥类似。此外，在圆形叙事脚本的发展链条中，也穿插了诸多不成文的社会行为规范、惯例，如喝完牛奶要擦嘴的卫生习惯、在纸上而非墙上或窗帘上画画的规矩、在自己创作的作品上签名的署名习惯等。“要是你给老鼠吃饼干”系列图画书的目标读者群体为 3~8 岁儿童（kidsbookseries.com），圆形虚构性叙事脚本通过一种兼具趣味性与逻辑性的方式，有效地将现实物理世界的诸多知识传授给儿童，对此类规则、惯例的掌握，能够扩展儿童关于社会性生存的认识，通过积累知识形成内化的认知模式，从而更加从容熟练地在现实世界生存、生活，理解他人的行为，对于其未来进一步适应现实物理世界也大有裨益，为下一步的认知更新、迭代打下基础。

当然，图画书虚构性叙事脚本所能提供给儿童的，远不止物理世界层面的生存生活知识。除了现实物质世界，儿童生活所要面临的另一个庞大而复杂的世界便是观念世界，包括伦理世界与美学世界。其中，与现实生活关系最为紧密的便是伦理世界。下文将就虚构性叙事脚本中的伦理知识对于儿童适应现实伦理世界的帮助展开论述。

2.2 伦理知识：认知伦理世界

现有的文学伦理学及文学伦理学批评研究早已通过诸多案例呈现了文学的伦理教诲作用，正如聂珍钊（2014：13）所言，文学是道德的产物，其“在本质上是关于伦理的艺术”，而儿童文学的诞生更是无法摆脱其教诲属性。伦理世界中庞杂的伦理道德网络为许多隐形法则所规范，其具有社会通约性，往往无须言说但人人了悟。不过，此“了悟”并非一日之功，而是需要从小学习、积累。虚构性叙事脚本便为儿童提供了大量的人际关系学习素材、是非善恶辨析素材，亦即伦理知识，从而使其更好地适应现实伦理道德世界，将人际关系中的伦理道德规范内化于心，明确个人责任与义务，形成基础性的伦理道德观念。

图画书中的虚构性叙事脚本往往情节简单，但内容精炼，其中蕴含的诸多伦理性因素，启发儿童对于友情、亲情乃至爱情等伦理关系的启蒙，帮助儿童明辨是非善恶，实现道德启蒙，为儿童打开通往伦理道德世界的大门。圆形虚构性叙事脚本作为有效的认识启蒙脚本之一，在伦理知识的传递方面也起到特别的效果。我们仍以《吃饼干》为例，故事中，小男孩与小老鼠之间的互动更多是小男孩在满足小老鼠的需求，表现为对小老鼠有求必应、鞍前马后地照顾，因此，除了广泛意义上社会成员之间的“爱护”，二者一方单纯索取一方单纯给予的互动模式更多地体现为养育初期父子关系的暗喻。叙事中呈现的小男孩无微不至的殷切表现，与小老鼠“衣来伸手饭来张口”“坐享其成”的姿态相映成趣。儿童在阅读中，首先会自然将自己代入与自身形象相似的小男孩中，随着阅读的深入，又会因为小老鼠举止与自己日常行为的相似性，从而也会将自己代入小老鼠的身份当中，儿童在认知上便会初步理解有关父子责任的伦理关系：首先，小男孩将会意识到，自己有一天也会成为父亲，也需要去照顾别人，而此时，自己正是被照顾的“小老鼠”，于是从这层伦理认识上出发反照现实，儿童便可懵懵懂懂地体悟父母照顾自己的不易，体悟到自己未来为人父、为人母所要经历的不易。结尾处“要是你给老鼠吃饼干，他就会……”的设计，将故事重新带回到开头，这种首尾相接的叙事模式一方面体现出照顾子女日复一日的辛劳，一方面也暗示了父子伦理的循环延续。此外，在故事的循环链条中，有几个环节是小老鼠主动为自己剪发并承担打扫卫生的责任，因其暗喻着故事外的儿童读者，无形之中会启发儿童树立为自己以及自己的行为负责的观念。而这一朴素的道理，实际上也隐含了引导儿童独立自主地承担人生责任、为人生负责的教诲意味。由此，便也引出此类圆形虚构性叙事脚本对于儿童认知的深层意义，即承担个人责任。承担个人责任不仅仅意味着自己对自己负责，同时也意味着承担个人对于共同体的责任，正如在父子责任循环中所强调的个人之于家庭中的责任。而这份责任延伸，便可拓展至个人之于社会的责任，之于人类共同的家园地球的责任。

就伦理知识而言，在图画书虚构性叙事脚本中，其人物设定、情节设计往往不可避免地涉及伦理道德知识的传递，而这份伦理知识的传递便能够帮助儿童获得伦理认知上的启蒙，更好地适应现实伦理世界，一方面在人际社会中处理好与他人的伦理关系，一方面又能够保持明辨是非的道德观念，同时能够树立自身的伦理责任，为自己负责的同时承担共同体责任。

2.3 审美知识：认知美学世界

图画书虚构性叙事脚本在传递物理知识、伦理知识之外，还能提供审美知识——同伦理知识一样，属观念世界的范畴，但伦理知识侧重个体在关系、在社会中的参与，审美知识的不同之处在于，它更指向儿童心灵内部。朱光潜（2008：4）在《谈美》中直言："人要有出世的精神才可以做入世的事业。"他强调，"把自己所做的学问事业当作一件艺术品看待"，"才可以有一番真正的成就"，同样是观念世界的审美知识，便比伦理知识而更为"出世"，其对于儿童认知的持续发展有着更潜移默化而幽深持久的影响。尼古拉耶娃（Nikolajeva，2014：22）定义的虚构性知识是指通过文学阅读活动获取的文学阅读愉悦，此处的审美知识便包含了其对于虚构性知识的界定。本文认为，图画书虚构性叙事脚本为儿童提供的审美知识，一方面包括"文学阅读活动获取的文学阅读愉悦"，另一方面，这种审美知识亦非单纯的感官享受，而是一种经过反省的艺术体验，需要儿童认知能力自觉或不自觉地参与。审美知识不以现实利害为判断标准，其与现实世界的相对距离，便给了儿童一个更为自由舒展的嬉戏空间、诗意空间。

首先，就文学阅读愉悦而言，圆形虚构性叙事脚本中的叙事循环可以在很大程度上满足儿童的阅读趣味。家长或老师不难发现，儿童在认知发展初期（大多与图画书阅读时期重合），热衷于重复聆听或阅读喜欢的故事。其原因往往并不是儿童忘记了情节，情况常常相反，儿童甚至能够背诵出故事中的文本。实际上，重复阅读的过程，是儿童加强、巩固自我认知的过程。在这一过程中，儿童能够预测情节、预测下文，满足了其在不稳定世界中获取确定性的需求。阅读中的循环与重复，对儿童而言是一种认知世界的练习，获得安全感、掌控感的练习。《吃饼干》自身的循环逻辑便符合儿童的这种认知需求，儿童能够从中收获无限循环的阅读满足。文本自身的无限循环能够额外增添阅读乐趣，其他循环叙事脚本的广受欢迎亦可证明，例如中文语境中"和尚讲故事"的童谣"从前有座山，山里有座庙，庙里有个老和尚，老和尚给小和尚讲故事：从前有座山……”，在一代代中国儿童中口口相传。“要是你给老鼠吃饼干系列”图画书全部以此类圆形脚本为基，其第一本书于1985年诞生（即《要是你给老鼠吃饼干》），很快受到了美国出版界的盛赞。其后陆续推出的《要是你给驼鹿吃小松糕》等8本书，蝉联《纽约时报》畅销童书榜70余周，可见儿童对此类叙事脚本的喜爱。（努梅罗夫，2017：编辑语）

此外，这种虚构性叙事脚本也向儿童展现了文学叙事中的框架性脚本之一，为其文学艺术审美能力的进一步养成进行了前期铺垫与演练。儿童在阅读《吃饼干》时，看到小老鼠与小男孩的互动、联想到其各自隐喻的现实人物、认识到小男孩身份的倒置，一步步走入文学世界的内部，从而初步领略文学世界衍生于而又超脱于现实世界的叙事逻辑，收获平行于现实生活的文学审美体验。圆形虚构性叙事脚本作为文化间共享的叙事模式，为儿童今后更广泛、深刻的文学阅读打下审美性的认知基础。对儿童而言，除了掌握有关现实世界、伦理世界的知识及规则，习得欣赏美学世界的审美能力更是认知发展的重要一步。正如哲学家保罗·霍尔默（Paul Holmer，1970：28）在评价 C. S. 刘易斯时所写：文学灌溉了生活的荒漠，图画书的虚构性叙事脚本同样为儿童展现了更为广阔的美学世界，儿童透过文学阅读拓展了生命体验。通过对于文学叙事脚本的积累，儿童的审美认知能力提升，在超越现实的文学体验中，成为认知更为成熟的个体。

除了现实物理世界、伦理道德世界，图画书的虚构性叙事脚本还为儿童提供了一个诗性美学世界。在其中，儿童不仅获得了认知发展需求的满足，还收获了开启更广阔美学世界的钥匙。而图画书中圆形叙事脚本这一趣味呈现，更有效率发挥了虚构性脚本在认知启蒙上的文学价值。

3 可能的认知壁垒与出路

图画书虚构性叙事脚本帮助儿童形成认识世界的高效认知模式，为其提供处理多样信息的认知框架，能够很大程度上提高其认知效率及准确性，从而认知能力得以提升。但与此同时，成形、固化的模式也容易导致过早得出结论，引起偏见、认知偏差乃至认知壁垒的产生。

以圆形虚构性叙事脚本为例，不断重复的脚本，在儿童读者头脑中固化为循环式的认知图式，固然便利了儿童对于世界的认知、接受与适应，但同时也将一种固定套路灌输进了儿童原本无限开放、无限可能的认知潜能中。认知能力的提升是一项终身事业，儿童要学会在约定俗成的认知模式与开放式的认知路径之间寻找平衡，才能在不同的认知发展阶段始终得以提升，否则前期积累的“高效”认知模式则更多地成为认知壁垒。

而打破认知壁垒、走出认知局限的出路便是更多脚本的接纳、更多认知模式的迭代组合，持续的阅读便是扩展认知边界的重要手段之一。内化的脚本形成的认知模式不是固定不变的，而是根据新的经验加以修改、完善以更适应现实需求。美国教育心理学家、认知心理学家杰罗姆·布鲁纳（Jerome Bruner，1990）也在研究中指出，儿童的认知能力、语言能力、社交能力都可以通过阅读获得提升。就儿童读者而言，可持续地提升认知能力一方面需要自身的不断阅读，另一方面也需要成年人的通力配合。儿童文学创作者不妨在考虑儿童接受度的情况下，尝试更多有趣、有效的叙事脚本创新，为儿童提供更多的认知可能性。家长则需要鼓励儿童大量阅读。儿童读者通过大量阅读，不断吸收、兼容并包，囊括更多的模式，从而使自己更加包容，对世界的认识也就更全面而不偏颇。

4 结 语

正如斯托克维尔（Stockwell，2005：6）所言，认知诗学是一种思考文学的方式。对于儿童文学而言，十分重要的一个侧面就是思考人类积累的诸项知识（从科学技术类知识到意识形态类知识）如何透过文学语言得以表达。本文在尼古拉耶娃提出的“文学作品提供虚构性知识（主要指审美知识）”的基础上，将文学语言提供的知识扩展为常识知识、伦理知识以及审美知识，提出图画书虚构性叙事脚本作为图画书知识资源的存在方式能够通过传递这三类知识从而使得儿童更深刻地认识现实物理世界、伦理世界及美学世界。其中，圆形虚构性叙事脚本因其重复、循环的特质，兼具趣味性和教育性，向儿童传递了认识世界、认识人生的有效认知模式，对于其认知世界、承担人生责任发挥了特殊的认知启蒙作用。

虽然本文就虚构性叙事脚本此类认知模式可能带来的壁垒提出了解决建议，然而就虚构性文学叙事脚本的跨文化传递而言，仍有许多问题值得考虑。例如，不同文化间默认的社会规范、生活习惯不同，其传递的知识资源是否不同？认知脚本是否不同？如果确有不同，对于译入语文化来说，是否比较难以产生共鸣？虚构性叙事脚本的认知启蒙作用是否还存在？若从最大程度发挥图画书的认知价值考虑，翻译中应强调原作叙事性脚本的文化特殊性还是文化通约性？随着这些问题的解答，相信学界对于图画书虚构性叙事脚本的认知启蒙价值将会有更深入的了解。

参考文献

[1] J BRUNER. Acts of Meaning. Cambridge: Harvard University Press, 1990.

[2] P HOLMER. C. S. Lewis: The Shape of His Faith and Thought. New York: Harper and Row, 1976.

[3] D C KIDD, C EMANUELE. Reading Literary Fiction Improves Theory of Mind. Science, 2013, 342 (6156): 377-380.

[4] M NIKOLAJEVA. Reading for Learning: Cognitive Approaches to Children’s Literature. Amsterdam/Philadelphia: John Benjamins Publishing Company, 2014.

[5] L NUMEROFF. If You Give a Mouse Series [EB/OL]. [2021-09-16] https: //www. kidsbookseries. com/if-you-give-a-mouse/

[6] P STOCKWELL. Cognitive Poetics: An Introduction. London and New York: Routledge, 2005.

[7] L ZUNSHINE. Why We Read Fiction: Theory of Mind and the Novel. Columbus: The Ohio State University Press, 2006.

[8] 劳拉·努梅罗夫. 要是你给老鼠吃饼干. 费利西娅·邦德, 绘. 杨玲玲, 彭懿, 译. 南宁: 接力出版社, 2017.

[9] 聂珍钊. 文学伦理学批评导论. 北京: 北京大学出版社, 2014.

[10] 朱光潜. 谈美. 北京: 北京大学出版社, 2008.

[11] 朱自强. 儿童文学概论. 北京: 高等教育出版社, 2009.

认知转向：儿童文学研究的新趋势

江璧炜

【摘要】本文厘清了文学研究领域认知转向的一些基础学理问题，梳理并剖析了国际儿童文学学界认知研究的基本走向，以成长研究为例指出该理论方法引入中国儿童文学研究领域的拓展可能性，意图为中国儿童文学的认知批评发展廓清道路。
【关键词】认知文学研究；认知批评；认知方法；儿童文学；跨学科

认知文学研究是一个伞形的学术概念，是从认知科学中汲取理论范式和话语资源的多种文学流派的一个集合。它从认知诗学这一流派和研究范式发端，已经发展出包括认知修辞学、认知叙事学、认知文化学在内的多种流派，可谓蔚为大观。与以往的跨学科不同，认知文学研究的理论资源来自认知科学这一前沿的仍在发展中的交叉学科，陌生而新颖的自然科学研究范式宛如巨石坠入学海激起众多学者的热议和关注，其中自然包括儿童文学研究界的有识之士。认知文学研究被引入儿童文学领域后，国际儿童文学学界多称之为认知研究（cognitive approach）或认知批评（cognitive criticism）。本文试图在厘清这一领域的一些基本状况的基础上，关注这一理论方法引入我国儿童文学研究的必要性与可行性。

1 文学领域的认知转向

随着 1977 年《认知科学》的创刊，1979 年认知科学学会在美国

作者简介：江璧炜，男，兰州大学文学院中国现当代文学研究所博士研究生，主要研究方向为儿童文学认知批评。

成立，以及1986年加州大学圣地亚哥分校成立世界上第一个认知科学系，随后与之相关的研究计划和学术机构接踵而至，一个致力于破解人类心智奥秘的跨学科领域——认知科学正式诞生（孟伟，2015：1）。它的研究内容包括感知、记忆、行动、语言、推理在内的人类心智活动，囊括了计算机科学、脑神经科学、语言学、心理学、生物学等学科的理论话语和研究方法。自其产生以来，认知科学至今已历经了三次革新，其研究范式主要从最初的信息加工认知理论，到联结主义认知理论，再转变为当下的具身认知理论。有学者认为它并非一门学科，而是多个学科的复杂合集；也有学者认为它看似松散，但形成了学科应有的某些框架和概念，但这两类对立观念都认为对心智的探索以及对科学方法的使用是认知科学的重要特征。笔者倾向于将认知科学视为一门还在完善阶段的学科，因为它虽有明确的研究对象，但在现阶段还未能展现出相对独立的学科话语体系，它的研究方法多为从其他学科的直接拿取或学科间的相互作用。不过，这并不影响认知科学的发展，正如劳拉·索斯伯瑞（Luara Salsbury）所说，“由于认知科学日益成为理解人类自身的一种主导性研究范式，因此，运用它的知识来形成阐释人类文化产品的各种方式也就越来越有影响力”（熊沐清，2019）。

认知科学的兴起引发了众多学科的“认知转向”，这种影响几乎遍及整个人文社科领域。认知诗学就是最先在语言与文学领域发端的交叉学科研究，以鲁汶·楚尔（Reuven Tsur）为首位提出者，彼得·斯托克维尔（Peter Stockwell）、玛格丽特·弗雷曼（Margaret Freeman）、乔安娜·盖文斯（Joanna Gavins）杰拉德·斯蒂恩（Gerard Steen）等为代表人物。此外，当下还包括以埃琳娜·塞米诺（Elena Semino）、乔纳森·库帕（Jonathan Culpeper）为代表的认知文体学、以马克·特纳（Mark Tuner）、乔治·莱考夫（George Lakoff）为代表的认知修辞学，以大卫·赫尔曼（David Herman）为代表的认知叙事学，以丽萨·詹塞恩（Lisa Zunshine）为代表的认知文化研究等。它们共享的理论源头均来自认知科学，都具有显著的探索人类“认知”与“心智”的特征，因此相当一批学者将这些文学领域运用认知科学相关理论范式的研究称为认知文学研究。它“是文学文本的一种批评分析模式（a mode of critical analysis），它的基本前提是这样的信念：心智及其推理过程，以及它的文化产品和情感经验，可以用生物的和进化的理论框架加以系统地分析”（熊沐清，2015）。

弄懂认知文学研究，我们必须厘清这样几个关键问题：

我们谈论“认知”和“认知转向”是在谈论什么？认知文学研究，或者说认知批评、认知研究等名称往往会引起人的误解，原因在于“认知”这一称谓的模糊性。“认知”是一个宽泛的术语，指的是“对使行为可以理解的活跃的（基本上是无意识的）心理过程的压倒性兴趣……”（Richardson，2004：2）。对某件事、某个人的思考，与本体论相对的认识论，往往是人们对“认知”的一般理解。然而“认知文学研究”等概念中的“认知”，必须关联以科学的方法来解释人是如何进行思考和感知的，它的理论话语必须建基在认知科学这一新兴的、仍在不断拓展的跨学科领域之上。“认知转向”就是以认知科学的视域对文学进行重新审视。

认知文学研究与以往的文学研究方法最显著的差异在哪里？首先，认知文学研究依赖于科学，运用诸多自然科学的研究手段。理查德森（Alan Richardson）和斯蒂恩（Francis F. Steen）指出，文学研究和认知科学共享对语言、精神行为和语言艺术品的共同兴趣，但对类似的阅读、想象参与和文本模式形成的现象有着明显不同的反应。“许多文学理论家和评论家一直在不断地工作，通过与认知科学中的一个或多个领域的对话来寻找灵感、方法和指导范式：人工智能、认知心理学、后霍姆斯基语言学、心理哲学、神经科学，进化生物学。”（Richardson & Steen，2002）人们试图以科学来为人文学科提供更多可能。其次，认知文学研究是一个伞形的话语和方法集合，囊括了众多认知文学流派和研究方法。这些流派之间可能共享一些资源和范式，但仍存在各自偏重的研究内容和方法。丽萨·詹塞恩（Zunshine，2015：3）在《认知文学研究的牛津手册》（*The Oxford Handbook of Cognitive Literary Studies*）中指出：“例如像神经美学、认知叙事学和新无意识，无论是在认知科学的研究领域，还是在它们发展的理论范式方面，几乎没有共同之处。”同时，以往的一些心理学或现象学可能涉及认知科学中包括的概念，文学研究也可能在某些方面运用了相关的范式，但并没有像认知文学研究这样以认知科学这一概念统摄丰富多样的研究行为。

认知文学研究的突破性表现在哪些方面？其一，认知文学研究是科学与文学的积极联姻，认知科学对人脑工作机制的探索，是解释文学活动发生的重要科学依据。将认知科学领域的一些理论资源和研究范式引入文学研究，比如科学实验的即时数据记录和对比，相较于以往一些印象式的文学分析，能提供更权威以及更精确的支撑。其二，以认知诗学、认知符号学为代表的研究流派和范式同时关注符号所联结的生理和文化信息，并打通了整个文学活动。斯托克维尔（Stockwell，2002：5）指出，认知诗学不局限于文学活动的某一点上，而是对作者、文本、读者三者之间都有所覆盖，并且“认知诗学从心理学和语言学两个维度，提供了一种讨论阐释的方法，无论它是世界的一个权威版本还是一个现成解释，也不管这些解释是如何在文本方面表现出来。从这个意义上说，认知诗学不仅是重心的转移，而且是对文学活动整个过程的彻底重新评价”。其三，认知文学研究的各种理论范式具有零散性，但中心都是为解答心智和认知机制，这使得它具有足够的灵活性与其他方面的理论进行结合，比如女性主义、生态主义等多个领域，可以在这些理论话语的语境中进一步探讨认知问题。赫尔曼（Herman，2007）就表明认知科学研究能帮助叙事学“后经典”研究方法更深入地展开。

认知文学研究有哪些被质疑的问题？冯军（2019）在《认知转向：文学研究的新机遇》一文中提到了当下国际上拉斯·博纳尔兹（Lars Bernaerts）等人概括的三种批判：一是“忽视传统（blindness to tradition）”。一些学者如莱恩（Marie-Laure Ryan）认为认知文学研究得出的结论可能是传统文学理论已经知道或不证自明的结论，还不能呈现具有新意的研究结果。二是“折中主义（调和主义）（eclecticism）”。认知文学研究是人文与科学的某种集合，显示出了博采众长的优点，但令人尴尬的是它和认知科学一样，缺乏一套系统而独立的理论话语和框架。各种理论拼贴在一起让人眼花缭乱，却很有可能并不兼容。三是“还原主义（reductionism）、极简主义（essentialism）”。认知文学研究中的认知脑神经研究等实证方法将文学活动简单化和还原了。这些科学方法将一种审美的艺术活动，变成了可精确推导的实验结果，抽取了个体、时代、地域以及社会差异，漠视了人的审美体验。冯军以极为包容的态度一一反驳了上述质疑，认为认知文学研究和传统文学并非简单的继承关系，两者侧重点不同。“认知研究范式与传统文学范式更大程度上是一种互补的关系，是对传统范式的‘认知升级’。”（冯军，2019）作为时代产物出现的认知科学还在不断地完善阶段，理应积极地看待它当前话语建构的缺陷。认知文学研究也不会变成“生物主义”中心论，它聚焦于人类的高级认知活动，只会在科学的帮助下深化“文学性”的相关研究。年轻的认知文学研究确实存在着不够成熟的事实，它还需要一定的时间去探索，但这并不妨碍学者们从认知科学中汲取灵感，为文学研究寻找新的可能。

2 儿童文学的认知批评实践

随着认知文学研究的蓬勃发展，国际儿童文学界积极聚焦这一文学的“认知转向”。他们理性看待认知文学研究中的部分争议，试图寻找认知文学研究与儿童文学这门学科的贴合性。投身其中的学者们惊喜地发现，认知文学研究能够帮助他们解决以往的某些困惑。比如，文学文本的意识形态究竟是如何影响儿童读者的？儿童读者是如何从作品中获取知识和培养自己的阅读技能的？落实于认知科学的认知文学研究让这些问题变得逐渐清晰起来。认知文学研究的潜力最先由儿童文学著名学者、前国际儿童文学研究会会刊主编约翰·斯蒂芬斯（John Stephens）挖掘出来，他将认知科学中的图式脚本理论引入儿童文学，用来考察他一直关注的意识形态传达问题。在图式脚本理论之后，映射、概念整合、概念隐喻、可能世界、具身认知等理论范式和概念术语陆续进入儿童文学批评领域，涉及文本改编、青少年主体建构、文学教育与阅读技能等问题，覆盖图画书、儿童诗、童话、儿童小说和青少年小说等多种文体。《儿童文学协会季刊》(*Children's Literature Association Quarterly*)于2018年9月开辟特刊以讨论认知方法在儿童文学上的应用，指出认知方法跨认知科学、语言学、教育，以及更多传统文学研究方法如叙事学、读者反应等，以形成关于读者和观众新的知识类型。这一特刊开辟的目的是旨在产出对认知方法对学界做出的贡献的最前沿概观。国外著名出版社约翰·本杰明斯(John Benjamins)推出了名为“儿童文学，文化与认知”(Children's Literature，Culture and Cognition，CLCC)的系列丛书，从2013年至2018年出版了10本，收录了包括玛丽亚·尼古拉杰娃(Maria Nikolajeva)、罗伯塔·塞林格·特瑞兹(Roberta Seelinger Trites)等在内的学术名家的作品。可以说，认知文学研究在儿童研究领域体现出了覆盖面广、黏合度强、认可度高的特点，以一种积极的进取姿态努力拓宽和加深了儿童文学的研究视域，呈现出儿童文学研究的新趋势。

总的来看，儿童文学的认知批评在实际应用上具体表现为如下特征：

第一，在进入文本具体分析的层面，可归纳为三种对“认知”的阐释模式，分别对应的是文本创作者和接受者的认知、文本人物形象的认知，以及同时包含前面两者。斯蒂芬斯最早在儿童文学领域尝试认知批评，其文章《图式和脚本：儿童文学中的认知工具和文化多样性的表征》(*Schemas and Scripts: Cognitive Instruments and the Representation of Cultural Diversity in Children's Literature*)主要以此来解释真实或隐含的儿童读者是如何与文本互动的，这成为儿童文学领域认知批评的主要模式。这篇文章以图画书为例，意在说明儿童文学一直试图介入不断发展变化的社会文化，从而肯定人类权利和人类平等的文化多元模式，而这一目标的实现就是在儿童文学文本中努力改变以往西方文化中常见图式和脚本的中心部分，从而使读者自身的图式和脚本进行更新或重建，进而影响读者对文本意义的创建，这一过程对于实现儿童文学多元表征是至关重要的

（Stephens，2011）。斯蒂芬斯用图式和脚本这种认知结构解释了阅读意义的获得以及文本传递意识形态的重要性，这一观点为后续学者打开了思路。在《青少年推理小说中的正义：一种认知阅读》（*Justice in Young Adult Speculative Fiction: A Cognitive Reading*）一书中，奥兹伊维茨（Marek C. Oziewicz，2015：9-10）也认为，“可以从作者的认知角度、读者的认知角度，或者作为隐含作者和隐含读者的文本来研究脚本”。对此，玛琳·奥克斯特兰德（Malin Alkestrand）和克里斯特佛·阿文（Christopher Owen）在《瑞典语和英语儿童幻想文学中人物的认知分析》（*A Cognitive Analysis of Characters in Swedish and Anglophone Children's Fantasy Literature*）一文中认为，斯蒂芬斯和奥兹伊维茨提出的方法存在使读者同质化的可能，即所有读者往往被视为一个无差别的实体。实际上，可以着眼于文本中的人物角色，对人物形象的认知层面进行考察，避免同质化的弊端。（Alkestrand & Owen，2018）这篇文章分别以瑞典语和英语的幻想小说为例，通过聚焦对文本中主角人物的认知，分析人物角色对其交叉主体位置的具身认知怎样推动文本情节和主题的发展。当然，一些研究认识到这两种阐释方式都具有合理性，比如在《将母性视为成熟：洛伊丝·劳里的〈儿子〉中的成熟脚本》（*Understanding Motherhood as Maturation: Maternity Scripts in Lois Lowry's Son*）一文中，作者一方面指出小说《儿子》中的女主角克莱尔从缺乏“母性”概念到逐渐觉醒——这是推动叙事的关键；另一方面指出读者正是通过概念隐喻这一认知机制实现对“母性”概念的理解（Deszcz-Tryhubczak & Marecki，2015）。由于母性经验尚未或者说有可能永远不会植根于一些读者的具身认知，读者只能寻求一个降级策略。《儿子》正是提供了概念隐喻“母性是成熟”，让读者从“成熟”这一概念来理解“母性”，实现了意义的传达。

第二，认知批评一方面和其他理论话语整合在一起，是对理论如何得以在认知层面具体运作的进一步阐释；另一方面也可能摒弃以往的理论呈现出截然对立的观念。这类研究往往从人类的认知机制和结构层面拓宽了以往的话语批评空间，并呈现出具有新意的成果。斯蒂芬斯（Stephens，2015）的文章《青少年小说中的认知映射和社会生态学》（*Cognitive Maps and Social Ecology in Young Adult Fiction*）通过认知地图和生态系统理论的联结为审视青少年小说提供了一种建设性的方法。生态系统理论和人类的认知映射机制对空间问题的共同聚焦，使得对于探究青少年小说中人物角色如何利用认知映射来理解自身与周围环境的关系、理解自我在世界中的位置起到了重要作用。玛丽·安妮·珊达（Mary Anne Shonda，2012）的文章《隐喻和互文：元功能幻想小说互文意义生成的认知研究》（"Metaphor and Intertextuality：A Cognitive Approach to Intertextual Meaning-Making in Metafictional Fantasy Novels"），指出儿童文学的学者们经常讨论互文性产生的幽默效果和意识形态功能，但未能说明人类的认知过程如何在互文性阐释中起作用。作者从隐喻研究领域和认知诗学的交叉领域中获取灵感，认为互文性阐释与隐喻性表达的认知机制是类似的。人类大脑中的隐喻阐释模型与不同的互文本一起工作，服务于不同的叙事功能，作者以幻想小说为例进行了相关阐释。相较于前面的研究，克伦·寇特（Karen Coats，2013）的《儿童诗的意义：一种认知方法》（*The Meaning of Children's Poetry：A Cognitive Approach*）一文则借助认知方法，批判了过往成人精英主义立场对儿童诗的偏见和矮化，提出一种全新的对于诗歌的模式转变，即从"儿童诗做了什么"而不是"儿童诗是什么"来进行审视，把儿童诗理解为孩子的使用而不是某种形式或解释。儿童诗营造了语言中的持有环境，帮助儿童管理感官环境，规范他们的神经功能，遏制他们的生存焦虑。孩子们的诗不是用语言代替感觉，而是通过强烈的节奏和声音唤起孩子的感官对象，从而将身体带入语言，从世界中的身体转变成语言中的身体。

第三，在儿童文学极为关注的阅读实践和教育问题上提供了必要支撑。这类研究对于儿童文学来说具有特殊意义，由于儿童文学自带的广义教育属性使其对儿童读者与文本之间的交流问题格外注意。儿童读者在阅读过程中是如何获得文本意义的？儿童读者能在阅读中习得哪些知识和文学阅读技巧？儿童文学著名学者玛丽亚·尼古拉杰娃（Maria Nikolajeva，2012）是关注此问题的代表人物，她谈及此类问题时指出，在以往的读者反应理论中读者是隐含的、被建构的，认知研究则关注无论是隐含的还是真实的读者，或者说两者的区别在认知研究这里并不重要。由神经科学支持的认知研究能帮我们用更科学、更精确的路径理解儿童文学的阅读是如何发生，以及阅读对儿童读者究竟会产生怎样的作用。她的文章《儿童文学的愧疚感，移情和伦理潜能》（“Guilt，Empathy and the Ethical Potential of Children's Literature”）基于最新的大脑研究，探讨了读者对文学的认知和情感参与的研究方向。文章认为，对于尚未充分理解基本道德问题的少年儿童来说，他们还没有达到理解虚构人物心理过程所必需的文学能力，文学作品中的情感表征可能会产生问题。文章指出文学为少年儿童读者发展移情技能提供了良好的培训领域，而内疚的替代体验暴露了读者广泛的伦理问题（Maria Nikolajeva，2012）。她在专著《为了学习的阅读——儿童文学的认知方法》（*Reading for Learning*: *Cognitive approaches to children's literature*）中进一步展开，此书认为在承认文学和阅读在教育和社会化青少年的前提下，无论是对于新手读者还是专业读者而言，通过阅读小说都可以加强和加速读者的各种文学阅读技能。这方面的技能包括：文字与小说的连接能力、情感反应、推理能力、移情、复杂的语言能力、自我反思能力等（Nikolajeva，2014）。作者具体分析了少年儿童读者可能经由何种认知机制与文本进行交流从而实现自我的学习。

第四，认识到具身认知研究范式兼顾生物性和社会性，贴合了青少年儿童的身心发展特征。具身认知是认知科学的最新范式，主张人类的心智和认知与身体构造、身体运动息息相关。认知不能脱离身体，而是与身体，以及身体运动水乳交融、浑然一体。而作为社会中的人，其身体活动不能脱离社会，始终处于与他人交往并受其影响的过程中，因此具身认知必然包含社会性。在许多关注认知文学研究的儿童文学学者那里，具身认知或具身体验成为不言自明的论述基础。罗伯塔·塞林格·特瑞兹（Roberta Seelinger Trites，

2014）就曾在《成长的文学概念化：青少年文学中的隐喻和认知》（*Literary Conceptualizations of Growth: Metaphors and Cognition in Adolescent Literature*）一书中明确了具身体验与青少年的紧密关联。认知语言学家认为语言是具身性的，青春期概念是一种话语的建构从而也是具身的。同时，她指出青春期是感知身体变化最明显的时期，从而更能理解通过具身性来进行表达的文本语言。在承认具身性存在的基础上，正是概念隐喻这种认知过程，脚本、刻板印象等认知工具，记忆、感知和情感等心智功能，概念整合这一认知能力等因素，共同影响了青少年小说中成长概念的形成。比如作者或读者的认知脚本、刻板印象的使用往往是携带一定意识形态的，有时构成小说的情节，影响着文本的叙事意义和阅读效果。记忆、感知和情感是塑造小说中人物角色和叙事进展的重要元素，也是读者能够理解文本的重要心智功能。

3　认知批评促进中国儿童文学研究理论话语创新

国际儿童文学学界对认知批评的热情产生了一批可观成果，呈现了上述所言的诸种特征。可以看到，认知批评既展现了一般性文学研究的创新潜质，对于儿童文学研究来说也发挥了格外的优势。那么，认知文学研究何以能够促进中国儿童文学研究理论话语创新呢？

朱自强（2006）曾在《对中国儿童文学理论研究方法论的思考》中指出，除了一般文学持有的绝大多数研究方法，儿童哲学的方法、深层心理学的方法、人类文化学和童年历史学的方法是与儿童文学的特性十分贴合的四种主要研究方法。相较于以往这些主要研究方法，认知批评的重要性在于它从认知科学的层面不仅为我们演绎了包括读者——主要是儿童在内的文学要素在文学活动中的位置和参与的科学机制，而且展现了文学文本作为演绎的中心场域所发挥的作用。李利芳（2013）曾在文章《当前儿童文学理论批评建设的几点思考》中就敏锐地感受到儿童文学研究应“从细读文本入手”，同时“向自然科学学习”。前者“能使我们牢牢握定研究对象，真正切实地面对研究对象，具体细致地掌握与理解研究对象。作为人文科学的文学研究其根本路径是审美感受与价值体验，这奠定了其主观性的基本特质”。后者提供的“自然科学的科学精神，做科学实验时的态度与方法，科学研究的姿态与工作状态，对对象的无穷逼近、解剖，对真理的不懈探求等”让研究更为客观。从理论上讲，认知方法可以辐射到儿童文学的所有文学类型中展开研究，因为认知方法以人类的心智和认知研究为出发点，其研究成果以助推人类的认知发展为目标。儿童经由故事形成认知结构，儿童认知能力的阶段性差异在儿童文学中都有对应体现。引入认知方法研究我国儿童文学，使得针对提升儿童认知能力的文学策略的实施更为切实具体，分级阅读的材料组织也更有学理依据与针对性。反之，作家根据不同年龄儿童认知水平及发展任务的要求，在文学设计中操作认知图式与脚本也更有科学依据，以使作品的可接受度更高。

我们可以以成长研究为例具体探讨认知批评引入我国儿童文学研究能够在哪些方面展开。成长是儿童文学常见的书写内容，也是教育者对少年儿童最广泛谈及的现实关切。对儿童文学中成长的研究主要可分为两类：一是对成长小说这一文类进行考察。曹文轩曾大力提倡成长小说的写作，在文章《论“成长小说”》中表明成长在少儿文学书写中的必要性，以及成长小说能够更合理地满足未成年人中高年龄段孩子的阅读需求。（赵郁秀，2002：135-153）张国龙（2013）致力于成长小说研究，在专著《成长小说概论》中以上、中、下三篇以及外篇对成长小说进行了总体性评述，包括本体特征辨析，概念厘清、叙述的基本结构模式等。二是对小说中的成长主题进行分析。如李学武（2003）的《蝶与蛹——中国当代小说成长主题的文化考察》一书涉及的文本包括成人文学和儿童文学，以“成长主题”为切入点对当代小说进行历时性的梳理与考察，探索新中国成立后小说中“成长主题”的嬗变过程呈现了怎样的成长书写以及成长叙事被怎样的社会文化因素所影响。但细数当下儿童文学成长研究的大多数文章，对“成长”的言说越来越泛化，真正有新意的论述并不多。认知批评的引入可以在这样一些方面拓展关于成长的研究空间：

第一，阐释文本的成长观念如何抵达读者。

大多数书写成长的儿童小说存在一个类型化的成长模式，特别是经典成长小说，往往书写青少年在与世界的互动对话中获取人生经验，增长见识，在身心方面共同成长。这种成长模式多次反复强化就成为一种有关成长的认知脚本。脚本（script）是解释了一系列项目或行为是如何被期待展开的长时记忆结构。奥兹伊维茨（Oziewicz，2011）就认为，“脚本是一种记忆结构，以及范式化的故事，用来存储我们对特定情况知识的一种方式……它们构成了人类理解的基础”。脚本往往能够被人们共同识别，比如“吃饭”脚本、“看书”脚本、“外星人造访地球”脚本，等等。斯托克维尔（Stockwell，2002：78）指出“一个脚本包含种种假定与这种情形有关的缺省（slot），除非我们已经被明确地告诉了如道具、参与者、发生条件、结果、事件序列这些东西”。这意味着即使简单的脚本也包含了丰富的信息，具有延伸和变化的可能。人们正是通过识别脚本达到交流的目的。因此，当读者们在阅读中摄入并不完整的成长脚本中的某个元素，他们也很有可能立马意识到这是一个有关成长的故事，从而引发相关思考。当然，叙事中脚本的变动很可能影响读者自身认知脚本的建构，斯蒂芬斯（Stephens，20110：12-35）认为作者在文本中改变某一特定脚本核心部分会使读者自身脚本进行更新或重建，进而影响读者对文本意义的创建。以此来观察当下许多青少年儿童喜爱的读物，就可以发现一些看似书写“成长”的作品并未真正彰显成长的精神，如“斗罗大陆”系列小说，这一在网络上有着超高人气的作品受到了许多少年儿童的追捧。以第一部《斗罗大陆》为例，该小说包含了常见的成长脚本，但成长脚本中最关键的“心理成长”元素被改写了。《斗罗大陆》第一部的主人公唐三是拥有完整记忆且穿越为新世界儿童的成人，这一设定决定了他在从幼童成长为成人过程中的心理成熟在一开始就已经满足了。《斗罗大陆》更替了个人成长中最重要的心理成长，并且将成长脚本中的重要内容更替为不断获取武力值参与竞争，使其呈现了狭隘的权力至上观念。《斗罗大陆》这类网络小说在很大程度上联结着年轻一代确立自身价值立场、建构身份认同的强烈愿望，通过认知批评可以科学深入地挖掘出这些文本何以呈现出狭隘偏执的内涵，以及这一“反成长”的价值取向又是如何可能影响读者的。

第二，明确具身体验在成长书写中的重要意义。

成长书写始终是和少年儿童的具身（embodied）体验密切相关的。“莱可夫等人（1980）早就指出，心智在本质上是基于身体的，人类的抽象思维并不是凭借抽象符号而进行的信息加工。抽象思维主要是隐喻的”，“莱可夫（2012）认为那些基本的隐喻都是一种具身的体验。这些具身的体验经常、反复的出现，就构成了我们的思维方式”（叶浩生，2017：50）。认知可以影响身体行为，身体经验也会对认知产生波动，同时这一身体性的行为感知也因其发生在社会文化场域中而具有文化性。懵懂无知的婴幼儿对身体的探索多来自成人的教育，而童年时期出现对身体的关注一般来说也不会过于强烈，自觉地、有意识地去探索身体多开始于青春期，这最关键的原因就是因为在他们发展出足够的认知水平后，意识到了自身身体正在发生显著的变化。可以说，正是青少年的身体变化以及对现实中身体的关注要求作家能对青少年的具身体验进行清晰的体察，同时将具身体验合理地置于青少年文学的书写当中。这表现在儿童文学中，最明显的就是对身体体验与自我主体形成之间关系的观照，认知批评可以指导我们对这一现象展开更具体的研究。如初潮常常是女作家们用以宣告少女角色告别童年、进入另一个生命阶段的标志。殷健灵就将这一宣告描绘得极其富有诗意。在《纸人》中，少女苏了了初潮的到来既是其成长过程中迈向青春期的关键，也是文本叙事中的节点。作家将寂静的冬天里苏了了周围的一切的细节放大，其眼所见，其耳所听，都是女主角内心的投射，由此烘托出例假这件事的发生对其内心所产生的非比寻常的震动，让这个十三岁的少女发出“让你像是不再属于自己”（殷健灵，2013：36）这样的感慨。特别是作家让“邻居家新生命的啼哭”（殷健灵，2013：36）出现在苏了了第一次例假后对周围的感知范围中，象征着苏了了另一层次生命状态的苏醒和诞生。莱考夫和约翰逊在谈及具身化的概念隐喻时指出，空间方位概念的基本元素“上—下”“中央—外围”等是构建人类其他概念的基础，情绪昂扬“向上”则是快乐的表现，反之则是低落悲伤（莱考夫，2015：14），“能否真正理解这些概念取决于人们是否能够理解人自身的身体”（袁小婷、叶浩生，2018）。当处于身心变化中的少年儿童读者阅读到这一部分，很容易对苏了了这一由自己为中心向周围辐射开来的拓展性的觉知感同身受，并在无意识间领略到一种积极情绪的隐喻。无论是苏了了这一少女形象，还是现实中的读者，他们对生命新层次的认识都是来自身体的积极参与。

第三，探究成长相关概念在时代社会中的恒与变。

在认知心理学家看来，图式（schema）是输入并存储在人脑中的一般性世界知识，是大脑对已有经验的反映或组织。人们在一定的语境下激活图式，并调用这种图式知识帮助自身理解和处理当前情况。通俗地来讲，就是利用人已有的稳定的知识结构积极地与现有信息进行结合，帮助认知和判断。斯蒂芬斯（Stephens，2011：12-35）指出，“一个图式通常由构成部分的网络组成，而且通过激发唤起了网络和它的相互关系，特别是关于这个网络的普通的和典型的东西。一个图式通过（a）命名而实例化，或者通过（b）引用一系列构成部分而实例化”。图式是一种认知工具也是一种表征工具，用图式去创作，必然会代入作家本人的文化、时代背景和意识形态，而这往往是无意识的。读者在接受的过程中也很可能会受这种文化、时代背景和意识形态的影响。图式成为观照时代背景、文化背景和意识形态的重要工具。少年儿童小说呈现了与“成长”相关的一些认知图式，通过对这些图式的历时性梳理，可以挖掘这些图式中的变化内容与稳定性框架的内涵、生成的原因。了解时代社会和文化因素如何影响了作者对这些问题的认知，从而影响少年小说的创作与读者对这些问题的理解。常新港是自新时期以来就辛勤耕耘的儿童文学作家，且对青少年的成长问题持续关注。常新港创作了他独特的青草意象，反复多次出现的青草成为认识他笔下不同时段、不同地域成长书写的关键图式。在早期刻画北大荒青少年成长的《青草的骨头》《青春的荒草地》中，青草图式的核心内容是平民草根以及不竭的生命力。在后来书写都市青少年成长的《灵魂草场之旅》《空气是免费的》中，青草又被赋予洁净、自由的意味。尽管青草图式始终为描绘青少年如何与不合理的成人社会抗争和积极成长而服务，是常新港设置的一个理想之物，但前者控诉的是那个混乱的年代和社会，后者则具体指向不合理的教育机制。青草图式的不同内涵，表征着不同的成长。

出于对现实青少年儿童成长的关心，儿童文学研究领域十分关注文学文本如何推动和促进读者的成长与主体建构，关注作者观念与文本意义如何与读者进行有效沟通，因此对科学理解文学交流模式的需求更为迫切。而实际上，这一部分在中国儿童文学的研究领域还并未得到足够的开发，认知文学研究在此呈现了拓展的可能。

认知文学研究给文学领域带来了思想革新，进一步推动了文学理论自身的发展，对于儿童文学这门学科而言，更是带来了贴合学科自身特性的研究契机。现今，认知文学研究相关理论方法在我国已成为学术界的热点，但就我国的儿童文学研究领域而言，这一研究方法才刚崭露头角。需要明确的是，绝对完美的理论方法并不存在，任何理论方法都具有进步的空间，理论的真实活力来自理性冷静的学术实践。因此我们在积极引进这一年轻的跨学科研究方法的同时，必须不断审查，避免对新方法新范式的生搬硬套和匆忙嫁接。总之，将认知文学研究引入中国儿童文学领域，是我们展开中西儿童文学研究对话的有力举措，也是儿童文学研究与成人文学研究进行互相印证的一个积极尝试，更是我们推动自身理论建构和学科建设的重要路径。

参考文献

[1] M ALKESTRAND, C OWEN. A Cognitive Analysis of Characters in Swedish and Anglophone Children’s Fantasy Literature. International Research in Children's Literature, 2018, 11: 65-79.

[2] K COATS. The Meaning of Children’s Poetry: A Cognitive Approach.

International Research in Children's Literature, 2013, 6 (2): 127-142.

[3] J DESZCZ-TRYHUBCZAK, M MARECKI. Understanding Motherhood as Maturation: Maternity Scripts in Lois Lowry's Son. Children's Literature in Education, 2015, 46: 190-205.

[4] D HERMAN. Storytelling and the Sciences of Mind: Cognitive Narratology, Discursive Psychology, and Narratives in Face-to-Face Interaction. Narrative, 2007, 17: 306-334.

[5] M NIKOLAJEVA. Guilt, Empathy and the Ethical Potential of Children's Literature. Barnboken, 2012, 35: 1-13.

[6] M NIKOLAJEVA. Reading for Learning, Cognitive Approaches to Children's Literature. Amsterdam, Philadelphia: John Benjamins Publishing Company, 2014.

[7] M OZIEWICZ. Restorative Justice scripts in Ursula K. Le Guin's Voices. Children's Literature in Education, 2011, 42: 33–43.

[8] A RICHARDSON. Studies in Literature and Cognition: A Field Map //Richardson, A. & E. Spolsky, eds. The Work of Fiction: Cognition, Culture, and Complexity. Aldershot: Ashgate, 2004.

[9] A RICHARDSON. & F. F. Steen. Literature and the Cognitive Revolution. Poetics Today, 2002, 23: 1-8.

[10] P STOCKWELL. Cognitive Poetics: An Introduction. London: Routledge, 2002.

[11] P STOCKWELL. Cognitive Poetics: An introduction. London: Routledge, 2002: 78.

[12] J STEPHENS. Schemas and Scripts: Cognitive Instruments and the Representation of Cultural Diversity in Children's Literature// Mallan, K. & C. Bradford, eds. Contemporary Children's Literature and Film. London: Palgrave Macmillan, 2011: 12-35.

[13] J STEPHENS. Cognitive Maps and Social Ecology in Young Adult Fiction. International Research in Children's Literature,

2015, 8: 142-155.
[14] R S TRITES. Literary Conceptualizations of Growth, Metaphors and Cognition in Adolescent Literature. Amsterdam, Philadelphia: John Benjamins Publishing company, 2014.
[15] L ZUNSHINE. The Oxford Handbook of Cognitive Literary Studies. New York: Oxford University Press, 2015.
[16] 冯军．“认知转向”：文学研究的新机遇.重庆社会科学，2019（4）：118-127.
[17] 李利芳．当前儿童文学理论批评建设的几点思考.学术界，2013（6）：34-41+282.
[18] 李学武．蝶与蛹 中国当代小说成长主题的文化考察.北京：中国社会科学出版社，2003.
[19] 孟伟．身体、情境与认知——涉身认知及其哲学探索.北京：中国社会科学出版社，2015.
[20] 乔治·莱考夫，马克·约翰逊．我们赖以生存的隐喻.何文忠，译．杭州：浙江大学出版社，2015：14.
[21] 熊沐清．外国文学研究“认知转向”评述.英美文学研究论丛，2019（2）：295-310.
[22] 熊沐清．文学批评的认知转向——认知文学研究系列之一．外国语文，2015，31（6）：1-9.
[23] 叶浩生．具身认知的原理与应用．北京：商务印书馆，2017：50.
[24] 殷健灵．纸人．北京：现代出版社，2013：36.
[25] 袁小婷，叶浩生．具身认知一体论：二元还是一元？．心理研究，2018，11（2）：100-105.
[26] 张国龙．成长小说概论．合肥：安徽大学出版社，2013.
[27] 赵郁秀．当代儿童文学的精神指向（第六届亚洲儿童文学大会文选 中英文本）．沈阳：辽宁少年儿童出版社，2002：135-153.
[28] 朱自强．对中国儿童文学理论研究方法论的思考．东北师大学报，2006（1）：80-86.

认知诗学“关键词”

认知女性主义文学批评

杜　坤

【摘要】女性主义文学批评在发展过程中广泛融合和吸收了从形式主义、马克思主义到新历史主义、后结构主义、文化批评等多种理论思路与方法，而认知女性主义批评作为认知文学研究中的一种范式，所依赖的学科背景、方法路径、研究内容大有不同。本文主要阐释认知女性主义文学批评的学理基础、研究问题、研究对象、研究方法和路径。结合具体的文学文本示例讨论认知女性主义批评所关注的主要问题，以期新的概念和方法拓展和深化女性主义文学批评研究。

【关键词】认知女性主义；性别差异；具身性；认知文学研究

伴随着近代科技和医学的发展，研究者们从心理学、生物学、解剖学、病理学、生理学、神经科学等多个学科角度论证和解释男女大脑功能差异和性别差异，以及诸如情感、记忆和学习等认知领域的研究发现。在此研究基础上，涌现出大量著作和文章，从性、性别、大脑、心智、感知等方面考察女性主义理论（Wilson，1998；Roberts，2007；Einstein，2007；Darlington，2009；Hines，2004；Fine，2010.），将当代女性主义理论的发展引入新的方向——认知女性主义（Cognitive feminism）。尽管女性主义学者强烈批判性别差异的存在，且心理学家研究证明男女性的大脑功能没有区别，

基金项目：国家社会科学基金项目“认知女性主义视域下美国南方女作家的社会焦虑研究”（19BWW074）的阶段性成果。

作者简介：杜坤，女，四川外国语大学博士生，讲师，主要从事英美文学、认知诗学和认知文学研究。

然而，倘若神经科学对大脑"性别差异"的一些新发现是无可辩驳的客观事实，女性主义批评的理论基石便会面临巨大挑战。因此，从认知科学、神经科学等学科视角重新考量和解释女性主义理论发展所带来的一系列科学的和社会文化的问题可以应对新的挑战。

1 认知女性主义简介

在 2015 年出版的《反对性别实践：巴斯克地区的政治想象》（*Marching against Gender Practice: Political Imaginings in the Basqueland*），作者约翰·帕特里克·林斯特罗斯（John Patrick Linstroth）在前言中阐明"我对女性主义与认知的关系理解为'认知女性主义'或'女性认知主义'（feminist cognitivism）"。他从认知人类学视角论述了性别身份，探讨"性别实践如何创造一个心智、认知和记忆的本体论和认识论框架以及结构化的实践模型"（xxvii）。然而从学理上讲，最为相关的研究是神经女性主义（Neurofeminism）。《神经女性主义：女性主义理论与认知科学的交叉问题》（*Neurofeminism: Issues at the Intersection of Feminist Theory and Cognitive Science*, 2012）是第一部将女性主义研究视角引入脑科学领域的论文集，明确提出将女性主义理论与认知科学研究结合。主要研究讨论四大问题：性与性别的差异、伦理道德、科学哲学和具身体验（embodiment）。由此可见，国外学者对认知科学、神经科学的视角考察女性主义的一些观点还是较为认可的，并在一定程度上积极推进。

20 世纪六七十年代，西方女性主义运动的第二次浪潮催生了女性主义文学批评和女性主义科学批评思想。随着女性主义对科学批判的加深，女性主义者提出要重新审视主流科学认识论和方法论，着重批评科学理论和实践中的男性中心主义，揭示其在科学事业中对女性经验的排斥与忽视。可以说，当代女性主义理论批评的矛头不仅仅局限于社会学和文化的层面，而且深入哲学和科学的层面，进一步从科学哲学角度支撑女性主义批评的论证。女性主义科学研究不仅回应了女性主义理论对性、性别和性别差异的质疑，而且还从女性主义和反激进主义等方面对身体、物质性、差异性、生物学和医学等方面产生了理论见解。从那时起，女性主义科学认识论与科学哲学就成为一个既定的研究领域，为女性主义神经科学研究提供了一定理论依据。

如果“没有几十年来女性主义对科学的介入，包括女性主义科学哲学、女性主义科学文化研究、女性主义对科学实践的批评以及女性主义关于性别和差异的理论等领域的大量学术研究，女性或其他边缘群体在不受歧视的情况下如何被纳入新的神经科学研究课题将不那么容易解决”（Bluhm et al.，2012：182）。神经科学研究为女性主义理论提供了宝贵的工具，它更深入地涉及世界的生物、地质、神经或物理模型（Wilson，2004：91）。所以，认知女性主义将研究基础建立在科学研究之上，可以得到最新的方法和新实验证据的批评和指正，因为诸如物理、化学、生物学、神经科学、认知科学等科学学科研究的可靠并富有成效的方法，源源不断地为研究提供着新的实验证据。同时，随着研究的深入和发展，认知女性主义研究的理论本身也可以依据自身不断修订，潜在的理论应用也会愈加广泛。当然还有其他非科学的理论依据也很重要，包括对经验的现象学描述、小说和故事中的叙述、对人类事件的历史描述等，从社会认知、认知人类学、经济学、哲学、历史等人文学科视角探索文化价值观、文化实践和制度如何塑造我们人类以及我们如何思考和行为。简言之，所有这些相关学科的解释方法和理论模型都得到了许多学科来源和方法证据的互涉支持。即使目前的认知科学和神经科学的研究成果不能断言它们是肯定的或绝对正确的，但是仍然可以从这些论据中得出试探性的结论，足以给出一个相对稳定的理论基础来推断认知女性主义所要关照的问题。

2 认知女性主义文学批评

众多文学批评者跨学科的研究都止步于人文学科内，对于科学领域内的研究成果知之甚少，即使是女性主义科学研究者也在一定程度上对文学与科学的结合持怀疑态度，而认知诗学和认知文学研究的出现则成功打破了学科间的藩篱。认知文学研究包括认知诗学、认知修辞学、认知文体学、认知叙事学、认知文化研究等范式。经过长期的孕育、发轫、生成和发展，现已衍生出认知生态批评、认知后殖民研究、认知女性主义、神经认知诗学、认知马克思主义、文学达尔文主义等范式或方法。认知女性主义文学批评旨在运用认知科学、神经科学等关于人类的性与性别、大脑与心智、感知与认知的研究成果的基础上，结合语言审美，重新审视传统女性主义文学批评关注的问题，阐释文学作品中人物各种类型的感知过程、性别与心智差异、具身情感和行为表达、记忆结构和语言操作、女性以及女同性恋的创作与阅读体验等等，探讨女性认知及其在文学、伦理道德、哲学上的文化力量。认知女性主义文学批评是一种“元批评”，它本身不是一套可以拿来就用的文本分析工具或技巧，而是一种立足于女性主义思想、运用认知科学相关学科理论、概念、方法和技术去分析文学活动、文学现象、文学产品、文学参与者（作家/演员和读者/观众）的文学观念和方法论聚合，旨在为文学研究和分析提供一种基于认知科学的女性主义立场、视域和路径。

女性主义文学批评和认知女性主义文学批评共同关注女性形象、女性阅读以及女性创作，针对（读者、作者、人物）情感与伦理道德、身份（种族、阶级）、性别等问题，从女性视角对文学作品进行解读，探讨文学作品中的女性意识，研究女性作家的立场、诉求、风格、视角等，努力发掘不同于男性的女性文学传统。不同之处在于研究问题和具体的研究方法。从文本的形式层面上讲，认知女性主义文学批评探讨了女性主义文学批评理论中没有关注到或关注不够的问题，如读者、作者、人物的意识和心智、思维风格等问题，采用认知语言学、认知文体学、认知叙事学的分析方法，结合女性主义叙事学、女性主义文体学的研究成果，从认知女性主义文体学（Cognitive Feminist Stylistics）和认知女性主义叙事学（Cognitive Feminist Narratology）角度解决心智在文本语言和叙事层面的表征形式，揭示语言背后的深层含义；对共同关注的问题，如《第二性》提出，至今仍是女性主义批评嘈杂纷争的问题，即男女两性性别差异的缘起和性别差异的内容以及情感研究和伦理道德等，再从认知角度重新分析进行“认知提升”，用认知科学的方法、手段（行为研究和实证研究）去解决文学中的认知问题。

由于认知女性主义是一种“元批评”，所以它的分析方法是一个开放性体系，修辞学的、文体学的、话语分析的、生态主义的、社会—历史的、叙事学的，不一而足，各种方法都能为其所用。在方法论上有两个原则：一是认知科学原则，即它采用的方法必须是源自认知科学、神经科学的。具体而言有两个方面：其一为形式研究，其二为意义研究。认知女性主义可以借鉴认知文体学、认知叙事学、认知诗学、认知修辞学的具体的文本分析方法对文本作形式研究，同时也可以借鉴认知科学中相关的理论方法，如心智理论（心智阅读）、社会认知、认知心理学、文学达尔文主义等，对文本以及文学活动提出某种意义阐释，这些理论方法为女性主义文学批评提供了强有力的分析工具，“他山之石，可以攻玉”，关键在于怎么运用这些理论。二是女性主义原则，任何方法的使用都应该服务于女性主义研究的目的和任务。如探讨情感、伦理道德在女性主义知识生产中的地位和作用，特别是在文本方法论中的地位和作用；可以依据认知文学批评的定量研究方法，考察具身性文本以及图像的力量以何种强度的身体方式感动观众，这种与文本分析不同的方式是对情感、具身性、伦理道德的定位考察，研究它们依赖的相互关系，据此，结合性别差异和社会语境等来阐释作品中性别歧视话语、女性体验、父权文化、男权思想等问题。

3　研究问题与视角探讨

认知女性主义文学批评虽然处于探索阶段，尚未形成系统的理论和方法，但是用认知批评方法重新审视文学、文化产品，深入探讨人类心智、性与性别等问题的发展势头逐步强劲，研究者越来越多。概括而言，与以往研究相比有两个新的特点：其一是与认知科学和神经科学的结合日益受到重视，因而给予了女性主义研究中的老生常谈的问题，如性别差异，一些新的、更科学的甚至是更符合人类认知的解释；其二是研究方法的多样性，对文学作品的定性研究方法和定量研究方法不再是文学研究者可望而不可即的研究领域。

3.1　具身性：身体、心智与情感

具身性是女性主义理论的核心问题，因为身体是性别差异的象征性建构的一个场所（Threadcraft，2016：207）。对于具身的女性主义者来说，他们发现身体可以被看作一个纯天然的产品，从根本上改变了将其置于社会的显著特点。（Young，2005）且越来越多的女性主义者从现象学的研究视角思考具身性，以对生命体的关注为基础，包括对女性怀孕、分娩和做母亲的生活体验的探究，也重新关注了我们作为有血有肉的人的体验（Schott，2010）。这是认知女性主义未来研究的主要方向之一：与生理学、药理学、进化理论、神经科学、认知科学等学科对生物性身体描述的结合将会对女性主义的身体理论产生重组作用，为探索“进入身体”“进入心智”提供新途径，使女性主义研究对身体、心智产生“更有活力”、更符合“生物性”和“社会文化性”描述。与传统女性主义文学批评的不同在于，认知女性主义文学批评更加注重挖掘身体体验背后的心智运作和情感表达，尤其是读者和人物，探讨人物对当前环境的感知、对过去事件的记忆以及对他人、对自己精神状态和性情的推断；读者如何将特定的文本细节解读为人物试图理解周围世界的信息，如何

从故事世界中的一个或多个角度对事件进行解释或概念化，等等；考察身体、心智以及情感在文本叙事和文体语言上的创新性表达，不再假设性别、种族、身份上的文化意义是任何特定叙事特征或语言效果的基础解释，而是试图处理它们之间相互关联、不断变化的关系。

聚焦语言如何将心智意识表征成身体状态，并进一步展现为具体情感，不失为一种新的研究视角。虽然 20 世纪 90 年代以来，具身性（embodiment）和物质性（corporeality）在女性主义的思考和研究中反复出现，对身体作为知识和经验问题的重新关注也凸显了对情感研究的新兴趣（Koivunen，2010）。但是，女性主义者对情感的研究仅定位于身体表征和描述方式对具身和身体物质的意义、知识和经验重要性，并没有采纳情感理论中心智具身性体验观点。情感作为“一种特殊的哲学工具”，试图通过“以心智和身体同时出现的形式”来弥合身心之间的分歧，“因为它们同时是心智的和身体的，也因为身体在情感体验中占据了中心位置”（Colombetti，2007）。因而，考察虚构人物语言、情感、身体、心智之间辩证表征关系是认知女性主义视角切入文本的一条途径。例如在《劝导》中，理查德森（Richardson，2002）认为简·奥斯汀转向了具身认识论，在描写段落和间接话语片段之间自由穿梭，这种方式不仅传达了意识的流动，也传达了意识的消逝。这样对主人公意识的创新表达方式既体现了对无意识心理活动和具身认知的新认识，也展现出一种表达意识体验变化的新模式。奥斯丁并没有使用太多有关身体器官的词汇，而是采用不同视角之间快速转换来表现具体的、紧张的情感。这样对文本细致深入的分析可以“阐明叙事是如何呈现虚构人物每时每刻的心理体验，以及这些体验是如何从人物对情境和事件的更广泛的认知和情感立场中获得的……人物在故事世界中行动和互动时的认知和情感状态、过程必须被理解为整个故事的核心事件或‘主旨’，而不是可以理解为从故事叙述中省略的可选的或次要的元素”

（Herman，2009：247）。

聚焦人物特殊情感状态如何通过语言和逻辑观点的表述来展现心智意识，或表征成身体状态，也不失为另一种新的研究视角。这些特殊的情感状态，尤其指具有创伤后应激障碍、焦虑症、抑郁症、边缘型人格障碍等在临床心理学中特定的疾病人群所展现出的情感。《住货车的女士》（*The Lady in the Van*）剧中的谢泼德小姐有明显的推理怪癖，源于她需要建立一种心理防御机制来对抗多年前无意造成一名摩托车手死亡的内疚感。麦金泰尔（McIntyre，2006）依据人物观点的语言构建的特质，考察人物视点（point of view）和心智风格（mind style）之间的关系。谢泼德小姐有缺陷的归纳推理是情感创伤产生的一种防御战术，这种策略的持续使用成为她性格的一个决定性方面，并产生了一种独特的思维风格：试图通过她所认为的逻辑推理来支持她的许多"论点"，而事实上她并没有完全理解逻辑论证是如何构建的，反映了她看待世界的方式和表现出来的思维方式如何运作以及她在文本世界的位置。在某种程度上，她对归纳逻辑的异常使用是一种真正的认知障碍。

如上述示例，对虚构作品的人物分析如同现实生活中的人物一样，首先应将对女性身体伤害或精神困扰的尊重导向女性自身的身体差异，而不是偏离男性标准或是种族、身份上的限制。在此基础上，把女性个人的心理或生物过程放在首位，定位健康身体的物理过程和思维的心理过程与社会结构之间的区别，这也是认知女性主义批评与传统女性主义批评的不同之处。

3.2 性别差异：大脑、语言、叙事

20世纪以前，男女两性的性别差异被看成一个客观事实，但在20世纪之后，在解构主义探索差异的语境中考察的是对差异的排斥，尤其是在女性主义精神分析中，"弗洛伊德专注于两性之间的'区别'（Entscheidung），拉康则关注两性之间的'关系'（rapport）"（Keates，

1992：403）。

在文学文本的研究中，针对语言和认知的关系，认知文体学家的贡献相对较多。再将性别差异纳入考量的范畴，他们更倾向于引入社会认知的相关研究，这样的跨学科互涉，会尽量避免一些研究者质疑文体学的认知发展：个人对文学的主观性解释凌驾于社会性之上（Jeffries et al.，2007：Ⅸ）。斯图尔特（Larry Stewart，2005）对十七八世纪英国小说词频的定量分析揭示了男女性作家在构建男性和女性叙述者方式上的显著差异：由男性建构的女性叙述者的语言往往比由男性作家建构的男性叙述者或由女性作家建构的男性或女性叙述者的语言更具有偶然性、自我参照性和社会参与性。以此研究为基础，斯图尔特依据社会认知研究中的归因理论，提出作者身份归因研究的方法，以区分同一作者创作的男性和女性的不同叙事声音（Stewart，2007：125）。他从措辞连贯性、自我指称代词和第三人称代词三个方面的定量分析考虑叙事声音，发现小说《帕梅拉》（*Pamela*）中男女书信差异的主要方面反映在对词汇的使用，与18世纪其他小说几乎相同，且帕梅拉语态的变化与她在不同时期的性别定位是一致的。

所以说，性别是复杂的，是一种特殊的社会情境，男性和女性如何在他们的体验中定位和表现自己不是一成不变的，性别、说话者的意图、观众和个人叙述的主题都是其中的一些变量。性别差异可以成为研究的一个重要因素，既可以产生富有成效的解释，也可以澄清叙事理论本身的局限性。但是，不能想当然地认为任何语言形式（包括那些在叙事中使用的语言形式）都可以以一种简单化的方式与性别差异联系起来，把与语境无关的意义强加到文本特征上，而是要认识到性别本身与一系列认知神经、进化心理、社会文化影响因素的相互关联性。

认知诗学的方法为回答旧的认识论问题提供了新的途径。中世纪女作家克里斯汀·德·皮桑（Christine de Pizan）的《妇女城》（*City of Ladies*）是西方女性主义七大奠基作之一。这部原女权主义文本（protofeminist text）从历史中凸显了模范女英雄形象。汉密尔顿（Hamilton，2002）从隐喻、类比和寓言着手分析，认为概念整合是文本理解的一种多样模式，是我们能懂古书的重要途径。他还发现传统女性主义对作品的解读过于强调男女之别。但如果认为男女性阅读过程中所涉及的实际认知过程是不同的可能更为牵强，因为在神经科学领域,还没有一项 fMRI 成像扫描阅读对象的研究表明在男女性读者阅读过程中存在显著的差异。

正如传统女性主义批评家从女性视角切入，注重文化意义上的性别差异，男性作为参照物和对立物被纳入研究视野，倾向于缩小甚至取消两性之间的差异。相反，神经科学家的研究一味追求差异的生物学解释而不关心性别与社会历史和文化变量之间的互动和影响，便也不可能得出令人信服的结论。然而，男女差异无论是从生理上还是文化上都是客观存在的。认知女性主义研究者在研究中须发生策略性转变：从生理、心理到文化进行具体研究，把生物性别与社会性别关系的思考置于这些发现的解释中，对女性特质给予积极正面解释，进而强调性别差异的多元化不仅是群体性的也是个体性的，这也是认知文化研究者一直强调的"认知的普遍性与文化的差异性。"

4 结 语

女性主义理论中反对女性作为一个受压抑的群体是具有一种非生物学的而是社会学意义上的同质性阐释。换句话说，认知女性主义批评要摒弃在"自然"和"文化"之间做一种激进的二元区分。生物有机体的自然属性与文化属性以某种方式共存、相互关联且错综复杂地交织在一起。反过来，如果没有生物体来实施，它就无法实现文化存在。在文学作品的分析和研究中，同认知生态批评、认知后殖民研究、认知空间批评等新型研究范式和方法一样，认知女性主义批评是认知文学研究中的一种新范式。它是继新历史主义、后殖民批评及文化批评之后在西方崛起的又一种具备科学性与合理性的文学批评流派，也是今后文学批评的重要维度。

参考文献

[1] BLUHM ROBYN, JACOBSON ANNE JAAP, MAIBOM HEIDI LENE. Neurofeminism: Issues at the Intersection of Feminist Theory and Cognitive Science. Basingstoke: Palgrave Macmillan, 2012.

[2] G COLOMBETTI. Enactive Appraisal. Phenomenology and the Cognitive Sciences. 2007 (6): 527-546.

[3] DARLINGTON CYNTHIA. The Female Brain, Second Edition. Boca Raton: CRC Press, 2009.

[4] EINSTEIN GILLIAN. Sex and the Brain. Cambridge: MIT Press, 2007.

[5] FINE CORDELIA. Delusions of Gender: How Our Minds, Society, and Neurosexism Create Difference. New York: W. W. Norton, 2010.

[6] HAMILTON CRAIG. Conceptual integration in Christine de Pizan's City of Ladies// Elena Semino&Jonathan Culpepper (eds.). Cognitive Stylistics: Language and Cognition in Text Analysis. Amsterdam and Philadelphia: John Benjamins Publishing Company, 2002: 1-22.

[7] HERMAN DAVID. Basic Elements of Narrative. London: Blackwell, 2009.

[8] HINES MELLISSA. Brain Gender. Oxford: Oxford University Press, 2004.

[9] JEFFRIES LESLEY, MCINTYRE DAN, BOUSFIELD DEREK.

Stylistics and Social Cognition. Amsterdam, New York: Rodopi, 2007

[10] KEATES DEBRA. Sexual Difference//Elizabeth Wright (ed.). Feminism and Psychoanalysis: A Critical Dictionary. London: Blackwell, 1992.

[11] A KOIVUNEN. An Affective Turn? Reimagining the Subject of Feminist Theory// M. Liljestrom and S. Paasonen (eds.). Working with Affect in Feminist Readings: Disturbing Differences. London and New York: Routledge, 2010: 8-28.

[12] LINSTROTH JOHN PATRICK. Marching against Gender Practice: Political Imaginings in the Basqueland. Lexington: , 2015.

[13] MCINTYRE DAN. Point of View in Plays: A Cognitive Stylistic Approach to Viewpoint in Drama and Other Text-types. Amsterdam and Philadelphia: John Benjamins Publishing Company, 2006.

[14] RICHARDSON ALAN. Of Heartache and Head Injury: Reading Minds in Persuasion. Potics Today, 2002 (1): 141-160.

[15] ROBERTS CELIA. Messengers of Sex: Hormones, Biomedicine and Feminism. Cambridge: Cambridge University Press, 2007.

[16] STEWART L LARRY. You Must Alter Your Style, Madam: Pamela and the Gendered Construction of Narrative Voice in the Eighteenth-Century British Novel. Lesley Jeffries, Dan McIntyre & Derek Bousfield (eds.). Stylistics and Social Cognition. Amsterdam and New York: Rodopi, 2007.

[17] STEWART LARRY. Empirical Analysis, Gender Assumptions, and the Language of Narration in Eighteenth-Century British Fiction. Empirical Studies of the Arts, 2005 (23): 65-77.

[18] THREADCRAFT SHATEMA. Embodiment// Lisa Disch and

Mary Hawkesworth (eds.) The Oxford Handbook of Feminist Theory. New York: Oxford University Press, 2016: 207-226.

[19] WILSON A ELIZABETH. Neural Geographies: Feminism and the Microstructure of Cognition. NY: Routledge, 1998.

[20] YOUNG IRIS MARION. On Female Body Experience: "Throwing Like a Girl" and Other Essays. New York: Oxford University Press, 2005.

前沿译介

文学方言的认知诗学研究方法

——彼得·斯托克维尔《作为社交指示语的文学方言》述评

邱小轻　邹　容

【摘要】彼得·斯托克维尔发现，学界长期以来运用社会语言学单一学科方法研究文学方言，仅将其视作真实性的一个指标，忽视了读者所受影响以及读者的积极作用。他指出，读者对文学方言使用者的态度在叙述与作者两个层面均受到操控，而且阅读效果、读者印象以及读者评估是阅读文学的关键。因此，他采用认知诗学视角，将文学方言视作社交指示语，分析 19 世纪和 20 世纪三个英国文学文本中的方言，从而论证方言能够清楚揭示作者、人物、读者各自的社会地位，并反映人物与叙述者的关系。可见，使用认知诗学方法研究文学方言能将读者纳入研究视野，从而能够更全面地把握文本意义。

【关键词】认知诗学；社交指示语；文学方言；读者；定位

0　引　言

彼得·斯托克维尔（Peter Stockwell）是认知诗学的奠基人和领军人（袁文娟、马菊玲，2012：634；杨波、王晔，2021：109）。他

作者简介：邱小轻，广东外语外贸大学英文学院教授，硕士生导师，主要从事叙事学、现当代童话改写、美国当代自然书写研究；
邹容，广东外语外贸大学英文学院硕士研究生，主要从事叙事学研究。

在 2020 年发表的论文《作为社交指示语的文学方言》（“Literary Dialect as Social Deixis”）中主张采用认知诗学方法来研究文学方言。他指出，学界对文学作品中方言的再现研究，多年来深受单一学科研究方法的制约，以致没什么起色（Stockwell，2020：359）[①]。这个单一研究方法主要是社会语言学，视文学虚构作品中的非标准语、地域方言与口音为真实性的一个指标，从属于性格塑造。厄尔祖拉·克拉克（Urszula Clark）则采用了多学科研究方法——文学研究、语言学、教学研究、社会语言学，以及话语分析，研究了地域方言与地方、身份的关系，取得令人瞩目的成果（358）。

克拉克的多学科研究方法及研究成果引发了斯托克维尔对文学方言的重新思考。他认为，多学科方法是文学作品的特点使然，因为文学作品既非民族志记录，亦非纯粹的美学物件。读者会运用他们的社会文化知识以及带着各种期待，来理解作者对人物的再现。因此，从认知诗学视角对社交指示语做进一步了解，有助于发现作者、人物、读者三者在文学体验中如何被定位。文学作品虚构场景中的地方口音和方言的再现也离不开读者的参与，因而涉及读者在阅读过程中对自身社会地位和身份的重新定位。（359）

至此，斯托克维尔阐明了研究方法——认知诗学，也交代了研究对象——社交指示语和文学方言。他紧接着从社交指示语的内涵说明文学方言是一种社交指示语，从文学方言的研究现状指出研究话语参与者、读者、作家的重要性，并用 19 世纪和 20 世纪三个英国文学文本为例，深入具体分析其中的方言，论证了方言能清楚揭示作者、人物、读者各自的社会地位，反映人物与叙述者的关系。

1 社交指示语的内涵

在众多研究指示语的学者中，语用学家斯蒂芬·列文森（Steven

① 文中的引用凡是只标出页码的，均引自彼得·斯托克维尔的论文《作为社交指示语的文学方言》。

Levinson）的研究影响深远。他指出，指示语（dcixis）是体现语言与语境关系的最明显方式（Levinson，1983：54）。他将指示语分成5个类别，包括人称指示语、时间指示语、地点指示语、语篇指示语，以及社交指示语（62）。其中，社交指示语是语言结构的某些方面，显示参与者的社会身份，或者参与者之间的社会关系，或者其中一个参与者与所指涉的人及实体的关系，主要包括各种敬语。（89-92）

斯托克维尔沿着列文森的思路继续研究社交指示语。在2002年的专著《认知诗学导论》（*Cognitive Poetics：An Introduction*）中提出了“认知指示语”概念，把指示语分成6大类，当时他用“关系指示语”指代社交指示语，将其界定为“那些显示了作者、叙述者、人物以及读者的社会观点和相对情境的表达用语，包括情态词、观点与视角的表达语，命名传统与称呼习惯，评价性的词语选择”（Stockwell，2002：46）。在2020年出版的第二版中，斯托克维尔采用了“社交指示语”一词替代“关系指示语”，并拓宽了它的内涵：“那些显示了作者、叙述者、人物以及读者的社会观点和所处境况的表达用语，包括情态词、观点与视角的表达语，命名传统与称呼习惯，评价性的词语选择，语域中社会关系的标示语等”（Stockwell，2020：54）。其中，增加的“语域中社会关系的标示语”指显示了说话者的社会地位的口音和语调等（360）。可以说，相较于列文森以及斯托克维尔本人之前的研究，这次他大大拓宽了社交指示语的含义，认为“只要标示出说话者与受话者不同社会地位的语言用法，均可视为具有指示语的特征”（359）。他指出，语篇的标记与标签既可视为语篇指示语，也可视为社交指示语，因为这些词语也标示了社会关系（360）。斯托克维尔界定清楚社交指示语之后，指明他现在要研究的就是口音和方言的书面再现所体现出来的社会定位（361）。

2 文学方言的研究现状

斯托克维尔首先指出文学方言研究所使用的两种传统方法的

缺陷。第一种非常类似方言学，把文学文本几乎看作社会语言数据，把录音出现之前的文学文本看作历史文献；第二种则研究方言的文体价值，把文学文本中的例子与现实生活中的事件进行比较，从中得出关于真实性的结论（362），比如社会语言学的研究目的是力证客观性。不同场景中的语言行为被尽可能中立地描述出来，研究者只是数据的收集者和描述者，并不参与到事件当中，也不探究所分析的群体的所思所想，而是力求客观描述能够观察到的行为、可以记录下来的数据等。文学语言学（即文体学，熊沐清，2008：300）也大同小异，将文本视为某种阐释的最终且唯一证据的依据（362-363）。

斯托克维尔接着指出，社会语言学与文学语言学的重大变革质疑这两种传统研究方法。社会语言学自从经历"批判"转向，便开始关注话语参与者的意识形态，还关注社会变量的复杂交错。文学语言学经历了"认知转向"后，则开始关注读者的经历，甚至作者的创作（363）。比如，霍德森（Hodson）以及许多研究者发现，作家对方言的再现不可能做到精确、系统、一致。克里斯滕森（Kristiansen）和德尔文（Dirven）则发现，作家会挑出一个方言变体的最明显特征，好让读者启动该方言与说该方言的群体的认知图式。

斯托克维尔选用狄更斯的名著《荒凉山庄》（*Bleak House*）中的一个情景，即"可怜的乔"（"poor Jo"，一个街头流浪儿）临死前的场景作为例子，论证作家在使用方言和口音等语言变体时不可能做到精确和系统。在这个选段里，医生艾伦·伍德科特（Allan Woodcourt）前来看望乔，他们之间展开了一段对话。艾伦使用的是标准英语，而乔使用的是非标准方言。为了更好了解乔所使用的语言，这里将他对艾伦问话的回答罗列如下：

> 'Never knowd nothink, sir.'
>
> 'No, sir. Nothink at all. Mr. Chadbands he wos-a-prayin wunst at Mr. Sangsby's and I heerd him, but he sounded as if

he was a-speakin to hisself, and not to me. He prayed a lot, but I couldn't make out nothink on it. Different times there was other genlmen come down Tom-all- Alone's a-pray-in, but they all mostly sed as the t'other 'wuns praued wrong, and all mostly sounded to be a-talking to theirselves, or a-passing blame on the t'others, and not a-talkin to us. We never knowd nothink. I never knowd what it was all about.'

'It's time for me to go to that there berryin ground, sir,' he returns with a wild look.

（363）

斯托克维尔分析道：在乔的言语里，有些词的拼写不规范，显示了 19 世纪中叶伦敦语的特征，如 knowd，nothink，wunst，heerd 等。事实上，作家对这些词语都做了改动，以保证可读性。此外，拼写存在不一致性：有些词语的拼写省去了后鼻音，如“prayin，speakin”，而有些则保留了标准拼写方式，如“talking，passing”。另外，还存在不同方言变体。作家的所有这些文体选择旨在引发读者启动关于工人阶层的言语认知图式，同时保留必要的真实性，但并非完全真实或精确（364）。斯托克维尔进而指出，批评者们由于聚焦乔的言语再现，而忽略了该片段中与非标准方言形成对照的标准英语（艾伦和叙述者均使用标准英语），因为该标准英语压根不起眼，以致被认为不值一提，这被一些批评者称为“标准语意识形态”在起作用。

斯托克维尔则认为，在叙述声音并非标准方言的少数文学作品里，这种叙述声音造成的效果值得关注。他以欧文·威尔士（Irvine Welsh）的名作《猜火车》（*Trainspotting*）的一个片段为例进行说明：

The magistrate's expression seems tae oscillate between pity n loathing, as he looks doon at me n Spud in the dock.

You stole the books from Waterstone's bookshop, with the intention of selling them, he states. Sell fuckin books. Mafuckin erse.

——No，ah sais.

（364）

在这个片段中，第一个句子是叙述者瑞顿（Renton）的话，使用的是非标准方言（苏格兰语，如“tae，doon，n'”），但又使用了偏高语域（“expression，oscillate，states”），之后又用了苏格兰语来呈现他的直接想法（“fuckin，Macuckin，erse”），从而凸显了治安法官使用的标准英语。此外，直接言语前面的破折号使瑞顿的否定语“No”产生了模棱两可效果，即究竟他否定什么：治安法官以为瑞顿否认偷书，而瑞顿否定的却是偷书之后拿去卖这件事。瑞顿与治安法官的不同言语风格造成的总体效果是作为叙述者的瑞顿处于掌控地位。在这个案例中，威尔士使用了大部分读者都已经内化了的认知图式，即标准语意识形态，来确立叙述者的掌控地位和凸显治安法官的自大，由此贬低了法庭体系。这种标准英语得到凸显、地域性非标准方言占主导地位的叙事作品，产生了列文森称为“内部异化”的现象，这是一种纯粹的颠倒（364-365）。

3 发挥定位功能的社交指示语

斯托克维尔接着指出，这种以方言为主导的颠倒性叙事会在不同程度上定位读者，意识到这点可以使我们了解到：即便一个文本的框架叙述是标准方言，又会是一种什么情况。已经被我们内化了的标准语认知图式使我们倾向于忽略标准英语，除非标准英语像《猜火车》那样被刻意凸显。人物使用的方言能起到干预框架叙述效果的另一种手段则是自由间接引语或反讽。在这些情形中，通常是经由叙述者而发生的转移，使人物引起读者的注意（365）。

斯托克维尔由此提到了对指示语的研究现状。他指出，杜臣（Duchan）等学者的研究已经使指示语成为认知诗学的重要研究对象（365）。他们的研究方法聚焦文本如何提示读者创造“指示转移”（deictic shift），即把读者的注意力投射到具有不同感知指示中心的文本世界。吉本斯（Gibbons）和威特雷（Whiteley）、麦克雷（Macrae）、麦克金泰尔（McIntyre）等学者均专门研究了文学文本中的指示转移。然而，斯托克维尔发现这些学者的研究范围过窄，或者只研究了指示语自我中心的各个方面，或者只聚焦社交指示语的某一、两个方面，如语篇指示语和复合指示语（compositional deixis，也翻成“架构指示语”）。而早在 2009 年出版的专著《文本肌理：关于阅读的认知美学》（*Texture: A Cognitive Aesthetics of Reading*, 2009）中，他就指出，可以对这种跨越文本世界边界的文本体验的意义进行探讨，包括情节、叙述弧、片段性信息（episodic information）、语气与氛围、反讽或讽刺或戏仿的意图、进行心智建模的人物、视角等。除了麦克雷，学界极少有人从认知诗学视角研究社交指示语，而斯托克维尔在对《荒凉山庄》和《猜火车》两部小说选段的研究表明：当叙述者的方言与人物的方言存在文本转移时，读者必须对这两种人物的关系进行判断（365）。

因此，斯托克维尔主张从认知诗学的角度研究社交指示语。他认为，当读者不断往前阅读时，不仅要对人物进行心智建模（mind-model），即在头脑中建构人物与叙述者的样子，而且还会建构他们自己与这两种人物的关系。在此过程中，读者本人也被心智建模，占据着一定社会空间。斯托克维尔紧接着引出了社会语言学的一个重要概念，即“交际适应理论”（Communication Accommodation Theory），即不同语言变体（口音、方言、语域）的使用者在交际过程中会向对方的话语模式靠拢。当然，说话者在多大程度上向对方靠拢，则取决于两者当时的文化差异与权力差别。在文学语篇中，读者也并非中立，而会带着先见，这种先见又会受到阅读的影响。

在阅读中，读者完成所有语篇行为：创建想象世界、建构叙述者与人物的心智（思维）、通过社交指示语确立这两者的关系。此外，默默阅读的读者也被定位，成为某种类型的读者（366）。

斯托克维尔这里采用的是布乔尔茨（Bucholtz）和霍尔（Hall）的社会语言学身份观，即身份最好被视为动态和生成的，而不是预先固定的，因而是一种社会文化现象（366）。在斯托克维尔看来，既然身份呈动态发展，那么阅读也应该是动态的体验，而不是静态和置身事外的行为。在社交指示语中，一系列社交变量比如认同、排斥等都是互相交错的，伴随着复杂的定位行为，如社会权力、社会性别与性属感知、阶级地位等。在文学虚构作品中，即使只存在一个叙述者和一个人物，但几乎总是存在多个心智（思维）。

斯托克维尔选用老女权主义者温尼弗蕾德·霍特碧（Winifred Holtby）出版于 1936 年的小说《南瑞丁》（*South Riding*）①的一个场景为例，展示读者在阅读中的心智建模活动，以及借助小说里的社交指示语来判断人物的社会身份。这部小说一开始就列出了多达 73 个有名有姓的人物，小说以位于英格兰北部的东约克郡一个虚构的县为背景，该县的名字“South Riding”的词源是“Thirding”（约克郡的三个县之一）。斯托克维尔选用的是小说开始不久的一个场景：叙述者透过 14 岁的女孩米琪·坎恩（Midge Carne）的眼睛和耳朵，描述她无意中听到女仆艾尔茜（Elsie）和奶农迪克森先生（Mr Dickson）之间的一段对话，当时，米琪害怕父亲（Robert Carne）归来。为了更好地了解斯托克维尔如何从认知诗学视角对该选段的方言进行分析，特将该选段完整复制如下：

> Mr. Dickson had climbed stiffly from the back of the float, let Dolly go loose, and clumped to the black door,

① 国内对温尼弗蕾德·霍特碧（Winifred Holtby）这部名为“*South Riding*”的小说采用了意译和音译相结合的方法，译成《南瑞丁》，而根据斯托克维尔对约克郡的方言和对该地方的认知，该小说名指的是东约克郡三县之一。

where Elsie had greeted him.

'Is Maister in?'

Then he had not found the body.

'He's at Flintonbridge, getting hisself made alderman. '

Like most of her generation and locality, Elsie was trilingual. She talked B. B. C. English to her employer, Cinema American to her companions, and Yorkshire dialect to old milkman like Eli Dickson.

'He's not, then, Astell's alderman. '

'Go on. '

'I've just heard it from Mrs. Tadman, who's been to Kingsport by bus, and got it from a chap in Flintonbridge. '

'Get away with you. Our Maggie saw Mr. Tubbs in Kingsport, Wednesday week, and he said it was sure as death. An *he*'s a councillor. '

'I tell you, Asteli's alderman. Socialist chap. They put it about that Carne's failing, and no one likes to county-court an alderman. '

'Failing? Mr. Carne. You're crazy. '

'Then why don't he do up my cow-house? That's what I say. He promised to do it a twelve-month back and now muck from yard's running right through to dairy. I'll be having government chaps to me...'

They went into the house. The back door clapped to.

It didn't mean anything. Nasty old man, with his little fringe of beard and greasy hat. He smelled.

（367）

斯托克维尔在展开具体分析之前指出，指示转移驱动读者的心智建模，读者把自己的心智投射到虚构世界中，而串起读者与人物的指示线（deictic thread）具有四个维度，分别是邻近、方向、转移、质量。他认为，在上述选段中，读者首先必须建构起一处由作者型叙述者确立的虚构地方，然后把注意力投射到14岁女孩米琪的心智（思维）中。选段中所有的命名类型、时间感知、感知的色彩、心理活动等，都是她的，而且均以她为参照来进行指示性描述（367）。与此同时，读者必须根据两个说话者——迪克森和艾尔茜——两者略微不同的言语模式来建构他们的社交指示语，因为叙述者并没有使用先行词来告诉读者哪个人物说了哪些话。叙述者注意到艾尔茜转换成方言的言语模式（"hisself"），而迪克森则呈现出本地人的言语模式，他的言语具有典型约克郡特征：①"Maister"而不是"Master"，"Why don't he"而不是标准英语"doesn't"，"12- month"指代"year"，"muck"指代"manure"；②完全省掉定冠词"the"。如果是一个不那么精准的作家，这个定冠词有时会被写成"t"，但霍特碧则完全省掉了这个定冠词，如"[the] Maister""Astell's [the] alderman""from [the] yard""through to [the] dairy"。此外，两个人物的措辞的细微差异还在于：迪克森说"He's not, then"，"then"的意思是"事实上，相反"；他使用完整的称呼"Mrs. Tadman"来称呼第三方，就像20世纪30年代的工人阶层那样，即使他们相识一辈子，而且彼此友好；他还使用"got it"，意思是"传闻到处散播"，对此，艾尔茜说"Get away with you"，意思是不相信该传闻。关于这个习语，斯托克维尔直觉这是约克郡方言中典型的女性用语。此外，艾尔茜还使用家庭代词"Our Maggie"，而且还使用习语"Wednesday week"，在这个语境，其意思是上周三。

斯托克维尔指出，对人物的言语特征的分析有时得依靠读者的图式知识（368）。他正是因为拥有女性工人阶层的图式知识以及约克郡习语的图式知识才得以对两个人物言辞的细微差别做出上述分析。他从选段中再取一例加以说明：选段中的短语"Go on"，大部分读者可能会理解成"接着讲吧"。然而，在约克郡方言背景下，该习语表达的是惊讶或者不相信。斯托克维尔之所以知道这点，是因为他注意到接下来的一轮对话中，艾尔茜用了意思相同的短语“Get away with you”（即“你这是在开玩笑”）。斯托克维尔发现，霍特碧在小说大部分篇幅里基本都避免使用非标准拼写，以此显示约克郡口音，她用不同的社交指示语特征来定位各个人物。

通过人物之间这些微妙的指示转移，读者得以按照人物的社会阶层、有偿劳动的等级、处于公共还是私人场所以及个性等因素来将他们归类（368-369）。读者还能分清每个人物相对于他人的地位，还能模拟他们对他人的看法。不过，斯托克维尔指出，他的上述分析不一定是标准分析，他是以 21 世纪英国视角来看待约克郡方言和约克郡的特点。他提醒大家注意的另一点是，小说的叙述框架也在把他建构成某种类型的读者，所以，他在定位小说人物的同时，也被小说定位。

4 作为社交指示语的文学方言的研究意义

在论文最后一部分，斯托克维尔论及社交指示语的具体表现形式，以及文学方言作为社交指示语的研究意义。

他认为，社交指示语可能出现在文学文本的五个地方：

第一，被报道的直接引语（reported direct speech）。这是社交指示语的关键场所。

第二，“闯入”被报道的直接引语的叙述者评论。这种评论有可能对口音和方言做出描述性概述，甚至有可能明显点出该方言将被如何看待。

第三，引用前后的报道性从句（reporting clauses as pre-quotatives or post-quotatives）。

第四，被引材料（quoted material）。该材料能拉近跟读者亲身经历的距离。

第五，叙述框架（narratorial framing）。叙述框架能让读者明白该往一个场景的哪个方向看，因为人物的言语或感知在到达读者之前，可能要先经过叙述指示中心（369）。

斯托克维尔强调，在寻找社交指示语的过程中，读者自身的位置以及自我感知均重要。他以亲身经历进行说明：当他回到英国提塞德（Teesside，位于英格兰东北地区）的家时，他很快就不再注意到当地口音，该口音变成不起眼的背景，因为该口音就是他的乡音。然而，当他观看一部带有提塞德口音的电视剧时，他会一直注意到该口音，因为此时他的身份发生了改变，即他已经被建构成一个观看者，从而将该口音视为非标准、非主流的语言。同理，在书面语中，由于标准英语无处不在，即使我们平常不使用，我们也不会将标准英语视作显眼的图像，而是将其看成不起眼的背景（369）。

最后，斯托克维尔还探讨了将文学方言视为社交指示语的四重研究意义：

第一，可以把读者定位和人物定位纳入指示语体系内研究。由方言特征显示出的社会身份可以用来测量跟读者以及跟其他人物的距离，由此形成的各种关系又可被读者用来评估人物对另一人物使用的方言会做出何种反应或者受到怎样影响。此外，还可以强调方言再现的复杂性（369-370）。

第二，使读者成为整体分析的一部分。读者运用他们的图式知识对人物以及叙述者有关的文本特征做出回应，从而成为一个参与者。

第三，就方言的感知、评估及象征意义而言，读者自己的方言、该方言与被再现的方言所具有的真实世界社会关系，都应纳入研究范畴，而不能视其为独立的语境，也不能当作背景，因为它们是文本意义的关键部分和语言部分。

第四，读者在阅读过程中建构自己，这再次证明读写能力扎根于我们的认知能力，说明社会语篇分析是对认知诗学理论的有效补充。

5 结 语

自斯托克维尔出版奠基性的认知诗学著作《认知诗学导论》近20年间，他一直在不断完善认知诗学学科体系。他在《文本肌理：关于阅读的认知美学》中研究了读者情感以及美学问题，引入了诸如“指示辫”“心智建模”（也被译成“思维模拟”）等新的理论术语，弥补了认知诗学偏重文本意义阐释的不足（袁文娟，2012：637）。在2020年《认知诗学导论》第二版中，他重新审视了社交指示语。此外，在这个再版中还从认知语言学的视角完善了图式理论和概念隐喻理论发展模式（杨波，2021：111）。在《作为社交指示语的文学方言》一文中，他强调了认知诗学研究方法的重要性。他从认知诗学的视角重新界定了社交指示语，大大拓宽了社交指示语的内涵，使之包括“语域中社会关系的标示语”，即显示说话者的社会地位的口音和语调等，以及所有标示出说话者与受话者的社会地位的语言用法。这样，文学方言就可被视为社交指示语来研究，在分析文学方言时就能关注到说话者的社会关系、读者的社会定位、叙述者与人物之间的关系等，从而丰富了以往对文学方言的单薄研究成果。

斯托克维尔对19世纪和20世纪的三个英国文学文本的方言进行了具体深入的分析，充分展示了将文学方言作为社交指示语进行研究的可行性与有效性：既可以揭示作者、人物、读者各自的社会地位，又可以看清人物与叙述者之间的关系。斯托克维尔的阐释令人信服，充分实践了他在《认知诗学导论》中提到的认知诗学方法论，即“精确且系统地分析读者阅读文学文本时到底发生了什么”（Stockwell，2002：5）。

认知诗学的一个重点是读者的认知，因此，斯托克维尔从认知诗学的视角研究文学方言时，注意到读者与叙述者、与作者、与阅读本身均存在密切关系，强调读者是文本阐释的重要参与者，把文学方言视为社交指示语能更准确地把握方言在文学虚构作品中发挥的作用，从而更好地理解作品的意义。

参考文献

[1] S C LEVINSON. Pragmatics. Cambridge: Cambridge University Press, 1983.

[2] P STOCKWELL. Cognitive Poetics: An Introduction. London: Routledge, 2002.

[3] P STOCKWELL. Cognitive Poetics: An Introduction. 2nd edition. London: Routledge, 2020.

[4] P STOCKWELL. Texture: A Cognitive Aesthetics of Reading. Edinburgh: Edinburgh University Press, 2009.

[5] P STOCKWELL. Literary Dialect as Social Deixis. Language and Literature, 2020, 29 (4): 358-372.

[6] 熊沐清. 语言学与文学研究的新接面——两本认知诗学著作述评. 外语教学与研究，2008（4）：299-305.

[7] 杨波，王晔. 基于认知语言学的认知诗学研究——《认知诗学导论》第二版介评. 外语研究，2021（1）：109-111.

[8] 袁文娟，马菊玲. 从“只可意会”走向“意可言传”——《文本肌理：关于阅读的美学认知》评介. 外语教学与研究，2012（1）：634-638.

文学阅读与大学生社会认知发展
——论《阅读文学，阅读社会人生：文学教学的认知路径研究》

邵 宏 张 燕

【摘要】文学阅读不仅可以促进大学生的语言文化素养，还可以促进大学生的社会认知发展。阿曼达·塔克认为，认知文学研究致力于探索文学阅读和社会认知之间的复杂关系，但对于文学教学并不关注。因此阿曼达·塔克旨在拓展认知文学研究领域的范围，在其论文《阅读文学，阅读社会人生：文学教学的认知路径研究》中介绍了自己对于所教授的《文学导论》课程进行的认知取向的重新设计、教学实践过程，以及她通过所收集的定性和定量数据来分析认知文学教学路径能否用于培养大学生换位思考的社会认知能力。

【关键词】文学阅读；社会认知；文学教学；认知路径

0 引 言

近年来，英语教学中越来越多地融入了文学教学的元素。文学教学可以为学生提供更能创造性地体验和使用语言的机会，并能进一步提升他们所学语言方面的语感和意识（Daskalovska & Dimova, 2012）。课内外的文学教学不仅能激发高中学生的文学阅读兴趣和动

作者简介：邵宏，男，桂林电子科技大学外国语学院副教授，主要从事认知文学和教学研究；
张燕，女，桂林电子科技大学外国语学院教授，主要从事英美文学和认知文学研究。

机，而且还能有助于他们的人格发展和身份意识（Kalamees-Ruubel & Läänemets，2012）。融入了文学元素的语言教学不仅可以提升语言学习者的学习动机，同时也有助于他们的社会、情感和认知发展；为儿童语言学习者选择的文学文本既要满足他们的语言学习需要，也要满足他们的认知情感需要（Songören，2013）。文学在儿童人格发展中起着突出的作用，因为儿童读者会与故事类文学作品产生情感共鸣，这不仅对儿童人格发展，而且对整个学习过程都有积极的影响。罗马尼亚的小学课程设计者们已将文学文本融入课程教学之中，以达成上述教育目标（Stan，2015）。阿曼达·塔克（Amanda Tucker）于 2021 年在文学阅读与大学生社会认知发展的关系研究方面发表了最新成果《阅读文学，阅读社会人生：文学教学的认知路径研究》（"Reading Texts，Reading People：Cognitive Literary Science and Pedagogy"，2021）。塔克是威斯康星大学普拉特维尔分校人文社科系的英语副教授及大学通识教育系主任，她讲授一年级写作课程以及英国文学、爱尔兰文学和世界文学。她的研究兴趣包括现当代文学研究、国别研究、认知文学研究以及教学研究。在上述最新论文中，塔克认为，认知文学研究致力于探索文学阅读和社会认知之间的复杂关系，但对于文学教学并不关注。因此，她旨在拓展认知文学研究领域的范围，并在其这篇最新力作中介绍了自己对于所教授的《文学导论》课程进行的认知取向的重新设计以及教学实践过程，以及她通过所收集的定性和定量数据来分析认知文学教学路径能否用于培养大学生换位思考的社会认知能力，并提出该认知文学教学模式也可以用于其他类型的本科文学课程。

1 社会认知和社会智能

根据维基百科的词条解释，社会认知是心理学分支的子课题之一，它关注的是人们如何处理、存储和应用关于他人和社会状况的信息。它特别关注认知过程在社会互动中的作用。社会智能是了解自己和了解他人的能力。社会智能是通过与人交往的经验以及从社交环境中的成功和失败中学习并发展起来的。它通常被称为“机智”“常识”或“街头智慧”。

解读社会伙伴的意图和情感状态信息的能力对于恰当的社会互动至关重要。这个复杂的过程就是所谓的社会认知的研究领域（Di Tella & Miti et al.，2020）。社会认知包括了解其他人的意图和信念的能力（即心智理论，Theory of Mind）（Leslie，1987；Tettamanti et al.，2017），以及识别和分享他人情绪情感的能力（Lieberman，2007）。尽管社会智能和社会认知在人际关系和职业关系中起着不可或缺的作用，但过去十年的研究表明大众的人际关系能力正在大幅下降。康拉斯等人（Konrath，et al.，2011）和特文格等人（Twenge，et al.，2008）的研究表明，大学生理解他人的能力在下降，其以自我为中心的倾向越来越严重。美国大学和学院协会（AACU，Association of American Colleges and Universities）对雇主调查的结果（2015，2018）显示，尽管雇主高度重视口头沟通和协作能力，但是他们一再发现大学毕业生在这些方面表现得差强人意，尤其是当他们需要与来自不同文化的人合作时，他们沟通能力不足的缺陷就被更加突显出来。对于那些想要将社会智能融入文学课程的研究者来说，文学教学的认知路径将可以帮助学生建立对于社会互动的认同感以及提升其社会互动参与度。

2　文学的认知研究与社会认知

不正确的文学阅读视角会让读者对于社会现象、社会中的其他族群形成负面的刻板印象。于是，社会认知也受到了文学认知研究派别的广泛关注。正如伯克和特罗西安科（Burke & Troscianko，2017:5）所言，社会认知是六大认知文学主题之一。邓肯等人（Duncan et al.，2017：245）断言，“20 年来，在神经生物学和认知心理学领域形成了趋同的研究路线，积累起来的证据一致表明，小说阅读为什么以及如何能够增强读者的社会智能和认知同理心”。基德和卡斯塔诺（Kidd & Castano，2013：378）也认为，文学阅读可以提升读者的心智理论（ToM）；并且发现，不同的阅读材料中，具有艺术性和复调性的小说最能够促进读者社会认知的发展，因为小说特别能够唤起读者的心理过程去参与解读小说人物的主观体验。基德和卡斯塔诺通过一系列实验发现，进行小说阅读的实验参与者在一种叫作阅读眼神（Reading the Eyes）的常用心智测试中，与那些阅读通俗读物或是非文学作品，或是不阅读任何材料的实验参与者相比较，取得了更高的测试分数，即显示拥有了更强的社会智能。

认知文学研究者纷纷探讨文学阅读与其他非文学阅读不同的原因以及其不同之处。关于文学阅读过程中大脑运作原理的关键研究进展来自格瑞格（Gerrig，1993）的《体验叙事世界：论阅读的心理活动》（*Experiencing Narrative Worlds: On the Psychological Activities of Reading*）一书。在该书中，格瑞格探讨了文学阅读过程中读者的认知发生过程及认知效果。米奥尔和奎肯（Miall & Kuiken，1994）的陌生化理论为解读文学文本的文体特征提供了一个非常重要的框架，为文学阅读者带去了不一样的阅读体验。斯塔尔（Starr，2013）的审美体验神经模型和菲利普（Phillips，2015）研究的神经科学路径都进一步提升了我们对于文学阅读认知反应的理解。格瑞格和奥布莱恩（Gerrig & O'Brien，2005）通过获得个人记忆的方式探讨了高度个性化的文学阅读体验。格瑞格和芒佩（Gerrig & Mumper，2017）探讨了读者是如何与文学文本中的某些方面发生关联或是产生共鸣的。库兹米科娃和巴林特（Kuzmicova and Balint，2019）探讨了文学文本与读者个人化的关联。阿尔科恩和奥尼尔（Alcorn and O'Neill，2019）指出，认知路径的文学研究有一个共同的论点，即文学阅读能够激活读者的情感反应，而这种情感反应又能对读者的社会认知能力和决策能力产生极大的影响力。

3 文学教学的认知路径和社会认知能力的培养

以上富有开创性的认知心理学、神经科学和认知文学研究给予那些想要采取社会认知路径来进行文学教学的老师们以极大的启示。布雷彻（Bracher，2019）认为大脑认知过程研究可以用于文学教学，以培养大学生的同理心并促进其社会认知发展。然而，传统文学教学实践达不到这样的教学目标，他倡导一种专注于培养学生的社会互动认知图式的教学法。在他的论文中，布雷彻概述了课堂文学认知图式批评原理以及课堂活动和作业如何操作等。例如，布雷彻在布置文学作品《汤姆叔叔的小屋》（*Uncle Tom's Cabin*）的阅读作业要求时，提示学生"描述一个自己没能帮助别人但后来感觉后悔的个案，并且说明自己的反应对于自己和其他普通人有何启示"。塔克认为这种阅读任务助长了大学生以自我为中心的发展倾向，不会采纳布雷彻布置的这种阅读任务；相反，她会布置与布雷彻的阅读任务风格极为不同的认知文学取向的阅读任务，从而将认知文学研究视角引入文学课堂。

塔克的文学课程教学设计旨在引导大学生聚焦文学文本中人物的心声，利用认知文学研究的概念和视角来帮助大学生获得认知阅读策略，同时培养其社会认知能力。雅培（Abbott，2015）也利用沃尔冈·伊瑟尔（Wolgang Iser）的文学作品来阐释读者对文学的理解：叙事的关键不在于其叙述出来的要素，其焦点在于字里行间的意蕴，该语义空间包含了或不包含故事要素。任何创造性的文学文本都包含字里行间的意蕴，因为文学作品不可能提供所有的故事细节，以至于让读者的想象力失去用武之地。正是文学文本的这种认知文体特征将其与非文学文本区分开来。塔克的文学课程教学设计的理论基础也来自詹赛恩（Zunshine，2017）关于小说和心智理论方面的研究。心智理论的概念首先来自认知心理学，它是指一个人能够理解他人的内心世界的能力，即了解他人的信仰、情感和价值观如何塑造他人的行为。因此，读者可以利用心智理论来分析文学文本中人物的内心活动，读者与文学人物之间的共鸣也会影响文学文本的理解。基恩（Keen，2013）认为叙事共鸣就是通过阅读、观赏、聆听或想象关于他人的处境状况的叙事而产生的情感共享和换位思考的体验。如果读者达不到叙事共鸣，便不能理解人物心理及其行为动机，进而导致简化的、有害的刻板印象。

认知文学教学路径认为，传统文学教学过于依赖叙事的相关性及人物认同感，从而使得读者因其自身与人物的联系而抹杀自己与异质文学人物之间的重大差异性，因而不利于大学生社会认知能力的培养。塔克的文学课程教学设计旨在培养大学生深度理解和再现他人心理世界的能力，而不强调学生对文学人物的认同能力。大学生正是通过这种他者的视角来理解他人的不同观点以及用包容差异性的方式来待人接物，从而培养和应用自己的社会认知能力。

4 认知视角下的文学课程设计

塔克用认知文学研究视角对自己讲授的《文学导论》(*Introduction to Literature*)课程进行了重新设计。《文学导论》是各类大学都会开设的文学入门课程或者通识课程。她在该课程教学设计中强调该文学课程知识的可迁移性和课堂教学与作业布置的可操作性。该课程教学设计保留原课程的主干结构，融入了与社会认知培养相联系的作业和学习活动，但无须系统测试学生的社会认知能力。该课程相当灵活，重点在于讲授文学研究中的基本概念。本课程重要的学习成果之一是理解作为文化产物的文学文本并探索特定时空中的社会关系。文化语境的学习对于旨在培养大学生社会认知的文学教学来说至关重要。塔克做出的唯一课程结构设计变动是在学期开始增加了一个两周的入门单元。在该教学阶段，她结合文学文本向学生介绍基本的文学术语以及认知文学研究的重要概念，以便帮助学生将这些概念融入阅读策略之中。塔克利用爱丽丝·沃克(Alice Walker)的小说《日用家当》(*Everyday Use*)为例，来帮助大学生思考视角(point of view)、人物刻画(characterization)、叙事空白(narrative gaps)和叙事共鸣(narrative empathy)等认知文学概念。塔克通过以上概念帮助大学生提高自身的社会认知能力，希望大学生去理解文学人物的内心世界，而不是获得一个刻板空洞的人物形象。她鼓励大学生从不同的人物视角并结合当时的社会文化环境来理解人物的行为表现，从而获得一个丰满的人物形象。

在其文学课堂教学实践中，塔克要求学生避免过度阅读和不充分阅读这两种倾向。保持恰当的阅读程度能促进大学生社会认知能力的提高。不充分阅读会让大学生读者忽略文学文本人物内在的复杂性；过度阅读则会让读者带入自己的思想、价值观和体验，从而得出文本难以支撑的理解和诠释。基德和卡斯塔诺（2013）认为，正是文学文本中的复杂性促进读者的社会认知能力发展。福伊和格瑞格（Foy and Gerrig，2008）也认为，如果读者忽略文学文本的复杂性，通过文学阅读只是为了验证自己的社会知识，那么这样的读者是不可能加强自己的社会认知能力的。因此，塔克在整个学期的教学活动中，都鼓励学生参与课堂讨论，探讨文学冲突现象以及分析人物某种内心情感背后的原因，从而促进大学生社会认知能力的提高。在课外的作业和任务中，塔克要求学生进行需要融入社会认知因素的文学分析和诠释。在整个学期中，学生需要完成四人小组的合作阅读写作活动；其任务要求包括人物刻画分析、视角分析和叙事共鸣分析。该任务锻炼了学生的心智理论能力，锻炼了学生全面深入的人物分析能力。课外作业中也可以包含论文写作，论文写作也可以锻炼学生的心智理论能力，让学生有机会运用心智理论探索所选文学人物的内心世界和行为动机。这种认知路径的文学课程教学设计可以促进学生的参与度和学生对于课程价值的感知，以及促进学生的文学理解能力和与他人沟通的能力。

5　大学生文学阅读前后的换位思考能力和社会认知能力评估方法

评估社会认知从学期开始到学期结束这段短时期后的可能变化是具有极大难度的任务。塔克在其研究中使用到的评估测量工具有 2 种：一种是定量测量，另一种是定性测量。定量测量工具改编自戴维斯（Davis，1983）的人际反应指数（Interpersonal Reactivity Index，IRI）。该测量工具是一份问卷调查，要求受访者分别从性格倾向性方面的 4 个相互联系但又彼此不同的范畴即同理心关怀（empathetic concern)、个人苦恼(personal distress)、幻想(fantasy making)和换位思考(perspective taking)来做自我评估。人际反应指数问卷调查量表有上述 4 个范畴,每个范畴包含 7 个问题,总共 28 个问题。量表采用李克特五级评分(0~4),每个范畴的量表得分范围是 0~28 分之间。7 个换位思考范畴的问题显然与社会认知有关,因为这些问题要求受访者评估自己在日常生活中能够自发接受他人心理视角的倾向性。尽管塔克只关注换位思考方面的问题,但是她还是调查了其他范畴的问题,以免问卷调查太过于重复枯燥。

塔克也用定性测量方式评估了大学生的社会认知能力,目的是验证认知文学教学路径的有效性。她采用系列问题访谈方式,逐步获得大学生对于其生活中最近遇到的冲突事件的反应和态度:首先要求学生简要概述冲突事件;接着要求学生解释冲突过程中的思维过程和感受;最后要求他们陈述冲突的解决方式以及他们自己对于冲突结局的评价。为了保护受访学生的隐私,所有收集到的数据来源都用编码来替代。编码可以帮助匹配受访学生学期初和学期末的受访数据。定性测量的设计可以帮助研究者判断大学生是否能够将心智理论和换位思考能力从文学文本分析迁移到现实生活中去。

塔克所采用的两种社会认知能力评估方式都有局限性:该研究没有采用控制组,因此,用这两种测量工具测得的社会认知能力变化不一定完全来自课程设计方案,也有可能由外部因素造成。人际反应指数量表采用自我报告的测量方式,可能不经意测到的受访者社会认知变化是来自外部环境因素或元认知因素,而不完全是来自性格倾向的变化。人际反应指数量表有可能制造某种需求效应,因为大学生通过课程活动和教学活动意识到课程的教学目标就是换位思考能力的培养,从而在回答问卷问题时受到自己对课程和对教师的印象的影响。定性测量获得的社会认知能力变化也有可能是来自外部因素的影响,而不是来自内部因素。研究中的一个难点在于学生描述出来的冲突事件对于换位思考能力的挑战度不一样。有些冲突发生在受访者和与之关系亲密的人之间,而有些冲突则发生在受访者和与之关系不亲密的人之间。所描述的冲突范围也大相径庭,从决定要参与什么社会活动到意外怀孕事件，无所不包。假定需要社会智能来解决的冲突复杂度相同，测量社会认知的内在挑战度一致，那么其局限性便可以预测，从而有助于指导数据分析。比如说，学生描述了不相同的冲突事件，比较他们的回答可能得不到有效的结论；但是，将学生个人的回答与他们的人际反应指数得分做比较，便可能得出有效的分析结论。

计算人际反应指数量表的得分比较容易，但是评估受访者关于最近人际冲突事件的系列问题的反馈就费力得多。塔克和本科教学研究助理一起评估学生的反馈，看他们是否在处理冲突事件时用到了换位思考的方法。在统一了评估标准后，她和本科教学研究助理开始分头评估学生的反馈。对于评估不一致的学生回答，她们都会见面讨论，以得出统一的分数。在学生的系列问题回答中，任何考虑到他人视角、想法或感受的成分都会被记为换位思考的正得分；反之，学生做不到上述方面，便会被记录为换位思考方面的负分。对于学生没有真正参与的冲突事件，或者没有他人真正参与的冲突事件，会被排除在评估分析之外。

塔克收集的数据来自 2017 年秋季学期和 2018 年春季学期的《文学导论》课程，每个学期都有 24 名学生。但只有 34 名学生（每个学期 17 名）签署了知情同意书并在学期初和学期末完成了上述社会认知调查任务，他们的反馈和回答被用于了评估分析之中。鉴于样本量少，塔克没有采用像 T 检验这样的统计分析手段，而是采取了人文学科常用的分析手段。

6　分析大学生文学阅读前后换位思考能力变化规律

参与研究的大学生在两个学期末获得的人际反应指数换位思考方面的平均分（18.909）略微高于其两个学期初在该项目的平均分（17.969）。如果分学期来看，两个学期末的人际反应指数量表换位思考方面得分均显示提高。2017 年秋季学期初的该项均分是 19.3，该学期末的该项均分是 20.5，提高了 1.2 分。而 2018 年春季学期初的该项均分是 16.7，该学期末的该项均分为 17.41，提高了 0.71 分。从受访者个人的成对数据显示，总共 33 个学生中（排除了一个学生的异常数据），18 位学生在学期初到学期末这段时间里提高了自己的人际反应指数换位思考方面的得分。7 位学生报告了相同的该项得分，而 8 位学生的该项得分下降了。从分学期的成对个人数据来看，2017 年秋季学期中，16 位学生中有 8 位提升了自己在上述项目上的得分。而 2018 年春季学期中，17 位学生中有 10 位提升了自己在上述项目上的得分。

在定性反馈的基础上，“学生是否提高了自己将课堂所学的换位思考迁移到现实生活中去的能力”这一结论尚不明确。33 位参与研究的学生在学期初和学期末的调查中都回答了关于冲突事件的开放性问题。排除五个没有论及人际冲突的回答，两个学期里一共收集到 61 个定性回答。38 个回答（占 62.3%）没有报告考虑到了冲突事件参与他人的视角。比较学期初和学期末的定性回答后，发现采取了换位思考的学生数量有少量的增长；同时，没有采用换位思考的学生数量相应地少量下降。在学期初，有 20 位学生没有采用换位思考，11 位学生采用了换位思考，2 位根本没有写人际冲突。在学期末，18 位没有采用换位思考，而 12 位采用了换位思考，3 人根本没有写人际冲突。分学期的数据显示了极大的差异。在 2017 年秋季学期中，在解决冲突的过程中，利用了换位思考的学生数从学期初到学期末增长了一倍（从 4 人增加到 8 人）。而没有采用换位思考的学生数同期下降了（从 10 人下降到 6 人）。在 2018 年春季学期中，利用了换位思考的学生数从学期初到学期末实际上下降了（从 7 人下降到 4 人）。而没有采用换位思考的学生数同期增加了（从 10 人增加到 12 人）。总而言之，学生的定性回答表明，大多数学生无论是在学期初抑或是在学期末都没有采用换位思考来解决自己所描述的冲突事件。这一结果与上文中特文格和康拉斯等人的元分析结果相一致。

审视学生个人的人际反应指数量表得分可以帮助我们更进一步地了解学生换位思考能力的变化。当学生被问及牵涉到他们自己情感状态的具体问题时，比如“即便我对某人很生气，我还是会替他们考虑一下”或者“即便我确信自己是对的，但我还是会花时间聆听别人的意见”，学生们往往不愿换位思考，结果上述两个问题的人际反应指数量表得分便会很低（分别为 2.06、2.18 分）。但学生们在这个具体问题“我经常会从朋友的角度看问题，从而更好地理解我的朋友”的两个学期的期末问卷中，获得了超过 3 分的最高分。这表明，通过文学阅读的认知路径，学生们愿意走出自我中心，在现实生活中采用换位思考来处理问题。第 329 号学生的换位思考方面的人际反应指数量表得分，从期初的 25 分急剧下降到 3 分。从其定性人际冲突描述上看，329 号学生的换位思考能力非常低下，并且保持不变的状态。该项目得分的急剧变化只能表明，该学生期末时更能准确地评估自己的换位思考能力，且其自我认知方面的调整表明其社会认知能力加强了。第 409 号学生的换位思考方面的人际反应指数量表得分与总体均值保持一致，具有代表性。其该项目期初得分为 16 分，期末得分为 17 分。这个得分变化与该学生的定性人际冲突描述基本一致，表明其在解决人际冲突的过程中提高了自己换位思考的能力以及人际沟通能力。个体的相关调查数据表明，能采取换位思考来解决问题的学生往往对于冲突的结局表示满意。

7 结　语

换位思考不是解决人际冲突的万灵药，也不能抹去人际互动的复杂性。人际反应指数量表得分往往反映换位思考的倾向性，而定性的关于人际冲突的描述往往可以表明学生实际换位思考的行为和能力。定量数据和定性数据之间的不匹配表明社会认知测量工作面临的巨大挑战性，这表明社会认知的测量需要多样的测量手段和工具。文学阅读与教学促进大学生社会认知发展的功能反映了该类教学的人文价值。文学教学不仅可以提升大学生的语言能力和语言审美修养，还可以促进大学生的全人发展，并能够充分发挥高等教育教学的“教书育人”功能。

参考文献

[1] H P ABBOTT. How Do We Read What isn't There to be Read? Shadow Stories and Permanent Gaps// Zunshine L. (ed.) The Oxford Handbook of Cognitive Literary Studies. Oxford: Oxford University Press, 2015: 104-119.

[2] M ALCORN, M O'NEILL. Adaptive Affective Cognition in Literature and its Impact on Legal Reason and Social Practice. Poetics Today, 2019, 40 (3): 499-518.

[3] American Association of Colleges and Universities. Fulfilling the American Dream: Liberal Education and the Future of Work. Available at: www. aacu. org/leap/public-opinion-research (accessed 19 April 2021), 2018.

[4] Association of American Colleges and Universities. Falling Short? College Learning and Career Success. Available at: www. aacu. org/leap/public-opinion- research/2015-survey-results (accessed 19 April 2021), 2015.

[5] M BRACHER. Can-and-Should Literary Study Develop Moral Character and Advance Social Justice? Answers from Cognitive Science. Poetics Today, 2019, 40 (3): 519-541.

[6] M BURKE, E TROSCIANKO. Cognitive Literary Science: Dialogues between Literature and Cognition. Oxford: Oxford University Press, 2017.

[7] N DASKALOVSKA, V DIMOVA. Why Should Literature be Used in the Language Classroom?. Procedia-Social and Behavioral Sciences, 2012 (46): 1182-1186.

[8] M DAVIS. Measuring Individual Differences in Empathy: Evidence for a Multidimensional Approach. Journal of Personality & Social Psychology, 1983 (44): 113-126.

[9] M DI TELLA, F MITI, et al. Social Cognition and Sex: Are Men

and Women Really Different?. Personality and Individual Diffcrences, 2020 (162): 110045.

[10] C DUNCAN, G BESS-MONTGOMERY, V OSINUBI. Why Martha Nussbaum is Right: The Empirical Case for the Value of Reading and Teaching Fiction. Interdisciplinary Literary Studies: A Journal of Criticism and Theory, 2017, 19 (2): 242-259.

[11] J E FOY, R J GERRIG. How Might Literature do Harm?. Style: A Quarterly Journal of Aesthetics, Poetics, Stylistics, and Literary Criticism, 2008, 42 (2-3): 175-178.

[12] R GERRIG, E O'BRIEN. The Scope of Memory-based Processing. Discourse Processes, 2005, 39 (2-3): 225-242.

[13] R J GERRIG. Experiencing Narrative Worlds: On the Psychological Activities of Reading. New Haven, CT: Yale University Press, 1993.

[14] R J GERRIG, M L MUMPER. How Readers' Lives Affect Narrative Experiences// Burke M. & Troscianko ET (eds) Cognitive Literary Science: Dialogues between Literature and Cognition. Oxford: Oxford University Press, 2017: 239-258.

[15] K KALAMEES-RUUBEL, U LÄÄNEMETS. Teaching Literature in and outside of the Classroom. Procedia-Social and Behavioral Sciences, 2012 (45): 216-226.

[16] S KEEN. Narrative Empathy. The Living Handbook of Narratology. Available at: www. lhn. uni-hamburg. de/node/42. html (accessed 19 April 2021), 2013.

[17] D C KIDD, E CASTANO. Reading Literary Fiction Improves Theory of Mind. Science, 2013, 342 (6156): 377-380.

[18] S H KONRATH, E H O'BRIEN, C HSING. Changes in Dispositional Empathy in American College Students Over Time: A Meta-Analysis. Personality and Social Psychology Review, 2011, 15 (2): 180-198.

[19] A KUZMICOVA, K BALINT. Personal Relevance in Story Reading: A Research Review. Poetics Today, 2019, 40 (3): 429-451.

[20] A M LESLIE. Pretense and Representation: The Origins of "Theory of Mind". Psychological Review, 1987, 94 (4): 412. https: //psycnet. apa. org/doi/10. 1037/0033-295X. 94. 4. 412.

[21] M D LIEBERMAN. Social Cognitive Neuroscience: A Review of Core Processes. Annual Review of Psychology, 2007 (58): 259-289. https: //doi. org/10. 1146/annurev. psych. 58. 110405. 085654.

[22] D S MIALL, D KUIKEN. Beyond Text Theory: Understanding Literary Response. Discourse Processes, 1994, 17 (3): 337-353.

[23] N M PHILLIPS. Literary Neuroscience and History of Mind: An Interdisciplinary FMRI Study of Attention and Jane Austen// Zunshine L. (ed.) The Oxford Handbook of Cognitive Literary Studies. Oxford: Oxford University Press, 2015: 55-82.

[24] S A SONGÖREN. The Place of Children's Literature Texts in Teaching German as a Foreign/Second Foreign Language. Procedia-Social and Behavioral Sciences, 2013 (70): 1825-1830.

[25] R V STAN. The Importance of Literature in Primary School Pupils' Development and Personal Growth. Procedia-Social and Behavioral Sciences, 2015 (180): 454-459.

[26] G G STARR. Feeling Beauty: The Neuroscience of Aesthetic Experience. Cambridge, MA: MIT Press, 2013.

[27] M TETTAMANTI, M VAGHI, B G BARA, S CAPPA, I ENRICI, M ADENZATO. Effective Connectivity Gateways to the Theory of Mind Network in Processing Communicative Intention. NeuroImage, 2017 (155): 169-176. https: //doi. org/10. 1016/j. neuroimage. 2017. 04. 050.

[28] A TUCKER. Reading Texts, Reading People: Cognitive Literary

Science and Pedagogy. Arts and Humanities in Higher Education, 2021, 0 (0): 1-17.

[29] J M TWENGE, S KONRATH , J D FOSTER, et al. Egos Inflating Over Time: A Cross-Temporal Meta-Analysis of the Narcissistic Personality Inventory. Journal of Personality, 2008, 76 (4): 875-928.

[30] L B ZUNSHINE. Theory of Mind, and Pedagogy: Cognitive Construction of Social Class. Eighteenth-Century Fiction, 2017, 30 (1): 109-126.

理论与实践的对话：评巴克兰德的《叙事与叙述：电影故事讲述之分析》

范司永

【摘要】《叙事与叙述：电影故事讲述之分析》是沃伦·巴克兰德历经多年电影理论研究与实践检验的成果结晶。该书阐述了叙事、叙述和叙事代理人的主要观点以及他们如何在叙事电影中展现，由此，作者提出了“电影的成败取决于叙事的有效性”核心观点，并通过多部经典电影的故事讲述分析进行检验。本书的作者为电影学界的电影叙事学研究提供了一个绝佳的范例。

【关键词】沃伦·巴克兰德；叙事与叙述；电影故事讲述

2021年面世的由沃伦·巴克兰德历经多年电影理论研究与实践检验的力作《叙事与叙述：电影故事讲述之分析》系作者在牛津布鲁克斯大学连续通过讲座、研讨会和放映的影片做出的检测，特别是为纪念两位导师爱德华·布兰尼根（1945—2019）和托马斯·艾尔塞瑟（1943—2019）在过去30多年里的学术影响和支持的结晶成果。从叙事电影的独特视角，作者在本书中提出的核心论点是，电影的成败取决于叙事的有效性（Buckland，2021：viii）：一是电影制作实践中电影故事叙述的基本要素单独或协同作用于对电影整体设计；二是使用特定的叙事要素创造一个有序的叙事结构。此外，叙事、叙述和叙事代理人是规范的经典好莱坞电影创新的原理，也

作者简介：范司永，男，湖北文理学院外国语学院副教授，博士，主要从事文艺学和英语语言学研究。

是电影叙事学研究的基础。

作者继承了西方基本理论研究和批评实践运用相结合的学术研究范式。首先，作者概述了叙事、叙述和叙事代理人的理论研究，绘制了它们的历史发展脉络，确定了它们的属性，并解释了他们与叙事一起工作，控制观众进入叙事，并沿着叙事、叙述和叙事代理人如何在影片中展现。然后从四种具体的叙事电影实践来验证电影故事讲述的分析过程，作者认为叙事、叙述和叙事代理人是电影故事讲述的核心要素，经典好莱坞电影是典型的理想（Buckland，2021：117）。当代好莱坞电影、女权主义电影、全球艺术电影、谜题电影和视频游戏逻辑主导的电影为规范的经典好莱坞范式提供了交替的故事讲述模式。

通览全书，除前言和尾声之外，主要内容包括两个部分的八个章节，形式展呈为理论探讨和实践验证的互动，组织结构严谨，论证逻辑缜密，为叙事电影研究提供了一套行之有效的方法论，最值得称道的特色主要体现在五个方面。

第一，作者采用了跨学科独特的叙事研究视角，从宏观总体上，将电影视作一种讲故事媒介，从理论上探索叙事、叙述和叙事代理人是如何融入经典好莱坞电影形式之中（该书第一章）。或者说，电影制作的技术形式（剪辑、灯光、摄像机移动、摄像机放置等）如何服务于视觉愉悦和故事叙述逻辑。汤姆·甘宁曾经暗示，早期景点电影有自己独特的审美体系，一种以场景或吸引物故事化的具象表述方式。叙事电影通过对电影的空间和时间操纵来讲述而不是展示，从而形成了一种新的观看模式：观众不是从超然的视角去观察一个奇观，而是被电影的虚构叙事或故事世界所吸收。从叙事批评实践上，作者以叙事电影《快乐鞋店售货员》为例，力图证实“在叙事电影中，既有展示者，也有叙述者。电影是在同一时间里展示和叙述的。展示者和叙述者被整合到叙事电影之中”（Gaudreault，2009：83）。作者借此概述了从“景点电影”向“叙事整合”电影的转变，检验早期电影中叙事、叙述、叙事媒介和偷窥癖是如何塑造（暴露、炫耀、窥淫等镜头特写）电影形式的、如何体现父权制（满足鞋店售货员的欲望或电影观众的欲望）价值观的。

第二，作者主张使用特定的叙事要素创造一个有序的叙事结构，向观众限制和披露这种叙事方式，展示叙事电影的创造力和独创性（第二章，该书重点部分）。经典好莱坞的故事之所以被定义为"经典"，正是因为其叙事结构的要素被强烈的因果逻辑联系在一起，即人物、动作和动作之间的内在关联性。作者从三个方面梳理了叙事理论家利用特定的叙事要素创造出不同类型的叙事结构，经典好莱坞创造性的"新故事"正源于此。

作者回顾了早期经典好莱坞故事的叙事结构。在《民间故事形态学》中，弗拉基米尔·普罗普从 100 个俄罗斯民间故事中提取出他认为是《好莱坞故事》中的叙事结构（Propp，1968）：按相同的时间顺序排列的 7 个行为体和 31 个叙事功能（普罗普已将继承确立为叙述原则）。托多罗夫将叙述中的功能序列简化为初始平衡、破坏平衡的外力、平衡的恢复（托多罗夫呼应列维-施特劳斯，在叙事的定义中添加"转变"）。A. J. 格雷马斯将普罗普的人物类型简化为更普遍的叙事结构（Greimas，1983，第 10 章和第 11 章）：6 个行为体被组织成 3 个二元对立（主体/对象、发送者/接收者、助手/对手）成对功能的网络，并重新定义为更抽象的三种关系——否定、反对和矛盾——的网络取代了普罗普的顺序因果关系。

作者探讨了新好莱坞故事的叙事结构。爱德华·布兰尼根认为，因果链并不是故事结构中行为联系的唯一方式。爱德华·布兰尼根在《叙事理解与电影》中确定的叙事要素之间的关系（Branigan，1992：26-27）：松散的（如连续、时序排列、常规、中介原因）或者强烈的（如必要或有利原因、直接原因、唯一原因）。如果叙事结构的关系松散，叙事的时空顺序就较弱；如果其关系紧密，意味着叙事的时空关系会强化，这是经典叙事的特征之一。此外，叙事也可以通过双焦点的行动链结构、转折、障碍、最后期限、阐述和描述等手段进行组织，例如，克里斯汀·汤普森在《新好莱坞故事讲述》中将叙事结构划分为准备、复杂行动、发展和高潮等四个组成部分。许多经典叙事都是双聚焦的，交织着一种类型叙事和浪漫叙事（Thompson，1999：37-44）。

作者还探讨了特定导演的叙事结构生产了创造性或独特性的“新故事”。作者认为，希区柯克的经典好莱坞电影《西北偏北》（1959）、《惊魂记》（1960）和《艳贼》（1964）之间存在潜在的相似性，他们的叙事结构、人物、主题等（或者他要求编剧重写故事），遵循预先设定的结构。詹姆斯·邦德系列《量子危机》（2008）是对一些叙事功能、主题和人物（有时是种族主义、性别歧视和种族歧视）进行了重新发明、重新设计，通过叙事顺序的倒置、关键要素的重复等，展现更深层次的创造力和艺术生产，即创造力是在现有的行为体和功能的新组合和重组中发现的，导致了现有叙事的变体（Buckland，2021：28），或者说“新故事总是仅仅作为旧故事的组合或变体出现”（Propp，1968：112）。

第三，作者在第三章探讨了电影叙述的基本要素以及中介作用的问题。电影叙述依赖于组织和控制向电影观众呈现叙事信息的“技巧”以及“叙事媒介”（Buckland，2021：29），主要通过人物、叙述者和作者的主观性呈现叙事信息，因而电影叙述在叙事与观众之间发挥重要的中介作用：观众—叙述—叙事。“叙述探究的焦点从发生了什么转移到如何以及何时我们知道发生了什么”（Branligan，1992：86）。即是说，叙述的研究侧重于如何重组叙事行为，当观众接收到这些行为的信息时，这些行为又是如何在到达读者或观众之前通过人物和叙述者过滤的。叙述对叙事信息的控制有时以欺骗性和非交际性的方式呈现，不可靠地传达一个人物的经历或故事事件而具有欺骗性，因而叙述不一定是可靠的和交际性的。

电影叙述的关键在于观众与叙事行为和媒介之间的关系。根据布兰尼根的理论，就身份识别、观点和焦点而言，在镜头中可以通过四种聚焦类型进行识别：客观镜头（非聚焦）、外聚焦镜头（意识）、内聚焦镜头（感知）、内聚焦镜头（体验）（Branligan，1992：100-107）。他们通过不同的叙述者（潜在叙述者和人物叙述者）来体现。潜在叙述者（故事世界之外）直接控制客观镜头，基于特定视角从文化、性别、种族和记忆等方面，以一种超现实的方式描绘人物的过去。人物叙述者（故事世界之内）执行一系列动作的角色，有时用画外音或者停止行动，面对摄像机直接向观众讲话。叙述从根本上重新组织了叙事的时间性，通过多个人物代理来构建。故事的动作和事件是通过导演高度程式化和不同寻常的电影技术，通过人物叙述者直接对着镜头，通过人物对遥远过去的记忆来调节的。此外，作者借鉴了彼得·沃伦的《解释学代码》和爱德华·布兰尼根的《叙事理解和电影》两部力作中的理论资源，讨论了叙述操纵的潜在作用。例如，在希区柯克的《后窗》、芬奇的《消失的爱人》、斯皮尔伯格的《侏罗纪公园》、莫法特的《魔鬼》等好莱坞电影中，高度程式化的叙述操纵导引观影者能够“看到什么、知道什么，以及向其他人揭示什么或者隐瞒什么”（Bordwell，1985）。

第四，作者在第四章中探讨了电影叙述的发音和自反性的问题。从发音的角度，作者提出了“发音的标志”“表达”“话语”“故事”和“自反”等概念（Buckland，2021：49），回指了第一章中的“叙事代理人”。电影是通过一种发音行为过程形成的。克里斯蒂安·麦茨认为，电影作为话语，其发音标志是可见的，而作为历史记录，其发音标志是隐藏的（Metz，2016：10）。电影的生产过程被省略，隐藏了创建和接收活动的主观痕迹；作为话语的电影使用一些技术来强化制作过程的宣示，如慢动作和快动作、看镜头和定格帧。经典的电影之所以经典，是因为它的技术（剪辑、剪裁上的视线匹配、动作上的匹配、镜头的移动等）隐藏或压制了它的发音标志，致使从特定政治角度说话的意识形态显得客观和中立（Buckland，2021：

50）。作者认为，现代主义电影在叙事幻觉和物质现实之间设置了对立，其中自反性通过暴露影片的物质现实来吸引人们对叙事错觉艺术性的关注，后现代电影暴露的这些痕迹不代表政治姿态，也不是揭露电影的实际物质性质，其中自反性只是创造了一种明显的文体特征。

第五，作者将本维尼斯特的“发音理论”（Benveniste，1971）和克里斯蒂安·麦茨的非人格化 11 种发音类型（画外音、书面表达形式、二次屏、发音、风格等）作为主要的参考点，以韦斯·安德森的电影《布达佩斯大饭店》作为主要的分析对象，强调电影叙述的客观表达。发音的标准理论检验了外部的“力量”（代理人、叙述者等）创建文本并组织文本，标识发音的内部（文本）标记。例如雷蒙德·贝洛尔的文章《希区柯克，宣讲者》（Bellour，1977）认为电影导演就是一个发音者，强调了麦茨在其非人格化的发音理论中边缘化的外部因素。在《艳贼》中，希区柯克是一个宣讲者，是掌握画面的代理人，然后将叙事分割成镜头和场景，从特定的视角——父权欲望的逻辑——将其组织起来。

第六，作者在本书第二部分“故事讲述的类型”，通过一系列当代好莱坞电影案例研究，概述了当前电影界流行的叙事和叙事实践发展趋势：从女权主义叙事和女性电影人到艺术电影、谜题电影、受视频游戏逻辑影响的科幻电影。在第五章，为对抗父权叙事，作者将女性置于叙事中心，女性身份的主流电影——莎莉·波特的《奥兰多》从“主题、自我表达、叙事与叙述、女性主义死亡美学”等 9 个特征超越了经典叙事传统，融入了“结局，夸张，第四种造型”等颠覆性元素，呈现了一个确定女性主义导演文本标记和女性主义称呼形式的框架，构建了女性的“另一个愿景”（赋予女性气质的故事世界）。在第六章，作者通过大卫·林奇的独立美国电影《内陆帝国》（2006），重点分析艺术电影的叙事和叙述方面的优势和价值，即艺术电影的方法没有告诉我们“电影意味着什么，而是它如何意味着什么，即构成了诗学而不是解释学”（Buckland，2021：93）。在第七章，谜题电影丰富和更新了讲故事，挑战了关于代理、身份、记忆和时间的根深蒂固的文化观念，执行了经典电影或艺术电影无法传达的附加制作任务，但不完全拒绝叙事和叙述方式，如2004年的《蝴蝶效应》（Branligan，2014：233-64）。在第八章，作者认为，受视频游戏逻辑影响的科幻大片是利用数字技术创建影片的混合叙事结构。视频游戏逻辑将影片推向一个非自然或不可能的世界，如电影《黑客帝国》《源代码》和《盗梦空间》均创造了与现实世界不同的想象世界，体现了瑞安的“最小偏离原则”（Ryan，1991：51）、阿尔贝的“不可能”（Alber，2009：79）、理查德森的“不可信”（Richardson，2015：3）等不可靠叙述原则。

综上，巴克兰德的《叙事与叙述：电影故事讲述之分析》不仅讨论了叙事、叙述和叙事代理人的理论问题，还提供了一套电影分析的方法。方法之所以重要，是因为它们充当了一个恒定的参考点——一组标准的、共享的实践——指导对特定电影或电影序列的分析。遵循一种方法能准确地告知读者电影分析是如何进行的，以及如何获得结果。作者对电影的分析是一个开放的、可逆的过程。此外，每个理论及其方法为检验电影的一个方面提供了指导电影分析的框架。每种理论方法仅仅考察了电影的一个方面，同时排除其他方面，进而使研究更加集中。总而言之，该书的作者为电影学界的电影叙事学研究提供了一个绝佳的范例。

参考文献

[1] ALBER JAN. “Impossible Storyworlds—and What to Do with Them”. StoryWorlds: A Journal of Narrative Studies 2009 (1): 79-96.

[2] BELLOUR RAYMOND. “Hitchcock, the Enunciator”. Camera

Obscura 1997 (2): 67-91.

[3] BENVENISTE ÉMILE. Problems in General Linguistics. Trans. by Mary Elizabeth Meek Coral Gables: University of Miami Press, 1971.

[4] BORDWELL DAVID, JANET STAIGER, KRISTIN THOMPSON. The Classical Hollywood Cinema: Film Style and Mode of Production to 1960. London: Routledge, 1985.

[5] BRANIGAN EDWARD. “Butterflfly Effects upon a Spectator”. In Hollywood Puzzle Films, edited by Warren Buckland. New York: Routledge, 2014: 233- 264.

[6] BRANIGAN EDWARD. Narrative Comprehension and Film. New York: Routledge, 1992.

[7] BUCKLAND WARREN, ed. Puzzle Films: Complex Storytelling in Contemporary Cinema. Oxford: Wiley-Blackwell, 2009.

[8] BUCKLAND WARREN. Narrative and Narration: Analyzing Cinematic Storytelling. New York: Columbia University Press, 2021.

[9] GAUDREAULT ANDRÉ. From Plato to Lumière: Narration and Monstration in Literature and Cinema. Trans. by Timothy Barnard. Toronto: University of Toronto Press, 2009.

[10] A J GREIMAS. Structural Semantics: An Attempt at a Method. Trans. by Dan-iele McDowell, Ronald Schleifer, and Alan Velie. Lincoln: University of Nebraska Press, 1983.

[11] METZ CHRISTIAN. Impersonal Enunciation, or the Place of Film. Trans. by Cormac Deane. New York: Columbia University Press, 2016.

[12] PROPP VLADIMIR. Morphology of the Folktale. (2nd ed.) Trans. by Laurence Scott. Revised by Louis A. Wagner. Austin:

University of Texas Press, 1968.

[13] RICHARDSON BRIAN. Unnatural Narrative: Theory, History, and Practice. Columbus: Ohio State University Press, 2015.

[14] RYAN MARIE-LAURE. Possible Worlds, Artificial Intelligence, and Narrative Theory. Indiana: Indiana University Press, 1991.

[15] THOMPSON KRISTIN. Storytelling in the New Hollywood. Cambridge, MA: Harvard University Press. Todorov, Tzvetan, 1971. "The Two Principles of Narrative." Diacritics 1999 (1): 37-44.

